The woman was pregnant!

"Stay!" Tristan commanded his K-9 partner, and Jesse dropped down with a grunted protest.

A woman appeared in the window. Dark hair. Pale skin. Freckles. Very pregnant belly that wasn't cooperating as she struggled to crawl through the opening.

Ariel Martin. The newest teacher at Desert Valley High School. Smart. Enthusiastic. Patient. He'd heard that from more than one parent. He'd even heard it from Mia.

"You okay?" he asked, running to her side.

She shook her head, dark gray eyes wide with shock, a smear of blood on her right hand. She'd cut herself. It looked deep, but she didn't seem to notice. "There's a gunman. He tried to shoot me."

The words were calm, crisp and clear, and they chilled Tristan to the bone. Two women had already been murdered in Desert Valley. Was Ariel Martin slated to be the third?

New York Times Bestselling Author

Shirlee McCoy

and

USA TODAY Bestselling Author

Valerie Hansen

Dangerous Secrets

Previously published as *Secrets and Lies* and *Search and Rescue*

HARLEQUIN® LOVE INSPIRED® CLASSICS

ISBN-13: 978-1-335-06127-0

Dangerous Secrets

First published as Secrets and Lies by Harlequin Books in 2016 and Search and Rescue by Harlequin Books in 2016.

Special thanks and acknowledgment are given to Shirlee McCoy and Valerie Hansen for their contributions to the Rookie K-9 Unit miniseries.

This edition published by arrangement with Love Inspired Books.

www.Harlequin.com

Printed in U.S.A.

CONTENTS

Aside from her faith and her family, there's not much **Shirlee McCoy** enjoys more than a good book! When she's not teaching or chauffeuring her five kids, she can usually be found plotting her next Love Inspired Suspense story or wandering around the beautiful Inland Northwest in search of inspiration. Shirlee loves to hear from readers. If you have time, drop her a line at shirlee@shirleemccoy.com.

Books by Shirlee McCoy

Love Inspired Suspense

Military K-9 Unit

Valiant Defender

FBI: Special Crimes Unit

Night Stalker
Gone

Mission: Rescue

Protective Instincts
Her Christmas Guardian
Exit Strategy
Deadly Christmas Secrets
Mystery Child
The Christmas Target
Mistaken Identity
Christmas on the Run

Classified K-9 Unit

Bodyguard

Visit the Author Profile page
at Harlequin.com for more titles.

SECRETS AND LIES

Shirlee McCoy

As for God, his way is perfect; the word of the Lord is flawless. He is a shield for all who take refuge in him.

—*Psalms* 18:30

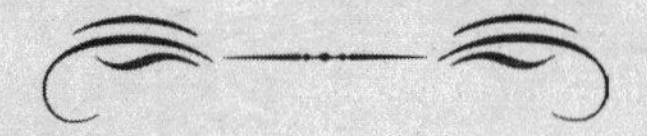

To my fellow Rookie K-9 Unit authors. Val, Dana, Lynette, Terri and Lenora, working with the five of you was such a privilege and a pleasure! We made quite a team, and I'm so glad that I got to be part of it!

ONE

The soft buzz of her cell phone pulled Ariel Martin's attention from the ninth-grade English paper she was grading. It was good that she'd been engrossed in the essay—the student had obviously done an outstanding job. It was not so good that long shadows had drifted across the classroom floor while she was reading. It was late. Later than she'd realized.

She grabbed her phone and read the text that had come through.

Want to grab some dinner later, Ari?

"No, Easton. I do not," she muttered, shoving the phone back in her purse without responding.

Easton Riley was a nice enough guy—a math teacher who'd coached the football team to regional victory the previous year—but she wasn't interested.

She had her hands full teaching summer school, tutoring on the side, getting the classroom ready for the long-term sub who'd be taking over from mid-September through December when she had her baby. The last thing she needed or wanted was a relationship complicating things. She'd lived that for five years—always at another person's beck and call, always worrying about what someone else wanted or needed.

She hadn't thought marriage would be that way. She'd thought it would be a mutual effort—two people working together to reach a common goal. She'd been wrong. She had the divorce papers to prove it, filed in Nevada and finalized three weeks later. Not what she'd wanted. She'd wanted couples counseling and pastoral help. Mitch had wanted someone else.

That had hurt. What had hurt more was how adamant he'd been that she get rid of the baby she learned she was carrying a week after Mitch had filed for divorce. An abortion, that's what he'd demanded. He'd even tossed cash at her, screaming that she'd better get rid of the kid or he'd do it for her.

That had been the first time she'd been scared of her ex-husband. There'd been other times after that. The fact that he'd died in a fiery car wreck a month later should have given her a sense of relief, but she'd felt trapped by all the memories—good and bad—of their marriage. Las Vegas had never been her dream. It had been Mitch's. They'd graduated from the University of Arizona and chased after the things he'd wanted—money, fast cars, expensive toys. She'd been happy to go along for the ride, because she'd loved him.

Love wasn't all it was cracked up to be.

She'd learned that the hard way, and now she was back in her old hometown, teaching at the high school she'd attended, trying to get ready for the daughter she'd be raising alone.

"We'll do great, munchkin," she said, standing and stretching a kink from her back. She glanced at the clock that hung above the classroom door. 5:45 p.m.

Mia McKeller's brother was late. Again.

Ariel understood that the guy was busy. The Desert Valley police had had their hands full the past few months—murders, drug runners, attacks, arrests. Rumors and speculations had been running rampant through the town, and Ariel had wondered if she would have been better off staying in Vegas. At least there, she had some anonymity. There'd been no sweet old church ladies knocking on her door in the evening, handing her casseroles and asking questions about her married state, her plans for the baby, her decision to raise her daughter alone. In Desert Valley, everyone seemed to know everyone else's business. If they didn't, they wanted to know. The problem was, Ariel didn't want to explain her marriage, Mitch's death, the fact that she wasn't nearly as sorry about it as she should be. She didn't want to lie, either, so she found herself hedging around questions, giving half answers and partial truths. She preferred authenticity, but it was hard when there were so many things she couldn't or wouldn't say. Yeah. She preferred straight-up answers.

She also preferred being on time.

Something that Tristan McKeller seemed to be opposed to. At least when it came to his meetings with her.

He seemed like a nice guy. They'd spoken on the phone several times, and he'd gone out of his way to introduce himself at church. She hadn't needed the introduction. She'd seen him in town, walking with Mia and his K-9 partner. Her first thought was always that he made a handsome picture—tall and dark-haired, one hand on his sister's shoulder, the other on the dog leash. Her second was always that he really seemed to care about Mia.

And yet, he couldn't seem to make it to their meetings on time.

She grabbed her cell phone, checking to make sure she hadn't missed a call. Tristan had had to cancel two previous meetings due to his job as a K-9 officer. He'd apologized profusely, and she'd been happy to reschedule, but summer school was drawing to a close, Mia's English grade wasn't improving, and if she didn't pass, she'd wouldn't be able to join her friends in tenth grade the following year. As Mia's guardian, it was up to Tristan McKeller to ensure his sister was aware of the ramifications of her decisions to not turn in assignments, not attend class, not participate.

Of course, he'd assured Ariel that he'd been talking to Mia, working with her and trying everything he could think of to motivate his sister. Nothing was working, and they were going to have to come up with a new plan. She'd explained it all to him Sunday morning when he'd pulled her aside after church and asked if Mia's grades were improving. He'd wanted to be prepared for bad news at the meeting, he'd said, a half smile softening the hard angles of his face.

She'd noticed that.

Which had irritated her.

No more men. Ever. That was an easy enough promise to keep to herself.

Ariel sighed, grabbing the writing prompt she'd be using for Monday's composition class. She might as well get it photocopied now, because she had a feeling Tristan would be canceling again, and once she heard from him, she was going home. She had a crib to put together. The baby was due in five weeks. Plenty of time to get the nursery ready, but whenever she got started, she thought about how it was supposed to be—two people choosing colors, two people picking wall art, two people putting the crib together—and she stopped.

She couldn't keep stopping.

Babies came whether the parent was ready or not.

She walked out of the classroom, the smell of chalk dust and floor cleaner filling her nose. Desert Valley High was smaller than the Las Vegas prep school where she'd spent the first five years of her teaching career. The main hall split into two wings, and she turned to the left, bypassing the girls' restroom, the library, the cafeteria. The teacher's lounge was just ahead, the photocopy machines tucked into a cubby there.

She walked into the room, smiling at the little sign one of the teachers had hung on the refrigerator door—a smiley face with Smiles Don't Happen Here scrawled across it.

Not true, of course.

Desert Valley High was a nice place to work—good teachers, good principal, good kids, supportive parents. A dream come true, really.

If a person still had dreams.

Ariel's had all died when Mitch had thrown the cash at her and screamed that he wanted her and the baby gone from his life.

"Cut it out," she muttered, sliding the prompt into the copy machine and closing the lid. The last thing she needed to do was dwell on the past. She had an entire future to plan out and live. She also had a baby who would need her to be strong, focused and positive.

Somewhere in the school a door slammed shut, the sound faint but audible. Tristan McKeller. It had to be. The rest of the staff had gone home for the night. Ariel had been alone in the building since the head custodian, Jethro Right, had told her to lock the main doors when she left.

That was one of the nice things about being in a

school this size. She had a key to the main door and could come and go as she pleased.

She left the machine and hurried into the corridor.

At least, she *tried* to hurry. The baby was gaining weight rapidly at this point, the heaviness of the pregnancy slowing Ariel down more than she'd imagined it would. She'd always been an athlete—cross-country, volleyball, soccer. She'd had to slow down the past month or so, but she still walked every day and coached the girl's track team.

By the time she reached her classroom, she was slightly out of breath, her heart racing as if she'd done the hundred-yard dash. The door was closed, no light spilling out from beneath it. Had she closed it? Had she turned off the light?

She couldn't remember doing either, and she hesitated, her hand on the doorknob, a shiver of warning working its way up her spine. There'd been moments since she'd left Las Vegas when the old fears had haunted her, when she'd found herself checking and rechecking the locks on the windows and doors of the little house she lived in. She'd found out a lot of things about Mitch after he'd died, things that had made her question herself and her ability to judge people, that had made her wonder if her entire marriage had been based on lies. According to the police, she'd been married to a criminal—a guy who'd laundered money through the casino where he'd worked, an arsonist who'd collected money after helping others commit insurance fraud. If he were alive, Mitch would be in jail.

He wasn't, and sometimes Ariel thought that the people he owed, the ones who the police said always played for keeps, might come after her to get what they were owed.

She shivered, backing away from the door. She couldn't imagine Mia's brother walking into her classroom, closing the door and turning off the light, and she really didn't think she'd done either of those things herself. She'd heard a door slam. Someone was in the school. Anyone who had any business being there would make themselves known, not wander around stealthily turning off lights.

She'd left her purse in the room, her wallet, her phone, but she could get those later. There was nothing wrong with being careful, after all. Nothing at all wrong with waiting for someone else to walk her into the room.

Heading up the corridor, she thought she heard the soft swish of a door opening behind her and turned, then saw her door swinging open, a man stepping out. Thin. Tall. Face masked by a stocking or a ski mask? He had something in his hand and raised it. A gun! She darted around the corner as a bullet slammed into the wall near her head. Plaster and cement flew into her hair, pinging off her cheek.

She didn't stop. She could hear his feet slapping against the tile, knew he'd be around the corner in heartbeat.

Run! her mind shrieked, her body clumsy with eight months of pregnancy, her legs churning in slow-motion, time speeding forward, the footsteps growing closer.

She ducked into the resource room, slamming the door closed, her hands trembling as she turned the lock. She stepped to the side just as a bullet flew through the door and smashed into a shelf of books that lined the far wall.

She had to get out!

The window was the only escape, and she ran to it, clawing at the lock mechanism. It didn't budge.

Behind her, something slammed into the door. Once. Twice. The door shook, and she knew it wouldn't be long before it flew open and the gunman appeared, weapon drawn and ready.

Please, God, please! she prayed frantically as she searched the room for another way out. There wasn't one, but an old computer monitor sat abandoned on the floor, wires tossed on top of it. She lifted it and slammed it into the window. A tiny hairline crack appeared. She slammed it again, and the glass cracked more. Behind her, the assault on the door continued, the wood starting to splinter and give.

Please, she prayed again as she lifted the monitor and threw it with all her strength.

Glass shattering.

Rookie K-9 officer Tristan McKeller heard it as he hooked his K-9 partner to a lead. The yellow lab cocked his head to the side, growling softly.

"What is it, boy?" Tristan asked, scanning the school parking lot. Only one other vehicle was parked there—a shiny black minivan that he knew belonged to Ariel Martin. He was late to their meeting. That seemed to be the story of his life this summer. Work was crazy, and his sister was crazier, and finding time to meet with Mia's summer school teacher? Nearly impossible. He'd already canceled two previous meetings. He couldn't cancel this one. Not if Mia had any hope of getting through summer school and moving on to the next grade. That's what Ariel had said when he'd pulled her aside at church last Sunday.

She can do it, Tristan. She's smart enough. We just

have to find the right motivation. We'll talk about it at the meeting. You are going to be there, right?

Of course, he'd assured her that he would.

What he hadn't done was assure her that he'd be on time. A good thing, since it looked like he was going to be more than a few minutes late. Jesse was still growling, alerted to something that must have to do with the shattering glass. Kids fooling around and busting school windows? A ball tossed the wrong way, taking out a streetlight?

He hoped it was something that innocuous, but he wasn't counting on it. Things had been happening in Desert Valley, a string of crimes that seemed to have surprised everyone in the small town. Drug runners. A dirty cop. Murder.

"Find!" he commanded, and Jesse took off, pulling against the leash in his haste to get to the corner of the building and around it. Trained in arson detection, the dog had an unerring nose for almost anything. Right now, he was on a scent, and Tristan trusted him enough to let him have his head.

Glass glittered on the pavement twenty feet away, and Jesse beelined for it, barking raucously, his tail stiff and high.

"Front!" Tristan said, and the dog returned to him, sitting impatiently, his dark eyes focused on the window.

"Stay!" Tristan commanded, and Jesse dropped down with a grunted protest. He wanted to keep going, but Tristan couldn't risk him cutting his paws on the shards of glass.

A woman appeared in the window. Dark hair. Pale skin. Freckles. Very pregnant belly that wasn't cooperating as she struggled to crawl through the opening.

Ariel Martin. The newest teacher at Desert Valley High School. Smart. Enthusiastic. Patient. He'd heard that from more than one parent. He'd even heard it from Mia. The few times Tristan had spoken to Ariel, he'd been impressed by her interest in his sister, and he'd felt confident that she could help Mia regain her academic grounding. If Mia would let her.

"You okay?" he asked, running to Ariel's side.

She shook her head, dark gray eyes wide with shock, a smear of blood on her right hand. She'd cut herself. It looked deep, but she didn't seem to notice. "He's got a gun. He tried to shoot me."

The words were calm, crisp and clear, and they chilled Tristan to the bone. Two women had already been murdered in Desert Valley. Was Ariel Martin slated to be the third?

"Who?" He grabbed her arms, hauling her through the opening.

She landed on her feet, her body trembling. "I don't know. He was wearing something over his face."

"But you did see a gun?" he asked, wanting clarification before he called in a gunman on the loose.

"Saw it. Heard the bullet slam into the wall. Saw one go through the door. He was trying to get into the resource room where I was hiding, but I think he heard your dog barking and left." Her voice trembled, but she didn't hesitate, the words flowing out easily. Truth did that to people. This was no overly imaginative person freaked-out about something that *might* have been seen. This was a woman who'd been terrified by a very real, very imminent threat.

Her safety was first, but Tristan wanted to go after the guy now, before he had a chance to run. If this was connected to the other murders, this might be the break they'd been looking for. Ariel had seen the guy. Not his face. But his height, width, maybe his skin tone.

He called dispatch and asked for backup as he led Ariel to his SUV. The sooner they hunted the perp down and took him into custody, the safer everyone in the vicinity would be.

He couldn't leave the victim, though. Not until he was certain the gunman wasn't hanging around, waiting for another opportunity to strike.

"Do you think he's gone?" Ariel asked.

"Yes."

"But you don't know. Not for sure. He could be in the building somewhere, or heading around the side of the school," she responded, just a hint of a tremor in her voice. Despite her advanced pregnancy, she was fit and muscular, her legs long and slim, her arms toned. He'd noticed that the first time he'd seen her. She'd walked into church with her head high, her shoulders squared, her belly pressing against a flowy dress, and there wasn't an unattached guy in the congregation who hadn't sat up a little straighter. A few months later and her belly was bigger, but she still looked confident and determined. Being shot at could shake the toughest person, though, and it had obviously shaken her.

He opened the passenger door, helped her into the seat.

"I do know for sure," he assured her. "Or at least, Jesse does." He pointed to his K-9 partner. The dog was relaxed, his tail wagging, his scruff down. He'd be growling or barking if he sensed danger. Instead, he'd loped back to their vehicle, not even a hint of tension in his muscular body.

Good, but not good enough for Tristan. He wanted to search the school, make sure the guy hadn't left anything behind—firearms, bombs, some kind of accelerant that he could use at a later date to cause mass casualties. Not likely, but it was always better to be safe than sorry.

Same for Ariel. Aside from her paleness and the cut on her hand, she seemed to be doing okay. It was better to get her checked out at the hospital, though, and make certain there wouldn't be any complications with her pregnancy. He called dispatch with the request for an ambulance as he opened the back of the SUV and pulled out a first-aid kit.

"I don't need an ambulance," Ariel protested.

He ignored her, pulling on disposable gloves and lifting her wounded hand. "This is deep. You'll need stitches."

He pressed gauze to the wound, and she winced.

"Sorry." He didn't ease up on the pressure, though. She'd bled a lot. Probably more than she realized.

"It's fine." Her free hand lay against her belly. No ring on that one or the one he was holding. He knew she was a widow. He'd heard rumors that her husband had died shortly after she'd found out she was pregnant. He hadn't asked for details, but he'd wondered. Mia really liked Ariel, and Tristan figured it took a special kind of person to win his sister's affection. He'd imagined that Ariel must be gentle, quiet, maybe a little sentimental, but taking off her wedding ring so soon after her husband's death didn't seem sentimental at all.

Then again, maybe it was. He didn't know much about those kinds of things, and he didn't know Ariel well enough to ask. What he did know was that she deserved better than this.

He met her eyes, saw fear in the depth of her dark gray gaze.

"It's going to be okay," he said.

"I hope so."

"It will be. The ambulance should be here soon. They'll triage this before they transport you," he said, and she frowned.

"Like I said, I don't need an ambulance."

"You're nine months pregnant—"

"Eight, and—"

Whatever she planned to say was cut off by a police cruiser's siren. The vehicle screamed into the parking lot, lights flashing, tires shrieking as Eddie Harmon's car squealed to a stop beside Tristan.

Eddie jumped out of the car, his uniform shirt pulled tight across his stomach, his shoes scuffed and pants wrinkled.

"What's going on here? Got a call about a gunman?" He eyed Ariel, taking in her bleeding hand and her very pregnant belly. "I'm assuming it was a false alarm, maybe a misunderstanding?"

Of course he'd assume that. Eddie liked to take the easy route to police work. His focus was on his family and his upcoming retirement rather than his job. He wasn't a bad cop, but he wasn't a good one, either.

Tristan would have preferred to have one of the K-9 officers there. He trusted Eddie to do his job, but he hated to leave Ariel with a guy who probably wasn't going to take her seriously. She looked too pale, too vulnerable, and he was tempted to stay right where he was until the rest of the K-9 team arrived. But, every minute he waited was another minute the perp had to escape.

"There *was* a shooter," Tristan assured him. "I'm going to take Jesse into the building and secure the scene. There's an ambulance on the way. Can you stay with the victim until it arrives? Until we know what the perp is after, we can't assume he's not going to try to strike again."

"In other words, you want me to take guard duty," Eddie said, crossing his arms over his belly and eyeing Tristan dispassionately.

"Right."

"I guess I can do that." Eddie shrugged. "Easier than walking around the building looking for the perp."

That's exactly what Tristan figured he'd say.

He met Ariel's eyes. She still looked scared. She also looked exhausted, her face pale, her cheekbones gaunt. He hadn't noticed that before, but then he'd been telling himself for months that he shouldn't be noticing anything about Mia's teacher. His life was filled up with work and with his sister. He didn't have time for relationships. Especially not complicated ones. A pregnant widow? That was way more than he had room for in his life.

"This might take a while. When I finish, I'll check back in with you."

She nodded, and he called Jesse to heel and jogged to the building. The perp hadn't gone out the front. Jesse would have scented him when they'd walked back to the SUV.

"Where is he?" Tristan asked, and Jesse's ears perked, his nose going to the air and then the ground. Tristan would have preferred to have Shane Weston and his apprehension dog, Bella, there tracking the perp, but waiting was out of the question.

"Find him!" he urged, and Jesse ran to the back of the school, nosing the cement path that led to double-wide doors. They yawned open, the corridor beyond silent and empty. This had to have been the entrance point. The exit point, too, if the guy was gone.

Tristan followed the dog across the threshold, calling out as he entered the building, warning that police were present. No response. He hadn't expected one. He really didn't expect the perp to have hung around.

Jesse tugged him through the hall, passing classroom after classroom. The lab stopped at room 119, sniffing the floor before walking inside. There, he nosed around near a teacher's desk, sniffing a dark blue sweater that hung over the back of a chair. He huffed quietly and left it, continuing across the room to a storage closet that stood open.

Had the guy been in the closet? Maybe waiting for Ariel to return to the classroom? The thought turned Tristan's stomach. Master police dog trainer Veronica Earnshaw had been murdered in her place of employment, shot to death while microchipping a new litter of puppies for the Canyon County K-9 Training Center. Since then, Desert Valley had been on edge. That wasn't the first murder in the area. Five years ago, K-9 officer Ryder Hayes had lost his wife on the night of the annual Desert Valley Police Department dance and fund-raiser. She'd been shot and killed while carrying her dress home just hours before the party.

The perp had shot at Ariel. Was this newest incident somehow related to the other two?

Jesse left the closet, tracing a path from there back to the desk and then out into the hallway. They moved through the dimly lit corridor, the dusky sunlight barely penetrating this far into the building. They reached the corner where the east and west wings jutted to either side of the main building, and Jesse barked, prancing around what looked like bits of concrete and wallboard.

"Front!" Tristan commanded, and the dog returned, dropping down on his haunches.

"Stay!" he said, motioning for the dog to lie on the floor, then moving past and looking at the debris that littered the gray-white tiles. A chunk of wall had been blown from the corner, the bullet still lodged in concrete. Tristan called for Jesse and continued on past several closed doors. He didn't need the dog to show him where Ariel had been hiding. The door to the room had been shot through, the old wood caving in from the force of a foot kicked into it over and over again. Another few well-placed kicks and the door would have caved in, giving the gunman a clear shot at his intended victim.

A random act of violence?

Tristan didn't think so. Everything about this seemed premeditated—the perp hiding in the closet, the mask that had hidden his features, the determination to get through a locked door. The guy had been after blood, and if Tristan hadn't had a meeting scheduled with Ariel, he might have gotten it.

God always has a way.

It's what his father had told him over and over again. It's what Tristan's mother had repeated during Tristan's challenging teenage years. Since they'd died, Tristan had been too busy trying to raise Mia to spend much time trying to figure out what God's way was.

Maybe that had been his mistake. Maybe it was the reason why Mia was struggling so much in school and with making friends. Becoming a K-9 police officer had seemed like the perfect transition from being an army dog handler into civilian life, but that wasn't the reason Tristan had signed on to the Canyon County K-9 Center Training Course. He'd joined in honor of his army buddy and good friend Mike Riverton who'd died the previous May.

Mike had sung the praises of the K-9 program, and he'd been trying to get Tristan to apply. Then Mike had died—killed when he'd fallen down steep stairs at his home. That's the story Tristan had been told, and that's what the medical examiner's records said, but Tristan wasn't buying it. A guy like Mike—trained in mountain climbing and free-climbing rock walls—would never have fallen and not been able to catch himself.

Yeah. Things around Desert Valley weren't what they'd seemed when Tristan had moved there for the program. Small towns, he was learning, often hid big secrets.

He frowned, his thoughts going back to Ariel, the way she'd looked when she'd been struggling to escape through the broken window, the fear in her eyes, the subtle trembling of her voice.

Sometimes, small towns also hid murderers.

Not for long, though.

Tristan knew the Desert Valley PD was closing in on the killer. He was certain it was just a matter of time before the perpetrator was found. But, time wasn't anyone's friend when a murderer was on the loose.

A murderer, he thought, eyeing the splintered door and the bullet hole, *who might have just attempted to strike again.*

TWO

She'd almost died.

Ariel couldn't shake the thought, and she couldn't ignore it as an EMT leaned over her cut palm, eyeing the still-bleeding wound.

"You're going to need stitches," the young woman said brusquely. "We can transport you to the hospital for that, or you can go to the clinic. Your call."

"I'll go to the clinic," Ariel responded by rote.

If she'd died, the baby would have died. Thinking about that was worse than thinking about herself, broken and bleeding on the floor of the resource room.

She shuddered, and the EMT frowned.

"Are you sure?" she asked, her tone a little gentler. "You seem shaky, and they could check on the baby. It might give you a little peace of mind."

Aside from the guy who'd shot at her being thrown in jail, there wasn't much of anything that could give her that. "I'm sure."

The woman nodded, pressing thick gauze to the wound and wrapping it with a tight layer of surgical tape. "That should hold it until you get to the clinic. Have someone drive you. Husband, family."

"All right." Except that Ariel didn't have a husband and she didn't have any family. She was making new friends at church and at work, but even after five months, they weren't the kind of relationships she could count on in a pinch.

If the principal came to check out the damage to the school, she'd probably offer to give Ariel a ride. Pamela Moore's daughter, Regina, had been Ariel's best friend from kindergarten through their sophomore year of high school. They'd stayed close after Ariel had moved away, and when Regina had taken her dream job working as NICU nurse in Phoenix, Ariel had cheered her on.

Regina had been the reason Ariel had been offered the job in Desert Valley. She'd contacted her mother, pleaded Ariel's case and gotten her an interview for a job that had opened up when another teacher had gotten married and left town.

It had seemed like a God-thing, the opportunity coming out of left field at a time when Ariel had been desperate to get away from Las Vegas and all the memories it held. She'd wanted a quiet little town to raise her daughter in. She'd wanted a safe environment where everyone knew everyone and where small crimes were considered a big deal. She'd thought that was what Desert Valley offered, all her sweet childhood memories leading her to believe the place would be perfect. Now, she wasn't so sure.

Several Desert Valley police vehicles had pulled into the parking lot and K-9 teams were spread out across the school grounds. Ariel could see a female officer walking through the gym field, her long hair pulled back in a ponytail, a golden retriever trotting in front of her. Ellen Foxcroft. A nice young woman who everyone in town seemed to like. Her mother was a different story. Marian Foxcroft was notorious for sticking her nose in where it didn't belong. She had money and influence in Desert Valley, and she wasn't afraid to throw both around to get what she wanted.

Unfortunately she also had enemies. She'd been attacked a few months ago and left in a coma. It was one of the many crimes that had been taking up the front page of the town's newspaper.

Ariel had tried not to pay much attention to the stories. She had enough stress and worry in her life. She hadn't wanted to add to it, and she'd been afraid…so afraid that she'd made another mistake—just like the one she'd made when she'd married Mitch.

She touched her stomach, feeling almost guilty for the thought.

"Ma'am?" the EMT said. "Would you like me to call someone for you?"

"No. I'm fine." She stood on wobbly legs and moved past the EMT just to prove that she could. Her keys were in her classroom. So were her purse and her cell phone. The house she'd bought with money her great-aunt had left her a decade ago was only two miles from the school, but walking there wasn't an option. Not with the gunman still out there somewhere.

Had Tristan found any sign of the guy in the school? Was he okay? She'd watched him walk toward the building, and she'd wanted to caution him to be careful, because the gunman had meant business. He'd been bent on murder, and if Ariel had walked into her classroom, she'd have probably been shot before she'd even realized she was a target.

She shivered, rubbing her arms against the chill that just wouldn't seem to leave her.

"You holding up okay?" someone asked.

She turned and found herself looking into Tristan McKeller's dark brown eyes.

"I was just thinking about you," she said, the words escaping before she realized how they'd sound. "What I mean—"

"Is that you were wondering if I'd found the gunman?" he offered, and she nodded.

"Yes. And if you were okay. Apparently, you are."

"I am, but the gunman is still on the loose. We've got a couple of K-9 teams trying to track him. Hopefully, we'll have him in custody soon. You said he was wearing some sort of mask?"

"It seemed like it. I only got a glimpse as he was coming out of my room."

"Were you heading there when you noticed him?"

"I was on my way back from the Xerox machine. I'd heard a door slamming shut, and I thought it was you." She spoke quickly, filling him in on the details and doing everything in her power to not allow emotion to seep into her voice. Breaking down in front of people wasn't something she liked to do. Even when Mitch had screamed at her, telling her that the baby she was carrying would ruin his life, she hadn't cried.

She finished and Tristan nodded. "Matches with what I saw. There's a bullet slug in the corner of the wall and one through the door into the room where you were hiding. If you'd been standing in front of the door—"

"I made sure that I wasn't." She cut him off. She didn't want to speculate, she didn't want to imagine. She'd been spared. Her baby had been spared.

God looking out for them?

She wanted to believe that.

She'd been trying hard to believe that everything that had happened—all the difficulty and trouble—would turn out for the good. There were days, though, when she questioned His goodness, wondered if He'd decided to turn His face away from her.

"Smart thinking, Ariel. It saved your life." His gaze dropped to her stomach, to the baby bump that pulled her silky summer top taut over her abdomen. "And your baby's. I guess you decided against the ambulance ride?"

"I'll get stitches at the clinic." Maybe. Or maybe she'd use a couple of butterfly bandages and hope for the best. The last thing she wanted was to walk out of the local medical clinic alone after dark, and there was no way she was going to ask Principal Moore to go with her. Not when the gunman was still on the loose. What if he came after Ariel again? What if someone else was in the line of fire?

The thought made her stomach churn.

"You're new to town," Tristan said, the comment taking her by surprise.

"I've been here for a few months, and I lived here when I was a kid," she corrected, not quite sure where he was going with the conversation.

"You were in Las Vegas prior to your move?"

"Yes."

"And your husband—"

"He was my ex, and he died a few weeks before I accepted the job offer here."

His expression softened, as if he realized there was a lot more to her story than anyone in town knew. "Had you been divorced long?"

"I'm not sure what that has to do with anything."

"Most violent crimes aren't committed by strangers. Most involve people who know each other. Is there a new relationship? A boyfriend? Ex-boyfriend? Someone who might be holding grudge?"

"Do I look like I have time for another relationship?" she asked with a laugh that she knew sounded bitter and hard.

She swallowed down the emotion, tried again. "There's no one else. My ex-husband died three weeks after our divorce was finalized."

"Can I ask the cause of death?"

"A car accident. He drove off a hillside and crashed into a tree. The car burst into flames on impact."

"I'm sorry."

"Me, too. He wasn't a very nice guy, but no one deserves that."

He studied her for a moment, his eyes such a dark brown the irises were nearly invisible. They reminded her of Mia's, the lashes black and thick. Mia, though, always looked sullen. Tristan looked concerned.

"I'm sorry," he repeated, and she tensed, not comfortable with the pity she saw in his eyes.

She didn't need anyone to feel sorry for her. She just needed to move on with her life, make a safe home for her baby and create something out of the nothing she'd been left with when Mitch had told her they were done.

"Like I said, so am I, but there's nothing I can do to change it. All I can do is make a good life for our child." *My* child was what she'd wanted to say, but Mitch would always be part of their little girl's life, the shadowy parent who existed as nothing more than a name, a photograph, a hole in the heart.

"It's still tough, Ariel. There isn't a woman on the planet who doesn't deserve better than what you got. It's getting late, and you need to get those stitches. How about I follow you over to the clinic? Jesse and I can escort you in and then follow you home when you're done." He touched his dog's head, and the yellow lab seemed to smile, its tongue lolling out.

"I—"

"You know it's the safest thing, right? Until we find out who this guy is and why he took a shot at you, you need to be cautious."

She knew. She didn't like it, but she knew.

"All right," she conceded. "But I'd rather just go home. A couple of butterfly bandages will take care of this."

Tristan didn't agree with the butterfly bandage idea, but he wasn't going to argue. Ariel knew what she wanted and after being married to a *not very nice* guy, she probably didn't need anyone telling her what decisions to make.

"That's fine. I'll walk you into the school. You can get your things and then we'll head out."

"You aren't needed here?" she asked as they headed across the parking lot.

"I was off duty when I arrived. The chief assigned the case to someone else."

"It's probably for the best," she said, brushing a few strands of hair from her cheek, the bandage on her hand crisp white in the fading light.

"Why do you say that?" He led her through the front door and into a wide lobby. Posters hung from walls, announcing clubs that would be meeting again in the fall.

"Mia," she responded. That was it. No other explanation.

"You think I should be spending more time with her?" He tried to keep defensiveness out of his voice, but he was feeling it just the way he did every time some well-meaning neighbor or church lady or school counselor pointed out that Mia needed more attention and time than what he was able to provide.

"I have no idea how much time you spend with her. I just know it can't be easy raising a teenager. Especially one who's been through a really difficult loss."

She was right about that.

He'd been an only child until he was seventeen, and he knew nothing about kids or teenage girls. He was learning, but it was a slow process. One that Mia didn't seem to have much patience for. "Mia has been through a lot. The last couple of years have been hard on both of us."

"I know, and I have a lot of sympathy for both of you, but hard times aren't an excuse for poor work." She stopped short and looked straight into his eyes. He was struck by that—by the directness of her gaze, the unapologetic way she pointed out the truth.

"I've told her that a dozen times."

"Probably a dozen too many. Kids like Mia need structure. They need consequences, too."

"I hope you're not talking about me letting her fail, because I'm not willing to do that."

"If she doesn't improve her grade in my class, she's going to fail, and there's nothing either of us can do about it." She sighed and started walking again. "I was thinking more along the lines of grounding her until her grades come up."

"I've done that. I've also made her come to work with me on her days off, so that I can make sure she's not goofing off. None of it seems to matter. She still turns in shoddy assignments."

"When she turns them in at all," Ariel added, and

he couldn't argue the point. Mia had received zeros on her last three assignments.

"I've been thinking about hiring a tutor to work with her. She hates the idea." It was the only option they hadn't explored. He could hire someone, see if that person could help nudge Mia into focusing on school again. "She's a smart kid. Before my parents died, she was in the gifted program."

"I know. I saw her records. Her standardized test scores are high, too." She stopped at the yellow police tape that blocked off one corridor of the school. "Tutoring will help, but she needs to know that people are invested in her life."

"She's got plenty of people invested. She just isn't appreciative of the fact," he muttered.

"Fourteen-year-olds seldom are." She smiled, but her gaze was focused on the hallway beyond the tape. "I guess I should get my things," she said quietly.

"I can get them for you," he offered. "If you'd rather not go back to the classroom."

"I'll have to go back Monday, so I may as well face it now." She lifted the police tape and shimmied under it, her advanced pregnancy not seeming to hinder her movements.

Up ahead, rookie K-9 officer James Harrison and his bloodhound, Hawk, crisscrossed the hallway, moving from side to side and back again.

"We're moving through," Tristan said, and James gave a brief nod, his focus on a wadded-up piece of paper that lay on the glossy tile.

"Anything interesting?" Tristan asked, and James finally looked up.

"I'm not sure. Hawk alerted here, so I'm going to process it like it is. It could have just been left behind by a kid and kicked by the gunman when he ran through." He shrugged, his gaze shifting to Ariel. "We'll figure it out though, and get this guy behind bars as quickly as possible."

He was trying to reassure her, but Ariel didn't look convinced. She looked tense, her arms crossed protectively over her stomach, her bandaged hand resting on the swell of her abdomen.

"I appreciate that," she said. "I'll feel a lot safer when he's in custody."

"Do you have any idea who it was?" James asked, opening up an evidence collection kit. He took a quick photo of the paper, then put on gloves and lifted it.

"No, but I don't think he's anyone I know."

"You didn't see his face?" James carefully opened the sheet, studying words that were scrawled across it.

"No. He was wearing a mask of some sort. I already explained everything to Officer McKeller."

"I know it's frustrating, but you'll probably be explaining things to a lot of people, Ms. Martin," James responded. "Unfortunately, that's the way these cases usually work. Lots of questions asked over and over again. Did the chief give you permission to leave the scene?"

"She's been cleared to go," Tristan responded. "I'm going to escort her and make sure she arrives home safely. At this point, that's my top priority."

She tensed at his words, but she didn't protest them.

"Good," James said. "If the guy was planning this, if he found out information to help him achieve his goal, there's no guarantee he won't go after her somewhere else." He held up the paper, so that Tristan could read the handwritten words.

Desert Valley High School
Room 119
Ariel Martin

They were scrawled in black ink, every *i* dotted with a circle. The *A* underlined.

Ariel took a step back, her gaze focused on the paper, her face leeched of color. Freckles dotted her nose and her cheeks, giving the impression of youth, but there was maturity in her eyes—a deep knowledge of what it meant to struggle, to suffer and to survive.

She'd been through a lot. Now she was going through more. That bothered him. It made him want to do everything in his power to keep her safe.

"Are you okay?" he asked, and she nodded.

"Yes. I..." She pressed her lips together, sealing in whatever she'd planned to say. "You'll think I'm nuts."

"There are a lot worse things that people can be," he responded, and she smiled, a dimple flashing in her right cheek. She had a pretty smile, a soft one.

"True. The thing about the letter...the writing looks really familiar."

"A student?" James suggested.

"No. My ex-husband."

"Did you part on good terms?" James asked. "Is it possible—?"

"He's dead." Tristan cut in. There was no sense walking down that road. A dead man didn't write notes. He didn't carry a gun. He didn't stalk his ex.

"That blows a hole in my theory, then," James responded, carefully placing the note in an evidence bag.

"What about the writing made you think of your ex?" Tristan asked Ariel.

"Mitch always underlined the *A* in my name, and he always used circles to dot *i*'s."

"That's information anyone could have known," he pointed out. "Friends, coworker, family. Most would have seen his writing at one point or another."

"He didn't have family. It was one of the things that brought us together. Two college students with no one." She blushed, shook her head. "It's an old story, and there's no reason to tell it now. I can get you a list of Mitch's associates, but I can't guarantee that I know all of them. He was involved in some things I didn't know about until after he died."

"Affairs?" James asked bluntly, and Ariel shrugged.

"I found that out before we divorced. After he died, the police started questioning me about other things. He'd been involved in a money laundering scheme in Las Vegas and insurance fraud in Nevada and several other states. If he'd lived, he'd have been arrested." She said it as if it didn't matter, her face and voice devoid of emotion. It had to have hurt, though. It had to have made her doubt all the things she'd thought were true about herself and her relationships.

"I'm sorry, Ariel," Tristan said, and she offered him that same soft pretty smile.

"So you keep saying. Sorry doesn't change things, though, and it's not going to help you figure out who tried to shoot me. I'm not familiar with any of the people who were involved in criminal activities with Mitch, but I can print out a list of his work associates and friends and swing it by the police department tomorrow. I may have a sample of his writing, too. If that will help."

"It will," Tristan said. "I'll talk to Chief Jones and see if we can send the paper for handwriting analysis. The state crime lab should be able to process it."

"You want me to handle that while you escort her home?" James asked.

Tristan met Ariel's eyes. She didn't look any less tired than she had a few minutes ago, and he thought she needed to be home more than she needed to wait around the crime scene while he did something another officer could handle. "Sure."

"Okay," James said. "Come on, Hawk, let's see what else we can find."

The bloodhound offered a quick bark in response and moved down the hall, ears brushing the ground as he moved.

Ariel must have taken that as her cue to leave. She headed down the hall, moving toward her room at a half run that Tristan didn't think could be good for her or the baby.

But, then, what did he know?

He'd never spent much time around pregnant women. He didn't know what the protocol was for exercise this late in a pregnancy. She was in good health and very fit. If she wanted to jog, who was he to question her? If she wanted to run away from her problems, who was he to tell her it couldn't be done?

Obviously, the discussion about her ex had been painful. It was just as obvious that she was done talking about it.

That was fine.

For now.

He kept silent as he followed her to her room. She stopped at the yellow crime-scene tape that blocked her path. Fingerprint powder coated the doorknob and the edge of the door. More dusted the wall.

"This isn't going to be fun on Monday," Ariel murmured.

"We'll have things processed and cleaned up by then." He lifted the tape, and she walked across the threshold and straight to her desk. She grabbed her sweater, opened a drawer and took out her purse.

"You want to check to make sure everything is there?" he asked, and she opened the purse, pulling out a cell phone and a wallet.

"Credit card. Debit card. Cash." She listed the items one at a time as she looked through the wallet. "Everything is here."

"Keys?"

She lifted a key ring. "Here."

"Anything else you want to grab? You may not be able to get in here tomorrow."

"I can access lesson plans and grades online. I have what I need." She slid into the sweater, then hitched the purse onto her shoulder. Nothing about her was fancy or overdone. Very little makeup, hair pulled into a ponytail, clothes understated. Her emotions were understated, too. No panic or tears or frantic speculating. She seemed determined to hold herself together.

That was good. It was easier to get information from people who were clearheaded. Tristan might not be working her case, but he could pick her brain, see if the ex-husband who'd died might be the key to the attack. One thing he couldn't do was walk away and not worry about the case or Ariel. He couldn't know for sure, but he thought that Ariel might have come to Desert Valley to escape her past and to try to create a more peaceful future. He wanted to make sure she was able to do both. He also wanted to know if the attack against her was personal.

There was a big part of him hoping that this newest trouble wasn't related to the other crimes that had happened in town. Desert Valley PD was under pressure to solve two murders and investigate two suspicious deaths. Plus there was the attack on Marian Foxcroft, which had to be related. They'd been hunting for a killer for months and still had no suspect.

If Ariel's shooter proved to be connected, they might have to shift their focus, stop looking for an opportunistic murderer and start looking for a serial killer.

THREE

Ariel wouldn't fall apart.

She absolutely refused to.

And not just because Tristan was beside her, his dark gaze focused on her, his eyes filled with concern and compassion.

No. She wouldn't fall apart, because if she did, she wasn't sure she'd ever pull herself back together again.

Legs trembling, heart racing, she still managed to walk out of the school and make her way toward the minivan she'd purchased a week after the divorce was finalized. Mitch had wanted the Jaguar, and she'd been happy to give it to him. She'd still had plenty in her savings account, all the money from her great-aunt's estate that Ariel had refused to allow Mitch to spend on trips or expensive toys because she'd wanted to buy a house one day. It didn't have to be big. Just cute and cozy with a nice fenced yard.

How many times had Mitch laughed at that dream? Told her that high-rise condo living in the city limits was more their style?

More *his* style, but she'd never said that, because she'd loved him and she'd wanted him to be happy. Plus, there'd been a part of her that had thought that eventually he'd get tired of the fast-paced, high-flying lifestyle and settle into the kind of pedestrian family life Ariel remembered from childhood. Before her parents had died, she'd had the pretty little house, the big yard, the fresh-baked cookies when she got home from school. At least, she thought she'd had it. She'd visited the house when she'd moved back to Desert Valley and realized it wasn't nearly as pretty as she'd remembered it, the yard not as spacious. That hadn't bothered her. She still cherished the memories she had of her time in the house, but she also realized they'd been made even more beautiful by the time that had passed since she'd been there.

Time changed memories and tricked the mind. Sometimes it made the past into what a person wanted it to be. Sometimes it made connections that weren't really there. Was that what had happened with the handwriting on the piece of paper? Had it only seemed to be like Mitch's writing because Ariel had been terrified, the memories of Mitch's last words to her, still haunting her mind and her dreams?

"Get rid of the baby or I'll do it for you!"

An idle threat is what she'd thought, words meant to manipulate her into giving him what he wanted—freedom from her, from every obligation and burden that marriage and family brought.

She'd despised him for that for way too long, wasting weeks fuming over what he'd asked her to do, and then he'd died, and she'd had nothing to do with her anger but let it go.

So, maybe all those pent-up memories and emotions had made her see what wasn't on the piece of paper. Maybe the writing had been nothing more than a note scribbled by a student who'd needed to find her class.

She fished her keys out of her purse, unlocking the minivan as she reached it. She could feel Tristan standing behind her, his presence both disconcerting and comforting.

"I'll follow you to your place," he said as she climbed into the vehicle.

She wanted to tell him not to bother. Not because she didn't appreciate the offer, but because she didn't want to start needing someone again.

Isn't that why she'd been with Mitch? Because she'd been alone in the world, and she'd needed someone to connect with, someone to call family?

Look how well that had worked out.

She'd ended up married and alone. Then, she'd ended up divorced and alone. Now, she was alone and in trouble. It would be nice to rely on someone else. Especially when her entire life seemed to be falling to pieces. But, needing someone left a person vulnerable. She'd learned that lesson a little too late to save herself from heartache, but she'd learned it well.

She wouldn't make the mistake again.

On the other hand, she wasn't foolish enough to think she didn't need protection. With a gunman on the loose, his motive unclear, she couldn't turn down Tristan's offer.

She was too afraid.

"Sounds good," she said, fumbling with her seat belt, because she didn't want to look into Tristan's eyes again. There was something unsettling about him, about the way that he looked at her, the way he really seemed to see her.

"Let me," he offered, taking the belt from her clumsy bandaged hand and reaching over her stomach. He snapped it into place easily and moved back quickly, but for some reason, her cheeks heated, her face flushing a dozen shades of red.

"When you get to the house, stay in the van until I check out your property, okay?" He closed the door before she could respond, jogging to an SUV and opening the back hatch for his dog. Jesse jumped in, the lab's golden fur nearly white in the evening light.

It took a couple of seconds for Ariel to realize she needed to start the van and a couple more to actually do it. By the time she drove out of the parking lot, her cheeks had cooled.

Delayed reaction from the attack. That's what she told herself as Tristan's SUV pulled onto the road behind her.

She wasn't sure she believed it.

Night would fall soon, blackness shrouding the quiet street where Ariel lived. She'd chosen the location purposely—close to school and the town's business district, but far enough away that she could have the solitude she needed. The house had been on the market for a while. A fixer-upper that no one had wanted to put the time and money into, the two-story farmhouse stood on a double lot that backed to a wide swath of open land. She'd purchased the place well under market value, and she'd been spending most of her free time getting it ready for the baby.

Mitch would have laughed at the idea, but she'd known she could make the old house into a comfortable home. Eventually, she'd invite people over, do a little entertaining, get back into the swing of being the person she'd once been.

She pulled into her driveway, Tristan right on her bumper.

He was out of his SUV before she could open her

door, motioning for her to stay where she was as he attached Jesse's lead. The dog jumped from the back of the SUV, his blond tail wagging, his face set in what looked like wide-mouthed grin. He looked like most of the yellow labs she'd seen—stocky body, broad head, short coat. He was fitter, though, his lean body made for the work he did. In other circumstances, Ariel would have been amused by the perpetually happy dog. Right then, all she wanted was to get into her house, close all the shades and hide from the world.

Tristan made a sweep of the yard, walking Jesse along the perimeter and then to the front door. Finally, he seemed satisfied and jogged to the van.

"Ready?" he asked, opening the door and offering her a hand out.

"Not really," she responded, the honest answer slipping out as he walked her up the porch stairs. An old swing hung from the eaves, the metal chains creaking as she unlocked the door. Across the street, Edna Wilkinson's porch light went on. She'd probably noticed the strange SUV in Ariel's driveway and wanted to get a better look.

"You're scared," Tristan said as she led the way into the house.

"I'd be foolish not to be." She turned to face him, was surprised at how tall he suddenly seemed. At least eight inches taller than her, and she wasn't short. "Someone nearly killed me. That's not something I can put on the back burner and worry about later."

"You're right, and I can assure you that the Desert Valley police are taking this seriously."

"They take every case seriously, don't they? Look at what they've accomplished these past few months. Cracking down on that extortion ring and putting corrupt police officer Ken Bucks behind bars. Finding the bank heist money that was hidden outside town."

"Yes," Tristan responded. "Sometimes, though, it helps to be reminded that you're not alone in your struggles."

The words echoed the thought she'd had at the school—the one about being alone and in trouble—and her cheeks heated again. "Yes. I guess it does. Thanks for escorting me home, Tristan. I appreciate it."

"It sounds like you're kicking me out."

"Just giving you the freedom to go back to whatever you were doing before you saved my life."

"I was heading for a meeting with you," he reminded her, a smile in his eyes.

She couldn't help it. She smiled in return, some of the tension she'd been feeling slipping away. "I'd forgotten all about that."

"Tell you what, how about I take a look at the locks on your doors while I'm here? Make sure they're strong enough to keep someone out? Then, we can discuss my obnoxious sister and her academic troubles."

"She's not obnoxious."

"Much?" he asked, and she laughed.

"That's better," he commented, as he fiddled with the bolt on the front door.

"What's better?"

"You don't look like you're going to shatter anymore. This bolt looks good. Let's look at the back door." He said it all so quickly that the first few words almost didn't register.

By the time they did, he was halfway down the hall, heading to the back of the house.

"I wasn't going to shatter," she muttered, hurrying after him.

"I didn't say you were. I just said you looked like you might." He'd reached the mudroom and the door that opened from it into the backyard.

"I'm not the kind of person who shatters when things don't go her way," she replied, but he was turning the lock, frowning at the door, and she wasn't sure he heard.

"This could be a lot stronger, Ariel," he finally said.

"I can have it replaced."

"You could also put a door between the mudroom and the kitchen." He touched the doorjamb that had once housed an interior door. Someone had taken it down before Ariel had bought the property.

"I think the one that goes there is out in the shed behind the house. I found it there after I moved in."

"I've got the day off tomorrow. How about I stop by and hang it for you? Two layers of defense are better than one."

"I can do it." Probably. Although, lately the pregnancy was making her tired. The further along she got, the more difficult everyday tasks became. She tried not to dwell on that. She tried not to think about how much more difficult it would be to parent alone than it would have been to parent as a team.

"Just because you can do it, doesn't mean you have to. If you don't want to accept the help as a gift, you can point me in the direction of a good tutor for Mia and give me a pass on being late to our meeting today. I did miss…what? Two previous meetings?"

"You also saved my life, so you've already earned the pass on that, but…" She hesitated, not sure about the offer she was about to make. She liked Mia. The teen had a great vocabulary and a flair for words. She also had a chip on her shoulder and an attitude to go with it. "I've been doing some tutoring on the side, working with some of the local kids getting them ready for SAT and ACT tests. I'd love to work with Mia."

"I couldn't ask you to do that."

"I offered. Just like you offered to put up my door. Bring her over tomorrow. While you're fixing the door, I'll help her with the paper that's due Monday."

"She has a paper due Monday?"

"Yes, and two extra credit assignments due by Friday. If she doesn't get As, she's not going to pass my class."

"It would devastate Mia to be held back a year."

"I know. If I could make an exception, I would. I can't."

"I wouldn't ask you to. She needs to pass on her own merit. It's not like she's not capable of it." He ran a hand over his hair, rubbed the back of his neck. He looked exasperated and worried. Like any parent would be if his child were failing. Only Mia wasn't his child. She was his sister. That had to be complicating the dynamics between them.

"Were you and Mia close before your parents passed away?" she asked, and regretted the question immediately. It was too personal, something that he might discuss with a counselor. Not his sister's teacher.

"I joined the military when I was eighteen. Mia was one. I guess you could say we barely knew each other before I became her guardian. I saw her during my leave, but that wasn't enough to create the kind of bond that would make this situation easier."

"I guess it's my turn to say I'm sorry," she said, her heart aching for what they'd both lost.

"It's been hard, but we're doing okay, slowly getting to know each other better. I think we'll both survive her teenage years."

"Think?"

He laughed, the warmth of it ringing through the quiet house. "I should have said 'survive with our sanity intact.' Now, how about we stop talking about my sister and finish looking at your locks?"

He walked to a window, frowning at the wood pane and old fashioned lock. "It would be very easy for someone to break the lock and climb in the window."

"That's a cheerful thought," she muttered, her heart thrumming at the thought of a masked intruder entering the house while she slept.

"What's through here?" He pushed open pocket doors that led into the office. There'd been a desk there when she'd moved in—an old rolltop that still stood against the wall. Light from the hallway filtered in, but she'd closed the shades earlier, and the room seemed dark and dreary.

She flicked on the light, waiting as Tristan checked a front window. It was newer than the one in the parlor, but he still didn't seem happy. "Definitely need some updating here. How about we do this—I'll work on getting the house more secure while you work on helping my sister pass ninth-grade English?"

It was a decent deal, but she didn't want to become fodder for the town rumor mill. If Edna saw Tristan hanging around, she'd spread the news lightning fast. Before anyone even asked for the truth, the entire town would think that she and Tristan were dating.

"I—"

Jesse growled, the hair on the scruff of his neck standing up as he moved toward the window, nosed the shade. He didn't look happy anymore. He looked ready to attack.

Tristan took Ariel's arm, nudging her into the hall. "Wait here."

"What—?"

"Stay here," he cut her off, flicking off the light and plunging the hallway into darkness.

Tristan didn't wait for Ariel to respond. He assumed she'd do what he'd asked her to. For the baby's sake as much as her own.

He jogged back into the office, called for Jesse to heel and then made his way to the front door. Someone was outside. That much was certain. Jesse knew the difference between a person walking past and someone lurking nearby. He only barked when he sensed danger.

He was barking loudly, doing everything he could to get his message across.

"Cease," Tristan commanded, and Jesse went silent.

The office window looked out into the backyard. They'd go out the front, move around the side of the building, and hopefully surprise whoever had been trying to peek inside.

The sun had set, hints of light still flecking the horizon and turning the evening a dusky blue. There were few houses on Ariel's street, the dead-end road isolated. Maybe she'd intended it that way, but it wasn't the best situation for a woman alone. A *pregnant* woman alone. She might be fit and tough, but the baby would slow her down if she ran into trouble.

He surveyed the front yard, eyeing the house across the street. The lights were on there, a Toyota Camry parked in the driveway. To the left, a small rancher stood about a half-acre away. To the right, an empty lot stretched toward a fenced property. Plenty of places for someone to stay hidden. Watching a house like Ariel's was as easy as taking out binoculars and looking through them. She had no large trees. No shrubs. Nothing to block a person's view of the front door.

That worried him.

Someone had been outside.

He was certain of that. Jesse never issued a false alert.

The gunman? If so, the guy was taking his sweet time acting. He could have fired a few shots in the window in the hope of hitting his target. That's what he'd done at the school, firing blindly as Ariel disappeared around a corner, and then again while she was on the other side of the door.

Why wait this time?

The question made him cautious. He didn't pull his gun, just let Jesse have his lead, following the dog around the corner of the house. Tristan stopped there, listening to the night sounds—a few birds calling in the distance, an animal rustling in the bushes a few feet away.

Not a sound from the backyard. No footsteps. No sign that the perpetrator was attempting to enter the house, no indication that he was leaving. But someone *was* there. Jesse clawed at the ground, twitching in his desire to finish what they'd started.

Tristan held him back, creeping closer to the edge of the house and peering around the corner. He could see someone, a dark shadow backlit by the porch light, pressing against the screened window.

A man?

If so, he wasn't a tall one.

"Police!" Tristan warned. "Don't move."

The person jumped, nearly falling over in his haste to move away from the window.

"One more step, and I'll release my dog," Tristan warned.

The person either didn't hear or didn't care. He took off, running down the porch stairs, flying across the yard, a hood pulled up over his hair and shrouding what looked like a pale face.

Caucasian. Five-six. Slight build.

He filed the information way as he released Jesse's lead.

"Get him!" he commanded, and the dog took off, closing in on the perpetrator in the blink of an eye.

FOUR

A woman screamed, the sound chilling Ariel's blood. She wanted to run outside, see what was going on, try to help if she could, but Tristan had been right—she had more than herself to think about.

She pressed against the hallway wall, her heart thundering in her chest, her stomach in knots. Everything had been fine that morning. Sure, she'd had the eerie feeling she was being watched as she'd left for school. Sure, she'd thought she heard someone walking through the hallway behind her as she'd made her way to her classroom, but she'd always had a big imagination, and she'd chalked it up to that.

No way could anyone have followed her from Las Vegas. Even if someone could have, why would they? She had no enemies. The only person she'd given the police information about was dead.

She should be safe and happy and preparing for her daughter's birth. She wasn't any of those things, and if she was honest with herself, she had to admit that she hadn't been in months.

The house fell silent, whoever was outside was quiet. Jesse wasn't barking. The woman wasn't screaming. Tristan was obviously handling whatever he'd found.

Whoever he'd found?

Had there really been someone outside the window? Jesse had sure been acting as if there was.

The faint sound of voices drifted into the house. A man's. A woman's. Or, maybe, a girl's. No gunshots. No more screams. Whatever danger had been there seemed to be gone. She turned on the light, the crystal prisms on the chandelier sending rainbows across the gleaming floor. Tristan had closed the door when he'd walked outside.

She could open the door, go outside and see what was going on.

Or…she could stay where she was and hope that Tristan returned eventually.

She'd never been one to wait around for others to do what she could. She walked to the front door and had her hand on the knob when someone knocked.

She jumped back, biting back a scream.

"Ariel?" Tristan called through the thick wood, and she opened the door.

Tristan looked furious.

That was her first thought.

Her second thought was that he had good reason to be.

His sister, Mia, stood beside him, her face set in the perpetual scowl that Ariel had been seeing every day for weeks.

"Mia!" she said, surprised that the teenage girl was on her front porch. "What are you doing here?"

"That's exactly what I was trying to find out," Tristan muttered, giving his sister a gentle nudge into the house.

"I…" Mia began, and then shook her head, her straight dark bangs falling across her eyes.

"Spill it," Tristan demanded, and Mia scowled.

"How about we discuss it over some lemonade or ice tea?" Ariel suggested. There was no sense standing in the foyer staring each other down, and it was obvious Mia had no intention of speaking. Not yet.

"I don't believe in rewarding poor behavior," Tristan replied. "She was outside looking in your back window. That doesn't earn her a glass of lemonade."

"What does it earn me? More time alone at the house?" Mia retorted.

"No phone," he growled. "No TV. No visits with Jenny, either."

That seemed to get Mia's attention.

The teen scowled and crossed her arms over her stomach. "That's not fair. I only came here because I heard someone had been shot at the high school. I knew you and Ms. Martin were supposed to be meeting there."

"You went to the school?" Tristan's jaw tightened. "I told you to go straight home after school and get some of the work that you're missing done."

"I did go straight home."

"And then you went to the school?"

"No, I went to Jenny's house. She lives right behind Ms. Martin's place."

"Jenny Gilmore?" Ariel knew that the two girls were best friends, but she'd had no idea that Jenny lived on the property behind hers. She'd been too busy trying to get ready for the baby to do much more than introduce herself to the neighbors who lived on her street. No way would she have walked the mile and a half through scrub and trees to knock on the farmhouse door.

"Yes. She lives with her grandmother."

"I did know that. I just had no idea they were so close. I would have gone and visited before now."

"Her grandmother doesn't like visitors," Mia said quickly. "She doesn't hear all that well, and she's really ancient. She gets tired out."

"And, yet, you decided it would be a great idea to spend the evening with her?"

"She gave me a ride, Tristan. And she was going to drive me home."

"Do you really think I want you riding around with someone who is *ancient and tired out*?" Tristan's blood was obviously boiling. It was just as obvious that he was trying to keep his temper under control. "Mia, I have talked to you about this dozens of times. You can't leave the house without letting me know where you're going."

"I called you at work. You weren't there."

"You knew I wasn't there."

"No, I—"

"Tea or lemonade?" Ariel cut in. She figured that if she didn't, the two would be arguing all night.

"Neither," Tristan responded. "But thanks. We're going to get out of here. I'll be by tomorrow morning to put in the door. If you have any trouble before then, don't hesitate to call 911." He pulled a business card out of his pocket, scribbled something on the back and handed it to her. "That's my personal cell phone number. I think the one you have on file at the school is my work number. If you even have a feeling that something isn't right, I want you to call me. Don't worry about being wrong or bothering me for nothing. I want to be bothered, and I want to check out anything that seems even a little bit suspicious."

"I appreciate that, Tristan."

"Don't just appreciate it. Act on it. You can't take chances, Ariel. You've got two lives depending on you."

He took his sister's arm, tugging her back outside.

Ariel stood in the doorway as they walked to his SUV, his words echoing in her head. She hadn't needed the reminder that it wasn't only her life on the line. Every minute of every day, she felt the heaviness of the baby, the life wiggling and kicking and growing inside of her, and she felt the weight of her responsibility to her daughter.

Tristan opened the back hatch of the SUV, and Jesse jumped in. Then, he turned to face the house, his expression hidden by the darkness.

"You'd better head inside," he called, and something in her warmed at his words, at the fact that he hadn't been so focused on his sister's trouble that he'd stopped worrying about her.

"I will."

"Now would probably be best. Lock the doors and pull the shades, and stay away from all the windows. Okay?"

"You don't think the guy from the school is going to come here, do you?"

"I think it's always better to be safe than to be sorry. I'm going to ask Chief Jones to send a patrol down your road a few times a night until we figure out who was at the school."

"Thanks."

He nodded. "Mia and I will be here early. I can install an alarm system if you want. That might make you feel more secure."

Nothing was going to make her feel more secure.

Not until she knew exactly what was going on.

She closed the door anyway, sliding the bolt home, and that little bit of warmth she'd felt when Tristan was there seeped away.

She should have felt safe in her little house on her

quiet road. She should have felt as though everything that had happened at the school was just a fluke, some weird anomaly that wouldn't be repeated. She couldn't help thinking about Mitch, though, about the trouble he'd gotten himself into before he'd died.

He'd been in deep with people who'd had a lot to lose if his crimes were discovered. The Las Vegas police had assured Ariel that none of those people would care about coming after her. She had no information about Mitch's contacts, no knowledge of anything besides the basics—trips he'd taken for *work*, dates and times that he'd left and returned. She'd always kept a calendar, and she'd had every one of his trips jotted into it.

The police had used that to tie Mitch in with arsons that had occurred at businesses all over the country.

Insurance fraud.

No one had been hurt except the companies that had to pay out millions of dollars.

Typical of Mitch, he'd probably thought that made it okay.

Just like cheating on her because she was boring was okay.

She winced at the memory. The look on his face when she'd confronted him, the complete lack of remorse had shocked her.

Or, maybe it hadn't.

She'd realized long before then that he wasn't the man she'd thought she'd married.

She turned off the downstairs lights. She probably needed to eat, but she wasn't hungry. She was just tired. For the first time in a long time, she wished things could be different, that she had someone in her life who could stand beside her, offer her support, give her all the things she'd thought that Mitch would.

Tristan had done that to her.

He'd reminded her of what it felt like to have someone care. Sure, he was just doing his job, but she'd still felt safe when he was nearby. She'd needed that. Maybe she still did.

"It's just us, though, sweetie," she said, patting her belly as she walked up the stairs. "And, that's going to be just fine."

The baby kicked as if she agreed.

That was something to smile about.

No matter what happened, they really would be just fine.

Ariel had to believe that. She had to trust in it. God had a way of making things okay. She just had to keep moving forward, keep praying, keep hoping.

Everything else would come together in its own sweet time.

Tristan didn't say a word to Mia as he drove home.

He was afraid of what he might say and of how it would sound. He was angrier than he'd been in a long time. His sister had a right to be confused and maybe a little unsure. They'd moved from the only home she'd ever known so that he could attend the program at Canyon County K-9 Training Center.

She didn't have the right to wander around town without permission. Especially not when there was a murderer on the loose.

He'd told her that. Repeatedly.

Yet, she'd still gone to Jenny's without permission, left there to go to Ariel's house. Also without permission.

Ariel…

He'd hated leaving her alone at the house.

He needed to call Chief Jones and make sure that an officer would patrol her street for the next few nights. It wouldn't take Tristan long to secure her house. It might take less time for the perpetrator to return to finish what he'd started in the school.

His hand tightened on the steering wheel, his muscles tense at the thought of Ariel being attacked again.

"You're mad," Mia accused, finally breaking the silence.

"Shouldn't I be?"

"No, because it's all your fault I keep getting into trouble. You forced me to move here."

A lie, and she knew it. They'd both agreed it would be a good move. "That's not true."

"It feels like it is," she responded sullenly.

He pulled into their driveway, then grabbed Mia's hand before she could get out of the car and run inside. "We're not finished our conversation."

"We never have conversations. You just sit and tell me what you think I should do."

"Is that how you see things?" he asked, because he tried to be open with her. He tried to listen to what she had to say.

She sighed. "No. Not really."

"Then, what's going on?"

"I keep telling you nothing is going on."

"You were a straight-A student in Phoenix, Mia. The work here isn't any tougher."

She dropped her gaze, fiddling with one of the dozen bracelets she had on her wrist.

"Mia?" he prodded, and she shrugged.

"I told you I was going to do better, and I will."

"Ms. Martin said you have an assignment due on Monday."

"I'll do it."

"And extra credit assignments due by Friday."

"I'll do those, too."

"While you're working so hard on those, who's going to take care of Sprinkles?" he asked, pointing to the puppy that was standing in the living room window, barking frantically for them to come in the house.

"I'll take care of her, too."

"Mia, a puppy deserves more than what you're giving her," he said gently, because he didn't want to make accusations, and because he knew teenagers were notoriously bad at taking responsibility. Still, he'd only gotten the puppy because his coworker Ellen Foxcroft had suggested it might be good for Mia.

Mia looked at the puppy, and her face fell. The next thing he knew, tears were streaming down her face.

She jumped out of the car, ran to the house and was inside before he opened the hatch and let Jesse out.

He followed her inside and found her in her bedroom, the little brown-and-white mutt they'd adopted from the shelter in her lap. The puppy was licking the tears off her face.

She didn't look at Tristan as he crossed the threshold, checked the lock on her window and pulled down the shades.

He wanted to say something that would bridge the gap between them, he wanted to tell her that he understood how it felt to be a teenager, that he knew how easy it was to get distracted by friends and movies and books.

He didn't think she'd hear what he was trying to say, though.

Lately, all they did was butt heads.

It had to be something that he was doing wrong,

but no matter how hard he tried, he couldn't seem to make it right.

He walked back into the hall without saying a word, and was surprised when Mia called out to him. "I'll do better, Tristan. I told you I would, and I will."

He walked back to the doorway, stood in the threshold. "I know you want to do better, but improvement takes a lot of hard work and focus."

"I am focused. Jenny and I were working on our papers together. That's why I went to her house." She kissed Sprinkles's fluffy head, scratched the puppy's belly.

"It's not about you going to her house, Mia. I think you know that."

"I did call your office," she said, and she was finally looking straight at him. He could see the young woman she was becoming. Not the little girl she'd been. Not the shy preteen he'd moved in with after their parents died. In a few years, she'd be an adult, independent and ready to face the world.

He had to prepare her for that.

And, it terrified him more than just about anything else he'd ever had to do.

"You should have called my cell phone."

"I know."

"Then why didn't you?"

"Because I thought you'd say no."

"I would have."

She nodded. They were at a stalemate. Just like always.

"Jenny is a nice girl, Tristan. She doesn't do the kind of stupid things other girls our age do," Mia said.

"What stupid stuff?"

"Chasing boys. Wearing clothes that are too mature. Swearing. Drinking."

"Who's drinking?" he asked, and she sighed.

"You're missing the point. Just like you always do." The barb hurt, but he kept his mouth shut and let her finish. "Jenny doesn't get into trouble. She likes animals. Just like me. She loves dogs. We have a lot in common."

"Including failing ninth grade."

She flushed. "That was stupid of both of us. I told her that today. I told her that we have to get serious if we're going to graduate and go to college."

"And she said what?"

"She agreed. That's why we were working on our English assignments together."

He wanted to believe her. He really did, but he'd heard the same thing a dozen times before, and he'd seen no improvements in Mia's grades or her behavior. "Tomorrow, we're going to Ms. Martin's house. She's going to tutor you while I—"

"Are you kidding me?" she nearly shouted.

"No."

"I can't have my teacher tutor me. Every kid in town will find out and be talking about it."

"You should have thought of that before you decided to fail summer school. We need to be there early. I've got a meeting in the afternoon that I can't miss. Set your alarm for seven."

She frowned, but didn't say another word.

Which was better than usual, so he'd just have to be thankful for it and move on. "Dinner will be ready in a half hour."

"I ate at Jenny's."

Another thing they'd talked about. Jenny's grandmother was on a fixed income. She couldn't afford to feed another teenager every night. Even if she could, she shouldn't have to.

He let it drop.

He'd been letting a lot of things drop lately. For the sake of harmony. Which they never seemed to have anymore.

If his mother had been around, she could have given him some advice. Of course, if she'd been around, she'd be raising Mia, and he'd still be in the army. He'd loved the military, but it wasn't the life he'd wanted for his sister—traveling from place to place, making new friends every couple of years. She'd needed stability, and he'd wanted to offer her that.

The gig in Desert Valley was supposed to be short-term.

That's what he'd told Mia when he'd talked to her about it the previous year. He'd been certain he could get assigned to the K-9 unit in Phoenix. He'd grown up there, had attended school there, and because of that, he had friends and connections in the area. His parents had lived in the same house for thirty years, and their neighbor was the chief of the police department. When he'd heard about Tristan's plan, he'd promised him a position on the Phoenix K-9 unit.

That had seemed too perfect to pass up, and Tristan had offered his parents' house as a short-term rental to friends from church, moved Mia to Desert Valley and begun the program at the Canyon County K-9 Training Center. He'd assured his sister that they'd be heading back to Phoenix in a few months, that she'd be back with her old friends and in her old school.

Things hadn't turned out that way. Until the murders, suspicious deaths and attacks were solved, all five K-9 rookie graduates of the training center were assigned to the Desert Valley PD. Mia wasn't happy about it. Tristan couldn't blame her, but he was tired of the acting out, the poor grades, the bad attitude.

His coworker Whitney Godwin had assured him that Mia's behavior was normal for girls her age. Maybe, but Mia had always been like their mother. Kind, easygoing, quick to lend a hand. She loved her friends, loved animals, dreamed of being a veterinarian or a dog trainer.

She could be either of those things or both of those things. She was extremely bright and she used to be really driven.

That had changed in the past few months.

Tristan was praying it would change back. He didn't know how much more conflict either of them could handle. He had nightmares about Mia running away and taking to the streets.

"Don't borrow trouble," he muttered, walking into the kitchen and opening the refrigerator.

"Did you say something, Tris?" Mia called from her room, and she sounded just like she use to. Happy and well-adjusted. A teen who'd been through the death of her parents but who'd be just fine.

"Nothing important." He eyed the contents of the fridge. They were pitiful. A few slices of cheese, a third of a carton of milk, a couple of grapes and an apple. Which was odd, because there'd been a dozen eggs, a head of lettuce and a bunch of fruits and vegetables earlier in the day.

"We need to go to the grocery store," Mia said from behind him, her voice soft and just a little apologetic. "I kind of brought some things over to Jenny's when I went."

He turned to face her, his heart catching just a little when he looked into her eyes. They were almond-shaped like their mother's, the high arch of her brows exactly the same as their father's.

"You brought a lot of things over to Jenny's," he said, and she sighed.

"I got carried away. The thing is, they don't have much. Sometimes they've got a can of tuna and a box of toaster pastries. Jenny is always hungry, and we always have plenty." She shrugged. "I'm sorry, Tristan. I know I messed up again. Sometimes, I forget to use the brain God gave me."

"You were using your heart. That's just as important."

She smiled at that. Probably the first smile he'd seen in a month. "Thanks. If you want, we can go to the store now. We're almost out of puppy chow, and we can get some while we're there."

"We're out of puppy chow?" He opened the pantry where they kept it and saw the twenty-five-pound bag lying on the floor empty.

If there was three pieces of kibble in it, he'd be surprised. "I bought this four days ago," he said as much to himself as to Mia.

"Sprinkles is still growing. He needs a lot of food." Mia still sounded pleasant enough, but she'd balled her fists and looked ready for another fight.

She just might get it.

His day had started before dawn, and he'd been running ever since. He was tired, and he didn't want to deal with another crisis. Which this was about to become, because there was no way the fifteen-pound puppy could have eaten that much food that quickly.

"Mia," he said, lifting the empty bag, "What happened to the dog food?"

"I told you, Sprinkles ate it." Her cheeks were flaming red, and he knew she was lying. She knew that he knew, and that was going to make the entire conversation more difficult.

"Your puppy weighs fifteen pounds."

"He's a big eater."

"Then he's going to be awfully hungry tonight," Tristan commented, tossing the bag into the recycle bin.

"You're not going to get him more food?"

He would. The puppy didn't deserve to be punished for whatever Mia had done. "I spent a good amount of money on the food that was in that bag. It should have lasted weeks."

She didn't say a word, just dug in her pocket and pulled out a bunch of crumbled bills. "Here's my allowance. Use that to buy the stuff."

She tossed the money onto the counter and stormed away.

He didn't go after her. He wanted to, because he wanted to tell her that it wasn't about money. It was about trust. It was about the lies that she seemed to tell all the time lately.

He wasn't in the mood to start a war, though, so he left the cash on the counter, grabbed his keys and headed to the store.

FIVE

Late pregnancy made it difficult to sleep.

Fear made it even harder.

By five in the morning, Ariel had given up. By six, she'd showered, dressed and prepared a lesson plan for her tutoring session with Mia. The teen had a lot of work to do if she was going to pass the summer course. Tristan seemed determined to make sure she did, and Ariel hoped that Mia would go along with the plan.

She set a kettle on to boil, grabbed a tea bag from the cupboard and dropped it in a mug, resisting the urge to lift the curtains and look out into the backyard. All night long, she'd imagined someone sneaking through the empty field behind the house. She'd imagined the sound of glass shattering, imagined her own panic, her trembling fingers as she dialed 911.

She'd kept the card Tristan had given her on the table near her bed, and she'd memorized his number before she'd turned off the lights.

She'd been as prepared as she could be, her bedroom door locked, a butcher knife on her dresser, but she hadn't felt safe.

The kettle whistled, and she poured hot water over the tea bag, grabbed a couple of crackers from the cupboard and headed back upstairs. She had a small study there, a bedroom for the baby and one for herself. It was a nice-sized house on a nice-sized piece of land in a nice community.

She'd been excited to buy it and to begin her new life. When she'd gotten the job offer and moved to town, she'd told herself that she'd turned the last page of a really horrible book, and she was about to read a new one. Write a new one? It hadn't mattered to her. She was just glad to be done with the past. All the ugliness of it—the marriage that hadn't been anything like what she'd planned, the divorce, the horrible moment she'd learned the truth about Mitch.

But, yesterday? That had scared her. It had made all the things she'd ignored, all the tiny little shivers of fear, the moments when she'd felt watched and hunted, seem like more than her imagination working overtime.

Had she brought her Las Vegas troubles with her?

Was someone who'd been affiliated with Mitch coming after her? Maybe seeking revenge for something she didn't even know she'd done?

She'd called Detective Smithfield from the Las Vegas Metropolitan Police Department the previous night. He'd been in charge of the insurance fraud investigation against Mitch. He'd assured her that there was no one that would put her name together with Mitch's. She had nothing to worry about. The case was closed, the people who'd paid Mitch were in jail. No one had any reason to come after her.

But, someone had been in the school last night.

That person had nearly killed her.

A childish prank gone wrong?

That's what Chief Jones had speculated. She'd called him the previous night, too, and the conversation hadn't made her any more comfortable with the situation. They hadn't found the perpetrator. They hadn't been able to pull any prints from the doors. There were no security cameras in the school. The district was too small, money too tight for those kinds of expenses.

She frowned, settling into the chair and sipping her tea. Sunlight streamed through the window, dust motes dancing across the room. It was already warm, the unair-conditioned house still sweltering from the previous day. She planned to have central air installed at the end of August, when prices went down. Hopefully, Mia wouldn't be too miserable working in a hot house.

Who was Ariel kidding?

Of course, Mia was going to be miserable. And not because of the heat. No teenager wanted to be tutored by her teacher. Especially not a teenager who was already in summer school.

Had Tristan broken the news to her, yet?

Were the two going head-to-head over it?

Probably, and Ariel was just curious enough to want to call Tristan to see if he needed any help convincing his sister to attend the tutoring session.

She wouldn't, because it wasn't her business to get between the brother and sister.

She also wouldn't because she wanted to so much.

The fact was, she'd thought about calling Tristan a dozen times the previous night. Every creak in the house, every brush of branches against the siding, and she'd grabbed for the phone, her heart pounding frantically. She'd known there was no one in the house, but she'd almost called Tristan anyway. Anything to feel less alone.

She opened the window that looked out over the backyard, letting a balmy summer breeze into the room.

The sun had already risen over the trees, the gold-and-purple sky hinting at the beautiful day ahead.

She wanted so badly to be thankful for that.

She was *going* to be thankful for it. God had provided everything she needed and most of what she wanted. So what if her marriage had fallen apart, if her dreams had been shattered? She had new dreams to pursue. God would bless that. She had to believe it, or she'd spend her nights tossing and turning and worrying about the future.

She returned to her desk and thumbed through a few assignments that still needed grading. Monday would be there before she knew it, and she'd be back in the classroom.

At least that never changed—the chalky scent of the air, the waxed floors, the morose teens who, just a few years ago, were giggling little kids.

She took a sip of tea and caught just a hint of something in the air.

Gasoline?

Surprised, she walked to the window and inhaled. There it was again. The same acrid scent.

Odd. None of her neighbors were close enough for her to smell exhaust from a car or gasoline from an old lawn mower. Even if they were, it was Saturday morning, the street quiet.

She walked into the hallway and stood at the landing at the top of the stairs. Nothing there. Whatever she was smelling was outside, and there was no way she was opening a door to figure out what it was or exactly where it was coming from.

Not after what had happened at the school.

She'd almost died. The bullet had been inches from

hitting her. A little better aim by the gunman, and she'd be in a hospital or worse, and the baby…

She couldn't dwell on that.

If she did, she'd be too terrified to function.

She walked into the nursery. Nothing there. Into her room. Nothing. Finally, she returned to the study. The smell was stronger now, and it was mixed with something else.

Smoke?

Fire?

Her stomach churned, her heart skipped a beat as she ran back to the window. She expected to see something. Maybe a brush fire in the woods behind the house. Instead, black smoke billowed past the window, pouring up into the sky from somewhere right below.

The back porch?

Was it on fire?

Flashes of red and orange shot through the blackness, and she could feel heat simmering in the air.

A siren screamed, the shrill sound jolting her into action.

The fire alarm!

The house was on fire!

She ran to the bathroom and grabbed a towel, soaking it in water and wrapping it around her lower face. Smoke billowed up the stairs, filling the hall with noxious fumes. Was the fire on the porch? In the foyer? At the back of the house?

Glass shattered and black smoke poured up the stairwell, filling the upstairs hallway, seeping through the wet towel and into Ariel's nose and throat.

She coughed, gagged, her eyes streaming with tears as she dropped onto all fours, trying to get closer to the ground and away from the rising smoke and heat.

She needed to get out.

She needed to do it quickly.

If she hadn't been pregnant, she would have lowered herself out an upstairs window, dropped to the ground below and run to the neighbors to call for help.

She *was* pregnant, though, and she didn't want to risk harming the baby. She had to find another way out. *Quickly*, because the upstairs hall was dark with smoke, and she could barely see her hands on the floor.

She crawled in the direction of the stairway, the baby wiggling and kicking. Was she getting enough oxygen? Was the thick smoke hurting her?

Please, God, protect her. Please, help me find a way out.

Her hand slid over the lip of the first step, and she knew exactly how many steps it would take to get to the landing, how many stairs from there to the first floor.

One.

Two.

Three.

She counted mentally. The smoke was so thick her head swam, her lungs burned from lack of oxygen.

All she had to do was make it to the door.

She scuttled downward through the haze, moving as quickly as she could. Halfway down, she hit the landing. The smoke was thicker there, heat pulsing upward. Something thumped on the stairs below, and she thought she saw a dark shadow through the gloom.

A neighbor coming to help?

Tristan? Her heart jumped at the thought. Had he arrived with Mia, seen the fire and broken in to help her?

"Tristan?" she called, her voice muffled by the towel. "Up here!"

"Good," someone said. Not Tristan. She was sure

she'd have recognized his voice. A man, though. She was certain of that.

"Did you call the fire department?" she asked, and the man laughed, a mean, hard sound that made her blood run cold.

"Why would I?" he asked.

There was a flurry of movement, a flash of light and flames shot up from the bottom step.

She scrambled back the way she'd come, running from the spreading flames and from whoever had been standing at the bottom of the stairs.

Tristan saw the smoke before he turned onto Ariel's road—black tendrils spiraling up toward the sky. Not a typical sight in Desert Valley especially not at the end of a hot summer. He eyed the growing cloud. It wasn't from a fireplace or wood burning stove. Not from yard waste being burned, either. To him, it looked more like a structure fire. He scanned the houses that lined the street, and that feeling he got when things were off, the one that told him that danger was nearby, edged along his spine.

He and Jesse had trained in arson detection, and he could smell gasoline and burning wood in balmy morning air.

"Call 911," he told his sister.

Mia didn't ask why.

She pulled out her cell phone and dialed.

"The operator wants to know what the emergency is," she said a moment later.

"House fire," he responded, his gaze on that smoke as he rounded the corner onto Ariel's street.

Plumes of smoke speared the pristine sky, staining the bright blue dusky brown black. Now, he could see where they were coming from—Ariel's place. Smoke wafted up from the back of the house, and the front door seemed to be in flames, tongues of fire licking the old wood.

He slammed on the brake, shouting the address to Mia. She repeated it to the 911 operator as he got out of his SUV.

"Stay here," he commanded, then took off running toward the old house. By the time he reached it, the front door had been consumed, flames lapping up the frame and licking at the upper story. No way to get in there.

He raced to the back of the house, hoping to gain entrance there. The back deck was engulfed, the door beyond it hidden by flames.

Odd that both entry points were on fire.

The thought flitted through his mind. He tucked it away for later. Right now, he had to focus on getting to Ariel. If she was still inside, she didn't have long to escape before the entire house went up in flames.

He scanned the back facade, seeing a broken window on the lower level. He thought it opened into the office. A few shards of glass littered the ground, glinting in the early morning sun.

Had Ariel escaped through the window?

If so, why break the glass? Why not just open it?

He reached inside the broken frame and unlocked the window. It opened easily, the room beyond hazy with smoke.

"Ariel?" he called, his voice barely seeming to carry above the crackling of the fire.

He stepped back and shouted up toward the top floor of the house. If she was in there, if she was conscious, she'd be at the window upstairs, not hanging around in the downstairs where the smoke was thickest.

A second-story window *was* open, the curtains fluttering outside. "Ariel?" he yelled again.

Seconds later, she appeared, her face smudged with soot, her eyes wide with fear. She had something in her hand. A sheet? A couple of blankets. "The stairs are on fire," she called, her voice hoarse. "This is the only way out."

"Do you have a ladder in the shed?"

"I usually borrow one from the lady across the street."

He could run over there, but he thought they were running out of time. The heat from the fire burned his face, the smoke filled his lungs and he was outside the building.

"We don't have time. Climb out and drop down. I'll catch you."

"I'm thirty-six weeks pregnant!" she protested, but she was already moving, her leg sliding over the edge of the windowsill, her hands clutching the frame.

"You'll be okay," he assured her, sirens blaring in the background, someone shouting from the front yard.

A neighbor with a ladder?

He didn't have time to check.

"I'm not worried about me," she responded. "I'm worried about the baby."

"The baby will be okay, too. I'll make sure of it." He positioned himself below the window, reaching up as she slid her other leg over the window frame. He could see flames eating at the edges of the roof, moving along the frame of the house.

They had minutes. Maybe less. But, Ariel seemed frozen in place, perched in the window frame and unable or unwilling to go any farther.

"Ariel, you're going to have to do the first part. Just

hold on to the window frame, and let your legs drop. I'll be able to grab you and lower you down." He kept his voice calm, because he didn't want her to panic, but she needed to move. Quickly.

"Come on," he urged, and she finally did, shifting position so that she was facing the house, her feet against the siding. Her belly bumped against the house and he reached for her, grabbing her legs as she lowered herself farther down.

"Let go," he urged, all his training, all his work in arson investigation, telling him that if they didn't hurry, the house might collapse and take them both down with it.

An old building. Lots of wood. Plenty of accelerant. He could smell it in the air and in the smoke that wafted from the window.

"Let go!" he urged, and she finally did, dropping quickly, her weight falling against him, his hands sliding from her leg to her waist.

He had just seconds to set her on her feet, and then he was dragging her away, the house groaning and creaking as the fire ate it from the inside out.

"Thankfully you came when you did!" she said, her face stark-white, a streak of soot on one cheek. "I wasn't sure how I was going to get out without hurting the baby."

"You would have managed." He had no doubt about that. Whether she would have escaped injury was another story.

"Are okay?" he asked as they jogged around the side of the house.

She nodded, but her hand was on her stomach, the protective gesture worrying him.

"The baby?" he asked, and she offered a wane smile.

"I think she's fine. She's wiggling around like crazy. Must be all the excitement."

"Too much excitement. Let's get the medics to check you out." He gestured toward the fire truck and ambulance that were pulling up to the curb.

Ariel didn't argue. She must be as worried as he felt.

Heat from the burning house scorched the front grass and the small shrubs that edged the property, the building going up like kindling.

Ariel had escaped just in time.

A firefighter ran toward them. "Is anyone else in the house?"

"No," Ariel said, then she frowned.

"You're certain?" the firefighter asked.

She nodded. "There was someone, but I think he's gone. I think he started the fire," she responded, her gaze shifting to the house. "I was trying to get down the stairs, and he was there. I couldn't see well through the smoke. At first I thought..."

"What?" Tristan prodded, and she shrugged, her shoulders too thin beneath her T-shirt.

"I thought it might be you. I knew that you and Mia were going to be there soon, and I thought you must have arrived and seen the fire. I called out, and the guy responded. That's when I realized he was a stranger. The next thing I knew, the entire staircase was in flames."

Tristan didn't like the sound of that.

He also didn't like the fact that he'd smelled gasoline in the air or that the front and back entrances had been blocked by flames.

He wanted to ask her questions, see what else she remembered about the guy in the house, but the paramedics were there, pressing an oxygen mask to her face, taking her blood pressure, checking her pulse.

Two police cruisers pulled up in front of the house, a dark sedan right behind them. A woman jumped out of it. Short and wiry with huge round glasses and wide blue eyes, she looked as if she'd been pulled out of bed—her hair sticking out in several different directions.

She darted toward them, pink slippers slapping against the ground.

"Ariel!" she cried as she skidded to a stop a few feet away. "Are you okay?"

"Yes," Ariel mumbled through the oxygen mask.

"Are you sure? I was heartsick when I got the call about the fire."

"Who called?" Ariel took the mask off, and Tristan could see the wound from the previous night—the edges of the cut butterflied together, blood seeping out from under the bandages.

"Edna. She saw the smoke and called 911, then she called me. She was worried that..." Her voice trailed off.

"That what?" Tristan prodded.

"That fire might have been started by bad wiring and that Ariel might want to sue me since I was the Realtor who sold her the house. I told her that was total hogwash. Ariel would never do such a thing. I also told her to check and make certain Ariel wasn't in the house. She refused. She said Ariel might have spent the night with a *friend*." She eyed Tristan, and Ariel's pale cheeks went bright pink.

"Tristan is actually a—"

"Officer McKeller," Tristan cut in. "I'm with Desert Valley's K-9 Unit."

"Oh!" The woman's eyes widened, and she placed a wrinkled hand on her chest. "Edna didn't mention that."

"She couldn't have known. I escorted Ariel home

last night. I'm sure you heard about the incident at the school, Ms…?"

"Janice Lesnever." She offered her hand. "I've heard some good things about the new K-9 unit. Of course, the training center is fantastic. One of the best programs in the country, the way I hear things."

"It is a great program."

"Too bad so many people affiliated with it have died," Janice continued. "That's got to be hard on its reputation."

"What people have died?" Ariel asked.

"Accidental deaths," Janice hurried to assure her. "It's nothing to worry yourself about, dear."

Accidental?

Not the lead trainer's, Veronica Earnshaw. That was for certain. Officer Ryder Hayes's wife hadn't died accidentally, either. And, Tristan had his doubts about Mike, a rookie. Another rookie K-9 handler's death had also been ruled an accident, too, but K-9 officer Whitney Godwin didn't believe it. She knew Brian Miller well and insisted that he'd have never lighted candles in his home.

"How many people have died?" Ariel asked as the EMT, placed the oxygen mask back over her nose and mouth.

"You need to get plenty of oxygen to that baby, ma'am," the young man said. "We recommend that you allow us to transport you to the hospital. It would be best to have a doctor check things out."

"I need to speak with Chief Jones," Ariel said through the mask, the words muffled. "There was someone in the house with me, Tristan. I know he set the fire."

"Arson?" Janice looked shocked, her eyes wide behind her glasses. "Why would someone set fire to my house?"

Because Ariel was living in it?

After the attack the previous night, that seemed like the obvious answer.

"I'm not sure, but I plan to find out," Tristan responded.

Whoever it was, he meant business. Going inside a burning building to be certain your victim couldn't escape? That took a lot of guts or a lot of craziness. Either way, it also took a lot of knowledge about the way fires spread, how quickly they could move.

He'd talk to the chief about it. Once the fire was out and the scene cool enough to work, he'd bring Jesse in, see what kind of evidence the lab might be able to sniff out.

For now, he'd follow the ambulance to the hospital and wait with Ariel until the chief arrived.

"Everyone okay over here?" rookie officer Ellen Foxcroft called as she strode across the yard, her golden retriever, Carly, beside her. The dog pranced restlessly, ready for the work she loved to do.

"Looks like it," the EMT responded. "But we're going to let the doctors at the hospital make certain of it."

"I'd rather not," Ariel muttered, the words barely audible.

Ellen heard. She patted Ariel's shoulder. "You'll be fine."

"Not if whoever was in the house with me has anything to do with it."

Ellen met Tristan's eyes. "What's going on?"

"Arson."

"Did you get a look at the guy?" she asked Ariel.

"Not much of one."

"Any idea how he got inside?"

"Broken window at the back of the house. I think that was the entrance point," Tristan said.

"Are you going to take Jesse around to search for accelerants?"

"We're not going to be able to get close until tomorrow. The fire is still burning pretty hot."

"I'll take Carly around the perimeter of the property. She might be able to catch a whiff of the perp. It's worth a shot anyway."

She called the dog to heel and headed around the side of the house, bypassing firefighters who were already working to contain the blaze.

It would be difficult for Carly to track the perpetrator with so many scents mixed together at the scene, but Tristan knew that she and Ellen would work until Ellen was convinced there was no possible way to track the perpetrator.

"We need to head out," the EMT said as he and a crew member helped Ariel onto a stretcher.

"Maybe it would be better to wait here," Ariel responded, her face ashen, her pallor alarming. "Whoever started the fire might be waiting at the hospital to see if I show up."

"He's not going to get anywhere near you," Tristan replied, his voice hard with anger. Ariel had been attacked twice in two days. She was terrified, shaken. That couldn't be healthy for her or the baby.

He waved to Ryder Hayes who'd just gotten out of his SUV. The most experienced member of the K-9 team, Ryder had been on the force for five years. He knew the town and the people in it better than anyone else of the rookies.

Ryder jogged over, his K-9 partner trotting along beside him.

"Ellen radioed that this was arson," he said, not wasting time or words.

"It is."

"You've called the chief?"

"I'm about to."

"I'll question the neighbors, ask if any of them saw anything. Are you sticking around or heading to the hospital?"

Tristan didn't hesitate. He didn't look at Ariel for approval, either. Whether she wanted him there or not, he was going to the hospital.

"I'm going to the hospital. I'll bring Jesse back here once the fire marshal clears the scene."

"You don't have to—" Ariel began.

"I do. There's an officer waiting to escort you into the building. I'll be there soon." He brushed the smudge of soot from her cheek, nodded for the EMT to wheel her away.

"We're going find the person who did this," Ryder muttered, his gaze on the burning shell of the old house.

Easy words to say, but it might not be as easy to follow through on them.

They'd been searching for a murderer for months. So far, they'd come up empty. They were also looking for the person who'd nearly killed Ellen Foxcroft's mother.

And then there was Marco. The team hadn't been able to find the missing German shepherd puppy that had escaped—or had been set free by lead trainer Veronica Earnshaw—the night Veronica was killed. Where was that puppy? Based on the break-ins that had occurred at homes in town that had dogs, it was clear someone wanted to find that puppy. But why? And who?

And where could Marco be? He'd been missing for a few months. He wouldn't be the tiny puppy he'd been when Marian Foxcroft had first donated him and two other pups to the K-9 Training Center. How could he be so easy to hide? Tristan and his fellow rookies were missing something.

Yeah. They were batting zero, but eventually the tide would turn.

Tristan just needed to make sure Ariel stayed alive long enough for that to happen. Not just because it was his job. Because he cared. About Ariel. About her baby. They'd come to Desert Valley for a second chance. Tristan was going to do everything in his power to make sure that they got one.

SIX

Three hours after she'd arrived at the hospital, Ariel was cleared to leave. She'd already wiped sonogram gel off her stomach, replaced the cotton gown with her yoga pants and T-shirt, washed her face and hands and tried to fix her wrecked hair. She hadn't been wearing shoes when the fire began, but a nurse had provided socks that she'd slipped on her feet.

Now, all she needed were her discharge instructions and a ride. She also needed a place to go. That was a problem that she was still trying to work through. She wasn't brand-new to town, but she was new enough to not have the kind of friends who'd offer a room for a few months. That's what Ariel was going to need, because the house was a total loss. The fire marshal had stopped by to tell her the news. Not much left, is what he'd said. He'd asked about insurance, and he'd encouraged her to call her agent immediately.

She had, and she'd been assured that the house and everything in it were completely covered. She'd have a new home, new material items, new everything that had been lost.

In a few months that she really didn't have.

The baby would be there in weeks, and she needed

a place to bring her. A hotel room didn't seem like the kind of place a newborn should go home to.

The good news? The baby was fine. Her little heart was beating beautifully, her little arms and legs were wiggling happily. Ariel had watched her on the sonogram, listened to the rapid beat of her heart on the monitor, and she'd cried. Not big huge tears, because that wasn't her thing. Just teary-eyed relief at the fact that the person who had meant her harm hadn't been successful.

Now, Ariel was waiting for the discharge papers and for inspiration. She had no wallet, no cell phone, no money, no credit cards. No ID. She was wearing soot-stained clothes, and she had no way of getting anywhere. She also couldn't think of anyone she could call for a ride. Except for Tristan. His phone number kept floating through her head, and she kept hearing the words he'd spoken right before the EMTs had carted her away. Kept feeling his fingers sliding over her skin as he'd brushed soot from her cheek.

He'd walked into the triage room minutes after she'd arrived at the hospital, told her that there was a guard stationed outside the door, and then he'd disappeared. She hadn't seen or heard from him since.

Which should have been fine, but somehow wasn't.

She felt better when he was around. Less shaky. Less scared.

Twice, she'd nearly been killed.

Twice, she'd been saved by Tristan, and she was beginning to think he was the only one standing between her and whoever was trying to kill her.

A foolish thought.

Tristan was doing his job. Just like every other K-9 officer.

He wouldn't always be around. It was only through the grace of God that he'd been there the first two times.

Maybe she needed to leave town. Again.

Start over. Again.

Maybe she needed to come up with another job, another house, another life.

The problem was, she was about four weeks away from giving birth. No one was going to hire her before the baby was born. Getting a job after the baby was born might not be easy.

"It'll all work out," she assured herself, pacing across the hospital room, restless and uneasy.

"Knock-knock!" someone called cheerfully from the open doorway.

Ariel turned to face the speaker, smiling as she met Lauren Snyder's eyes. The pastor's wife had been kind and helpful from the first day Ariel had moved to town. She'd been the first one to show up on the doorstep after Ariel moved into her house. She'd had a bunch of kids in tow, each one of them carrying a dish of food. If Lauren hadn't been the busy mother of six children, she and Ariel would have been good friends by now. As it was, they were slowly getting to know each other over Sunday morning coffee at the church.

"Lauren! What are you doing here?" Ariel asked, surprised and pleased by Lauren's arrival. Lauren was the kind of woman who knew everyone, made friends wherever she went and who cared enough to help anyone who needed it. She'd have ideas for housing. She'd also tell Ariel what she needed to hear—that God was in control, that things would work out, that she just had to keep a steady course and trust that His plan was the best one.

"Doug and I got four calls about you. We would have

been here sooner, but the big kids all had sports events, and I had to find someone to watch the littles. Doug wanted to come ahead without me, but I said you'd need a woman's motherly touch not a gnarled old pastor's words of wisdom. He's parking the car." She bustled into the room, a large duffel bag slung over her arm, a tall take-out cup in her hand. "We drove by your place before we came. I wanted to see if we could salvage any of your things."

"How bad is it?" Ariel asked even though she knew.

Lauren sighed and shook her head. "The police wouldn't let us get anywhere close, but the firefighter Doug was able to talk to said the house was a complete loss."

"That's what the fire marshal told me."

"Honey, I'm just so sorry about that, but don't worry, we'll get it all sorted out."

"We? I think you're a little busy, Lauren. The last thing you need is another project."

"What's busy have to do with anything? We've got one opportunity to live this life well. I plan to be busy until the day I keel over."

"Why are we discussing my lovely wife's untimely demise?" Doug Snyder asked as he stepped into the room, his tall broad frame nearly filling the doorway.

"I was just explaining to Ariel that we plan to help her get through this crisis."

"Of course, we do."

"Really, I don't—"

"There's no sense arguing, Ariel," Doug said. "Lauren has already come up with a plan. Trying to stop her would be as useless as trying to rein in an ocean wave."

"What plan?" Anything would be better than the nonexistent plan that Ariel had come up with.

"Did you know that the church owns a parsonage?" Lauren dropped the duffel onto the bed, then handed the cup to Ariel. "That's one of those horrible healthy smoothies all the ladies at church are always talking about. I picked it up at the organic market. Banana, strawberry and spinach. It seemed like the least offensive of the choices."

Ariel accepted the cup, but didn't take a sip. Her stomach was still churning with anxiety. "Thank you."

"Thank me if it doesn't make you gag. If it does, I'll go get you a real milkshake. I might get myself one while I'm at it." She smiled and dropped down onto the edge of the bed, her dark hair springing around her head, threads of silver woven through it. "Now, about that parsonage. The church has owned it for eons."

"Fifty years," Doug corrected. "A member of the congregation lived in it for fifty years before that. From what I've heard, she married but her husband died during WWI. She never married again, never had children and when she passed away, she left the house to the church. We were offered the opportunity to live in it when we took the pastorate, but we already had four kids and another on the way. We opted to move into something a little bigger and use the parsonage for guest speakers and visiting missionaries."

"It's empty most of the time," Lauren added. "Which is a shame. It really is a pretty little house. It needs some work, but it's very livable. Doug already called the deacons, and they agreed that it would be the perfect place for you to stay while your new house is being built. Free of charge. Everyone agreed to that. A woman in your position shouldn't have to pay rent to stay in the church property."

"I really appreciate you thinking of me, but I couldn't

take advantage of the church's generosity." She'd like to, though, because having a place was a lot nicer than having to find one. Especially at this late stage of the pregnancy.

"How is it taking advantage?" Doug asked. "You've been working in the church nursery for a couple of months, you help with the AWANA program. You're a hardworking young woman who has come on some hard times, and I think that the church would be lacking in compassion if it didn't step in and help you out during this challenging time."

"It's right near the school," Lauren added. "Less than two blocks away. You've probably seen it on your way to work. It's an old bungalow with a bright blue door?"

She might have seen it, but she hadn't noticed. She'd been too focused on other things. Lesson plans, plans for the baby, moving on with her life.

"That *would* be really convenient."

Lauren smiled. "For me, too. Our place is around the corner, and after you have the baby, I'll want to come visit all the time. Now that Naomi is six, I'm missing the sweet baby and toddler years." Her youngest was a wild-child, climbing and jumping and squealing during Sunday school every day. She had her mother's zeal for life, that was for certain.

"If I moved in there, I'd want to pay rent. Otherwise, it wouldn't feel right."

"We'll discuss that with the deacons and the business committee. I'm sure that we can write up some paperwork that will make everything legal and nice. For now," Doug said, "let's just get you moved in for a few days. You can see how it works for you, decide if it's something you'd be willing to do for several months."

"That's sound good," Ariel agreed. She didn't have

any other options, and she was relieved to have this one. Once she got to the house, she could lock herself in and really think about her situation. She needed a plan. One that would keep her safe until the baby was born.

"Fantastic!" Lauren gushed. "Are you ready to go now? We can give you a ride, walk through it together and see if there's anything you'll need for the night. We've got a few ladies making meals and stocking the fridge—"

"Honey," Doug interrupted. "I told you to wait until Ariel agreed to the plan."

"I know, but I knew she'd agree. She's like me. Practical." She grinned. "We'll be fabulous friends one day. I just feel it. I'll bake cookies for you and your daughter, and you'll help my kids with their English papers."

It sounded nice. Like a little piece of the dream Ariel had once had.

"I'll help your kids with their English papers even if you don't bake cookies," Ariel said. If she was there long enough for that to happen. She'd planned to make Desert Valley her home. She'd planned to raise her daughter there, build friendships there, make a life that she could be content with there.

But, she couldn't do any of those things until the police found the person who'd tried to shoot her, the one who'd set her house on fire.

The same person?

Ariel thought so.

She was interested to hear what Tristan had learned.

If he ever returned.

"Oh, I'll be baking cookies," Lauren exclaimed. "My kids go through dozens a day. Speaking of kids, Rachel had a few things she thought you could wear. I bought them last Christmas, and she thought they were too fuddy-duddy for a fifteen-year-old. She packed them in the duffel. Simon grabbed toiletries from our supply room. I have no idea what he tossed in here." She lifted the duffel. "I'm hoping soap, shampoo, toothpaste and toothbrush, but it could very well be chips and soda. Fourteen-year-old boys have different ideas about necessities than adults."

Ariel laughed, some of her anxiety fading. She was still scared, still worried, but Lauren's good humor was contagious. "I have to wait for my discharge papers. Then I can leave."

"No problem. While we're waiting, we can make a list of things you're going to need right away. Is there paper around here? A pen?"

"I'll go find something," Doug offered, stepping out into the hall, and then back in.

"Never mind. Looks like the police are back. How about we go get a coffee while they talk to Ariel," he said, taking his wife's arm as Tristan stepped into the room.

He met Ariel's eyes and smiled an easy charming smile that made butterflies dance in her stomach. "I hear you're ready to go home."

"You hear right," she responded, her voice a little hoarse, her mouth a little dry.

From the fire.

At least, that's what she tried to tell herself.

She didn't believe it. Not when she was looking in Tristan's eyes, her heart galloping with something that felt a lot like joy.

"I got back just in time then." His gaze shifted to the Snyders. "Pastor. Lauren. It's nice to see you both," he said. "I'd have been up here when you arrived, but I was waiting for a coworker to pick my sister up."

"Mia was here?" Ariel hadn't realized that, but she probably should have.

"She wanted to come in to talk to you, but I told her to wait until you were a little more settled. She wasn't all that happy about sitting around in the hospital waiting room, so Ellen Foxcroft picked her up and took her to the station. She's going to do some schoolwork there while she waits for me."

"The paper that's due in a couple of days, I hope," Ariel said. It was a lot easier to worry about than everything else.

"That and a couple of extra credit projects. Ellen said she'll make her sit next to Carrie Dunleavy until she finishes."

"Carrie?" Ariel knew a few of the Desert Valley police officers, but she didn't know any of them very well. She couldn't remember Carrie.

"She's the shy, sweet young lady who works as the police department secretary, isn't she?" Lauren asked.

"Right. Hopefully, she'll be able to keep Mia on task. Although, if my sister had been a little more patient, she could have peeked in to say hello. Looks like they've unhooked you from all the machines."

"They unhooked the monitor twenty minutes ago. I'm just waiting for the nurse to come back, and then I can leave."

"You have a place to stay?" he asked.

"We're moving Ariel into the parsonage until her home is rebuilt," Lauren cut in cheerfully.

"That little house on Perry Drive?" Tristan asked, pulling out his phone and typing something into it.

"That's the one," Lauren agreed.

"I just sent a message to Chief Jones to let him know.

I'd like to come over and check it out, see how secure the place is."

"That's a good idea," Doug agreed. "If you want to wait with Ariel and give her a ride, Lauren and I can go over and unlock the place, air it out a little. I don't think it's been used since last Christmas."

"Sounds good," Tristan agreed.

No one bothered asking Ariel what she thought. One minute, they were all in the room. The next, it was just Ariel and Tristan. Alone together.

"There's no need to be nervous," Tristan said, his voice soft and soothing. As if he were afraid she was going to run screaming from the room.

She wasn't, but she probably should. Run. Not scream.

Tristan was trouble.

The kind that could break her heart if she let it.

"I'm not nervous." She paced across the room, fiddled with the strap of the monitor they'd used to track the baby's heart rate.

"No?" Tristan stepped up behind her, touched her shoulder, his fingers warm through her T-shirt. "Then why are your muscles so tense?"

"Someone tried to kill me. That would make anyone nervous."

It would make anyone nervous, but Tristan didn't think that was all that was bothering Ariel. He urged her around so that they were face-to-face, looked into her dark gray eyes.

"I make you nervous, too," he said, and she shrugged.

"You're different, Tristan. I'm not sure what to make of that."

"Different than who?"

She cocked her head to the side, studied him for a moment. "I'd say Mitch, but that would seem like an insult."

"Not really. Your ex sounds like a loser. I prefer to not be anything like that."

"I meant, it would seem like an insult to compare the two of you." She tucked a strand of hair behind her ear, the dimple in her cheek showing for just a second as she offered a quick smile. "Let's talk about something else."

"Like?"

"Did you find the arsonist?"

"No, but we've got teams out looking."

"So, I'm still not safe."

"No." He wasn't going to lie. "But the chief is already rolling patrol cars past the house on Perry."

"I can't believe the Snyders are offering it to me. I was so worried about where I was going to stay, and then they showed up." She grabbed a duffel from the bed, and would have probably hefted it onto her shoulder but he took it from her hands.

"And now you have one less thing to stress about." Although, she might be a little disappointed when she got a look at the place. The house on Perry was about twenty years older than the farmhouse Ariel had been restoring. Tristan passed the place every day when he dropped Mia off at school. He'd been on the volunteer list to mow the half-acre yard in the spring, so he knew exactly what kind of shape it was in. A Cape Cod style house built in the early part of the twentieth century, it had dormer windows on the upper story, a bright blue door and questionable front porch. That really needed to be fixed if Ariel was going to live there.

"I'm really thankful for that."

"Just so you know," he said, "the parsonage might

need a little more work than Lauren and Doug are anticipating."

"I don't mind work."

"You're a little bit pregnant," he pointed out, taking the duffel.

"That hasn't stopped me yet."

"At some point, you're going to have to slow down."

"I'll slow down when the baby is here. Until then, I've got to keep working." She brushed a lock of hair from her cheek, her hand shaking just enough for Tristan to notice.

"You sure you're doing okay?" he asked, wishing he had the right to tell her to sit down and rest for a while.

"I'm not even sure what okay is anymore," she responded, her eyes deeply shadowed, her face pale. She'd washed the soot from her skin, but Tristan could still smell the smoke on her clothes and in her hair.

"I'm sorry this is happening to you, Ariel."

"Yeah. Me, too. I thought when I left Las Vegas that everything would be better, that all the hard times would be over. I guess I was wrong."

"By hard times, you mean what happened with your husband?" He'd spoken with a detective in Las Vegas the previous night. Jason Smithfield had been happy to tell him what he could about Ariel's ex, but he hadn't been able to add much to what Tristan already knew.

"Ex-husband." She paced back to the open doorway. "I called the Las Vegas police last night and talked to the detective who worked my ex-husband's case."

"I spoke with him, too."

"Did you?" She turned to face him. "Detective Smithfield keeps assuring me that my problems have nothing to do with Mitch."

"He told me the same. I'm curious to know what you think. *Are* your new problems related to your old ones?"

"There haven't been new and old. At least, not that I'm aware of. Things have been off since before Mitch died. He filed for divorce right before I found out I was pregnant, and during those last few weeks that we were together, I felt uneasy."

"About?"

"Everything. I'd come home from work, and I'd feel like someone was in the house even though I knew it was empty. The phone would ring, and I'd pick up, but the caller would hang up. I started wondering if Mitch..."

"Was having an affair?"

"It's so cliché, isn't it?" she said with a sad smile. "The naive wife, thinking that everything is okay while her husband cheats behind her back."

"I'm sorry." He was, because he knew the betrayal had hurt. Still, after hearing the list of crimes her husband would have been charged with if he'd lived, Tristan thought Ariel was better off without the guy.

"I was, too. Now, I look back and wonder why I was so surprised by it." She shrugged as if it really didn't matter, but he knew it mattered a lot. He'd had a few friends who'd been through similar things. The hurt took a long time to heal.

"Anyway," she continued, "I was feeling...anxious, and I told him I was worried about us. That's when he broke things off. Three days after I left, he filed for divorce. I found out I was pregnant a couple of days later. He wasn't happy when I told him about the pregnancy. He wanted me to get rid of the baby."

"Nice guy," he muttered.

"Yeah. The thing is, I was never afraid of Mitch

until after the divorce. That's when he seemed to go a little…"

"Crazy?"

"Maybe. He was just really determined that I not have our baby. *My* baby," she corrected. "We both signed legal documents when we divorced. I promised to ask him for nothing. No child support. No contact. He promised to not ever seek visitation or custody of the baby."

"Seems cut-and-dried." It also seemed like the loser's way out. What kind of man walked out on his wife, filed for divorce, gave up all legal right to his child? Not any kind of man Tristan wanted to know.

"It was, but I guess it wasn't enough for him. He wanted me to have an abortion, and he just wouldn't drop the subject. He'd call three, four, five times a day. Finally, I threatened to get a restraining order."

"Did that stop him?"

"He died a few days later. I wish I could say that I was sorry when I found out, but I was mostly just relieved. I'd already been looking for a job, and I had a lead on the teaching position here. Everything should have been okay, but since the divorce, I've just never felt…safe."

"Even here?" he asked. What he wanted to say was that she was safe. That he'd make sure of it.

"For a while, I did. Then, I started to feel like someone was watching me. A couple of times, I thought I heard someone turning the back doorknob at the house. Once, I thought someone was outside the window at the school when I stayed late."

"You didn't think to call the police?"

"And say what? That I thought someone was stalking me? I didn't have any proof. Just weird feelings.

Besides, nothing ever happened, so I chalked it up to lack of sleep and an overactive imagination. Maybe it was. Maybe the things that have happened here have nothing to do with the past."

That was possible. Two women had been murdered in Desert Valley. Maybe the killer was ready to strike again, or maybe the past Ariel thought she'd left behind had followed her.

"I know we asked this already, but aside from your husband, was there anyone else in your life who might have wanted to harm you? Someone you might have forgotten? Maybe just a guy you went out with after your divorce? Someone you might have shown a little interest in?"

"I'm pregnant, Tristan," she said. "Do you really think I'd want to complicate my already complicated life by adding a guy to it?"

"Not every guy is a complication," he responded, because he could imagine helping her get settled in her role of mother, supporting her as she took on the responsibility of parenting her daughter. She had some tough times ahead of her, and if he let himself, he could picture what it would be like to be part of helping her get through them.

"I know, but anything extra in my life after the divorce would have been too much. I didn't date. I didn't go to parties. I didn't hang out at singles' retreats or go searching online for the perfect man."

"How about here? Anyone who's been hanging around you at school? Someone who might have asked you out?"

She hesitated.

"Who?" he asked, not even giving her a chance to deny it.

"Easton Riley."

"The football coach?" He knew the guy—big mouth, big muscles and a little too arrogant for Tristan's liking. It didn't surprise him that Easton had gone after Ariel. What surprised him was how annoyed he felt about it.

"He asked me to dinner a couple of times, but I've been too busy to take him up on the offer."

Good, he almost said.

"Did he seem upset when you refused the invitations?" he asked instead.

"Are you kidding? The guy goes out with a different woman every few days. The only reason he asked me more than once was because he's never heard the word *no* before, and he wasn't quite sure what it meant," she retorted. She must have realized how that sounded, because her cheeks went bright red. "What I mean is—"

"You don't have to explain. Everyone in town knows the guy is a player. I'm glad you didn't have to go out with him to figure it out."

"After being married to Mitch, I can spot one a mile away," she said dryly, as she walked to the open door and glanced out into the hall. "I wish the nurse would hurry. I'm anxious to see my new digs."

She was obviously also anxious to change the subject.

That was fine with Tristan. He'd gotten what he needed.

"I'll go to the desk and ask for the paperwork. Then we can get out of here."

"That's okay. I can wait a few more minutes."

"You shouldn't have to. I'll be right back."

He walked out of the room, pulling the door shut as he left. As soon as he was out of earshot of the room, he dialed Chief Jones's number. Easton Riley had been in town for a long time. As a matter of fact, Tristan was pretty sure he'd heard that the guy had grown up there. That meant he'd been there when Ryder's wife was killed. He'd been there when Veronica was killed, too. School had still been in session, and there'd been a ball game that weekend. Tristan remembered that because Mia had wanted to attend it with a freshman guy she'd met at church.

He'd said no.

They'd had a fight.

Typical stuff, but it had been enough for the game to be seared into his brain.

Had Veronica and Easton ever dated?

Had he and Melanie Hayes had contact with one another?

They were questions worth getting answers to, leads worth following. He left a message for Chief Jones, and then went to find a nurse.

SEVEN

It took Ariel three seconds to realize that she hadn't asked Tristan one question. It took her another second to realize that he'd asked her plenty, and that she'd answered all of them. He was much better at interrogation than she was. Which was a shame, because she needed answers.

Someone had tried to kill her twice. It seemed very possible that the person would try again. Unless the police could find him and put him in jail.

Tristan had mentioned that Officer Ellen Foxcroft would take Tristan's K-9 partner, Jesse, trained in arson detection, through her house, but he hadn't said whether or not she'd found the arsonist's trail. He also hadn't mentioned what kind of evidence had been collected from the scene, whether or not any of the neighbors had seen or heard anything.

Were there any leads?

Ariel had no idea, because she hadn't asked.

But, she would, because she had a whole lot riding on the answers. She had to decide whether to stay in Desert Valley or to leave.

She frowned, walking to the window that looked out over the parking lot. Sunlight streamed from a clear blue sky and glinted off cars that were three stories below. A few people walked through the lot, some of them hand in hand, some of them huddled in groups. One or two were alone. She found herself watching the loners, wondering if they wanted someone with them or if they were glad to be by themselves.

Ariel had never wanted to be the person walking alone.

Maybe because she'd lost her parents or because she'd never had siblings. Maybe because she'd felt a little lost when her great-aunt died. Whatever the reason, she liked having people in her life. She missed her Las Vegas friends. She missed her church there. She longed for the kind of connections that lasted. The ones that were there for decades.

Even before she'd met Mitch, she'd loved the idea of going home to someone, of lying in bed knowing that she was sharing space with a person who wanted to share it with her.

She'd wanted to grow old with someone. She'd wanted to hold hands late at night, talk into the early morning hours. She'd wanted a dozen things that were out of her reach now.

That was okay.

Or, it should have been.

Lately, she'd been wondering if maybe she could have those things that she'd once longed for.

Lately?

The last two days.

And, she knew why.

Tristan.

He seemed to fill her thoughts. His warm smile, the way he always seemed to be there when she needed him, those were heady things for a woman who'd been cheated on and tossed aside.

She could switch gears and change focus. She could be a single mother and raise her daughter without crying for all the things she didn't have, but she couldn't stop herself from wanting that deep connection with another person, that unbreakable bond that a couple should have.

She also couldn't hide from whatever seemed to be after her. That would only be putting off the inevitable.

At least, that's how it seemed to her.

She'd left Las Vegas, hoping that the anxiety and fear would stay there. It hadn't. She'd been more anxious since the move, more scared.

Now she was being terrorized by someone.

Would moving away keep her safe?

Or would she just be followed to the next town, the next job?

Footsteps tapped against the tile floor and she turned as a nurse walked into the room.

"Ready to go home?" the young woman asked.

"Yes." Even if home was temporary. At least she had somewhere to go.

"Great. Here are the discharge orders." The nurse handed Ariel a sheet of paper. "No follow-up necessary unless something changes. You'll be seeing your OB within the week, right?"

"Yes," Ariel assured her.

When the nurse left, Tristan took Ariel's arm, the duffel hanging from his other shoulder. "You want me to find a wheelchair? Usually they wheel people out of here."

"I can walk."

He glanced at her feet, raised a dark eyebrow. "In socks?"

"It's a warm day."

"Scorching might be more the word you're looking for. The sun is brutal and the pavement is hot. Your feet might burn. Even through the socks."

"After what happened this morning, that's the least of my worries."

"I know." He took her hand, pulled her to a stop. "I also know that you're trying not to think about that old house and all the things you had in it."

"Tristan—" she began, because he was right. She didn't want to think about it. She didn't want to talk about it. She just wanted to move on.

"It's tough. I'm not going to say it isn't, but you have people who care about you. We're going to make sure that you rebuild, that everything you lost is replaced." He was so sincere, his gaze so steady and reassuring that she could barely speak past the lump in her throat.

"Thanks," she managed to say.

"Thank me after we find the guy who burned your house down." He linked his arm through hers, led her into the corridor. "You game to go straight to the parsonage?"

"Where else would we go?"

"I planned to take you to your place to pick up your van, but I've got a meeting in an hour, and I need a little time to look at the parsonage. I want to check the doors and windows, see what kind of security system needs to be installed. The sooner that's done, the better."

"A security system wouldn't have helped this morning."

He paused, his dark eyes troubled. "You're right, but knowing you have one will still make me feel better."

They'd reached the elevator, and he pressed the button, urging her inside when the doors opened. He was wearing his uniform, and there was a smudge of soot on his shoulder.

She touched the spot, trying to rub the mark away.

"Don't waste your time, Ariel." He took her hand, squeezing it gently, his fingers warm and callused against hers. "It's not coming out until I toss it in the wash."

"I can do it for you," she offered, and wished the words back immediately. Doing laundry for Tristan was not a good way to keep some distance between them.

"I'd rather you do something else," he murmured, his thumb running along the back of her knuckles, sending warmth up her arm and straight into her heart.

She pulled away, the contact making her long for things she had no business even thinking about—this man, a future with him. "What?"

"Be careful. Be aware. Don't ever doubt your gut." The doors slid open, and they stepped out into the lobby. A few people were sitting in chairs there, reading or scrolling through their phones while they waited.

"I will be. I have been. I won't," she assured him.

"Good. I don't want anything to happen to you or the baby, Ariel. From what the fire marshal said, the entire back door of your house was consumed. The kitchen was gone. He thinks the arsonist threw gasoline on the door and then lit it. Pretty rudimentary, but very effective. Especially on an old house with lots of dry wood holding it together. If you'd been sleeping, you might not have made it out alive"

"Has any evidence been recovered?" She finally managed to ask a question. Not a good one, but it was a start. Maybe her brain was starting to function again, the shock of losing her house and nearly losing her life fading away and leaving room for rational thought.

"The house is too hot. It'll be another day before we can get in there."

"How about Ellen? Did she and her partner find anything?"

"Unfortunately, no. The area was too contaminated. Chemicals. People. Machines. Carly is a great tracker, but any dog would struggle under those circumstances."

"So, we're back where we were yesterday." She knew she sounded discouraged. She shouldn't be. She had an entire team of well-trained officers working to help her.

"Don't give up hope for a quick solution. I've got a call in to Chief Jones. I want him to do a background check on Easton."

Tristan clearly was leaving no stone unturned. "Do you really think he's behind all this?"

His tone gentled. "I don't know. But I *do* know that you're not the only woman in Desert Valley who's found herself in danger, Ariel." He tilted his head back, his frustration evident that a killer was on the loose in his town. "I have to check every possibility. Your life depends on it."

She looked at him, those blue eyes so serious. "I know that a woman was murdered a month before I arrived." The lead trainer at the K-9 center where Tristan had recently graduated. She'd also heard about the murder of another woman, a then–K-9 rookie's wife, but that had happened five years ago. "But, I don't see what that has to do with me or with Easton."

"Probably nothing, but I want to make certain there's no connection. Veronica was murdered. The wife of one of my coworkers was murdered. Marian Foxcroft was attacked in her home. It makes sense that those things might be related. If these attacks against you are, too, we need to look for the common denominator."

She nodded. She understood why he had to investigate Easton, no matter how unlikely it was that he was the killer—and trying to murder her. Then again, with everything that had happened in the past eight months, she could almost believe that a blowhard like Easton *was* a serial killer.

"Like I said, I don't know. I *won't* know until we do a little more digging." He opened the lobby door, and they walked outside.

He'd been right about the heat.

It was broiling, the sun beating down on Ariel's head as they crossed the parking lot. She could feel the pavement through her socks, searing the soles of her feet.

Maybe she should have waited for the wheelchair.

"Hot, huh?" Tristan asked as he opened the door of his SUV and helped her inside.

"I don't mind the heat. Unless it's pouring from the back of my burning house."

He smiled, reaching past her stomach and buckling the seat belt just like he had the previous day.

"I can buckle my own seat belt, Tristan," she said as he slid into the driver's seat.

"I figured you could."

"Then why did you do it for me?"

"Why wouldn't I do it for you?"

"Do you make it a habit of answering questions with questions?"

"Yes." He grinned and started the engine. "But, if you want to know the answer, I buckled it because the baby is starting to make maneuvering a little more difficult for you. I didn't think you'd want to waste time fiddling around with a seat belt when we could be heading to your new home."

He was right, and she wasn't sure how she felt about that.

In all the years she'd been married to Mitch, he'd never done something before she'd asked. He'd never lent a hand unless she'd nearly begged for help. She'd spent a lot of time telling herself it was because he viewed her as a strong, independent and capable woman. It had taken her a couple of years to realize the truth. He was so self-absorbed that he hadn't wanted to be bothered. He'd never noticed when she was sick, when she was hurt, when she was tired. If he did, he ignored it.

Had he been like that when they were dating?

She couldn't remember.

Or maybe she could, and she just didn't want to.

Mitch had been the perfect boyfriend. He'd bought the perfect gifts, said the perfect things, written the most beautiful notes, and Ariel had wanted to not be alone anymore.

"You okay?" Tristan asked as he pulled away from the hospital.

She nodded, because her throat was tight from tears she wouldn't shed. Pregnancy hormones. That's what she told herself, but she thought it might be a lot simpler than that.

The parsonage was about as safe as a chick in a hawk's nest. The window locks were ancient, the doors flimsy. If someone wanted to break into any of them, it wouldn't be a challenge to do it.

Tristan wasn't happy about that.

Ariel, on the other hand, seemed pleased, her smile genuine as she followed Lauren from one room to the other. The paint was worn, the wood floor dull, the air filled with a hint of age and must. She didn't seem to care.

"You can use all the furniture, Ariel," the pastor's wife explained as she led the way into a dining room with built-in cabinets. "Or, if you'd rather, you can buy new things, and we'll store these."

"No. This is perfect." Ariel ran her hand over the old dining room table. The top was covered with nicks and dents, but she seemed to like it.

"Let's go upstairs and look at the bedrooms. There are only two, but that will be perfect for you and the baby." Lauren grabbed Ariel's hand and hurried from the room.

Good. Tristan had a few things to say to the pastor, and he didn't want either of the women to hear.

"Pastor," he began, but Doug held up a hand.

"You don't have to say it. I know exactly what you're thinking. She's not going to be safe here."

"I want to put in a security system, new doors and windows."

"That's going to be quite an expense, but I think I can get the board's approval. With everything that's been happening lately, I'm sure they'll understand the need for extra precautions. In the meantime, maybe Ariel can get a dog. Something nice enough to be good with kids but mean enough to take a chunk out of anyone who was trying to hurt her."

"She's gone a lot. That will be hard on a dog."

"My wife and I could probably keep it for her during the day." He ran a hand over his dark hair. "The kids would love it. They've been begging us to let them have a pet, but our house is crazy enough without adding a puppy to it. This would give us an opportunity to see if we could handle it, and it would give Ariel the protection she needs."

"It's a good plan, Pastor. How about we talk to Ariel

about it, see what she has to say?" Tristan liked the idea. He liked it a lot, but if Ariel didn't, the plan would be out.

"Good idea. I've got to admit, I'm worried. Not just about Ariel. I was at the hospital, yesterday, visiting Marian Foxcroft. One of the nurses said she's showing some signs of improvement."

"Ellen said that she might be responding to voices. That's a good sign. One we've all been hoping for." That was something the team planned to discuss at the meeting. If Marian woke from the coma, she might be able to tell them who had attacked her.

Might.

Brain injuries were notoriously hard to predict. If she woke, if she remembered, if she could speak, maybe Marian was the key to solving Veronica's murder. But Marian Foxcroft was much more than someone who could aid in a criminal investigation. She was the mother of Tristan's colleague. He knew Ellen was hopeful that her mother would come out of the coma. Despite the differences between mother and daughter, Ellen was counting on her mother's full recovery. Tristan was praying that she'd got what she longed for. He knew how hard it was to lose a parent, and he didn't want Ellen to have to suffer through the pain of it.

"We've been praying for Marian. Plus, everyone in town is on edge. We need answers."

"We're working hard to find them," Tristan responded. He'd said the same to a dozen people in a dozen different ways. There wasn't much more he could add. He and the rest of the K-9 team were just as on edge, just as anxious for answers as the rest of the citizens of Desert Valley.

"I know you are." Doug was silent for a moment, his gaze darting to the staircase.

"There's something else," he continued quietly.

"What?"

"Lauren asked me not to say anything, but this isn't something I feel comfortable keeping to myself. I told her that I'd give it some time, but that I'd probably talk to you."

"About?" Tristan asked, his pulse jumping a notch, because he knew without a shadow of a doubt that the next thing the pastor had to say was about Mia. She was in the youth group at church. She was in the same peer group as the Snyders' son. She'd probably said or done something she shouldn't have.

"Last week, Lauren was in Nelson's Stock and Feed. It's right outside town."

"I know it."

"Andrew Casing is the owner."

Tristan could tell Doug was taking his time for a reason. "Right."

"His daughter is in the youth group, and she's been out for a few weeks, so Lauren stopped in to see if she was okay. Turns out she just had a summer flu. Anyway, Lauren decided to pick up a bag of cat food for our neighbor. Helen is getting up there, and it's not so easy for her to get around."

That was putting it mildly. Helen Erickson had smashed through the Snyders' fence a couple of weeks ago. She'd voluntarily relinquished her license after that.

"Anyway." Doug cleared his throat, obviously uncomfortable with what he had to say. "Lauren walked into the pet food aisle, and Mia and her friend Jenny were there. Jenny had a couple of cans of dog food, and she was trying to shove them into her pants pockets.

Mia didn't have anything in her pockets, not that I could see, but she did have a can in her hand. When they saw Lauren, they put everything back on the shelves and Jenny said she was playing a game, trying to see how many cans she could fit in her pocket."

"Sounds like a really stupid game," Tristan muttered.

The last thing he wanted to hear, the last thing he needed to hear, was that his sister was aiding a shop-lifter.

"It's possible that is exactly what Jenny was doing and that Mia wouldn't have let her friend steal—not with a police officer for a brother. You know that, right? Kids do all kinds of strange things."

"Anything is possible, Pastor, but a lot of them aren't very probable. I'll talk to Mia."

"I hope my telling you this doesn't change how Mia feels about Lauren. Mia needs a motherly figure in her life, and we were hoping that Lauren could be that for her. Unless, of course, you find the woman God's cho-sen for you. Then, she'll be all Mia needs."

The woman God had chosen for him?

The thought would have been laughable a few days ago. Now? He wasn't laughing. He was thinking about Ariel. The dimple in her cheek, the softness of her hair, the way she cared about her students.

"I won't mention Lauren," he promised, pushing thoughts of Ariel to the back of his mind.

"Thanks, and I'm really sorry about this. I know it's bad timing."

"I can't think of a time that would have been bet-ter," Tristan responded, glancing at his watch. He was supposed to be at the office in ten minutes. He needed to get moving, but he wasn't comfortable leaving Ariel by herself. Not in a house like this one. Not in any house, really.

He jogged upstairs, the narrow staircase and uneven steps concerning. There was no handrail, nothing to hold on to, and nothing to grab during a fall. That was another thing that needed to be changed. He doubted Ariel could see her feet, and the height of the steps were just uneven enough to be challenging.

According to the police report, that had been the reason for Mike Riverton's death—uneven stairs, steep grade, dark stairwell, no handrail. He'd fallen, hit his head on the cement floor and died from a brain hemorrhage. It had all looked good on paper, everything lining up and making perfect sense. Except for the fact that Mike had spent most of his adult life mountain and rock climbing. He knew how to balance. He knew how to catch himself. He knew how to fall without getting hurt. Tristan had seen him in action, and he knew just how good he was. Still, if it had only been Mike who'd died under unusual circumstances, Tristan might have been able to chalk it up to a bizarre accident. The year after Mike died, though, Brian Miller was killed in a house fire.

Both had been training at the Canyon County K-9 Training Center at the time of his death. Both had died on the night of the annual Desert Valley police dance. Just as Ryder Hayes's wife did.

Coincidence? Doubtful. And Tristan didn't believe much in coincidence.

This year, though, the night of the police dance, held a couple of months ago, came and went without trouble. No rookies were harmed or died under mysterious circumstance. One, James Harrison, had even set himself up as bait. No one took it.

He followed the sound of voices into a large bedroom to the left of the staircase. It needed a good cleaning, the wood floor coated with dust, the windows grimy but Ariel was smiling as if someone had just handed her the moon.

"Isn't this great, Tristan?" She waved toward a rocking chair that sat in the corner of the room. "There's even a place to rock the baby."

"It's perfect." Mostly because it was on the second floor, and there was a lock on the door. He checked it, made sure it was working. It wouldn't keep someone out for long, but it might offer a little extra time for help to arrive.

"Does it meet with your approval?" Lauren asked.

"It will once the doors and windows downstairs are changed." *And an alarm system is put in, and Ariel is trained in firearm safety and owns a Glock.*

"I wish there was something more we could do to make the place secure," Lauren responded, her gaze on the window and the sunlight that was streaming through it.

"Your husband suggested she get a dog."

"I don't have time for a dog," Ariel cut in, her dark blue eyes still focused on the rocking chair. Was she imagining sitting there with her baby?

"Pastor Doug said that his family could take care of it while you're at work."

"What?" Lauren squealed. "He did not say that."

"He did," Tristan responded, smiling as Lauren ran from the room.

"A dog isn't going to save me if some guy decides he wants to set this house on fire," Ariel said.

"No, but it will bark if someone gets close enough to toss an accelerant."

"I really don't have time. Dogs take training and attention and energy. I can give it attention, but I know nothing about training, and I definitely don't have the energy."

"There are older dogs at the shelter. We could find you one that is already trained, fairly low energy. Just a sweet old guy or gal who needs a home and would be happy to be your early warning system."

She frowned, smoothing the front of her shirt over her belly, her hand lingering for just a moment. "I'll have to think about it."

"Don't think too long, Ariel. Someone has come after you twice. There's no telling when he'll be back. As much as I want to be here for you every minute of every day, I can't. If I'm not here, and something happens to you, I'll live with the guilt for the rest of my life.

She frowned. "I'm not your responsibility, Tristan."

"Maybe not, but I care enough to want you safe."

Her expression softened, her eyes a pale dove gray, the rims nearly black. "I'm not even sure what to say to that."

"Just say thanks," he murmured, his hand gliding up her arm, settling on the firm muscle of her biceps.

She stilled, her eyes widening, her body leaning toward his just enough for him to know that he wasn't the only one who cared.

He could have leaned down then, touched his lips to her temple, to the hollow of her throat, to her cheek. He could have pulled her closer, tasted her lips, let himself give in to the feeling that the two of them were meant to be together. But it was too soon. For her. For him.

"Thanks," she finally whispered, stepping back, putting some space between them.

"You're welcome. Now, how about we go to the station together? I'm sure you have some questions you'd like to ask the chief. And I have a meeting. If I'm late, I'll never hear the end of it."

He offered his hand and she took it, her fingers curving through his. Her palm felt cool and soft, her grip light. When he met her eyes, she smiled. Not the easy smile he'd seen before. A tentative one that spoke of endings and of beginnings and of a dozen things he didn't think she was ready to say.

They walked out of the room like that and might have even walked down the stairs hand in hand if the stairwell hadn't been so narrow.

He wasn't sure what Ariel thought about that, but her cheeks were pink as she sidled past and hurried down the steps.

EIGHT

Tristan had never been much for meetings. He preferred action to long, drawn-out discussions. Especially discussions that reiterated earlier conversations, listed earlier facts, asked the same questions that had been asked before.

Thirty minutes after the team's meeting had begun, the chief was still doing that, reading notes from an old notepad.

A plate of cookies sat in the middle of the conference table, the goodies provided by the department secretary, Carrie, who sat in the corner with her computer, typing notes. She was a good secretary, quiet and efficient.

She also was a great baker.

Tristan snagged a cookie, mouthing "thanks" as Carrie looked up from her computer.

She blushed, her gaze dropping quickly.

As far as Tristan knew, she'd never married, didn't date and was so shy she rarely spoke to anyone but her coworkers and a few friends.

He was always kind to her, but she still clammed up when he asked her questions.

He grabbed another cookie, listening as Chief Jones listed the evidence found at the school. There hadn't been much. A few smudged fingerprints. A bullet casing. A spent shell.

"One thing we do know," the chief said, rubbing the bridge of his nose as he stared down at his scribbled notes. "The perpetrator did not use the same gun that was used to kill Veronica. It wasn't a Sig Sauer."

There was a murmur of voices from the team, all of them gathered around a conference table, most of them with their K-9 partners beneath their feet.

"Any idea what kind it was?" Ryder asked. He looked as though he hadn't slept much. Maybe his daughter had kept him awake. A single father, he worked hard to keep a balance between his home life and his work.

Tristan knew just how difficult that was and just how exhausting it could be.

"A Glock. Something anyone on the street could get his hands on easily enough."

"Which gives us just about nothing to go on," James Harrison said. His bloodhound, Hawk, raised his head from his paws, his long ears brushing the floor as he stood. James gave him a quick scratch behind the ears, but his attention was on the chief.

"Not nothing," the chief corrected. "We know what it isn't. It isn't a murder weapon."

"It could have been," Whitney Godwin replied, her blond hair falling across her cheek as she leaned forward. "Whoever fired it meant it to be. Just like he meant the fire this morning to be fatal."

"You're connecting two things that might not go together," Chief Jones said with a sigh.

That was enough to get everyone talking.

Twenty minutes later, they'd all agreed that the attacks on Ariel were related. What they couldn't decide is whether or not they were related to Veronica's death.

"The way I see it," Ellen said, brushing a few cookie crumbs from her uniform. "We've got two separate things going on. Ariel brought some sort of trouble with her. The rest? That's homegrown."

"Maybe," Tristan agreed, but right at that moment, all he could think about was keeping Ariel safe. No matter the cause of the attacks, no matter what they were connected to, he had to make sure they were stopped.

The chief changed the subject to the German shepherd puppy that had been missing since the night of Veronica Earnshaw's murder. They knew the lead trainer had been microchipping three donated puppies at the training center when she'd been interrupted by a killer. One pup escaped—or had been set free by Veronica with her last dying breath—and was last seen running down Main Street. A witness said she thought she saw a person on a bike pick up the puppy and ride off with it, but it was dark that night, the biker was wearing a hoodie and the witness couldn't even tell if it was a man or woman.

Tristan was frustrated by the lack of progress. "We have to find the missing puppy. Veronica's body was found by the open puppy gate in the yard—as though she'd dragged herself out there to let that puppy go. For a reason. And with all the break-ins in town of homes with dogs—someone is clearly looking for that puppy, too. Maybe the killer. Any more leads on that?"

"A guy just outside town insisted that he saw a kid walking a German shepherd puppy down the road," Shane Weston said, pouring himself coffee from a carafe that Carrie had brought in. "I checked it out, but there aren't any kids living near there, and no one else saw anything. I canvased the neighborhood and wrote up a report, but it's probably safe to say the lead is a dead end."

"Funny you say that," Ryder said. "I spoke to a few of Ariel's neighbors. I was asking about the fire, and one of them mentioned that she'd heard a dog barking earlier in the morning. A puppy yipping is how she put it."

"It might have been a coyote," the chief said, jotting something at the top of the notepad. "I've heard a few of them recently."

"Even if it wasn't," Whitney added. "There are plenty of strays around. Any one of them could have a litter of babies."

"Aside from the puppy, did any of Ariel's neighbors notice anything unusual this morning?" Tristan asked.

"Not until they smelled smoke. We should be able to get into the house tomorrow. The fire marshal said the structure is sound. The house was built on a slab, so there's no danger of a floor collapse. All that's really left are four walls."

"That's such a shame," Carrie Dunleavy, the secretary, spoke quietly, her voice barely carrying across the room.

"It is, and I've got a meeting with the town council to discuss it." The chief glanced at his watch. "Seems like all I'm doing anymore is running. A guy my age needs a little bit of a break. Before I go, do we have an update on the missing evidence box?"

The question brought everyone to attention, the entire team going still and silent. Last month, someone had entered the evidence room and taken all items found at the scene of Veronica's murder. There was no doubt it was an inside job. No one but a member of the Desert Valley police force and employees of the police station had access to the room.

"I'm afraid not," Ellen said, her fingers tapping against the tabletop. "We haven't found a match for the earring found in the evidence room, either. If we find that, I feel confident we'll find the person who took the evidence."

"And maybe Veronica's murderer," Tristan said. He didn't want to think that Veronica had been killed by someone he saw every day, someone he'd spoken to, probably joked with. Trusted.

But the evidence box had been there. Now it was gone.

The only person who'd be worried about what the evidence would reveal was the person who'd killed Veronica.

"Again," the chief said with a tired sigh. "Let's not connect two things that might not be connected. Just because the evidence is missing doesn't mean the murderer took it."

"I think you're wrong," Ryder said, the blunt comment not seeming to bother the chief at all.

"You might be right, Ryder. If you are, then someone we know well is a murderer. That's not something I want to spend too much time dwelling on. I've got to go. I'll see all of you tomorrow."

The chief walked out of the room, Ryder and Whitney following behind him.

Tristan needed to leave, too. He'd left Mia and Ariel in the interrogation room just off the main corridor. Mia had taken out her laptop without being prodded, and by the time Tristan walked out of the room she and Ariel were looking at the document Mia had been working on.

That had been nearly an hour ago.

More than likely, they were both anxious to leave.

Especially Mia who'd spent most of the morning at the station hanging out with Carrie.

Speaking of which…

He turned toward the secretary, waiting as she closed down her laptop and stood.

She must have sensed his gaze. She met his eyes, offered a timid smile. "Did you need something, Tristan?"

"I just wanted to thank you for hanging out with my sister this morning."

"It was no problem. She had work to do. That kept her occupied." She tucked a lock of brown hair behind her ear, her fingernails short and unpainted. Behind her, framed photos hung from the wall, group shots of different teams that had gone through the K-9 training program. Mike was in a couple of the group shots.

He took one from the wall, eyeing his old army buddy.

Old? Mike had been in his early twenties when he'd died.

"I'm not sure the chief would want you to take that," Carrie said, and Tristan was surprised by the comment and the protest.

"Don't worry," he assured her. "I'm not taking it. I just wanted to see how Mike looked after he graduated from the program."

"Why's that?" James asked, calling for his bloodhound to heel as he crossed the room and stared down at the photo.

"It's always seemed odd to me that he died from an accidental fall. The guy was part mountain goat." Tristan scanned the photo. He recognized a few of the people in it. The chief. Ryder. Carrie. She was in the background like always, her eyes wide, her hair swept up in some kind of fancy style.

"Even mountain goats fall sometimes, Tristan," James said.

Tristan barely heard. He was too busy studying the photograph. There was something odd about it. Something he couldn't quite put his finger on.

"Is there something odd about this picture?" he asked, handing it to James.

James studied it for a couple of seconds and shrugged. "Not that I can see. Why?"

"Something about it is bothering me, and I can't figure out what."

"Maybe seeing your friend alive and healthy?" James suggested. "That's got to be hard."

"I imagine that's what it is," Carrie chimed in, her brown eyes full of compassion.

"Maybe." But Tristan didn't think that was it. He handed the photo to Carrie. "I feel like it's something else, though. You're sure there's nothing odd about it?"

Carrie stared at the photo, tilting her head left, then right. "Not that I can see." She frowned. "Mike does look tired in the picture, though. Don't you think?"

"I didn't know the guy," James said. "So I can't say for sure, but he looks pretty wide-awake and healthy to me."

Tristan agreed. Mike looked exactly like he had every time he and Tristan had gotten together. His blond hair was a little longer, but other than that, he looked healthy, strong and a little full of himself. Just like always.

"Yeah. He looks good to me, too."

Carrie nodded. "You want me to hang this back up?"

"That would be great. Thanks, and thanks for the cookies. They were fantastic."

"I'm glad you enjoyed them," she murmured, her

cheeks pink, her eyeglasses falling down her nose a bit as she replaced the photo.

Tristan was tempted to look at it again, because he couldn't shake the feeling that he was missing something very important. The rest of the team had left, though, and he needed to get Mia back home. He worked the graveyard shift tonight, and tomorrow was church. He'd drop Mia off, pick Jesse up and get what he needed to fix Ariel's security problems.

It shouldn't take long to swap out a few doors and bolt a couple of windows.

He strode through the quiet corridor, the odd feeling that someone was watching him crawling along his spine.

It reminded him of what Ariel had said—the odd feeling that she wasn't alone, that someone was watching her.

He glanced over his shoulder and saw Carrie standing in the doorway, her brown eyes wide.

"Everything okay?" he asked, and she blinked.

"Carrie?" he prodded.

"Everything is great, Tristan. I was just...thinking about something. And trying to decide if I should print out the minutes of the meeting now or later."

He was tempted to tell her not to print them out at all. No one really read them. Except for maybe the chief.

"There's no time like the present to take care of business," he said instead. Carrie had always been nice to him, had been kind to his sister this morning and he didn't want to get her in trouble with the chief.

She nodded, sliding her glasses back up on her nose. "You're right. That's exactly how I always feel. Thanks, Tristan."

She scurried away, and Tristan walked to the end of

the hallway. The door to the interrogation room was open, and he could see Mia and Ariel sitting beside each other. They both looked relaxed, Mia smiling a little as Ariel said something to her.

That was a surprise. His sister didn't smile much anymore. At least, she didn't when she was around him. Ariel seemed to bring out the best in her. She probably brought out the best in all her students. She had empathy, compassion, humor. That was a great combination of things to have in a teacher. That was a great combination of things to have in a person, and Tristan couldn't deny how charming he found them.

She must have sensed his gaze. She glanced at the door, then caught his eye and smiled, the dimple in her cheek showing. "Is the meeting over?"

"For now. How's it going in here?" he asked as he stepped into the room.

"Good," Mia admitted, her normal teenage attitude gone. "We were talking about school."

"Yeah?" That was it. No questions, because he didn't want to bring back the sullen teenager he usually had to deal with. "I'm glad you were having fun. I've got some work to do over at Ariel's house. I thought I'd bring you a hamburger before I went over there."

"You've already done more than enough for me today, Tristan. Why don't you and Mia go home? You can work on the house another day."

"What house?" Mia asked, standing and stretching, her skinny body encased in her favorite jeans and T-shirt. "I thought your place burned down, Ms. Martin."

Ariel winced, but still managed to smile as she answered. "It did. I'm staying at the church parsonage until I can have a new house built."

"That little house near the school? The one with the pretty blue door?"

"That's the one," Ariel agreed.

"I heard the youth group has sleepovers there every year."

"I don't know anything about that," Ariel said. "But I can tell you that it looks like the perfect place for a bunch of kids to hang out."

"I heard there's a secret passage in the basement that goes to the church. Do you think it's true?"

"I don't know, but I'll check it out and fill you in on what I find."

"That would be awesome, Ms. Martin."

Mia sounded excited, and Ariel seemed just as excited to fill her in.

As Tristan watched his sister and Ariel talk, he wished he and Mia could share the same kind of easy back and forth. Ariel was a good influence on his sister. On him, too. He wasn't too sure how he felt about *that*, but he was going to go with it, see where it led. Where God led.

Ariel wasn't nearly as excited about the parsonage as Mia seemed to be, but she smiled and chatted about it anyway. Tristan stood a few feet away, watching the exchange. He seemed to hold back a little when it came to his sister. Maybe he was afraid he'd say the wrong thing and break the happy little conversation up. He cared about his sister. He wanted the best for her, but he had no idea how to deal with a teenage girl. Maybe Ariel could help him.

"You know what else would be awesome?" Ariel asked, keeping her voice light and her expression pleasant.

"What?"

"You passing my class so you could attend tenth grade in the fall."

"I'll pass the class if you host a sleepover." Mia laughed, the sound dying abruptly when she saw that her brother was watching.

Smile to frown in two seconds flat. Mia had perfected the art. Ariel had watched her practice it over and over again in the time she'd spent with Mia and Tristan.

There was no doubt that Tristan noticed. He didn't comment on it. Just offered his sister a smile.

"You ready to go?" he asked, and she nodded.

"I guess."

"How about you, Ariel?" he asked, and she found herself looking into his handsome face, his gorgeous dark eyes.

"What?"

"Are you ready to go? I'll give you a ride to the parsonage. The chief is going to have a patrol car parked outside today and tonight. We'll have one near the school when you return on Monday."

Was she ready to go?

No.

She felt safe at the police station, protected by Tristan and his fellow officers. She couldn't stay there forever, though. No matter how tempted she might be.

"Sure," she responded as cheerfully as she could.

Tristan didn't even crack a smile.

She was sure he knew she was terrified. He didn't feed her any false platitudes, didn't tell her that she shouldn't be scared. He just stepped aside so she could walk into the hall.

"You're not alone, Ariel," he said quietly as she moved past, the words barely carrying above the wild pounding of her heart.

She wanted to say something clever or strong, something that would let them both know that she was just fine. She had no words, though. Nothing to offer but a brief nod and a thank-you that she wasn't even sure he heard.

You're not alone.

Three words that she'd desperately needed to hear, because she had been feeling alone these past few months. Three words that reminded her that she wasn't walking the path by herself, that she had people who cared, a God who cared.

That she had Tristan.

Such a strange thought, because she'd had no intention of relying on anyone again. But maybe *reliance* wasn't the right word to describe what she felt when she was around him. Maybe *trust* was a better word. *Hope.*

She glanced at Tristan. He was watching her, his eyes shadowed with fatigue, a day's worth of stubble on his chin. He'd been working hard to find the person who was after her, and it showed.

"Thank you," she said again, and this time he heard, his expression easing into a soft smile that turned his eyes from nearly black to warm brown.

"Thank me by staying safe," he responded, pushing open the door and leading Ariel and Mia outside.

The sun was bright and hot, the sound of cars and voices drifting on the dry air. It might have been Ariel's imagination, but she was certain she could smell a hint of smoke in the air.

Or maybe it was on her clothes.

She needed to shower and change, and then she needed to get to work. Tristan had been correct about the house. As much as she appreciated what Lauren and

Doug were doing, there was no way she'd feel safe until she had new windows, new doors, a security system.

A dog?

She'd always wanted a dog. Yes, she was busy, but she'd have help caring for it. She was also scared and a dog would make her feel safer.

"I wonder what time the animal shelter closes today," she said as Tristan opened the SUV's door.

"Six. I volunteer there one Saturday a month," Mia responded, getting into the backseat, and then muttering something under her breath.

"What's wrong?" Tristan asked.

"I left my backpack near Carrie's desk. I've got to run in and get it. I'll be right back."

She was off like a shot, sprinting across the pavement, her dark hair flying out behind her.

"I remember being that age," Ariel commented as Tristan started the engine and turned on the air. "It's not easy."

"I know. I'm trying to be patient with her. I'm trying to remind myself that I've never been a teenage girl, and I have no idea what she's going through," Tristan responded with a tired sigh.

"You're doing great, Tristan." She meant it. Mia might be shirking her schoolwork, she might be skipping class, but she was a nice girl who really seemed to care about her brother.

"Tell me that when she's back in ninth grade this fall."

"There are worse things than being held back a grade."

"I guess that means you don't think she's going to pass your class?" He met her eyes, and she found herself studying his dark brown irises, finding the flecks of gold and green in their depths. He had long eyelashes, dark brows and tiny lines fanning out from the corners of his eyes.

"Actually, I think she will. The first draft of her paper is really good. But, what I said still stands. There are worse things than being held back. Mia is a great young woman."

"With attitude to spare."

"She's just trying to find her way."

"If finding her way includes standing by while her friend shoplifts dog food, then she's on the wrong path."

"Shoplifting?" That surprised Ariel. She'd seen the way Mia was with the other students in summer school. She shared lunches, baked cookies, treated everyone with respect. Sure, she was different than the other girls. She had her head screwed on a little tighter, was a little more aware of how fragile life was. She didn't care about the latest fashions or the cutest boys. That certainly didn't make her a bad kid or a criminal.

"Are you sure, Tristan?" she asked, trying to see some hint of doubt in his face.

All she found was fatigue and concern.

"I'm not sure of anything except that Lauren saw them at the local feed store. Jenny was shoving cans of dog food in her pockets. Mia was with Jenny."

"Jenny I can believe. Mia…she was probably in the wrong place at the wrong time."

"I keep telling myself that's the case." He offered a tired smile, and she was tempted to touch the arm he had draped over the seat, tell him that everything was going to be okay.

"For what it's worth, I agree with you."

"Thanks."

"For?"

"Giving me hope that I'm not failing my sister and raising a criminal. I'm going to have to talk to her about Jenny. Again. That kid is a bad seed."

"Not really. She's just a young kid who's been allowed to run wild. She's got a good heart."

"Maybe, but I haven't seen much of it. Ever since she and Mia started hanging out, my sister has been a walking talking attitude."

"Jenny calls her own shots. Maybe Mia is trying to do the same. The thing is, Jenny has been with her grandmother for five years, and she hasn't had a whole lot of rules. Plus, she's smart. She can skip quite a bit of school and still do okay."

"She's in your summer school class, Ariel. Obviously, she's not doing that well."

"Last year, she struggled. She struggled for the first few weeks of summer school, but she seems to be coming around. I'd say that has something to do with your sister."

"You're trying to tell me that Mia is a good influence on Jenny so I should continue to let the two of them hang out?"

"I'm saying that Jenny is the only real friend your sister has in school. They do everything together. If you try to break them apart, you're asking for more of the attitude Mia has been giving you. If you let them continue on the way they are, you might be surprised at how things work out."

"I just want Mia to make good choices," he responded, his gaze shifting to the front door of the police station. Mia had reappeared, the backpack tossed over her shoulder. She was skinny and gangly, her arms and legs too long for her frame, her hair a little too wild around her face.

She waved as she ran toward them, and Tristan sighed.

"I'll give it a little more time, but if she fails your class—"

"She won't," she assured him as Mia slid into the SUV.

"Won't what?" she asked, her dark eyes exactly like her brother's, her lashes just as long.

"Fail my class." Ariel said. "I have faith in you and so does Tristan."

Mia raised her eyebrows. "Please tell me that you weren't talking about me the entire time I was gone."

That got almost a smile out of Tristan.

"We were also talking about Jenny," he said, the smile fading.

"Because you hate her," Mia grumbled. "And you think I'm such a wimp that I can't make my own decisions."

They were about to have an epic battle, and Ariel had no idea what to say to stop it.

Tristan's cell phone buzzed, interrupting whatever he might have said.

He grabbed it and answered quickly, his expression hard, his gaze on his sister. "McKeller here, what's up?"

There was a moment of silence, concern deepening in his features. "They're certain about that?"

His gaze shifted, settling on Ariel and staying there as he listened to the caller. "Okay. I'll let her know."

He ended the call and shoved the phone back into his pocket.

"Let me know what?" she asked, because she had absolutely no doubt that caller had been talking about her.

"The note we found at the school yesterday? The handwriting on it *does* match your ex-husband's."

The words were matter-of-fact, but she could see the sympathy in his eyes, see the concern in his face.

She wanted to tell him not to worry, that she was fine, but her throat was clogged with fear, her heart pounding frantically. There were a dozen questions she needed to ask, a bunch of things she could have said.

Instead, she turned away from his brown eyes, his sympathetic look, and stared out the window, trying to think of some explanation for the matching handwriting.

"It can't be his," she said, and she wasn't sure if she was trying to convince herself or Tristan.

He covered her hand, his palm warm against her chilled flesh. "The handwriting expert with the state police says she's 99 percent certain that it is."

"He had to have written it before he died. Do you think...?" Her voice trailed off. She didn't want to voice the thought in front of Mia. She didn't want to ask the question that was filling her mind.

Could Mitch have paid someone to kill her and the baby?

Could he have arranged it all before he died?

He'd wanted them both out of his life. He'd threatened to get rid of the baby if Ariel wouldn't. Not just the first time she'd told him the news. He'd called her on numerous occasions, leaving messages in a cold tone that had left her terrified.

Get rid of the kid or I will.

She'd told herself that he hadn't meant it, but she'd never really believed that. The deadly serious tone of his voice had chilled her to the bone. If he'd been screaming, ranting, yelling, she might have been able to brush it off as emotions getting the better of him. He'd been calm, though. He'd wanted the baby gone, and he'd have probably been happy to get Ariel out of the picture, too. A clean break. Nothing to tie him to the past. He could have married the woman he'd been living with, talked her into all the things Ariel had refused.

He'd died, though, and that should have been the end of it.

Should have been, but someone wanted Ariel dead, and the only one she could think of who'd ever felt that way was Mitch.

Tristan squeezed her hand, the gesture gentle and comforting.

"I'm okay," she said as if he'd asked, and he nodded, his palm brushing against her knuckles, his hand sliding away.

"We'll talk more after I drop Mia off," he said, and she nodded, because there was nothing else she could do. They both knew she wasn't okay. They both knew that the information he'd shared changed everything and solved nothing.

Mitch had written the note.

Mitch had wanted her dead.

Everything that was happening was because of him, and she wanted to cry because of it, wanted to ask God why she couldn't just be free of the past.

You're not alone.

Tristan's words suddenly filled her head, chasing away some of the panic and the fear. She let them comfort her as he pulled out of the parking lot and headed home.

NINE

The drive to Tristan and Mia's place took minutes.

It seemed to take a lifetime.

By the time they pulled up in front of the brick rancher, Ariel's stomach was in knots, her mind filled with memories she'd been trying really hard to let go of.

Mitch at his best and at his worst. A man she'd thought she knew well who had turned out to be a complete stranger.

Someone who'd wanted her dead?

Who'd paid someone to make sure she and her child didn't live?

She shuddered.

"It's going to be okay," Tristan said as he opened his door.

"I'm glad one of us thinks so," she responded.

"It will be. Nothing can last forever. Eventually, we always get to the other side of our troubles." He glanced at his sister. "I remind myself of that every day. Come on, let's go inside. I have to get Jesse. We're working the graveyard shift tonight, and I'm hoping to take him to your house. He's trained in arson detection, and he might be able to sniff up something that everyone else has missed now that everything has settled down."

"Graveyard, again?" Mia cut in. "Are we ever just going to be a normal family with a normal schedule? The kind where the parent is actually home with his kid?"

"Eventually, but things are kind of crazy right now. You know that, Mia," Tristan responded, a hint of weariness in his voice.

Ariel had a feeling they'd had this conversation many times before and that it had accomplished absolutely nothing.

Talk was sometimes cheap. She remembered bottling up all the words she wanted to say in those final days of her marriage, shoving them down and keeping quiet, because it was the only way to keep the peace. That was something she'd coveted. Peace.

She hadn't had much of that when she was a kid. Her father had been an alcoholic, coming home at all hours of the night, tripping over things, breaking things, apologizing with slurred words and heaving sobs. By the time Ariel was nine, her mother had died of cancer, and she'd become her father's weekend caregiver, keeping the secret that her mother had kept for a decade because her father was a well-liked businessman, a deacon at church, a weekend drinker who went a little too far a little too often, but a good guy who'd loved his wife and his daughter.

He'd died while she was babysitting for a neighbor. It had been a Thursday night. Not a drinking night for him, but he must have decided he wanted to drink anyway. He'd emptied a bottle of Scotch and then gotten in the car to buy some more. He drove off the road before he reached the liquor store, flipping his car and dying instantly.

Another memory Ariel tried not to dwell on, and one

of the reasons she'd married young. Her great-aunt had taken her in after her father's death, and when she'd died, Ariel had been alone. She'd longed for someone she could connect with. She'd been desperate to have people she could call family.

Mitch had stepped into her life when she was just vulnerable enough not to notice his selfishness, his lies.

And, now, Tristan had stepped into her life.

Right when she'd decided she didn't need anyone. Right when she'd been determined to go it alone. She wasn't sure how she felt about that.

She followed Tristan and Mia to the front door of the house, only half listening to their conversation. The words seemed rehearsed, spoken so many times both had their lines memorized.

"Since you're going to be gone," Mia huffed, her backpack dragging on the ground. "I want to spend the night at Jenny's."

"Mia, I don't—"

His words were cut off by the revving of a car engine.

Ariel glanced toward the street and had just enough time to see a black car speed around the corner before Tristan yanked the door open, shoved Mia inside and nudged Ariel in after her. Mia tripped and went down hard, sliding across hard wood.

The door slammed, a burst of gunfire filling the sudden silence, Mia's screams mixing with the sound of a dog's frantic barking and a puppy's terrified howl.

"Tristan!" Mia wailed, and Ariel finally realized what he'd done—shut them in the house and shut himself out.

The first bullet missed Tristan by an inch.

The second one took a chunk out of his upper arm.

The third buried itself in the door frame.

The guy was still a bad shot.

Tristan wasn't. He'd been well trained by the army, and he knew how to take someone out. He pulled his service revolver, aiming for the windshield of the vehicle as the car sped by.

The bullet hit its mark, shattering the glass.

The driver kept going, and Tristan fired another shot, hitting the back tire.

The sedan swerved, speeding around the block and out of sight.

Tristan jumped into his SUV, wishing he had Jesse with him. There'd been no time to get Jesse from the house, though. Not if he wanted to catch the shooter.

And, he did.

No way was this guy escaping again.

Three attempts at taking Ariel's life.

This time, the perpetrator could have hurt Mia.

Tristan never should have brought Ariel to the house. Not while his sister was there. His mistake could have cost Mia her life.

He sped around the corner, heading in the direction the crippled vehicle had gone. He could see the sedan ahead, racing toward the main thoroughfare that led to the highway.

He called in his location and asked for backup, wishing he'd had time to get Jesse. If the driver of the vehicle turned off the road and jumped out, they'd be chasing him on foot. Jesse wasn't trained in apprehension, but he could take down a man if he had to, disarm one if he saw a gun.

Behind him, a K-9 vehicle sped out of a side street, lights flashing, sirens blaring. Fellow rookie K-9 officer Shane Weston. Tristan recognized the number on the

SUV, and he slowed down, let Shane take the lead. His K-9 partner, Bella, was trained in apprehension. If they could get the guy to stop, they'd have a good chance at taking him down.

Up ahead, the sedan blew through a stop sign and squealed onto the highway entrance ramp. The driver took the curve too quickly, and the sedan flew off the road, bumping down an embankment and into a ditch. The door opened, and a man tumbled out, racing away from the wrecked vehicle as Tristan stopped his SUV.

Shane was already out of his vehicle, Bella on a lead beside him, lunging toward the fleeing man.

"He has a gun," Tristan warned as he joined the two.

"And, I have Bella. Seems like he's at a disadvantage. Police!" he called. "Stop, or I'll release my dog."

The guy just kept running, sprinting toward a distant copse of trees. Maybe he thought he could find a place to hide there. If so, he knew nothing about the way K-9 apprehension teams worked. Bella already had the guy's scent. She'd follow it until she had him cornered.

"I said 'stop'!" Shane called again, then he unhooked Bella's lead and released her. The German shepherd bounded down the ravine, moving so quickly the perpetrator barely had time to respond. He'd pivoted and was turning back in their direction, when Bella hit him full force. The guy fell backward and lay still, Bella growling in his face.

Seconds later, Tristan had the guy by the wrists and was snapping cuffs into place. He patted him down, pulled out a wallet, a cell phone and a wad of twenty-dollar bills. He could feel warm blood oozing down his arm as he dragged the guy to his feet. He didn't care. He wanted answers, and the pasty-faced, pockmarked man Bella had apprehended had them.

"Keep that dog away from me," the guy howled, his mud-brown eyes focused on the shepherd.

She stood a few feet away, growling quietly, her hackles still raised.

Shane patted her back, hooking the lead back into place. "If you'd cooperated and stopped like you were told, she wouldn't have gotten close to you in the first place."

"I didn't hear you, so you had no right to sic her on me."

"You had no right to shoot at me, so I guess we're even," Tristan replied. "Or, maybe not. What you did was a felony. What my buddy did was his duty."

"I didn't shoot at you," the man spat, his eyes a little too small in his puffy face. He looked as if he'd had a few too many beers and a bit too much hard liquor. As a matter of fact, he reeked, the scent of stale alcohol wafting around him.

"Have you been drinking?" Tristan asked, opening the guy's wallet and pulling out a driver's license. Butch Harold. Forty-five. Five-foot-ten. Two-hundred-twenty pounds.

From Las Vegas, Nevada.

"Sometimes, a man needs a little liquid fortification," Butch responded, his gaze darting to Bella again.

"You're a long way from home, Butch. I guess there's a reason for that?"

"Had a job to do," Butch responded. "Now, I'm done. Let me go, and I'll just head on back the way I came."

"You tried to kill someone. You don't get a free pass on that."

"I wasn't trying to kill anyone," the guy yelled. "So, if you think that, you can just stop!"

"Tell you what," Shane said, walking over with Bella.

"How about I read you your Miranda rights, and then we discuss your reasons for visiting Desert Valley?"

"I'm not here for a visit," Butch said. "And I'm not telling you squat."

Shane ignored him, reading him his rights and then escorting him up the ravine. A squad car was there, Eddie Harmon standing beside it.

"This the guy who's been trying to kill the teacher?" he asked.

"I said I wasn't trying to kill anyone. Especially not some pregnant lady."

"How did you know she was pregnant?" Tristan asked.

"The guy who paid me said, I'd know..." Butch's voice trailed off, and he scowled. "You thought you had me, didn't you?"

"I *do* have you." Tristan tugged him to Eddie's car. "You want to transport him to the station? I'll help Shane collect evidence here, and then I've got to go check on my sister and Ariel. After that, I have some questions I'd like to ask this guy."

"I want a lawyer!" Butch yelled as Eddie opened the back door of his cruiser and shoved him inside.

"We'll get you one," Eddie promised, and then he slammed the door shut.

"Good job on the apprehension. Not that he looks like that much of a challenge. He put up a fight?"

"Bella took him down. The guy took one look at her teeth and gave up," Shane responded.

"She's a good dog," Eddie said, taking off his uniform hat and wiping sweat from his temple. "But that guy is drunk as a skunk. Do you really think he's capable of going after the teacher?"

"I don't think it. I know it. He took a shot at my

house. I think he was aiming for Ariel. It's hard to say, though. His aim stinks."

"Looks like it was good enough for him to take a slice out of your arm."

"He barely grazed it. I'm more irritated about the bullet slug in my door frame." Tristan took an evidence bag from his truck and dropped the wallet, phone and money into it. "These were on him. Want to take it back to the station? Show the chief the phone. He may be able to get some information off it. The rest you can lock in the evidence room."

"Who's to say the cash won't go missing after I put it there?" Eddie smirked.

"Or *before* you put it there?" Shane retorted.

"Now, wait a minute, Shane. I might joke, but I'm no crook."

Shane nodded, his attention on the sedan that was still nose-down in the ditch. "Let's check out the vehicle. Maybe good old Butch left some information that will lead us to the guy who hired him."

"If not, maybe attempted murder charges will loosen his tongue." Tristan followed Shane to the sedan and used gloved hands to open the passenger-side door. The gun was lying on the floor. A Glock. New.

"Looks like this could match the one that was used at the school." He checked the chamber, unloaded the pistol and dropped it into an evidence bag. He found a round of ammunition in the glove compartment. Registration for the vehicle. Not in the perp's name. A stolen vehicle? It seemed likely.

"I've got something back here, too." Shane lifted a paper bag from the backseat. "The liquid fortification. We can probably get some DNA evidence from it. Not that we'll need it. The guy is guilty as sin."

"We know it, but we still have to prove it in a court of law." Tristan handed him another evidence bag and popped the trunk. He expected to see something there. Maybe a few empty gas containers, matches. Something that would indicate that the guy had set fire to Ariel's house.

He found nothing. Not even a whiff of gasoline-soaked carpet.

"Strange," he muttered, lifting the carpet and opening the small hatch that contained the spare tire. It was there along with a tire iron and an electric jack.

"What?" Shane peered into the trunk, Bella's leash in his hand, the dog settled onto her haunches beside him.

"I thought I'd find something that linked him to the fire."

"Could be he got rid of the evidence. If I were him, I sure wouldn't be riding around with it in my car."

"I'd expect the gasoline fumes to soak into the interior. Leather and carpet can hold on to the scent for weeks."

Shane inhaled, shook his head. "I don't smell anything."

"I'll bring Jesse over later. If there's been gasoline in this car in the past few days, he'll know it. I need to check on Mia and Ariel first. Can you call this in? See if the chief wants a state evidence team to come out? Also, can you run the plates? The registration card doesn't have the perp's name on it. If the vehicle is stolen, that'll be one more nail in the guy's coffin."

"No problem." Shane strode to his car, speaking into his radio as he went.

Tristan followed more slowly, eyeing the black sedan and the shattered window.

The guy who paid me…

That's what Butch had said.

Butch from Las Vegas, Nevada.

He dialed Las Vegas Metropolitan Police Department as he climbed back into the SUV. He left a message for Detective Smithfield explaining what had happened and asking for any information that might be pertinent to the case.

Hopefully the detective would get back to him quickly.

If Butch had been telling the truth, someone had paid him to kill Ariel. According to Ariel there was only one person she'd ever been afraid of, only one person who'd ever threatened her. Since he was dead, there had to be someone else. Someone that Ariel didn't know about or hadn't thought about.

Her ex-husband's girlfriend?

Could she be jealous of the baby Ariel was carrying? Jealous of Ariel for having what she couldn't?

It seemed far-fetched, but it was all Tristan had.

He climbed into his SUV, waved at Shane and headed back to the house.

As touchy as the subject was, he'd have to ask Ariel about it. If she knew the name of the girlfriend, Tristan could do a little checking, see if the woman was still in Las Vegas.

Whitney and Ryder were standing on the front porch with their dogs when Tristan pulled into his driveway. Whitney was shooting photos of the door frame while Ryder crouched a few feet away. He stood as Tristan approached.

"I heard you got the guy," he said without preamble.

"Eddie is transporting him. I plan to stop by the station after I check on—"

The door flew open, and Mia ran out, throwing her

arms around Tristan the way she had when she was a little girl and he was her favorite big brother.

"I've been so worried." She sobbed into his shoulder. "Ms. Martin said you knew how to take care of yourself. She said you were going to come home to me, but Mom and Dad knew how to take care of themselves, and..." Her voice trailed off, and she backed away, her cheeks damp with tears.

"It's okay, Mia. I'm okay." His heart ached for the pain he'd put her through, for the fear she'd experienced. "Ms. Martin is right. I do know how to take care of myself, and I'm always going to come home to you."

"You're a police officer, Tristan. You don't know if that's true."

"I trust that it is, because I'm committed to being around for as long as you need me, and I really believe that God is going to let me do that." He smoothed her hair, looked into her face. Sometimes he forgot how much she'd been through and how young she really was.

"Yeah? Well, if you're okay, then why is your arm bleeding?" She grabbed his hand and dragged him into the house. Jesse was there, pacing the living room, obviously sensing the tension. Sprinkles was following his lead, sprinting from one end of the room to the other.

There was no sign of Ariel.

"Where's Ms. Martin?" he asked as Mia used a towel to dab at the slice in his arm.

"She called Pastor Doug and Lauren, and they came to get her. I think she said she was getting her van and then going over to the parsonage. Now that the guy who was after her has been caught, she thought it would be safe to be there."

"I need to call the chief and have him run some patrols by her house," he said out loud. He wasn't happy that she'd left, and he wasn't convinced that she was safe. If Butch had been hired by someone, Ariel could still be in danger.

"Why? Ryder Hayes said the guy who was after her had been caught. He told Ms. Martin that he'd been arrested."

Tristan hooked Jesse to his leash. That was the lab's signal that they were going to work, and the dog barked excitedly, tugging Tristan to the door. "Just to be on the safe side," he told his sister, opening the door and walking out into the warm afternoon. If the guy who'd shot at the house hadn't been caught, he wouldn't feel comfortable leaving Mia here. Still, he'd have one of the rookies drive by several times and keep a watch on the house.

Several neighbors were out in their yards, watching as Whitney and Ryder processed the scene. No doubt, the neighbors would stop by later to find out what had happened. He'd have to tell Mia not to open the door. He didn't want an overly dramatic version of the incident getting out to the public. Not after everything else that had been happening in town. The shooter was in police custody and no threat to the community.

He loaded Jesse into the SUV and drove back to the sedan, anxious to see if the lab alerted near the vehicle.

Shane was still at the scene, a county tow truck idling a few yards away, its driver scrolling through messages on his phone.

"That was quick," Shane said as Tristan let Jesse out of the SUV.

"Whitney and Ryder are processing the scene."

"Are your sister and Ariel okay?"

"Mia is fine. Ariel went back to the parsonage."

"You don't sound happy about that."

"Someone hired the guy who shot at us tonight. Until

we find out who. Ariel still isn't safe. I already sent a text to the chief and asked him to run patrols on her street, but I'm not sure that will be enough."

"There isn't a whole lot more that can be done."

"That's not what I want to hear," Tristan said.

"I know, because we all think we can solve the world's problems, right? We all think that we can keep the people we care about safe. Sometimes, though, we can't. So, all we can do is our best and then pray that it's enough." He opened the back of his SUV and called for Bella.

"I need to head back to the station," Shane continued. "The chief said we'll impound the car, keep it for evidence retrieval. It was reported stolen in Las Vegas a few days ago, so we've got more paperwork to fill out and more charges to press. John will tow the car to the county impound lot once you're finished here." He motioned toward the tow-truck driver.

"Sounds good."

"I'll see you back at the station." Shane hopped in his SUV and drove away.

Tristan grabbed Jesse's vest, the dog whining excitedly as Tristan buckled him into it.

"Ready to work?" he asked, and Jesse let out a quick sharp bark.

They made their way down into the ditch, the lab tense with excitement, his tail high and still.

He knew what he was looking for, knew what he should be scenting.

"Find," Tristan said, and Jesse lunged toward the sedan, his excited barks ringing through the hot afternoon air.

TEN

11:00 p.m. Too late to be awake, but the baby was restless.

Or, maybe, Ariel was restless.

She'd been living in the parsonage for nearly a week, going to church, to work, to the police station.

How many times had she been *there*?

A dozen?

More?

First, she'd gone to look at mug shots of the guy who'd tried to kill her. Butch Harold wasn't anyone she'd ever seen before. She'd told Tristan that. She'd told Chief Jones that. She'd signed a paper that said it. After that, she'd been asked to file a report on the incident at the school. She'd been called in to discuss the fact that Tristan and his K-9 partner had found no sign of accelerants in the car Butch Harold had used. The police hadn't found any empty gas cans near the house, either. No evidence of smoke or fire on the clothes Butch had been wearing or any of the clothes they'd taken from a duffel in the back of his car.

Was she certain someone had been in the house with her? She'd been asked that question so many times, she'd begun to doubt her memory and her answer.

If Butch had been in the house, something of his should have had evidence of it. The police had found a bag of his clothes in the car he'd been driving. Not a hint of smoke or soot on any of them. Tristan has brought Jesse to the vehicle, had the dog sniff every inch of it. He'd found no hint of an accelerant, not even a trace of smoke or fire anywhere on the vehicle. If Butch hadn't been in the house, someone else had been there.

That's what Ariel thought about every night. It's what chased her from sound sleep and woke her in a cold sweat. She'd close her eyes, and she'd smell the smoke, she'd see the shadowy figure, hear his voice, feel the heat of the fire chasing her back up the stairs, and then she'd lie in bed, the baby kicking and wiggling, imagining the parsonage going up in flames. Tristan checked in with her every day. He called in the morning, stopped by the school in the afternoon and escorted her home. He'd done everything he could to make her feel safe, but she still felt afraid.

She walked across the large bedroom, the old floorboards creaking beneath her feet. She needed to buy some throw rugs, a little bassinet for the baby to sleep in, a crib for the room across the hall. She'd been out twice since the fire, but replacing her phone and her bank cards had been a higher priority than stocking up on the things she'd need after the baby was born. She had managed to buy a couple of maternity outfits and a few small items that the baby would need, but at thirty-seven weeks, she was closing in on the home stretch. No one could predict how late or how early the baby would arrive, and sitting around brooding and worrying wasn't going to help Ariel prepare.

She opened the drawer in the bedside table and pulled out the notebook and pen she'd brought home from school. She'd make a list of what she needed, and she'd go out in the morning and spend the day shopping and preparing.

That would make her feel better about things.

She hoped, because she wasn't used to dwelling in her worries, and for the past few days that's what she felt like she'd been doing.

The truth was, she had nothing to be worried about. The attacks against her had stopped as soon as Butch Harold had been arrested. Since then, she hadn't felt hunted, she hadn't felt watched. There'd been no wiggling doorknobs in the middle of the night, no feeling that someone was standing just out of sight.

She'd walked to the school twice since the second shooting, and she hadn't felt anything but tired.

She was still afraid, though.

She kept running through the day of the fire, picturing the moment when she'd realized someone was in her house.

Not Mitch's girlfriend.

Ariel was certain the person was a man. Besides, Tristan had checked in on Mitch's girlfriend. A real estate broker in Las Vegas, Mora Hendricks had already found a new boyfriend. She insisted that she had nothing but goodwill for Ariel and the baby, and that she was disgusted with herself for ever getting involved with someone like Mitch.

Tristan hadn't been convinced of her remorse.

He'd told Ariel that Mora's new love interest was a married father of three with a healthy bank account and a lot of expensive things.

Ariel had been sorry for the guy's wife.

Eventually, she'd find out the truth, and her life would be turned upside down.

She'd told Tristan that.

He'd brought her a gift the next day. A huge sunflower that he'd picked from an empty lot at the edge of town, a reminder that good things could grow from tough times.

That's what he'd told her.

She still had the sunflower sitting in a tall vase that she'd borrowed from Lauren. It was down in the kitchen, right next to the window he'd replaced earlier in the week. He'd been keeping Ariel informed, filling her in on all the details of the case while he worked on making the parsonage more secure.

While he'd put in new windows and doors, Ariel had tutored Mia. A fair exchange. That's how Tristan put it. Ariel thought she was getting the better end of the deal. She had a new alarm system, windows that would be very difficult to jimmy open and doors with bolts.

All Tristan had was a sister who was suddenly attending every class and getting an A on every assignment. He also had a sister who seemed happy to sit at Ariel's kitchen table every evening, her puppy in her lap as she worked on her assignments. Jesse was always near the back door, lying with his head on his paws, his golden eyes tracking Tristan's movements.

Ariel had cooked dinner every night.

For all three of them.

She'd also bought dog food and a bowl. Not for the dog that Tristan still wanted her to get. For Jesse and for Mia's puppy, Sprinkles. Every night, she filled the bowls, and the dogs ate, while she, Tristan and Mia shared a meal. They'd talk about their days and their plans, laughing and joking like a family.

It was starting to feel normal.

That scared Ariel more than she wanted to admit.

She'd made peace with her life. Mostly. She'd accepted her new situation. She had every intention of raising her daughter alone, because she was afraid of being hurt again, of being disappointed.

But, maybe, she didn't have to go it alone.

Maybe she could let Tristan into her life. He cared, he was always there, offering sincerity and humor and sweet words that made her feel like she mattered.

She scowled, carrying the notebook and pen down the stairs and into the kitchen. She flicked on the light and sat at the table. Mia had left a jacket on the back of the chair, and Ariel had a feeling that if she looked around, she'd find more evidence of the teen's presence. A small dog toy sat on the floor near the back door. A pencil lay on the counter. The house looked lived-in and happy. Exactly the way she'd always dreamed her home would be.

"Focus," she whispered, staring at the blank page in the notebook. "Baby stuff. What do we need?"

Blankets.

Baby wipes.

Onesies.

Someone knocked on the back door, the sound so startling, the pen flew from her hand and skittered across the floor. She tried to jump up from her seat, but her stomach bumped the table, nearly overturning it.

"Who's there?" she called as she yanked open a drawer and looked for a weapon. Lauren had lent her some utensils. Forks. Spoons. A few dull steak knives.

She grabbed one of those, edging toward the door, her heart beating frantically. She should have grabbed her cell phone from the bedside table. She could have called for help, because there was no way anyone she knew would be knocking on her door at this time of the night and the old rotary phone on the kitchen wall no longer worked.

"I said," she repeated, the knife clutched in her hand. "Who's there?"

"Mia." The voice was faint, but unmistakable.

Ariel threw open the bolt, tugged the teenager inside and slammed the door closed again.

"What are you doing outside at this time of night?" she nearly shouted, and Mia winced, her eyes red-rimmed, her cheeks damp. She had her backpack over her shoulders and what looked like slippers on her feet.

Had she run away from home?

She'd been crying, and that was enough to stop the reprimand that was on the tip of Ariel's tongue.

"What's wrong?" she said. "What happened?"

"Jenny and I had a big fight," the teen sobbed.

"You were at her house?"

"Tristan said I could spend the night. It was my reward for doing so well in school this week." Mia swiped tears from her cheeks. "Now it's all ruined, because Jenny won't listen to me."

"About what?"

"Anything!" Mia dropped into a chair, her legs splayed out under the table, her hair hanging limply around her shoulders. She looked pale and tired, her eyes deeply shadowed.

"There must be something specific that you want her to do."

Mia hesitated, then shrugged. "It doesn't matter what it is. If Jenny doesn't listen, we're not going to be friends. I told her that flat out."

"What do you want her to listen to you about? It must be important if you're willing to break up your friendship over it?"

Mia shrugged again, but didn't respond.

"Mia?" Ariel prodded. "Do you really think you should throw in the towel over a disagreement?"

"It's not a disagreement," Mia responded. "She's wrong."

"About?"

"She..." Mia began, then shook her head. "Nothing."

"If it's nothing, then it's not worth giving up the friendship over."

Mia wiped a few pieces of dog hair from her jeans, but didn't speak.

Ariel knew enough about teen girls to know that she and Mia could dance around the issue all night and never get to the root of it. Better to give Mia the chance to tell Ariel when she was ready. She'd come for that reason.

"Does Tristan know you're here?" she asked.

"He should."

"What does that mean?"

"I sent him a text when I saw your light. I told him I was going to see if you were awake because Jenny's grandmother's place is pretty far away, and my feet are tired from walking."

It wasn't that far, and Ariel was certain Mia had walked the distance on more than one occasion. She didn't point that out, though.

"He hasn't responded?"

"Of course not. Tristan is always too busy with his job to be bothered with me."

"That's unfair, Mia. I think you know it."

"I called him from Jenny's. I left him two messages saying I wanted to go home. He's always told me that if I ever have a problem, he'll drop everything to help me. But, he didn't return my calls, and he didn't show up. So, I walked. And, let me tell you, it's creepy out there at night." Her voice broke, and the tears started falling again.

"Maybe you should have waited a little longer," Ariel suggested. "Walking around by yourself this time of night probably wasn't the best idea."

"I know. I was just so mad. I've helped Jenny dozens of times, but I can't keep helping her. Not when…"

"What?" There was something going on between the two girls, and Ariel didn't think it was a petty disagreement. Both were strong-willed and smart. Both were creative and imaginative. They were like two sides of the same coin, and there had to have been a really serious problem for Mia to walk away from that.

"Have you ever kept a secret and then regretted it?" Mia asked, her dark eyes staring straight into Ariel's.

"Only once," she admitted.

"Did people find out? Did you get in trouble?"

"Yes, and no. But, I missed an opportunity to help someone I loved. I might even have missed an opportunity to save his life. I'd hate to see that happen with you."

"Are you talking about your husband?"

"No. My father. It's a long story. Maybe one day I'll tell it to you. For right now, I'll just say that my father was an alcoholic, and I helped him hide it. He drove off the road and flipped his car. He was killed instantly. For a long time, I wondered if I could have saved him. If I'd just said the right thing to the right person, if he might have gotten the help he needed."

"It wasn't your fault," Mia said, patting Ariel's arm. "You couldn't have known he would drink and drive."

"Maybe not, but I did keep his secret. I've always wished I hadn't."

"That stinks," Mia said quietly, and Ariel knew there was something she was holding back, something about Jenny maybe. A secret that she'd been keeping and didn't want to.

"Mia, it's hard to break a trust, but sometimes we have to. For the good of the person we love."

Mia bit her lip, her gaze jumping away.

"I—"

The doorbell rang, and Mia jumped up, obviously relieved by the interruption.

"I wonder if that's Tristan," she said, the words rushing out.

She ran from the kitchen. Ariel followed more slowly.

By the time she reached the living room, the front door was open and Tristan was standing in the entryway.

He didn't look happy, but he sure looked good, his hair just a little long, his eyes that deep brown that she couldn't seem to stop looking at.

He scanned the room, spotted his sister and walked straight to her, pulling her into his arms. "I'm glad you're okay, sis. I've been worried."

"You're not mad?" Mia mumbled against his shirt.

"I might be later. Right now, I'm just glad you found a safe place to wait for me." He patted her back, met Ariel's eyes. "Sorry about this, Ariel," he said, offering an apologetic smile.

"It's okay," Ariel responded. "And I was awake, so it's not like she pulled me out of bed for a visit."

"We still owe you an apology," he said, and Mia sighed.

"I apologize, Ms. Martin. Next time, maybe my brother will pick up his phone when I need him, and I won't have to bother you."

Tristan's jaw tightened, but he didn't rise to her bait. "I was in a meeting, Mia. If you'd given me a little more time, I'd have picked you up at Jenny's house."

"You won't have to worry about it anymore," Mia said. "Jenny and I are no longer friends. Which is exactly what you were hoping for. Happy now?" She burst into tears and ran from the house.

Tristan rubbed the back of his neck and sighed. "I guess I'd better go deal with that."

"Want me to talk to her?"

"You've already done more than your fair share to help our family, Ariel."

"I'm hearing yes," she said, and he laughed.

"I must be thinking really loudly, but I can't ask you to help. Not tonight. It's late, and you and the baby need to rest."

"The baby is wide-awake, and so am I."

"Too much on your mind?"

"I keep thinking about the fire and about the guy who was in the house with me. If it wasn't Butch Harold, who was it?"

She grabbed her purse from a hook near the door, not waiting for him to tell her again that he didn't need her help with Mia. Being with Tristan and his sister was a lot more appealing than pacing her room or writing a list of things she needed for the baby.

"I'm glad you brought that up. I planned to stop by tomorrow to discuss a few things with you," Tristan said, taking her arm as she walked out onto the porch.

"What things?"

"I spoke with Detective Smithfield again. I asked him to send me a copy of the medical examiner's report. I also asked for a copy of the accident report that was filed after Mitch's death."

The words left her cold, and she stopped short, turning to face him as they reached his SUV. "Why?"

"He was being investigated for insurance fraud."

"I know."

"He burned down five businesses."

She knew that, too. "What are you getting at, Tristan?"

He watched her for a moment, and she knew when he spoke, he was going to say something she didn't want to hear.

"Mitch's body couldn't be identified. Not by dental records. Not by fingerprints. He was so badly burned, that there was really nothing left for the medical examiner except DNA, and Mitch didn't have family."

"I know that, too."

"Do you know that the fire at the accident site burned so hot the metal on the car melted? If the fire department hadn't arrived when they did, there wouldn't have been anything but ashes left."

That was something she hadn't known. "You're getting at something, Tristan. Why not just tell me what it is?"

Why not?

Because Tristan didn't think it was something Ariel would want discussed in front of Mia. He didn't think she'd want to discuss it at all, but he'd made the calls, he'd read the reports and he couldn't shake the feeling that they were missing something really important.

Something really obvious.

Like the fact that her ex was an arsonist whose name had been tied to several insurance fraud cases. Mitch had been paid good money to make fires look like accidents, and he'd been mostly successful. If an insurance company hadn't gotten suspicious, if they hadn't hired a private investigator to check things out, Mitch probably would have continued to get paid for burning buildings to the ground.

Yeah. The guy had known his way around a fire.

To Tristan, it seemed a little too coincidental that he'd died in a car accident that had caused a fire that burned so hot it had melted metal and destroyed all but a small amount of DNA. The medical examiner had written a grim report. No fingerprints. No recognizable feature. Teeth intact, but somehow Mitch's dental records had disappeared.

Another coincidence that Tristan didn't like.

"Tristan?" Ariel prodded, her face pale in the darkness. She hadn't been sleeping well. He'd noticed the dark circles under her eyes when he'd been at her house the previous day, noticed the narrow width of her shoulders, the thinness of her arms. She needed to eat and she needed to rest, but he doubted she'd do either until he gave her the answers that she wanted.

"How about we discuss it tomorrow?" he hedged, eyeing Mia through the dark glass of the SUV's back window.

She'd crossed her arms over her chest and closed her eyes. That didn't mean she wasn't listening to every word that was said.

"You don't want Mia to hear?"

"No, and I also don't want to keep you up any longer. You look tired, Ariel. That can't be good for the baby."

"It goes with the territory. I try to sleep. I can't. The baby keeps getting in the way." She touched her belly and smiled, but there was no humor in her eyes. She looked sad and a little worried, and he figured it would be a lot crueler to make her wait a few hours than to tell her something she might not want to hear.

"Tell you what," he said, opening the passenger-side door of the SUV. "If you really can't sleep, let's bring Mia home. We can talk after that."

She hesitated, then nodded. "All right, but I'll take my van. That way you won't have to drive me back."

"I'll end up following you back instead," he pointed out.

He opened the passenger door, and Ariel slid in without another word.

Mia was silent, too, her eyes still closed, her lips pressed together in an angry frown.

He'd have to talk to her, but first he needed to figure out the right thing to say. Not the snide remark he'd almost made before she'd stormed out of the house. Not a cut on Jenny's character or a cheer of approval over the end of the girls' friendship.

That wasn't what Mia needed or wanted from him.

The problem was, he had no idea what the right words were. He had no idea what it felt like to be a teenage girl who'd just broken up with her best friend. He also had no idea how to take back all the unflattering things he'd said about Jenny. If he'd kept his mouth shut, his sympathy might have sounded sincere. As it was, he doubted Mia would ever believe he was sorry about the situation.

The fact was, he wasn't sure he *was* sorry.

Jenny was a bad influence, and she had been from day one. The incident at the feed store had been the culmination of that. He'd asked Mia about it, and she'd denied everything. No way would Jenny ever shoplift. She and Jenny had been playing around. Jenny wouldn't have walked out of the store with dog food that didn't belong to them. That's what she'd said, and he'd wanted to believe her. She'd been working so hard at school and at home, that he'd let it go.

But, it had still been in the back of his mind.

Especially when he'd agreed to let her spend the night with her best friend. The one who was no longer her best friend.

He glanced in the rearview mirror, eyed his sister's pale face.

"I really am sorry, Mia," he said, and she opened her eyes, looked straight into his. He saw his mother in her gaze. He saw his father in the abrupt shrug of her shoulders.

"It doesn't matter," she replied.

"Sure it does," Ariel cut in. "It hurts when there's tension in a friendship."

"It wasn't a friendship anyway." Mia closed her eyes again, and that was it. The end of the conversation.

"There are all different kinds of friendships," Ariel said. "Some are meant to last for decades. Some last just long enough for us to find our way through tough times."

"I haven't found myself anywhere but in trouble since Jenny and I met," Mia muttered.

She sounded pitiful.

She looked pitiful.

"You've had fun with her, right?" Ariel asked.

"I thought I was having fun. Now, I just think I wanted a friend and Jenny was there. I guess when you don't have any other option, you take what's offered."

"Jenny is a nice girl. She just doesn't have as many rules as other kids your ages." Ariel seemed determined to make Mia feel better. Tristan could have told her it was a wasted effort. He'd spent the past few months doing everything he could to help Mia adjust to Desert Valley and their lives there.

"Whatever," Mia muttered.

"Mia," Tristan warned, because he could see where the conversation was heading. If things went the way they usually did, Mia's "whatever" would turn into some kind of angry rant.

She must have decided to skip that step and go straight to sullen moping, because she didn't say another word as he drove through Desert Valley and pulled into their driveway.

She was out of the SUV like a shot, sprinting across the dark front yard, racing up the porch steps and digging in her backpack at the same time.

Probably looking for her keys.

"Mia!" he called, planning to caution her, tell her to take things a little more slowly.

Too late.

She tripped on one of the porch steps, her gangly body flying forward. She landed with a loud thump, her backpack flying out of her hands, the contents spilling everywhere.

Tristan was out of the car and up the stairs before Mia was back on her feet. He took her sister by the arm, helped her back up, his heart heavy as he looked into her face.

He was failing.

By a lot.

The tears, the sadness, the anger? He had no idea how to deal with any of them.

Ariel didn't seem to have the same problem.

She patted Mia's arm, not even a little awkwardly. "That was quite a fall. Are you okay?"

"No!" Mia wailed, grabbing at one of the books that had fallen from her pack.

She picked it up, then reached for a sheaf of papers. As she snatched it up, something small and white bounced across the porch. A marble? Tristan grabbed it, planning to toss it in Mia's backpack, then realized he wasn't holding a marble. He was holding a pearl earring. Clip-on.

It looked exactly like the one found in the evidence room.

He went cold.

"Where did this come from?" he demanded, his voice harsher than he'd intended.

Mia looked up from the papers she was shoving in her pack.

"What?"

"This." He held the earring in front of her face, and she frowned.

"How should I know?"

"What is it?" Ariel asked, her hands filled with books and papers.

"It's an earring, and it was in your bag, Mia. It had to be. How else would it have gotten on the porch?"

"I have no idea." Mia took the papers from Ariel, shoved them into her bag and stood. "It's not mine."

"It fell out of your bag," he repeated.

There was no other explanation.

He'd heard it skitter across the porch floor. He'd seen it tumbling away from the things that had fallen from her pack. It had been in the bag. It had fallen out.

Now, she was saying she had no idea what it was or how it had gotten there.

"I didn't put it in my bag." She hefted the bag onto

her shoulder and scowled. "And, I didn't steal it. If that's what you're implying."

"I'm not implying anything. I'm asking very simple questions that you don't seem to be able to answer."

"I did answer. Maybe I just need to be a little more simple in my reply," she retorted. "I. Don't. Know."

She whirled away, stomping to the front door and unlocking it. Sprinkles barked excitedly as she pushed it open, and she lifted the puppy, cuddling him close as she disappeared inside.

"What's wrong?" Ariel asked, her gaze on the earring. "Do you think she took it from Jenny?"

"There was an incident at the station a few weeks ago. This is connected to it." He couldn't tell her anything more, and she didn't ask. Instead, she grabbed a sweater and a notebook that had fallen.

"What are you going to do?" she asked, and he could see the sympathy in her eyes and on her face.

She must have known how serious the situation was. She must have understood how much trouble Mia could be in.

"The only thing I can do," he responded. "I'm calling my chief."

ELEVEN

Mia was in trouble. The kind that tutoring couldn't get her out of. Ariel stood in the living room of Tristan's small home, waiting as he went to get his sister.

She couldn't hear what was said, but she'd heard enough of his conversation with Chief Jones to know that the earring Tristan had found might somehow be connected to Veronica Earnshaw's murder.

The police had been searching for the dog trainer's murderer for months. As far as Ariel knew, they had no leads. If the earring was one, Mia might be in even bigger trouble than Ariel thought.

She wanted to walk down the hall, see if she could do anything to help, but it wasn't her business, this wasn't her family, so she stayed where she was.

Jesse lumbered over, nosing at her hand, his velvety muzzle warm and soft.

"Hey, boy," she murmured, scratching him between the ears, her gaze on the hallway. Still not a sound. Whatever Tristan was saying to his sister, he was saying it quietly.

Finally, a door opened, and Tristan reappeared, his dark hair ruffled as if he'd run his hand through it several times. She wanted to smooth it down, tell him that everything would be okay, but he met her eyes, shook his head.

"I'm sorry, Ariel. We're going to have to talk another time. I've got to bring Mia to the station."

"That doesn't sound good."

"It isn't, and if she doesn't start talking, it will be even worse."

"She's fourteen, getting anything out of girls that age is difficult."

"Unfortunately, this isn't a good time for her teenage angst to be at full throttle. She's going to be in serious trouble if she doesn't open her mouth and speak up."

"I spoke up," Mia grumbled, stepping into the hall. She'd changed into dark jeans and an oversize sweatshirt. Despite her height and the hint of makeup around her eyes, she looked like a little kid, her hair pulled back into a high ponytail, her cheeks pink with anger or frustration.

"You didn't say anything that would help your case, Mia," Tristan said, smoothing his hair. He looked a hundred times more frustrated than his sister, but he kept his tone even, his expression neutral. "We'll drive Ms. Martin home, and then I'll take you to speak with the chief."

"Tristan, I didn't do anything wrong. I've never ever seen that earring before. That's the honest truth." Mia sounded desperate.

"Whether you did or not doesn't matter. You have to talk to Chief Jones," he responded, hooking Jesse to a leash and leading him outside.

Ariel followed, leaving the door cracked open, the sound of Mia's muttered response to her brother drifting out into the balmy night.

He heard.

She could see the tension in his shoulders, the hint of anger in his face.

"Is there anything I can do to help?" she asked, and despite herself, despite every warning in her head that told her that getting too close to Tristan and his sister would be a mistake, she touched his shoulder, her hand just skimming the warm fabric of his cotton shirt.

"I don't think there's anything anyone can do to help," he responded, his eyes dark in the porch light.

"How much trouble is she in?"

"It depends on how much she hasn't told me." He pulled a plastic bag from his pocket. He'd dropped the earring into it while he was speaking with Chief Jones.

"You're assuming that she hasn't told you everything."

"Aren't you? You've seen how my sister is. She keeps secrets if she thinks it will keep her out of trouble." he said, his focus on the earring.

"That maybe be true, but she's been trying the past week."

"Trying to what? Convince me that she's staying out of trouble while she's knee-deep in it?" He shoved the earring back into his pocket and sighed.

"She's not a bad kid, Tristan. She's just a kid," she reminded him. "They make mistakes. That doesn't mean they'll keep making them."

"Tell that to the chief, because he's going to want an explanation for how my sister got that earring, and her silence isn't going to be enough of an answer."

"Okay," she said, and he raised an eyebrow in question.

"Okay what?"

"I'll talk to Chief Jones. I'll tell him that Mia is a good kid."

He smiled, just a quick curve of the lips. "I appreciate the offer, but you need to get home."

"And you don't think my opinion is going to help?"

"We've had a lot of crime in Desert Valley recently, Ariel. Everyone is on edge."

"Including your sister. Maybe this time she needs more than her brother standing in her corner fighting for her. Maybe she'd like her teacher to be doing the same."

"And maybe she'd like people to stop talking about her like she's not old enough to make her own decisions," Mia blurted out from behind the door. Obviously, she'd been listening.

"Since you're standing right here—" Tristan opened the door, took his sister's arm "—we may as well get going."

"I'd rather not."

"I already explained that you don't have a choice."

"Well, then. I want Ms. Martin to come." She grabbed Ariel's arm.

"I don't think—" Tristan began.

"That I have a choice in that, either?" Mia nearly spat the words. "Then what do I have a choice in? You didn't let me stay where I had friends. You didn't let me decide to attend high school with all the people I've known my whole life. You made me go to a new church in a new town filled with a bunch of stuck-up brats who have all kinds of money and no sense. If Mom and Dad knew how unhappy I was, they'd hate you!"

She released Ariel's wrist and stomped down the stairs, climbed into the SUV and slammed the door.

"Wow," Tristan muttered, and Ariel's heart ached for him.

He was doing the best he could in a difficult situation, but sometimes a person's best wasn't enough to change things. She'd learned that the hard way.

"You've done everything you can to make her happy," she said quietly, and he met her eyes, shook his head.

"Obviously not."

"She's angry. She'll feel differently in an hour."

"She's been feeling this way for months. That's why she's doing so poorly in school. It's why she hasn't made more friends. It's why she hangs out with Jenny. She wants what she used to have. I took all of it from her, and she wants to make sure I know just how much she's suffering."

"You didn't take her mother and father. That's what she misses the most and that's what she wants the most."

"If I could bring them back, I would. She's not the only one who misses them, but I'm an adult, she's a kid, and I do understand how hard things are for her. What I don't understand is all the trouble she keeps getting into. She was always such a great kid. Never any kind of trouble for my parents. She and I always got along great. She was an ace student. I should never have brought her here."

He turned away, and she knew the conversation was over, that he didn't want to say anything else about his sister or their struggles. She could have honored that, kept her mouth shut, kept her thoughts to herself, but she knew how it felt to fail. She knew the sick churning feeling of regret.

She followed him, catching his arm when he would have opened the door to the SUV. "You made the best decision you could," she said. "Don't waste your time second-guessing yourself."

"It's human nature to doubt our decisions," he responded. "Especially when everything we're working to preserve is falling apart. If something happens to Mia because I moved her here, I'll never forgive myself."

That was another thing Ariel understood—how hard it was to forgive yourself. Forgiving others was so much easier.

"After my husband filed for divorce," she said, the words ringing out into the quiet night. "I was angrier at myself than I was at him. I thought that if I'd made a better decision, if I'd been more careful about the guy I'd chosen, if I'd worked just a little harder or done just a little more, things would have turned out differently."

"Your husband was a liar, a thief and a cheat, Ariel. That had absolutely nothing to do with you."

"Maybe not, but now I'm going to be raising my daughter alone. She's going to have a mother who loves her, but she won't have a father."

"You don't have raise her alone," he said simply, and she knew there was a question in the words, knew that he was asking if he might be included in her life and the baby's.

"Tristan," she began, and he held up a hand, stopping her words.

"I'm not asking you to offer your undying affection, Ariel. I'm just asking you to think about letting me into your life. Me and Mia. We're kind of a package deal." He smiled, and she found herself smiling in return.

He did that to her, made her feel like everything was going to be okay, like the things that seemed so overwhelming, so insurmountable, were tiny little blips on the radar of her life.

"It's a nice idea, Tristan."

"But?"

"No buts. Our friendship is new, and neither of us can know where it's going to lead."

Maybe not.

Probably not.

Tristan wasn't even sure what the next day was going to bring. He couldn't say for sure where his relationship with Ariel was going to lead.

He wanted to try, though.

He wanted to offer her the support she deserved. "We can know that we'll try, and you can know that I'll always be there for the baby. No matter what happens between us."

She didn't respond.

He hadn't expected her to.

She'd been through too much. She'd been betrayed and hurt, and he was asking her to put that aside, believe that something she'd stopped believing in was possible.

He could have pushed her for an answer.

He could have told her that they were heading in a direction together, whether either of them wanted to or not. Instead, he leaned toward her, brushed her lips with his. Just a gentle touch, one that gave her a glimpse into his heart.

He didn't care that Mia was in the car, didn't care that she might ask questions. He and Ariel had come too far together, and he wasn't willing to turn away from her.

"We have time," he said. "And I'm willing to wait."

He opened her door and helped her into the seat. Her stomach seemed to be growing a little more every day, her small-boned frame barely able to accommodate the baby. The bigger her stomach got, the thinner her arms and legs seemed to be, the gaunter her face.

That worried him.

"You need to eat more," he said, and she laughed shakily.

"That was a quick change of subject."

"You didn't seem excited about the other one. I thought I'd switch things up."

"I'm eating." She patted her belly. "But I can't fit much in anymore. The kid is taking up more than her fair share of space."

"You need to pop that little girl out," Mia said absently, her head bent over her cell phone. Hopefully, she wasn't texting Jenny.

He wouldn't put it past her, and he almost warned her to put the phone away and not give Jenny any information about the earring or the fact that they were heading to the police station.

Sure, Mia had said Jenny wasn't her friend anymore, but that meant nothing.

Knowing her, she'd tell Jenny even more, if he warned her against it. Just to spite him, because that's what she lived for.

Not nice.

The words whispered through his mind, and they sounded just like his mother's. She'd said that to him when he was a kid, poking fun at another child or one of his teachers.

"Not nice, Tristan. You never know where someone has come from or what they've been through. You might be laughing at a person who's got nothing but sorrow in his heart."

It had taken him a few years to understand what she'd meant. He'd finally gotten it when he'd heard a group of his friends laughing at Lyle Henry. The kid had holes in his shoes and smelled like cigarette smoke. Everyone knew that his mother had died when he was six, and the teachers made certain that he wasn't picked on. Not to his face. Behind his back, kids whispered, they talked and they laughed.

Tristan had often joined in. Childish jokes. Harmless fun. Until he'd heard his friends laughing and had seen Lyle just a few feet away, cheeks red, eyes lowered. He'd heard every word. The next day, he hadn't come to school. The day after that, he'd been absent, too. By the end of a week, Tristan had felt bad enough to ride his bike to Lyle's house, knock on a front door that had peeling paint and splintered wood. An old man had opened the door, a cigarette dangling from his lips, the stench of it drifting in the air. When Tristan asked for Lyle, the guy had told him to come in.

The place had been filthy, the carpets layered with grime, the walls dingy from smoke. Lyle had shuffled down steep stairs, hitching up pants that were too big, his hair cut in some awful style that Tristan had known the other kids would make fun of.

Right on the wall behind him, there was a picture of a woman with a pale, pretty face. Next to her, a smaller, younger version of Lyle. In the picture, he was clean, his hair nice, his smile happy. In the picture, he'd looked like a normal average kid. Like Tristan or any one of his friends.

And, that's when Tristan had known just how cruel he'd been, just how wrong.

He didn't want to make the same mistake with his sister.

She hid her sorrow well, but she was still feeling the loss of their parents. He'd be a fool to ignore that, to not take into account how much it impacted her actions.

He settled Jesse into his crate, slid into the driver's seat, the tension in the vehicle thick and uncomfortable.

There were a lot of things Tristan could have said, a lot of questions he wanted to ask. Somehow, the match to the earring that had been found in the evidence room had been in Mia's bag. There had to be a reason for that, and there had to be an explanation.

Mia had insisted she had no idea.

He could choose to believe her, choose to stand by and support her, or he could choose to believe she was lying. Ariel had been right when she'd said that Mia was a good kid. She'd made mistakes, but she'd been working to correct them.

He shifted, turning so he could look at his sister, see their parents in her face.

"Mia," he said, and she stared him down, mutiny in her eyes. "Before you talk to the chief, I want you to know something."

"That you think I'm a loser?" she muttered, tears in her eyes.

"That I believe you. We'll figure out how the earring got in your backpack. *I'll* figure it out. All you have to do is keep moving in the direction you've been going. Good grades. Good attitude."

He turned away before she could respond, but caught the look of surprise on her face. He shoved the keys in the ignition and starting the SUV.

Chief Jones was waiting for them. He was pretty certain several other members of the K-9 team would be at the station. A match to the earring they'd found in the evidence room—near where the Veronica Earnshaw evidence box *should* have been—was something they'd all been waiting on. If they could figure out where it had come from, they might just find Veronica's killer.

He backed out of the driveway, surprised when Ariel

leaned close, her lips almost touching his ear, as she whispered, "Good job."

"We'll see," he responded, and she chuckled.

"We already saw." She backed away, shifted so that she was looking out her window. "I've been thinking about what you said. About Mitch and the car accident he was in."

Obviously, she didn't want to wait to have their discussion. He glanced in the review mirror. Mia had earbuds in and was bopping around to some song or another. "What about it?"

"I never understood why Mitch was so determined that I not have the baby. Even after we got divorced. It made no sense. He wasn't going to have any legal obligation. I'd signed papers that released him of his financial responsibilities, but he wouldn't let it go."

"I think we've established that your ex wasn't a very moral guy. He wanted his freedom."

"From me? From the baby? He had it."

True. Tristan had seen the legal documents. "Maybe he was motivated by spite," he suggested. "He didn't want you to be happy. Or..."

He stopped before he said it. The thing that had been nudging the back of his mind, the idea that he couldn't quite shake.

"What?" she asked, her voice tight.

She knew what he was thinking.

He was almost positive that she did.

"Like I said before," he responded, "it's convenient that there was no way to identify Mitch's body. It was his car. His gender. His height. Body type. Those things all match, but the only way to know for sure would be to compare his DNA with a relative's."

That was it.

He didn't say anything else, just let the words hang there.

They were nearing the police station when Ariel finally spoke, her voice just loud enough to be heard above the soft rumble of the engine. "The baby is his only living relative."

"I know."

"If he were alive, he'd want to start again, right? Doing what he's been doing to make money?" she continued as if he hadn't spoken. "Or maybe living off money he's made from other schemes. The police were investigating several arsons, but had only been able to tie him to five. He could have made a boatload of money and socked it away overseas."

"He was smart enough to do that, and probably greedy enough to keep working his angle, making money off insurance fraud," Tristan agreed. He'd read up on the guy, talked to a few people who'd worked with him. Most people hadn't been fond of him, but they'd all agreed he was smart and he knew how to work any system to his advantage.

"He's also smart enough to know that the police might get suspicious if there are more fires, ones that match his MO." She tapped her fingers against her thigh. "They might want to check the baby's DNA, see if it matches the DNA extracted from the victim of the car accident. DNA from new crime scenes, too. If it did, they'd be hunting him down, and they'd find him. He would have to know that. If he were alive," she said the last part so quietly he almost didn't hear.

It was what he'd been thinking, though, what he'd been worrying about.

If Mitch was alive, that would explain everything.

If he was alive, that would give Butch Harold a really good reason to keep his mouth shut about the person who'd paid him to kill Ariel. A guy who wanted to get rid of his own child wouldn't hesitate to kill a hired lackey.

It was something Tristan planned to discuss with Chief Jones.

He touched Ariel's hand, found himself linking fingers with her, offering comfort that he knew she needed. She needed more than comfort, though. She needed her ex found, and maybe, too, she needed to know just how much Tristan cared.

"It's going to be okay, Ariel. I'm going to figure out what's going on. If your ex is alive, I'm going to make sure he doesn't get anywhere close to you."

She squeezed his hand in acknowledgment but didn't speak as they pulled up in front on of the police station and parked beneath a glowing street light.

TWELVE

Mitch. Alive.

Those two words ran through Ariel's head over and over again, chilling her blood and making her stomach churn. She tried to drown them out by listening to the K-9 officers who were gathered in a conference room nearby. She could hear bits and pieces of their conversation, but not enough to be interesting and not enough to drive those words out of her head.

Mitch.

Alive.

It had never occurred to her before. She'd never even considered the fact that he might not have died in the accident, that someone else might have been behind the wheel of the vehicle.

If it was true, if Mitch had faked his death, everything else made sense. The eerie feeling that she was being watched, the odd sense that she wasn't alone.

She shivered, pacing across the small room Tristan had left her in. He'd said he'd be back soon. That had been a half hour ago. She hadn't heard from him or anyone else since.

Obviously, the interview with Mia wasn't going well. The teenager had secrets, but Ariel didn't think the earring had anything to do with them. She'd looked genuinely surprised to see it, genuinely confused as to who it might belong to.

She'd also seemed stunned when Tristan had told her that he believed her, that he'd figure things out.

Tristan was a good guy, the kind of guy that Ariel had been looking for when she'd found Mitch.

"You were such a fool," she muttered.

"What's that?" Tristan asked, his voice so surprising that she startled, nearly tipping over as she whirled to face him.

He stood in the open doorway, his eyes shadowed, his jaw covered with stubble.

"Just talking to myself," she responded, her cheeks hot. "How's everything going?"

"The way I expected. Mia is insisting that she knows nothing about the earring."

"I don't think she does."

"Me, neither. The problem is, I'm sure she's hiding something. She's nervous and edgy, and it's making all of us suspicious."

"Including you?"

"Something is going on with her, Ariel. I just wish I knew what." He ran a hand down his jaw, shook his head. "But, I don't want to keep you here any longer. We're all taking a ten-minute break, so I can give you a ride home. I want to leave Jesse at your place—if anyone comes near your house, he'll alert you. The moment he does, call me and 911." He patted the lab's head and was rewarded with what Ariel was certain was a doggy smile.

Ariel nodded. "I don't mind staying, though, Tristan. I did tell Mia that I'd be here for her, and I'd like to at least say goodbye before I abandon her."

"I don't think it counts as abandoning her when I'm forcing you to go." He offered a weary smile. "For the baby's sake, you really do need to rest, Ariel."

He was right.

She knew it, but the thought of going home to the empty house, even with Jesse, made her sad.

"All right. I'll leave, but tell Mia—"

Someone knocked on the doorjamb, and secretary Carrie Dunleavy walked in. She smiled shyly, holding up two disposable cups. "Coffee, Tristan?" she asked, holding one toward him.

"Thanks, Carrie. You're a gem."

She blushed and held the other cup out to Ariel.

"This is hot chocolate. Lots of real milk and just a little chocolate. I didn't think you'd want a lot of caffeine." Her gaze dropped to Ariel's stomach, and she blushed again.

"That's really thoughtful of you," Ariel said, taking the cup and smiling at the woman. Ariel appreciated how kind Carrie had been to Mia when Tristan had needed a safe place to leave the girl the other day.

"Very," Tristan added. "Especially considering that your shift ended hours ago. Did Chief Jones call you back in?"

"No." Carrie's blush deepened, her skin suddenly the color of a ripe tomato. "I was out on my way home and saw a few of the K-9 officers walking across the parking lot. That seemed odd, so I decided to stop in and see if I could assist anyone. I was really sorry to hear that your sister had been taken in for questioning."

Tristan frowned. Ariel had the feeling he didn't like word of that spreading. "Who told you that?"

Carrie bit her lip. "Ellen mentioned it. But, she didn't say questioning," she hurried to add, clearly hoping to make Tristan feel better. "She just said that you'd brought Mia in to speak with Chief Jones. Did something happen? Is Mia okay?"

"She seems to be," Tristan responded kindly, but he was still frowning, his gaze focused on Carrie.

"Great. Good. I'm going to see if anyone else wants coffee."

"Or, you could go home. It's past midnight," Tristan pointed out. "You're working the early shift, right?"

"I'm a night owl," Carrie said with a nervous laugh. "I don't mind being out until the wee hours of the morning. I'll just check in with the chief and see if he needs anything."

She scurried from the room.

"Carrie seems very dedicated to the police department," Ariel said, sipping the sweet chocolate.

"Yeah." He frowned.

"What's wrong?"

"I don't know. Just something at the back of my mind that I can't quite catch hold of. Every time I see Carrie, I think there's something I'm not putting my finger on, then she runs off and it's gone. I think I'll have a chat with her later. See if I can figure it out. Come on. Let's get out of here." He took her arm, his fingers caressing the inside of her elbow, and for a moment she was back at the house, his lips brushings hers, a million butterflies taking flight in her stomach.

She'd been trying to forget about the kiss, trying to tell herself it had meant nothing, but she'd known it meant way more than that. She'd felt it to her soul, the gentleness of the touch, the promise in it.

"I've been thinking about your ex," Tristan said as he led her into the hall.

The words were a splash of ice water in the face. "What about him?"

"He was a criminal. A liar. A cheat."

"No need for the reminder, Tristan. I'm very aware of what he was."

He nodded, eyes filled with concern and compassion. "I know, and I'm sorry. The thing is, Mitch was also a fool, Ariel. He didn't value what he had. If I were ever in his position, if I ever had the love of a woman like you, I would know exactly how blessed I was."

"I—" she began, not sure what she was going to say.

"Tristan!" Mia called, her voice ringing through the hallway, her feet tapping against the floor as she raced toward them. Her eyes were wide with fear, her face leeched of color. She was crying again. Silent tears that streamed down her face.

"What happened, Mia?" Tristan pulled her into his arms, patting her back the way he probably had when she was a tiny kid and he was an awkward teenager.

"Carrie said you'd left me."

"No!" Carrie called, hurrying toward them. "You misunderstood, Mia. I didn't say he'd left you. I said, he'd left."

"Same thing!" Mia cried.

"What's going on out here?" Chief Jones asked, stepping into the hall, Ellen Foxcroft and Ryder Hayes and their K-9 partners beside him. "Mia, I thought we agreed that you'd stay in the interview room and wait while I made a phone call."

"I was going to, but Carrie—"

"I didn't say that your brother left you," Carrie snapped, the harsh tone so surprising that everyone went silent. "Sorry," Carrie mumbled. "I…just. That's not what I said."

Mia's face crumpled. "You *were* going to leave me, weren't you, Tristan? Because I've been such a brat. You were going to let them take me off to juvenile hall."

"Hon," Chief Jones said, his voice gentle. "We weren't going to take you anywhere. We just wanted the truth."

"I told you the truth!" she cried. "But not about everything. I'm really sorry, Tristan. I should have told you from the very beginning."

"Told me what?" Tristan looked as confused as Ariel felt, his dark eyes jumping from his sister to Chief Jones and then settling on Ariel.

"Help me?" he mouthed, and she moved a little closer, touched Mia's shoulder.

"Mia, what's going on? You're carrying too big a burden for someone so young, and it's making you do all kinds of things you normally wouldn't. If you share the weight of it with us, we can help."

Mia wiped tears from her cheeks and took a shuddering breath. "I just don't want to get Jenny in trouble. She didn't mean any harm."

"Didn't mean any harm when she did what?" Tristan asked,

"That puppy that went missing from the training center the night the trainer was murdered? The one that everyone is looking for? Jenny found it, and she took it to her grandmother's house. She's been keeping it in her grandmother's barn. That's what we were fighting about tonight. I told her she had to turn the puppy back over to the training center, and she said she wasn't going to do it."

For a moment, everyone was silent, then they were all talking at once. Chief Jones telling Tristan that they needed to get to the Gilmores' house. Ellen saying that she'd call the K-9 training center and get the microchip reader. Ryder speaking on his radio, talking to another K-9 officer.

Ariel could sense the excitement, the anxiety, and she took Mia's hand, starting to lead her away from the group.

"Hang on for a minute, okay?" Tristan said, snagging Ariel's wrist, his fingers warm, his touch light. He was looking into her eyes, and she couldn't stop looking back, seeing the intensity in the blue of his gaze.

"Should we call Jenny's grandmother?" Ellen asked, and whatever seemed to be between Ariel and Tristan disappeared. "Let her know we're on the way?"

"And give Jenny a chance to hide the puppy?" Ryder responded. "I don't think so."

"Me, neither," Chief Jones agreed. "Tristan and Ryder, why don't the two of you head to Jenny's place? Ellen, want to call the new trainer? Ask Sophie to bring the microchip scanner here? We'll meet in my office ASAP and get the chip read. Hopefully, we'll get the answer we're looking for."

"Answer to what?" Ariel asked.

"The question of who murdered Veronica Earnshaw," Chief Jones answered grimly. "Carrie, can you…"

His voice trailed off. "Where did she go?"

"Probably too much action for her," Ryder commented. "You know how she is. She's quiet, and she doesn't like a lot of commotion. She'll turn back up eventually. She always does. Let's go get that puppy, Tristan."

Getting the puppy was Tristan's first priority. Otherwise, he'd have gone looking for Carrie. There was something he was missing about her, and he wanted to know what it was.

First, though, they had to get the puppy and have the microchip scanned. If Veronica had been able to leave a clue about her murderer, that's where it would be.

"All right. Let's go," he said, as anxious as Ryder was to get going.

"You can't just go barging in on them," Mia protested. "Jenny's grandmother is old. She'll freak out and have a heart attack and die, then Jenny will never forgive me!"

"We can't wait, Mia," Tristan responded as patiently as he could.

He was angry, and he thought he had a good reason to be. Mia had lied. She'd helped her friend keep a puppy that didn't belong to her—a puppy the police had been searching for for months now. He thought about the empty dog food bag, the incident at the feed store. It all made sense now. Mia wouldn't have wanted the puppy to go hungry. She'd have made sure it had food, but she would have drawn the line at stealing. She'd probably been trying to convince Jenny to put the food back when Lauren spotted them.

"Tristan, seriously, you have to listen to me. Jenny loves that puppy. She's going to be heartbroken if you take it."

"Sweetie," Ellen said gently. "My mother donated the puppies to the training center, and that's who they belong to. No matter how much your friend loves the puppy, it's not hers."

"But—"

"You know," Ariel broke in, the cup of chocolate still in her hand. It made him think of Carrie again, of that niggling thing that he couldn't quite pull from his mind. “It might be best if a woman went with you, a woman who’s not a police officer. And someone Jenny’s grandmother knows. I’ve been out there a couple of times to visit. She might respond better to me than to anyone else.”

No, Tristan was going to say, because she looked exhausted, and he wanted to ask Ellen to drop her off at her place.

The chief had other ideas. He nodded. “That’s a good idea, Ariel. I sure appreciate your help in the matter.”

“It’s no problem. I’d hate for Ms. Gilmore to get confused or upset about the situation. She might be afraid that you’re going to bring Jenny to juvenile detention, but I’m sure that’s not your plan.”

It wasn’t a question, but the chief shook his head. “It’s not. We want the puppy back, and I’m sure we’ll have a few things to say to Jenny, but if she’s been taking good care of the puppy, we may be able to just let it go. We’ll have to discuss it later.”

“She is taking good care of the puppy,” Mia said earnestly.

“I’m sure,” Ariel responded. “She’s a good kid. She’s made a childish mistake, but I think we can all understand it. She found the puppy and then couldn’t bear to give it back. What she did was wrong—she knew the police were looking for him, but I do hope she can pay for her crime by doing community service, perhaps volunteering at the training center. Since she’s only fourteen, I’d be happy to accompany her.”

Tristan might not have been so forgiving, but Mia looked so relieved and Ariel made a good case. He kept his mouth shut.

“Ellen, is there any chance you can drop my sister off at our place?” he asked.

"I don't want to go home. Jenny is my friend—"

"That's not what you said an hour ago," Tristan pointed out and was rewarded with a scowl.

"I still like Jenny. Even if we aren't friends. I don't want her to get in trouble because of me."

"If she's in trouble, it's because of her actions and it has nothing to do with you," Ariel said gently. "Now, how about you do what your brother wants without arguing? The sooner we get this over with, the sooner Jenny can make amends and move on."

It seemed to be the right thing to say.

Mia sighed. "All right. Fine. I'll go home."

"And stay there?" Tristan prodded.

"That, too."

Good. That was what he wanted to hear. The last thing he needed was his sister running to rescue her friend.

Her friend who'd been hiding the puppy the team had been searching for.

"Hard to believe, isn't it?" Ryder asked as Ellen led Mia away.

"That a teenage girl could fall in love with a puppy?" Ariel responded before Tristan could. "Not really. I've seen the picture of the German shepherd puppy. He's every kid's perfect dog."

"That two teenage girls could keep a puppy hidden for so long. Especially when an entire town was looking for it," Ryder said.

"The Gilmores are pretty far outside town," Tristan said, calling to Jesse and then heading down the hall. He was anxious to get a look at the puppy Jenny was keeping. It was possible Mia was mistaken, that Jenny had found some other dog.

It was possible, but he didn't think she *was* mistaken.

The timing was too perfect, the change in Mia's attitude coinciding with Veronica's murder, the missing puppy, the other crimes that had been happening in town. He should have seen the connection sooner, but he'd been so caught up in the investigation, so certain that his sister was just rebelling because she didn't like Desert Valley, that he hadn't looked any further than that for an explanation of her behavior.

"There is no man so blind as the one who will not see," he muttered as he opened the door to his SUV and helped Ariel in.

"What's that?" she asked, her mouth curved in a half smile.

"Just thinking that I should have realized what my sister was hiding. Now that she's told me the truth, it seems pretty obvious. Dog food missing. A sudden interest in all things puppy."

"Lots of girls that age love animals."

"Maybe so, but—"

"Don't waste time looking back, Tristan. Take it from someone who's been there and done that—it won't change anything. All it can possibly do is make you doubt yourself."

"Is that what you've been doing?" he asked as he pulled out of the parking lot. "Doubting yourself?"

"Absolutely," she responded without hesitation. "I question everything I think, every decision I make, because of Mitch."

"Maybe we both need to be a little kinder to ourselves," he said.

"Okay. You first."

That made him laugh. A surprise, because he wasn't in a laughing kind of mood. If Mia was right about the puppy, the key to finding Veronica's murderer had been right under his nose for months.

Right under his nose. Living in his house. Lying every day.

He frowned, glancing in his rearview mirror. Ryder was right behind him, his SUV's strobe lights on. He was as anxious to find the truth as Tristan. Maybe even more so. Tristan had been hoping to find answers to his friend Mike's death. He hadn't believed the rookie K-9 officer's fall down the stairs was an accident, and he'd been determined to learn the truth.

There'd been no clues, though. No hint that Mike hadn't just taken a hard fall down the steps.

Ryder's wife *had* been murdered, though. She'd been shot. Just like Veronica. Was it possible that finding Veronica's murderer would lead them to Melanie's? That's what the team was hoping for, and they were about to find out.

The Gilmores' farmhouse was just ahead, the old structure a hulking black shadow against the dark sky. There were no lights on in the house, just a lone bulb glowing from the porch.

Tristan parked the SUV and climbed out, opening the back hatch for Jesse. Ariel was out of the vehicle before he got to her door, her face pale in the moonlight.

"I feel bad waking them up," she whispered as Ryder got out of his car and released his K-9 partner from the back.

"We don't have a choice. If the puppy is here, we need to find it." Tristan called Jesse to heel and headed up the rickety porch stairs. The place had seen better days, but he knew Ms. Gilmore did her best. On a limited income, with limited health and energy, she was raising a difficult teenager.

He knocked on the door and thought he heard a puppy barking somewhere in the distance.

The old barn?

That's where Mia said it would be.

"How about I go over to the barn and take a look?" Ryder suggested, Titus sniffing the ground beside him. The dog scented something.

"Let's both—"

The door creaked open, and an old woman appeared, her white hair wild around her head, her wrinkled face slack with surprise. "What in the world is going on out here? My granddaughter said there were police cars outside, and I guess she was right."

"Actually, Ms. Gilmore," Ariel said, smiling kindly at the older woman. "We're here to speak with Jenny. I'm her teacher, Ariel—"

"Martin. I'm old. Not senile. What has that girl done now?" The older woman sighed, opening the door wider and gesturing for them to enter. "Jenny!" she called.

There was no answer, and Tristan met Ryder's eyes.

"The barn?" he suggested.

"I think so," Ryder replied as Titus began to bark frantically, pulling at the lead and lunging toward the still-open door. A shadow was moving near the edge of the driveway, darting through sparse trees and heading toward a distant outbuilding.

"Let's go," Tristan commanded, running back outside with Jesse.

He didn't release the dog, just let him have the lead as they raced toward the retreating figure.

THIRTEEN

Tristan and Ryder were gone just long enough for Ariel to explain the situation to Ms. Gilmore. The older woman seemed more annoyed than angry, her eyes red-rimmed with fatigue as she puttered around the kitchen, putting on a teakettle, her old housecoat at odds with her perfectly styled hair. She had clearly rushed to powder her face before she'd answered the door. There were specks of powder on her cheeks and a dusting of it across her nose. She'd tried for mascara, and it had smeared, dots of it staining her cheeks. She had rings on every finger. Earrings on both ears. One pearl. One gold stud. Clip-ons. One of them dangling precariously.

"I just don't understand that girl at all," Ms. Gilmore said, pouring hot water over a tea bag and handing Ariel a cup. "I've tried so hard to instill good values in her, and then she up and does something like this. Stealing a dog? It's just unconscionable."

"She might not have known she was stealing it, Ms. Gilmore," Ariel said, shouting a bit since the woman was hard of hearing. "When she first found it, she might have thought it was a stray."

"When she first found it, yes, but after that, there

was no excuse. And, I'm sure her sweet little friend was telling her that." She shook her head, white curls bouncing around her head, the loose earring flopping around. "I suppose I'm going to have to bring her to that counselor she was seeing after her mother died. She's in the next town over, though, and it's a long drive at my age. Maybe—"

Whatever she was going to say was cut off by the sound of a door opening, dogs barking, men talking and a girl yelling very loudly, "It's not fair! Sparkle is mine. I found him, and you can't just take him away."

"I guess that is my cue to do something," Ms. Gilmore murmured, hurrying out into the foyer.

Ariel followed.

Tristan and Ryder were there, Jenny standing between them with a big German shepherd puppy sitting at her feet. It was a handsome dog, big feet and young thin body. Calm. Not barking or jumping. As a matter of fact, it looked like a younger, thinner version of a few K-9 dogs she'd seen.

"Hi, Jenny," Ariel said, and the teen's eyes widened.

"What are you doing here?"

"Is that any way to talk to your teacher?" Ms. Gilmore snapped, marching over to her granddaughter, her blue eyes blazing. "I cannot believe that you've caused this ruckus, Jenny Lynn. I really can't."

"I didn't cause it. Mia did. If she hadn't opened her big mouth—"

"She did the right thing," Ariel cut her off. "You know it, Jenny."

"The right thing is not to squeal on your friend," Jenny said.

"It is when your friend is doing something she shouldn't," Tristan said quietly, and Jenny blushed.

"Okay. So, maybe it isn't her fault. Maybe it's mine, but I love Sparkle, and I didn't know he was missing from the training center when I found him. He was just a little baby, and he needed someone to love and care for him. I thought I was doing the right thing."

"Until you heard we were missing a dog and kept him anyway?" Ryder asked, and Jenny's flush deepened.

"I'm sorry. I should have brought him back, but by that time, I already loved him so much." A tear slipped down her cheek and she wiped it away.

"I understand, honey," Ms. Gilmore said, leaning in and giving Jenny a hug.

Jenny sobbed and knelt next to the puppy, pulling him into her arms. The dog licked her cheek, put a paw on her thigh.

"I guess you have to take him," Jenny said morosely, kissing the dog's snout and standing. "He knows all the basic commands, and I've been working with him on puzzles, he's really good at finding anything I hide." Her voice broke, but she seemed determined not to let another tear slip out.

That made the situation even sadder.

At least, to Ariel it did.

Jenny was a tough girl because she'd had to be, but she'd shown a softer side on a few occasions, and she'd obviously done a great job caring for the puppy. He looked healthy and happy, his tongue lolling out as he watched Jenny intently.

"He's going to miss me so much," Jenny whispered, and then she took off, running up stairs that creaked and groaned beneath her light weight.

"I know she's going to have to be punished for this, but it almost seems like giving up the dog is punishment enough," Ms. Gilmore said, shaking her head sadly, the force of the movement loosening her dangling earring. It flew off, clattering onto the floor.

Tristan bent to retrieve it, seemed to freeze as he grabbed the old pearl clip-on.

"We need to get back to the station," he said abruptly, handing Ms. Gilmore the earring and calling for Jesse to heel.

That was it.

No explanation.

He just sprinted out the door and ran toward his SUV.

Ariel was doing her best to rush after him, when he stopped short, turned toward her.

"Sorry about that," he said with a tense smile, returning to take her arm and walk her the rest of the way. Slowly. As if she was fragile and delicate.

That would have made her laugh, if he hadn't looked so upset, his blue eyes shadowed, his jaw tight.

"What's wrong?" she asked, as he opened her door.

"Did that earring remind you of anything?" he asked.

She started to shake her head, then realized that it did. It looked something like the one that had fallen out of Mia's bag. "I guess it does look a little like the one Mia had in her bag. You don't think she stole it, do you? Because it isn't a match to the one Ms. Gilmore was wearing. It looks like it, but it's not the same."

"No. But I know what's been bothering me. I know why every time I see those earrings or see Carrie Dunleavy, I have the feeling I've missed something."

"What—?" she started to ask, but he'd backed away.

She watched as he jogged to Ryder's vehicle, the strobe lights flashing across his face as he said something that Ariel couldn't hear.

Whatever it was got Ryder moving. He lifted the

shepherd puppy into the back of the SUV and whistled for his partner who jumped in beside Sparkle.

"I'll meet you back there. Hopefully, Sophie has already arrived. I want the microchip read now," he said, his voice gruff. Then, he was in the SUV and speeding away.

Tristan loaded Jesse into the back of the vehicle, then jumped into the driver's seat.

"Seat belt?" he asked as he started the engine.

"Yes."

That was it.

The sum total of the conversation.

Tristan didn't speak another word as he drove back to the station. He didn't say anything as he helped her from his SUV, then ran to greet Ryder and the puppy, Jesse prancing beside him.

She followed as they walked into the lobby and through the long hallway. She could hear voices. Men and women speaking in hushed tones and in loud ones.

She wasn't sure she should be there, because she could feel the frantic energy in the building, feel the tension that seemed to fill it.

She wanted to suggest that she go home. She could have easily walked, but the thought of Mitch potentially being alive, maybe waiting for her to let down her guard, sealed her lips.

Tristan glanced over his shoulders, met her eyes. "Just give me a few minutes, and I'll take you home," he said as if he'd read her mind.

"Okay," she responded, but he was already moving toward a conference room, the door opened to reveal a crowd of people and dogs.

Chief Jones stood near the doorway, his back to the hall, his hair mussed. He'd been looking tired lately, the unsolved cases taking their toll on him. Ariel had heard the discontented murmurings of more than one Desert Valley resident. The chief of police was being blamed for the fact that Veronica's murder hadn't been solved, and for the fact that the murder of Ryder Hayes's wife was still being investigated five years later. Then there'd been the missing puppy, the attack on Marian Foxcroft and the string of break-ins that had been occurring since the puppy disappeared.

None of those things had been resolved, and Chief Jones was the obvious scapegoat. People were whispering that he should retire, and Ariel was certain he knew about it.

A young woman stood beside him, long blond hair spilling down her back. She held a white wand-like device in one hand, a collar and leash in the other.

The lead dog trainer who'd taken Veronica Earnshaw's place. Sophie Williams. That was her name. Ariel had heard a lot about her from Mia and Jenny. The two girls were fascinated by everything and anyone who had anything to do with dogs.

The trainer must have heard them approaching. She turned, her attention going straight to the puppy.

"Is this Marco?" she asked, crouching and holding out her hand.

"Yes," Tristan responded. "Is Carrie around?" he asked, and Sophie frowned.

"I have no idea. I haven't seen her since I got here. Why?" She attached the collar to the puppy and snapped on the leash. The dog seemed unfazed by the commotion and not in the least bothered by the other dogs that were gathered with their handlers.

"I wanted to speak with her."

"This is the second time you've asked about her, Tristan," Chief Jones said. "What's going on?"

Tristan stared at him. "The pearl earring found in the evidence room near where Veronica Earnshaw's evidence box had been. The matching earring found skittering out of my sister's backpack. I think I've seen those earrings before. He walked into the room and took a photograph from the wall. It looked like a group shot taken at a Christmas party, a bunch of men and women smiling happily at the camera.

Tristan studied it for a moment, then shook his head. "I don't know how I missed it. Look." He jabbed at the photo, his finger touching Carrie's face.

"What?" Ellen said, leaning a little closer, her eyes going wide. "Carrie is wearing the earrings. The exact match for both earrings."

"What?" Chief Jones snatched the photograph from Tristan's hands, his face going pale as he studied it. "No way. There is no way she stole that evidence."

"How else do you explain the earring?" Tristan asked. "She had access to the evidence room. She also had access to my sister's backpack. They hung out here together a couple of times while Mia was waiting for me."

"But…couldn't be it a coincidence?" the chief sputtered, clearly unable to believe the longtime department secretary could be guilty. Of much more than stealing evidence. And planting evidence.

"She probably thought she'd throw us off her trail. You noticed the picture the other day," Shane pointed out. "You said something to me and her about it."

Tristan nodded. "Right. Where is she?"

"Hold on!" the chief growled. "Before we go chasing her down and accusing her. Let's read that microchip."

* * *

Tristan waited impatiently while Sophie scanned the puppy. He didn't need more evidence. He already knew the truth. Carrie was somehow involved in Veronica's murder.

"That's it," Sophie said, eyeing the small screen on the front of the scanner. "Oh boy," she murmured.

"What?" the chief asked, and she turned the scanner so everyone could see it.

Carrie D DVPD.

"We need to find her. Now." Shane Weston headed for the door, brushing past Tristan in his hurry to find Carrie.

Tristan was in a hurry, too, but he couldn't leave Ariel standing around the police department, and he wasn't going to let her return home alone.

He took her arm, leading her out of the conference room that was suddenly filled with people voicing opinions and making plans. He'd be part of that. Eventually.

Right now, Ariel was his priority.

She looked exhausted, her eyes deeply shadowed.

"If you need to stay," she began, and he shook his head.

"It won't take long to get you home and make sure you're safe. I want Jesse with you."

"I really don't mind waiting. It seems like you have a lot of things to work out here."

"We've got a good team. They'll make the plans while I drop you off. We'll follow through on them later."

"What's going to happen to the puppy?" she asked as he backed out of his parking space and headed across town.

"I'm not sure. We'll talk to Sophie, see what she has to say and then make a decision."

"Sophie is the new lead trainer, right?"

"Yes. She took Veronica's place." He didn't mention the murder. She didn't ask about it. Ariel seemed to understand the boundaries he had, the fact that his job wasn't always something he could discuss.

He liked that about her.

He liked a lot of things about her.

Including her willingness to be there for her students.

"It was nice of you to go out to the Gilmores' place tonight."

"I was just doing my job, Tristan."

"I don't think your job requires late-night visits to students," he responded, and she laughed quietly.

"In a town this size, it does. In Las Vegas, I taught five classes every day. Thirty students in each one. I only got to know most of them on a surface level. Here, I get to know them individually. When you know someone, you can't ignore the troubles they might have. You can't just turn your back and walk away when you know they're hurting."

"Some people can."

"You couldn't," she pointed out, and he knew she was right.

He'd be heading back out to the Gilmores' tomorrow, checking in on Jenny and her grandmother, making sure they were both doing okay. He might even try to help Jenny find a dog she could train and keep, because he was beginning to think Mia was right. Jenny wasn't a bad kid. She just needed a few adults in her life that could steer her in the right direction.

"You're thinking about Jenny, aren't you?" Ariel asked as he pulled onto her street.

"How did you know?"

"Just a guess. I was thinking about her, too. The

puppy seems to be doing really well. She did a good job with him. Maybe in addition to volunteering at the K-9 training center, she could get a little extra training from someone on your team? Someone who might be able to get her turned on to K-9 training as a career choice."

"By someone, I'm thinking you mean me."

"Someone needs to care, Tristan."

She was right, and he would have told her that, but Jesse barked, the sound ringing through the vehicle.

Odd, because Jesse almost never barked.

Unless he sensed danger.

"What is it, boy?" Tristan asked, and the dog barked again, a loud fierce sound that made Tristan's hair stand on end.

He glanced in the rearview mirror, sure he caught a hint of movement in the darkness, a shadow darting from one tree to another.

They were close to the parsonage. Just two houses down. He could see the lights from her front porch, a light in the window upstairs.

He kept driving in that direction, pretending he hadn't seen the guy scurrying through the darkness, but Ariel sensed the trouble the same way he had, and she twisted in her seat, her belly brushing his arm as she leaned over to get a better look.

"What's going on?" she whispered as if she was afraid whoever was outside might hear her.

"Maybe nothing," he responded, but Jesse growled, the sound low and mean, the harshness of it a warning that there *was* something wrong, and that Tristan had better be prepared for it.

He called his location in on the radio, asking for backup as he pulled into Ariel's driveway. He knew most of the rookies would be looking for Carrie Dunleavy, but at least one of them would respond to Tristan's call. The area around her house seemed empty, the early morning silence eerie.

Jesse growled again, this time lunging at the back window, his claws scrabbling against the kennel.

"Someone is out there," Ariel said, so quietly he almost didn't hear.

She'd found his hand, holding on as if her life depended on it, her skin cool and dry against his palm.

He didn't think she realized it, but he did, and he squeezed gently, offered her the only reassurance he could.

"It's going to be okay," he said, his attention focused on the porch, the light and what looked like a small string that seemed to hang from it.

A fuse of some sort?

At the end of the street, strobe lights flashed, and he knew his backup had arrived.

"Stay here," he said, opening the door.

"He's out there, Tristan," she replied, holding on to his hand when he would have pulled away. "I know he is."

"Your ex?"

"Who else would hate me and the baby enough to do this?"

"If it is him, I'm going to put a stop to this."

"He knows how to use a gun," she said, and he touched her cheek, looking into her eyes. He wanted to escort her to the house and lock her safely inside, but that string was bothering him. If it had been there before, he'd have noticed.

"I do, too. Shane just pulled up. I need to talk to him. Stay here."

She nodded, finally releasing his hand and offering a halfhearted smile. "Be careful."

He didn't need the warning.

If Mitch really was alive, the guy had nothing to lose and everything to gain by escaping.

He nodded, closed the door and opened the back hatch for Jesse. The dog had barely jumped from the back when he started barking, the loud, sharp warning that said he scented something.

Shane Weston was already out of his vehicle, K-9 partner, Bella, at his side.

"He's alerting?" he asked.

"Yeah."

"Where'd you see the guy?"

"A couple houses to the east."

"I'll head in that direction. Ellen and Whitney are on the way over."

"Ryder?"

"Heading to Carrie's place with James and the chief. Do you really think she murdered Veronica?" he asked.

"How about we handle one problem at a time?" Tristan responded, clipping Jesse to his lead, and then giving the dog the command to find.

The lab took off running, nose to the air, heading straight for the house and that small piece of string that was twisting just a little in the warm summer breeze.

FOURTEEN

There were people everywhere.

Police officers. Bomb squad. Neighbors.

Ariel could see them all from her position in the window of Millie Raymond's house. The older woman had offered to let her sit there while the explosive experts disarmed the bomb that had been left in the porch light fixture.

Mitch's doing?

She had a horrible feeling it was.

Tristan and Shane were out with their K-9 partners, and Ariel needed to remember they were trained for this. They'd find Mitch just as they'd found the thug he'd hired.

She needed to have faith.

"You know what you need, my dear?" Millie said as if reading her mind, her voice a little shaky with age. She'd lost her husband a few years ago, and she'd filled her life with charitable work. She served food at the local mission and rocked babies in the NICU. Apparently, she also took care of terrified neighbors.

Faith, Ariel thought. *That's what I need.* "What?"

"A nice cup of tea. Let's go in the kitchen, and I'll make you some."

Ariel managed a smile. "That's okay, Millie. I'm fine."

"Fine? You've been sitting there for three hours watching the sun come up and all those people run around outside. That can't be good for the baby."

"Tristan said that if I came over here with you, I should stay where he could see me."

"Tristan… Good-looking guy."

"Yes. He is."

"He's also a nice young man. I've seen him over at your house on several occasions."

"It's not my house," she hedged, because she didn't feel like discussing her love life with Millie.

Her love life?

The thought almost made her laugh.

Except that she felt something every time she looked into Tristan's eyes. Something warm and nice and just a little exciting. Something that she should ignore but couldn't seem to.

"You know what I mean, dear. He's been at the parsonage with his sister, helping you out."

"I've been tutoring Mia."

"It will be hard to step into a teenager's life, but I'm sure you're up to the task."

"What are you talking about, Millie. Tutoring her isn't the same as stepping into her life."

"No. It isn't," the older woman said, smiling slyly.

"Whatever you're thinking, stop."

"I'm thinking romance and candles and all the wonderful things a woman your age should have."

"How about I just take a cup of tea instead," Ariel responded, forcing herself to stand. Outside, the sun was just beginning to rise, the first rays of it tingeing the morning with purple light. Across the street, the little parsonage was lit like a Christmas tree, spotlights turned to the porch where several men were working to remove evidence.

There'd been enough explosives to take down the entire house. Tristan had told her that when he'd helped her out of the car and walked her to Whitney's vehicle. He'd wanted her to go to the police station, but Millie had been standing on her front porch watching the action, and she'd offered to bring Ariel inside.

"Just stay where I can see you, okay?" he'd whispered, his lips brushing her hair.

And, she'd told him that she would.

"I've got a wonderful Earl Grey," Millie gushed, leading the way through the small bungalow and into the kitchen. It was at the back of the house, butting up to trees and open land. A pretty property that Millie's husband had bought when they were newlyweds. There were pictures of the life they'd lived together on every wall and every shelf, candid shots and posed ones of the couple growing old together.

Such a nice dream.

One Ariel wished she could still have.

"Do you take cream with your tea? Sugar?" Millie poured hot water into a teacup, dunked a tea bag in it. She had no finesse, but what she lacked in grace, she made up for in enthusiasm. Tea splattered over the rim of the mug as she handed it to Ariel, dropped onto the pristine floor.

"Oh dear!" Millie grabbed a rag. "I'm getting clumsier every day."

"Me, too," Ariel responded, taking the rag from her hand. "I'll do this. You go ahead and make your cup of tea."

"Tea? I'm not pregnant. I'm having soda. High-octane. Which…" she whispered, "means it's caffeinated. A woman my age needs all the help with energy that she can get."

She wobbled over to the fridge, yanked the door open as Ariel bent to clean the floor, her stomach making the task more difficult than it should have been.

She swiped at the drop once. Then again, trying to get to her feet when glass shattered, pieces of the window flying into the room landing near her hands, in her hair, on her skin.

Millie screamed, the sound echoed by a loud pop.

This time a bullet smashed into the wall behind Ariel.

She scrambled away, grabbing Millie's arm and dragging her into the hallway. It was a shotgun-style house, and she could see the front door from there. She could also see the back door, the little windows in the top panel, the man who was peering in.

Mitch! His face, his eyes, everything as familiar as breathing.

He shouted something, the words lost to the frantic gallop of Ariel's heart. Then he stepped back, and she knew what he planned. She shoved Millie forward, covering the older woman as the glass in the door shattered, bits of wood flying into the hallway.

He was coming in, and he didn't care that there were police everywhere, that he was going to be caught, that he might die.

All he cared about was paying Ariel back for whatever it was he thought she'd done. Getting pregnant? Insisting on having the baby?

Surviving when he'd wanted her to die?

She grabbed Millie's hand, dragging her to the door as another bullet slammed into the hallway. She didn't hear the explosion, just felt it, the air charged with her fear and Millie's, the sharp scent of gunpowder mixing with it.

He had to have a silencer on the gun, and she had no idea if anyone across the street knew he was there, but the door was just ahead, escape within reach.

She grabbed the doorknob and released the bolt with Millie shrieking beside her.

Behind them, the back door flew open, banging against the wall as Mitch barreled into the house.

She shouldn't have looked back. Ariel knew it, but she couldn't help herself. She glanced over her shoulder as she managed to open the front door and shove Millie outside.

And, he was there, his face filled with rage, a gun in his hand.

"You should have listened to me, Ariel," he said, his voice cold. "You should have gotten rid of the baby."

His hand tightened on the gun, and she knew he was going to pull the trigger, knew she'd never make it outside before the bullet flew.

She dived through the front doorway, Millie's squealing shrieks still ringing through the air, the sound of other people shouting, of dogs barking, of Tristan yelling her name filling her ears as she tumbled onto the porch and rolled to try to protect the baby.

A gun.

A silencer.

Mitch.

Tristan could see them all as he raced across the street. Jesse snarled and snapped beside him, and he let the dog go, ordering him to cease, as he aimed for the guy in the front door of the old bungalow, shouted for him to drop his weapon.

Wasn't going to happen.

Tristan knew it.

Mitch was committed to his course, and that course was murder.

Ariel scrambled across the porch, trying desperately to grab Millie's hand and drag her away. They weren't going to make it. Not before Mitch could fire again.

"Drop the weapon," Tristan commanded again.

Mitch ignored him. Ignored the commands of Whitney, Ellen, Ed and Shane.

He raised the weapon, aimed at Ariel.

Tristan fired.

One shot, and it was a good one.

Mitch went down, the gun clattering across the old floorboards and falling onto the ground.

Everyone moved at once. Shane sprinting to the perp's prone body, checking his vitals, shaking his head.

Dead.

Tristan couldn't rejoice in that, but Mitch had gotten what he'd been asking for.

He bypassed the fallen gunman and knelt beside Ariel. She had her arms around Millie murmuring words of comfort, her gaze on Mitch and the blood that was staining the ground near him.

"I'm sorry," Tristan said, touching her chin, forcing her to look in his eyes.

"Don't be," she responded, her voice shaky. "He would have killed me, Tristan. He didn't care if he died doing it."

"Ms. Millie," Whitney said, moving in and putting her arm around the older woman. "Let's get you out of here."

"I can't leave my house," the older woman wailed. "My back door is broken. Someone might walk in and take my valuables."

"Officer Harmon will keep an eye on things here," Whitney assured her. "I promise. Now, how about I drive you to the clinic and have a doctor check you out. Just to make sure you're okay." She led Millie away, and Tristan wrapped an arm around Ariel's waist, helping her to her feet.

"Are you okay?" he asked, his lips brushing her soft hair.

"I think so." She stepped back, ran a hand over her belly, then brushed bits of glass from her hair. She had a tiny cut on her cheek, and he pressed the edge of his sleeve to it.

"You must have been hit by a piece of glass."

"I'm really fortunate I wasn't hit by more than that. I should have stayed at the window. Next time—"

"Let's not have a next time, okay?" he said. "My heart can't take it."

She smiled at that, a shy curving of the lips that made him think of early morning walks and late evening talks.

"Tell you what," she said, leaning on him a little as he led her past Mitch and away from the house. "Let's not have this kind of next time. Let's have something better. Something that doesn't take a few years off each of our lives."

"Like?" he asked, calling to Jesse who ambled over, moping a little because he'd been kept out of the action.

"Breakfast? Or lunch? Or even dinner?" she suggested.

"No teenage sister?" he guessed, and she frowned.

"Of course, teenage sister. And, her friend. Jenny

needs some adults in her life who can put her on the right path. I don't see why we can't be that for her."

"We? As in the two of us together. That could lead to something, Ariel. You know that, right?"

"Yes," she said, then smiled again. "I like the idea of that, Tristan. A lot. You remind me of all the dreams I used to have. The ones where some nice guy came along and swept me off my feet and I lived happily ever after. I'm falling for you, but… I've got a lot of baggage to work through, a lot of fears I need to let go of." She glanced back at the house, at Mitch's body now covered by a white sheet, and her smile fell away.

"I didn't want him to die," she said quietly. "But, I'm not sorry that I'm finally free."

"I understand," he said, turning her away from the house again, leading her across the street to his SUV. "And, I'm not going to lie. I'm afraid, too. It's not like I'm winning father of the year with my sister. I don't want to mess things up with your daughter."

"You're doing a great job with Mia," she said, touching his cheek.

"I guess we'll ask her what she thinks in a couple of years." He smiled. "So, we'll take things slow. Maybe we'll find what we're both looking for. How does that sound?"

She looked into his eyes, silent for moment, and then she nodded. "I think that sounds like more than I ever thought I could have."

He lifted her hand, pressed a kiss to her palm and curved her fingers over it. "You're much more than I ever thought I'd have. Keep that in mind, okay? When my sister is going nuts, and I'm going nuts, and life is so crazy that you think I've forgotten about you."

"I will. As long as you keep it in mind when the baby is here, and I'm distracted, and life is crazy, and you wish you'd found someone without all the baggage I'm carrying."

"We make quite the pair, Ariel," he said, and he meant it in the best possible way.

She squeezed his hand, her gaze shifting to a point just beyond his shoulder. "We do—"

"Tristan!" Ryder called, and Tristan glanced over his shoulder and saw his coworker striding toward him.

"What's up?"

"I got a search warrant for Carrie's place."

"That was quick."

"The judge is very aware of what's been going on, and he agreed that we have probable cause." Ryder's gaze shifted, dropping to Ariel's hand. The one Tristan was still holding.

He didn't let go.

He wasn't going to make a secret of his feelings.

"You want me to conduct the search with you?" Tristan asked.

"Chief Jones got the call that things were under control here. He said grab the first K-9 officer I saw. You're it."

"Where is he?" Tristan asked, opening the back hatch of the SUV. Jesse jumped in, settling into the crate with a satisfied sigh.

"Back at the station, fielding questions from a few concerned citizens who heard there was a bomb in town. He's up to his eyeballs in citizen complaints, so I told him we could handle the search."

"Give me five," Tristan requested, and Ryder nodded, striding toward the group working evidence recovery. He turned to face Ariel again. "I'm going to have to go."

"It's okay."

"You should be able to get back in the parsonage soon. Or, I can have Ellen bring you to my place."

"Stop worrying," she said with a smile. "I'm out of danger. The baby is fine, and I think I can handle finding my own ride to wherever I want to go."

"Where would that be?"

"Anywhere you might show up later," she responded, grinning broadly as she turned away. "We still have breakfast, lunch and dinner to do, Tristan. I won't forget if you don't."

He wouldn't, but she didn't give him time to say it. She walked to the parsonage and started talking to Ellen, offering a quick wave in Tristan's direction.

And, he knew he was lost.

Sunk into that thing he'd never thought he'd feel.

Not just like. Love. The kind that really would last forever.

He got in the SUV, following Ryder over to Carrie's place. The small house wasn't much to look at from the outside. Just a small brick rancher, the lawn green and pretty enough.

Ryder was already at the front door, Bella beside him as he dug through a potted plant.

"Looking for an extra key."

"She keeps one here."

"And, you know this why?"

"She's mentioned it before. I think after my wife was killed." He frowned. "Yeah. That was it. She said that if I ever needed a place to go, somewhere where I wouldn't be reminded of what I'd lost, I could come here and chill. There'd always be a key in the potted plant." He smiled grimly, pulling a key from the dirt. "I guess she wasn't lying."

"You sure she's not home?" Tristan asked, knocking on the door.

"Her car isn't here. There's no garage. We've already put out an APB on her and the car." Ryder shoved the key into the lock. "I don't know about you, but I'm shocked that Carrie is connected to Veronica's death. But the microchip points to her for a reason. She stole the box of evidence on Veronica's murder for a reason. She has to be guilty."

"I'm as shocked as you are," Tristan responded, walking into a small sparsely furnished living room. "But why kill Veronica? What was her motive?"

"No clue," Ryder added. "But now I know why she was always around when anyone needed anything—she was keeping tabs on us."

"Always around *period*," Tristan said, pulling on a pair of disposable gloves and lifting the couch cushions. Not even a crumb was hidden beneath them. "How about we start in a room visitors normally wouldn't see?" Ryder suggested. "We can work our way to the front rooms."

They headed down a narrow hall. No photos. No pictures. Nothing to give any hint of who Carrie really was.

The first room to the left was her bedroom, the frilly bedspread and drapes a pale pink that even Mia would have turned her nose up at. They looked through drawers, lifted the mattress, hunted under the bed. Everything was neat and organized, devoid of any hint into Carrie's personality.

They did the same in a spare bedroom, then walked to the end of the hall and tried the door there.

"Locked," Tristan said, wiggling the knob a second time. "Wonder why?"

"Let's find out." Ryder jimmied the lock and pushed open the door. The room smelled like rotten rose petals, the air thick and musty.

"What is that stench?" Tristan muttered, feeling for the wall switch and turning on the light.

It wasn't a white light.

No. This one was pink, the weird glow barely illuminating the room. Heavy drapes were pulled across a lone window, and one piece of furniture stood against the far wall.

A bench?

Table?

Tristan walked into the room, wrinkling his nose at the cloying scent of dead flowers. Jesse growled, his hackles raised. Apparently, he didn't like it, either.

"What is that?" Ryder said, the tension in his voice matching what Tristan was feeling.

There was something really off about this.

He approached the table, realizing there were photos on it and on the wall beyond it. Photos of people.

No. A person.

Photos of…

He glanced at Ryder, his colleague's expression one of shock—and horror. Almost every picture on the wall was of Ryder. Smiling. Frowning. Standing with his wife, her face cut out of the photo.

"She did it," Ryder said, the words hoarse, his voice tight. "She killed my wife."

"You don't know that," Tristan said, but the proof was staring them in the face. Or, at least, the evidence that it might be true. Every photo of Ryder and his wife had Melanie cut out. There were other photos, too, and Tristan lifted one, studying it carefully.

Mike. Standing in a group of people. Only someone had drawn a red X through his face. Brian Miller was in another picture, his face crossed out, too. A photo of Veronica lay on the floor, the same red X through her face.

"She was nuts," Ryder muttered.

"She *is* nuts," Tristan corrected. "Now that we know it, we can stop her."

"From what? Killing again? Because based on what I'm seeing here, we've already let her get away with four murders."

"Right, and I think we can also say," Tristan responded, lifting one of the many photos of Ryder, "that you might be her next target."

"Forewarned is forearmed," Ryder growled, then he turned on his heel and stalked from the room. "I'm calling the chief. We need some more manpower here. We've got a lot of evidence to collect."

And a lot of ground to cover if they were going to find Carrie and stop her before she could strike again.

Tristan set the photos down, took out his phone and started snapping pictures, documenting the shrine that Carrie had created. A shrine to a man that she'd loved so obsessively, she'd been willing to commit murder to have him.

The team would gather to discuss Carrie's murder trail, but Tristan was sure she'd murdered Ryder's wife, Melanie. She'd murdered the rookies. She'd murdered Veronica Earnshaw. And she'd attacked Marian Foxcroft. What Tristan wasn't sure of was the connections—Melanie's murder made sense, given Carrie's obsession with her husband, Ryder. But how did that lead to Mike Riverton's murder? To Brian Miller's? To Veronica's? Why had she attacked Marian?

For those answers, they had to find Carrie. They'd already turned the town upside down. They'd searched every alley, looked in every empty building. So far, they'd come up empty. Tristan didn't want to think that she'd escaped, but he had the sinking feeling she was far away from Desert Valley.

It didn't matter.

They'd hunt her down. No matter how far she'd gone.

FIFTEEN

Three weeks after Carrie had disappeared, and the town was still talking about the manhunt for her.

Ariel tried not to worry about it. She tried not to think of how hard Tristan and the K-9 team were working. Long days, long nights. Tristan looked exhausted, and she wanted nothing more than to see him finally solve the cases that had been haunting him for months.

She sighed, trying to keep a cheerful smile in place. The youth group at the church had planned a baby shower for her, and the kids would be upset if she looked as worried as she felt.

Balloons hung from the rafter of the church's fellowship hall. Pink streamers decorated the windowsills, and a huge white cake with bright pink icing sat in the middle of a table at the front of the room. A dozen smaller tables were spread throughout the large area, covered with plastic tablecloths and silver-and-pink glitter. Pink-and-white mints sat in tiny bowls, and daisies poked up from jelly jars. The flowers, more than anything, made Ariel smile as she sat and watched a bunch of teens play a game that involved changing a doll's clothes and diaper.

The fastest would win the grand prize.

Which was apparently a night babysitting Ariel's daughter.

That had made her laugh.

It seemed every teenager in the church was eager to help out. Most here were students, and they'd insisted on throwing her a baby shower. With the help of the social committee, they'd pulled it off.

In wonderful, wacky teenage style.

Even with the baby kicking and wiggling and keeping her awake at night, Ariel felt good. Soon, her daughter would arrive, and she'd begin her life as a mother. She'd set up the nursery in the parsonage, painting the walls and trim a pretty butter yellow and a bright crisp white.

At night, when nightmares woke her, she'd walk into the room and think about the years to come. All the good things that would eventually overshadow the bad.

It would take time, but eventually the image of Mitch staring at her through the glass in Millie's door would fade. She'd be left with little of the bad and a whole lot of the good.

Like Mia and the way she'd blossomed, accomplishing more academically in a few short weeks than most kids did in months. Mia had been making friends, too. Lots of them. Now that her secret was out, now that she no longer had something weighing on her heart, her true nature was coming out, and the other kids were responding.

Jenny had changed, too. She'd become happier, kinder, more responsible. She'd apologized to the police department for keeping the puppy, and she'd even visited Marian Foxcroft in the hospital, apologizing for taking the pup who Marian had donated to the center. According to Ellen, the teen had promised to volunteer at the center, work hard and pay the training center for whatever the lost puppy had cost.

No one wanted her to do that, of course.

The apology had been enough, and the puppy had been so well trained, so well socialized and healthy, that Ellen had gifted the puppy to Jenny. Sophie was helping Jenny train Sparkle, and teaching her a few tricks of the trade. That had given Jenny something to work toward, something to be proud of. That had shown itself in her schoolwork. It hadn't improved as much as Mia's, but she'd passed her summer courses and would enter tenth grade in a few weeks.

Both girls were excited about that. Summer school had ended a week ago, but Mia and Jenny visited Ariel often, stopping by the house with tales of their dog-training adventures, plans for their tenth grade year and lots of girlish giggles.

And, then, of course, there was Tristan.

Having him in her life was the biggest surprise and the biggest blessing Ariel had ever received.

As if her thoughts had conjured him, Tristan walked into the room, Jesse trotting along beside him. They'd been working, and Tristan was in his crisp blue uniform, Jesse wearing his work harness. They made a handsome pair and Ariel wasn't ashamed to admit she noticed.

She'd also noticed just how hard the two had been working recently. Hour after hour chasing down leads, trying to stop Carrie before she struck again. Despite the best efforts of the Desert Valley PD, the secretary hadn't been found. She'd apparently gone deep into hiding, and everyone on the force was working overtime trying to find her. There'd been little information released about her, little said to the public, but rumors were rampant. People whispering about obsessive love, murder, a secret shrine. Someone who worked on the police force had said that Carrie had been completely enamored of Ryder, and that she'd have done anything to have him.

Ariel was pretty sure the one who'd been spreading the rumors was Eddie Harmon. He'd been inside Carrie's house. He'd seen what she'd been hiding. And he liked to talk almost as much as he liked to spend time with his family.

Ariel hadn't mentioned the rumors to Tristan. She was sure he'd already heard them.

She also hadn't joined in the gossip, and she didn't ask Tristan to tell her more than he'd been able to. He didn't need that kind of pressure, and she cared too much to burden him with her own curiosity or the curiosity of others.

He did look tired, though—his eyes shadowed and a day's worth of stubble on his jaw—and that worried her.

"You look happy," he said, leaning in and offering her a sweet kiss that made her toes curl and her heart sing.

"I am. This is more than I could ever have hoped for."

"You hoped for less than pink glitter and baby-changing games?" he teased, picking up a handful of gaudy faux gems that one of the girls had tossed on the table.

"I just hoped for peace," she said seriously, because she wouldn't ever downplay how much he meant to her, how much this new beginning meant. "And I got joy and happiness and friendship. And love. That's a lot, Tristan, and I'm so thankful for it."

He smiled gently. "I'm thankful for you. You're a

little bit of sanity in my crazy world. Sometimes I need that way more than I'm willing to admit."

"Rough workday?" she asked, taking his hand and pulling him into the chair beside her.

"Sad workday. The more we learn about Carrie..." He shook his head. "Let's just say that it's rough for all of us, but especially for Ryder."

"I wish there was something I could do, some way I could help."

"You're helping by being here." He tucked a strand of hair behind her ears, his fingers skimming across her skin. "By being you. I still can't believe how fortunate I am. I came here thinking I'd go through training and go home. God had bigger plans than that. Better ones."

"Eventually you'll find Carrie. When that happens, will you stay in Desert Valley?" She hoped he would, because she loved the little town, but if he left, she thought that she'd leave, too. Wherever Tristan and Mia were, that's where she wanted to be.

"That depends," he responded, his gaze on his sister. Mia was frantically yanking clothes off a doll, her hair pulled back, her face wreathed in a smile. She was laughing so hard, she could barely get a diaper from a package on the table.

"On Mia?" Ariel asked, because she thought that the teenager was doing well, but she could understand if Tristan decided that returning to Phoenix would be best for Mia. He'd made a promise when they'd come for his training, and she knew he didn't want to break it.

"Mia is happy. She told me that she wants to stay here forever." He turned his attention back to Ariel, and she looked into his dark eyes, saw the future there, written in the love that shone from the depth of his soul. "Whether I stay depends on you, Ariel. Mia and I both want to be wherever you are. We've talked about it, and we agreed. She wants to be a big sister, and I want to be a father, a husband, a best friend. I know I'm not going to be perfect at it, but I hope you'll give me the chance to try. Love isn't about one moment, right? It's about all the moments added together to make a beautiful life. I want that with you. Every moment. The good ones and the bad ones."

He took something from his pocket, and her heart jumped, her pulse raced and all the noise from the teenagers and the church ladies faded as Tristan opened a small box and took a ring from it.

"This was my mother's ring. I was talking about getting you one, and Mia suggested it. She said that I should make my proposal romantic, but I'm not that kind of guy. Besides, the baby could come any day, and when she's older, I want to say I was her father from the very beginning. Will you marry me, Ariel?"

She nodded, her hand shaking as he slipped the ring on.

She hadn't expected to find love again, but maybe she'd never had it the first time, because the way she felt with Tristan? It was like every dream she'd ever had coming true, every blessing she'd ever longed for being handed to her.

She didn't realize she was crying until he wiped a tear from her cheek.

"Happy tears?" he asked.

"Happy for what I have. Sad because I wasted so much time finding it."

"No, you didn't," he whispered as he leaned in and kissed her tenderly. "You got here just at the right time to meet me and Mia, to touch our lives, to steal my heart. I promise I will never betray you, I will never lie to you and I will always love your daughter just as much as I love the children we will have together."

"*Our* daughter," she murmured against his lips, and she felt him smile, heard someone clapping. Softly at first, and then more loudly as the teens realized what had happened, and the church ladies rushed to tell the world, and everything Ariel had ever wanted was suddenly hers.

* * * * *

Valerie Hansen was thirty when she awoke to the presence of the Lord in her life and turned to Jesus. She now lives in a renovated farmhouse in the breathtakingly beautiful Ozark Mountains of Arkansas and is privileged to share her personal faith by telling the stories of her heart for Love Inspired. Life doesn't get much better than that!

Books by Valerie Hansen

Love Inspired Suspense

Military K-9 Unit

Bound by Duty

Classified K-9 Unit

Special Agent

Rookie K-9 Unit

Search and Rescue
Rookie K-9 Unit Christmas
"Surviving Christmas"

The Defenders

Nightwatch
Threat of Darkness
Standing Guard
A Trace of Memory
Small Town Justice
Dangerous Legacy

Visit the Author Profile page at Harlequin.com for more titles.

SEARCH AND RESCUE

Valerie Hansen

Seek, and ye shall find; knock,
and it shall be opened unto you.
—*Matthew* 7:7

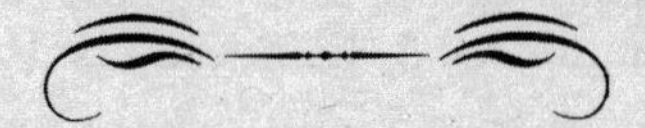

As I have continued to write book after book, it has occurred to me that I can never fully acknowledge all the amazing folks who have helped and encouraged me along the way. This book is dedicated to all those unsung heroes who are ready to share a smile or a hug no matter what their own needs may be.

And, as always, to my Joe, who is with me in spirit.

ONE

Sophie Williams faced Desert Valley's new police chief, Ryder Hayes, with a smile, hoping he wouldn't ask what she was up to and object before she had a chance to convince him she was acting for his benefit.

Anybody would be tense about taking over as chief after Earl Jones finally retired, but Ryder had received a double whammy. He'd discovered that he'd been working beside his late wife's murderer, and the killer of others, for over five years. Former police department secretary Carrie Dunleavy had fooled everyone and had disappeared weeks ago, just as Ryder and his team had discovered she was the killer they'd been after for months. The whole town was unbelievably on edge. No wonder the new chief had been a tad short-tempered lately.

"I'm going to make a quick run to town and back," Sophie told him, noting his scowl in response.

"Be careful. You may have been a cop once," Ryder said, "but you're a dog trainer now."

That was a low blow. Sophie clenched her jaw while the chief brushed a speck of lint off his dark blue uniform and continued as if clueless. "We all have to be on guard," he said. "There's no telling where Carrie is or whether she's through killing people. There's nothing normal about Carrie. I have a feeling she's sticking close to town, watching us."

Given the shrine to Ryder that had been found in Carrie's home, Sophie had to agree. Carrie was in love with Ryder, had killed his wife, had killed two rookie K-9 officers who were like stand-ins for him. Why she'd murdered Sophie's predecessor, lead dog trainer Veronica Earnshaw or had attacked prominent resident Marian Foxcroft, no one knew yet. Until Ryder and his rookies had answers, until Carrie was behind bars, everyone had to be careful. Sophie nodded. "I'll keep my eyes open." She tossed back her shoulder-length blond hair and faced him with a determined look.

He arched a brow. "Are you carrying?"

"Of course." She patted a flat holster clipped inside the waist of her jeans and further hidden by her blue T-shirt. "I won't be out and about for long. I'm going to the train station to pick up a dog."

"Why didn't you say so in the first place?"

"Because I wanted to surprise you."

She watched Ryder stroke the broad head of the old yellow Labrador retriever at his feet. The Desert Valley K-9 training center hadn't been running regular sessions since the last rookie class had been temporarily assigned to help in the investigation of the murders and attacks they now knew Carrie had committed. Therefore, Ryder was highly likely to suspect Sophie was picking up a potential replacement dog for him.

"I don't appreciate that kind of surprise," he said.

Sophie rebuked him gently. "Look. Poor old Titus is more than ready for retirement. We both know that. And your little girl will love having him as a full-time pet. It's not as if you're abandoning him."

Ryder passed his hand over his short, honey-colored hair, clearly frustrated. “Lily already plays with Titus every night when I go home. He and I are a team. It’s as if he can read my mind. This is *not* the right time to trade him for a newer model.”

“Maybe it isn’t for you,” Sophie said. “But what about what’s best for your dog? We both know he’d keep going until he dropped in his tracks because he’s so dedicated. Is that what you want?”

“Of course not.”

“Then trust me.” She began to grin as she headed for the door. “The paperwork’s all taken care of. I’ll be back in a flash.”

She was still smiling a few minutes later when she parked at the small railroad station and climbed out of her official K-9 SUV.

Dry August heat hit her in a smothering wave. Thankfully, the scheduled train was already there so she wouldn’t have to stand on the outdoor platform for long.

Sophie was always eager to get a new dog but it was not normal for her to feel this nervous. That was the chief’s fault. He’d planted seeds of apprehension when he’d suggested that Carrie might still be in the vicinity, and that possibility kept Sophie from fully enjoying herself.

A sparse crowd was beginning to disembark as she approached. She shaded her eyes. *There!* A slim, young police cadet had stepped down and turned, tugging on a leash. The welcome sight brightened her mood. Grinning, she offered her hand to the courier. “Hello! I’ve been expecting you. I’m Sophie Williams.”

“This is Phoenix,” the young man said, indicating the silver, black and white Australian shepherd cowering at his feet. "I hope you have better success with him than we did."

"I've read his file." She let her free hand drop in front of the medium-size dog, ignoring him as he sniffed her fingers. As soon as the three-year-old canine began to visibly relax, she said, "You can pass me the leash now."

"I don't know, ma'am. He's pretty skittish. You sure you don't want me to walk him over to your car and crate him for you?"

"That's the last thing I want," Sophie said. "Did he give you trouble on the train?"

"Not to speak of. I kept a good tight hold. He mostly just sat on my feet and shook a lot."

She grasped the end of the leash, gave it slack and took several steps back before asking. "Is he shaking now?" The way the courier's eyes widened almost made her laugh. Instead, she politely bade him goodbye, turned and walked away with Phoenix at her side. Every maternal instinct in her was on standby, yet she knew better than to fawn over the dog too soon.

"You already have a lot in common with your new partner," Sophie said softly, watching Phoenix's ears perk up. "He's hard to get to know, too, although who can blame either of you? He lost his life's partner and, in a way, so did you when your handler died in the line of duty."

As they approached the parking lot Phoenix hung back, putting tension on the leash.

"Heel," Sophie ordered, firmly but calmly.

The dog refused to budge.

She faced him, the leash slightly loose. "What is it, boy? We were doing so well. What's scaring you?"

Phoenix was sitting with his back arched and head lowered as if trying to hide in plain sight.

The poor animal was terrified. Sophie's heart went out to him and she broke her own rule. Gathering the leash as she slowly edged closer, she dropped into a crouch so she and Phoenix were eye to eye.

A loud bang echoed fractions of a second later. Sophie recognized a rifle shot and instinctively ducked before she'd fully processed what was happening.

The already-traumatized dog surged toward her. She opened her arms to accept him just as a second shot was fired. Together they scrambled for safety behind her SUV.

She was reaching up for the door handle when a third bullet took out the windshield.

Shouting for bystanders to take cover and waving them away, Sophie drew her weapon and cocked it, prepared to defend herself—and praying she wouldn't have to.

Ryder was livid. And more afraid than he dared let on. "I *told* her to watch herself out there. Who called it in?"

"Sophie was the first. She said she was ready to return fire but never did get a bead on the shooter."

"Description?"

The dispatcher shook her head. "Some callers said it was a man and some said a woman."

Ryder rounded on the pack of rookies who had been made his temporary deputies. "Let this be a lesson to all of you. Never let your guard down. Now get your dogs and gear and let's roll." He pointed to the bloodhound's handler, James Harrison. "Especially you and Hawk. I want *evidence*."

"Yes, sir."

The chief glanced over at the whiteboard as he prepared to leave the police station. It was all there. Every victim's photo, including that of his late wife, Melanie. It didn't matter how much it hurt him to keep seeing her picture, it had to stay posted. She was an integral part of Carrie's crime spree; the beginning, the key, for the simple fact she happened to be married to him.

Ryder tore himself away and raced for his car. Enough people had already died at the hands of the madwoman who wanted him, or his blond look-alikes, to fulfill her distorted sense of romantic destiny. It must stop now. They were not going to lose one more life. Not on his watch.

Sirens howling and lights flashing, he and the others pulled out onto Desert Valley Road. Ryder floored the accelerator. Multiple incoming reports had not mentioned any victims, but he needed to see for himself. Sophie Williams might be hardheaded but she was a great dog trainer. He'd hate to lose her.

Was that the only reason his pulse was pounding? he asked himself. Probably not. It was true that all his deputies and the staff at the training center were special to him, yet he and Sophie had occasionally seemed to connect on a deeper level. Which was another strong reason for him to keep his distance. If Carrie imagined that he and Sophie were even good friends it might be enough to put the innocent trainer in the crosshairs. Which was exactly where she had ended up today.

Ryder's pulse jumped as he skidded to a stop outside the Tudor-style depot. There she was! Sophie was not only on her feet, she was pointing and apparently giving directions to other arriving officers.

Ryder hit the ground running. "Keep your head down."

"The shooter's long gone," she called back.

He stopped beside her, on high alert despite her assurances. "You okay?"

"Yeah. I hate to think what might have happened if I hadn't bent over when I did."

Ryder's jaw clenched. He started to grab her arm, then stopped himself. "Get in the car and fill me in."

"It's too hot for that."

"I'm running the auxiliary air in my unit. Come on."

"Titus is with you?"

"No. I left him in my office." When Sophie didn't move quickly he scowled. "Well?"

"Just a second. I need to coax Phoenix to come with us on his own. I don't want to muscle him into obedience."

A mottled, grayish muzzle poked from beneath the damaged SUV as Sophie spoke softly and reached out. Ryder didn't know what to say. If that sorry excuse for a K-9 cop was supposed to be his new partner, the obstinate trainer had better rethink her plans. No way was he going to accept a trembling basket case in place of a heroic partner like Titus.

The new dog slunk over to Sophie and pressed against her lower legs as she straightened. "This is Phoenix."

"Um..."

"He'll come around. He's already better than he was when he arrived. I had a courier bring him so he wouldn't be frightened by being treated like freight."

"I don't think it helped," Ryder said flatly. "If he crouched any lower he'd be crawling on his belly like a commando."

"Trust me." Sophie gave him a slight smile. "I really believe you and this dog will work out together.

He needs a strong, seasoned handler like you, and you need a replacement partner."

"I need a good partner, emphasis on *good*."

"He will be. You know we don't have the funds right now to bring in a fully trained K-9, and this one deserves a second chance. If it happens he doesn't work out, we can think about pairing you with one of the younger dogs. They're just not ready yet."

"If you say so." He opened the rear door and waited until Sophie managed to load the dog, then held the passenger side for her. As she slid into the car he was struck by her courage and calm expertise despite the danger she'd just faced. That was part of the problem he had with her. She was very good and she knew it, which made her far less tractable.

Ryder smiled to himself. If she'd gotten a dog with those same tendencies she'd have been quick to send it away as a pet or maybe farm it out to the service dog program that Desert Valley Police Department rookie Ellen Foxcroft had recently started.

He could tell Sophie was studying him as he slid behind the wheel. When she asked, "Why are you grinning?" he decided to tell her.

"Just thinking. If you got a dog half as obstinate as *you* are, he'd wash out of the program in a heartbeat."

"There's a fine line between being dedicated and being foolish. I see myself as dedicated."

Although he wanted to remain aloof he couldn't help chuckling. "Dedicated to running things your way, you mean."

She shrugged, reflecting wry humor in her twinkling hazel eyes. "Hey, if my way is the best way, why not?"

Ryder sobered immediately and glared over at her. "Just make sure it doesn't get you killed."

Sophie knew she had barely cheated death at the railway depot. In order to cope and remain functional, she usually relegated troubling thoughts to a separate part of her psyche. This time, however, it was a bit harder to do. The tight expression on Ryder's face didn't help.

Sophie was half-turned in her seat, checking on the condition of the dog in the back, when the vehicle began to move. "Hey! Where are we going?"

"Away from here," he said.

"Why? I told you the danger is over. It has to be with all those K-9 rookies milling around. What did you do, bring the whole team?"

"Yes."

Viewing his profile, Sophie admired his strong jaw and muscled forearms. He was every bit a chief, in demeanor as well as appearance. The way he carried himself spoke more loudly than words, and his pristine blue uniform fit perfectly, unlike the way the previous chief's shirt had strained to stay buttoned over his ample stomach.

Ryder apparently sensed her attention because he glanced to the side. "What?"

"Nothing." Sophie was afraid she was blushing. "I was just thinking."

"About the shooter?"

"Right. The shooter. Why assume it was Carrie? I mean, would she suddenly switch to a rifle when her previous weapon of choice was a handgun?"

"Why not?" Ryder said, continuing to cruise slowly down Main, "She shot my wife and Veronica, but she pushed rookie Mike Riverton down steep stairs and burned down rookie Brian Miller's house with him in it. Carrie has no known MO when it comes to how she murders her victims."

Shivering with those memories, Sophie said, "I just can't see Carrie accurately aiming a rifle. She's too scrawny to hold it steady."

"Maybe. Maybe not. She did miss."

"Well, somebody did. Too bad it wasn't caught on surveillance cameras."

Nodding as if pondering the attack, Ryder pulled into a deserted parking lot and stopped beneath a shade tree, letting the engine idle to keep the vehicle cool. "If not Carrie, then who?"

"How should I know?" She raised both hands, palms up, and shrugged. "I was too busy taking cover to make notes. All I know is there were three shots and they all seemed to be coming from the east side of the depot building. Whoever it was took a big chance of being spotted. Somebody *must* have seen something."

"We'll sort that out back at the station after I've read the reports. That's one reason I deployed all the K-9s. We may as well make full use of them while they're still temporarily assigned here."

Sophie sighed. "I suppose so. I'll be glad to get back to running new training classes but I will miss these rookies when they move on. They've kind of grown on me."

"Me, too," Ryder admitted. "It's nice to have more officers. Particularly when their salaries are being paid by the richest woman in town."

"Marian Foxcroft." Sophie thought of the woman who'd arranged to have the newly graduated rookies stay on to solve the murders and mysterious deaths over the past five years. Someone had attacked Marian in her own home—and that person was very likely Carrie Dunleavy. Why, was a question no one had an answer to. "I hope she recovers from her head injury, for her sake and for poor Ellen's." Sophie knew that Ellen Foxcroft, one of the rookies, hadn't been very close to her mother before the attack. Everyone was pulling for Marian. Sophie decided to change the subject. "It's nice to be able to have all the rookies' partners around for a little longer, too."

"Right. The dogs, too." He cast a quick glance over his shoulder. "Well, all except for one. What possessed you to send for—Phoenix, is it?"

"Yes. Phoenix. We have him on a trial basis, just in case he doesn't work out, but I think you're going to be surprised. Besides, he was a bargain."

Ryder arched his brows. "I don't doubt that."

"Hey, don't criticize him before you give him a chance. At one time, this dog was very good. He can be again."

"What happened to him?"

Taking a deep, calming breath Sophie explained. "He lost his partner in the line of duty. They were ambushed in an alley. Even though he was wounded, too, Phoenix stood guard over his fallen partner until reinforcements arrived."

"And after that he stayed scared?"

"Not exactly. Several other officers tried to work with him. When that failed, he was sent to rehab training in the southern part of the state, then reassigned, but he was too emotionally fragile to be of much use."

"You think you can cure him?"

"I think I understand him. That's a start." She hesitated. "Been there, done that."

Ryder was shaking his head. "So, you expect to convince a dog that the death of his handler was inevitable because that's what you've been telling yourself about the loss of your own partner, back when you wore a badge?"

Wondering if she would be able to sound logical, Sophie paused to gather herself. Her mouth was dry, her palms damp. She knew full well that her narrow focus on the criminal she and her former partner, Wes Allen, had been pursuing was what had cost him his life. Acting as his backup, she'd failed to notice a hidden gunman—until it was too late. Wes had died on the spot and it was her fault. She'd left the force shortly thereafter.

Sophie suppressed another shiver. Here in Desert Valley she had colleagues who would probably understand. One of them was sitting next to her. Confiding the full extent of her lingering guilt and pain, however, was out of the question.

"That all happened long ago," she said. "I've found my niche training dogs for law enforcement."

"It's still excess baggage. We all carry plenty."

She could tell by the faraway look in his blue eyes that he was remembering his wife, the mother of his little girl. At least he still had Lily to give him solace. Sophie had nothing left but her work.

Pressing her lips together tightly she considered her personal life. Her best friends were dogs—and that was just the way she wanted it. People had hurt and disappointed her as far back as she could remember. Listening to her parents quarreling, she had often hidden in her room, hugging the family dog and trusting him to keep her safe. Law enforcement had seemed the perfect career choice at the outset but she had quickly realized she was not equipped to accept loss, particularly the death of her own partner. In turning to K-9 training she had, in a way, gone back to the solace she'd found as a frightened child. Not that she was about to admit it.

"I've recovered from my past," Sophie finally said. "You will, too. Just give it time."

Ryder was shaking his head. "No. I don't ever want to forget."

A sense of melancholy enfolded her. She had never come close to finding the kind of love and devotion this man held for his late wife, nor did she ever hope to. A lifelong commitment was the kind of thing dreams were made of and she knew better than to entertain such fancies.

She had her job, her dogs and a career many people coveted. Heartfelt prayer had led her to Desert Valley and circumstances were keeping her here. That was enough. It would have to be.

A sidelong glance at Ryder convinced her further. He needed her help and that of the dog she was preparing for him. Call it a job or a ministry or whatever, it was why she was where she was at this moment in time. She would not waste the opportunity.

While it was wrong to think of hugging away his pain, it was right to support his rise in rank. Merely the fact that he had been promoted to police chief while still technically a K-9 cop was a wonder. Keeping him active and qualified with a dog for as long as he wished to be was up to her.

She closed her eyes for a moment and thought. *Father, thank You. Please stay with me.*

"You okay?" Ryder asked.

"Fine." Her voice had a catch in it the first time so she repeated, "Fine."

"Do you want me to drop you back at the training center or take you home?"

"Home, please," Sophie said. "I want Phoenix to get

used to living with his handler again. We may as well start right away."

"You won't take any unnecessary chances? Promise?"

"Cross my heart." She made the motion.

"Okay. I'll go in ahead of you and check your house."

Her "No," came easily.

"No?"

Sophie was nodding. "Thanks, but no thanks. That won't be necessary. If there's anything wrong at my place the dog will alert."

"How? By ducking and shaking the way he did at the depot?" The chief sounded cynical.

Reminded of the shooting incident and the way her own hands had trembled in its aftermath, Sophie covered her emotions by shrugging and saying, "Whatever."

To herself, she added, *That will make two of us feeling fearful.* All her previous efforts to escape the rigors and threats of active law enforcement had been rendered ineffectual the moment those shots had been fired. If she had not been going home with a dog, traumatized or not, she might have welcomed human intervention.

Ryder was adamant. "Look. Until we know whether or not the attack on you was random, I'm going to pull rank. I'm inspecting your house when we get there. Is that understood?"

Sophie was so relieved she nearly sighed aloud. Instead, she purposely pouted, scooted lower in the seat and folded her arms, making sure her courageous image remained unspoiled. "Yeah, I get it."

In truth, she was thankful. The house she'd been renting for several years sat on a double lot on East Second Street and backed up to undeveloped land, a quiet location that had seemed ideal until she'd started feeling vulnerable.

Right now, she'd have gladly settled for high stone walls instead of wire fencing, and maybe a turret with an armed guard or two, preferably one like Ryder Hayes.

If he turned up anybody hiding in her house, waiting to hurt her, she didn't know what she'd do. But she was pretty sure she knew what Ryder would do—whatever it took to see that she was taken care of.

TWO

Ryder had figured Sophie's objections to his entering her home had been based on its messy condition. One look had immediately changed his mind. She was a good housekeeper. The dishes were washed, the bed made, and a vacuum cleaner stood sentinel in a corner of the living room. There were slipcovers on her padded furniture and an extra throw on the sofa. He could understand that when a person kept bringing new dogs home.

Satisfied that she'd be fine, he divided the remainder of his day between his office and the depot crime scene. He was a methodical investigator. Usually. This time he felt as if he was missing something, some clue that would better explain why Sophie had been targeted. But what?

After being fooled so thoroughly by Carrie, he found himself mistrusting everyone, a trait which had gotten him into hot water with Sophie after her predecessor, head trainer Veronica Earnshaw, had been murdered at work. Unwarranted suspicion and hurt feelings at that time meant he'd have to be doubly sensitive about how he chose to dig deeper into Sophie's past. Looking for someone who may have held a grudge since her days as a police officer was going to be his first objective.

The most logical choice was to simply question her, although he hadn't gotten very far when he'd tried that before. There were cut-and-dried facts in her file, sure, but that wasn't the same as getting her input on old cases.

Planning to speak with her the following day, Ryder put Titus in his car and started for Lily's babysitter's house. Passing the veterinary office adjacent to the training center, he did a double take. There was only one old car he knew of that lacked a backseat and was decorated with decals of various dog breeds. Sophie Williams was out and about.

He parked at the curb. Bypassing the deserted front counter he headed down the hall to the exam rooms. Phoenix was perched on a stainless steel table while Sophie comforted him.

Her eyes widened. "Oops. Caught me."

"You *promised* me you'd stay home today."

"I believe I promised I wouldn't make any unnecessary trips." She'd looped an arm over the trembling dog's shoulders while Tanya Fowler, the veterinarian, held a stethoscope to his ribs.

"This is necessary?"

"Yes," Sophie replied.

"And why is that?"

"Well, you wouldn't want a sick dog to contaminate our working teams or facility, would you?"

He eyed the shaking canine. "He's sick?" Judging by the way Sophie's cheeks bloomed even before she answered, he doubted it.

"Um, no, Tanya says he's healthy." Sophie brightened. "But you have to agree. We did need a professional opinion."

"And now we have one. Let's go. I'll follow you home and check the place again."

"Don't be silly. There's no reason for you to go to all that trouble. I told you, I'm armed."

"A handgun is no defense against a rifle unless your attacker runs out of ammo and tries to club you with it."

The face she made at him was hilarious. Rather than smile and lose authority he turned away and pointed to the door.

Although Sophie didn't hurry, she did comply. Giving the vet a brief hug and thanking her, she lifted Phoenix down and started for the exit.

Ryder let her pass before he allowed himself to grin behind her back. Of all the trainers and handlers he'd ever known, this one was the most admirable—and the most hardheaded. She had a quick answer for everything and a dry wit that often surfaced at the most needed moments. Working in law enforcement was tough, particularly for men and women who were in it for altruistic reasons, and they often needed the kind of emotional release that laughter provided.

Sophie was out the door and halfway to her car before he stopped her. "Wait. You forgot something."

"What?"

He'd already scanned their surroundings, satisfied they were safe for the time being. "You never once checked for threats. You just barged out the door as if you were the only person in town."

"Like I keep telling you, Phoenix will let me know if there's danger."

"Sure. After he has his own nervous breakdown."

The view of Sophie, chin held high, her eyebrows

arched and her hands fisted on her hips, was so cute he could hardly keep a straight face.

"I'll have you know he saved me at the depot this morning. If he hadn't held back I might not have bent over and could have been shot."

That was enough to ruin Ryder's day. "Why is this the first I'm hearing about a connection?"

She shrugged. "Actually, it just occurred to me when you questioned his abilities."

"*You* didn't hear or see anything to make you duck?"

"Nope. The first I knew I was in trouble was when the bullets started flying. Which reminds me. How long do you think my SUV will be out of service? I like my car but it lacks a certain dignity."

"If I had my way you'd be stuck in your office for the rest of the year. Or longer."

It was the rapid way Sophie's expression changed that focused his attention. She was clearly trying to maintain her bravado and failing miserably. What had he said or done to trigger such a transformation? Even shortly after the shooting that could have taken her life, she hadn't looked this doleful.

Concerned, Ryder approached. "What is it? What just happened?"

"Nothing."

He reached out, not quite touching her shoulder, and heard an unexpected growl at his feet. Wonder of wonders, the usually shy dog had stepped in front of Sophie and was prepared to defend her.

"Whoa." Ryder withdrew. "Maybe there is hope for Phoenix after all."

"There's hope for all God's creatures, given the right environment and enough love," Sophie said. "Now, if you'll excuse me, I'll be going."

She let the dog jump in before she slid behind the wheel of her decal-covered car.

Because he assumed she'd take off as fast as possible, Ryder jogged back to his idling patrol unit, unlocking the door remotely. Titus was panting but comfortably cool thanks to a special air-conditioning system that functioned whether the car was moving or not.

It was easy to follow her to the small house on Second Street. Ryder stayed in his car and observed, just in case. The usual spring was missing from Sophie's step. She was almost plodding, as if bearing a heavy weight on those slim shoulders. Seeing such a change come over her—and linger—had him worried.

Somehow, he had caused emotional injury to someone he admired, and for the life of him he couldn't figure out what had happened. They'd been talking about her SUV and he'd made some sarcastic remark about wishing she were stuck in her office, but surely that couldn't have been enough to instantly depress her.

Puzzled, Ryder kept watching and mulling over the problem until Sophie and the dog were safely inside. Whatever he'd done had also bothered the new dog so it must be something simple. Intuitive.

"I raised my voice?" he muttered. "I was just worried about her but…" *But perceived anger had demoralized her.* Perhaps Sophie's mood had had less to do with what he'd said than it did with his forceful delivery.

So, who had verbally abused her in the past? And why were the residual effects lingering in her twenties?

A strong urge to climb out of the car and apologize was not easy to quash. Surely there would be a better time to speak with her in private and express regret. Besides, it might be too soon to approach after inadvertently hurting her.

That was what bothered him the most, even though it had been unintentional. He would never purposely harm anyone.

"Except for Carrie," Ryder murmured. It would be better for all concerned if he were not present for the capture. His respect for the law was strong, yet he didn't want to have to put it to the ultimate test.

Modern laws didn't allow "an eye for an eye" biblical justice. God forgive him, he sorely wished it did.

Before releasing Phoenix, Sophie led him on a comprehensive tour of her house, allowing him to sniff to his heart's content now that she was sure he was healthy. It was good to have a dog underfoot again, even if she was going to eventually have to relinquish him to a new partner.

She stroked the top of his head and saw his stub of a tail begin to wag. "That's right, boy. I'm one of the good guys. You can trust me. Now let's see if I can trust you."

She unsnapped the leash. At first, the timid dog stayed close to her, not venturing far until he caught a scent and put his nose to the floor.

"You have natural ability and curiosity," she said, keeping her voice gentle. "Good boy." The stubby tail wagged faster. "I can get you over your fear. I know I can."

So, who's going to help me? Sophie asked herself. It had been a long time since she'd had such a strong flashback to her dysfunctional childhood, and even longer since she'd let it show enough to be noticeable. What was the matter with her? Chief Hayes—Ryder—was liable to think she was as unstable as the new dog.

"I'm not. Not at all," she insisted. "There must be lots of people who don't like to be yelled at." And, to be totally honest, Ryder had not actually shouted. Maybe it was his reference to her being stuck in her office, combined with a harsh tone, that had pushed her panic button. As a child she'd spent long hours hiding in her closet and had even crawled under the bed a time or two, seeking escape from her parents' anger. By themselves, her mother and father were generally amiable, but put them together and they didn't seem to know a civil word.

"Which is why I love dogs," she reminded herself, smiling at her new boarder. "Come, Phoenix."

His ears perked up and he stopped to look at her. Pleased, she repeated, "Come," and turned to walk away. To her delight, the mottled gray Aussie trotted along behind. By this time his short tail was wagging his whole rear end.

"Good boy. Sit," Sophie commanded. Phoenix plunked down so fast it was a blur. She made him wait while she entered the kitchen, then released him to join her.

"You are going to be perfect for the chief," she told him. "Now, let's get you food and water bowls and fix a place for you to sleep in my room. Are you hungry?"

Two leaps and a skid on the slick, marbled vinyl floor took Phoenix straight to the refrigerator. Tongue lolling, he danced in circles.

Sophie had to laugh. She cupped his furry face on each side and gazed into his light brown eyes, positive they reflected intelligence. "Dogs eat dog food out of bowls in this house," she told him. "Didn't they teach you safety in those other places?"

He barked in her face. "Eww, dog breath," she joked. "Follow me and pay attention. Lesson one is going to keep you from getting poisoned."

Sadly, it was necessary to teach working dogs to ignore treats from strangers in order to protect them. The Canyon County Training Center did allow their graduates to eat from a human partner's hand, but only when given a specific command.

With Phoenix close at her heels, Sophie pulled out two weighted dog dishes and placed them on a mat beside the back door. The expression on his face when he saw they were empty made her laugh again. "Patience, buddy. I'm working on your dinner."

He watched her every move, quivering with excitement before she released him to eat. Then he approached his food as if he'd been starving. That kind of dog could be harder to train to leave food fragments alone but considering his rapid improvement she felt confident he was a quick learner.

As soon as he'd licked up the last crumb and polished the food dish with his tongue, Sophie accompanied him outside.

The instant his paws hit the porch, Phoenix bristled and began to growl. Sunset was casting her small backyard in long shadows, the lingering heat making portions of the ground shimmer.

Sophie followed the dog's line of sight to her chain-link fence and past it to a stand of ancient ponderosa pines. The climate might not be conducive to grass and a lot of greenery but it was perfect for drought tolerant trees and scrub brush. Normally, that kind of growth made it easier to spot threats but at this time of day every silhouette seemed to mask danger.

A gust of wind lifted her hair, bringing a welcome draft of cooler air. She squinted to see what was bothering Phoenix. If he was the kind of dog who alerted at every lizard or blowing leaf he might not be suitable after all.

Opening her mouth to speak, Sophie never had the chance. Phoenix leaped off the porch without touching the steps and tore toward the wire fence. His bark was fierce, his hackles bristling.

When she saw the problem her heart skipped a beat. A large rattler was coiled, ready to strike, mere feet in front of the dog. If she called him now and he turned his back on the reptile he was sure to be bitten!

Although she was still armed she didn't want to shoot so close to civilization unless she had to. Praying silently, she slipped off the porch and opened the door of her metal toolshed.

A broom would only irritate the snake and a shovel was too unwieldy. A hoe, however, was ideal. If she couldn't scare off the rattler she might be able to pin its head long enough for Phoenix—and herself—to escape. It wouldn't be the first snake she'd routed since coming to Desert Valley, but it was the first incident involving a working dog. If the fangs pumped venom directly into a dog's head, the chance of survival wasn't good.

Phoenix was still barking when Sophie approached behind him. Too bad she and the Australian shepherd didn't know each other well. If they had, she would be able to better predict his reactions.

Staying to one side, Sophie inched closer. There was no way she could swing faster than a snake could strike. The trick would be getting the metal blade of the hoe between it and her dog, then trying to pin it or push it away. If it had recently fed and was only defending itself, it might turn and flee.

Another short step closer. And another. She extended the hoe. The snake's forked tongue flashed out, its mouth opening. She could see folded fangs descending. It was ready. So was she.

Phoenix backed up slightly. The rattler's head rose. Sophie was out of time and she knew it. She thrust the blade forward. Her aim was accurate. With one lunge she managed to force the viper's triangular head to the ground.

Startled, Phoenix jumped back. He began to circle her, barking, while the snake writhed, struggling to get free. As soon as she was certain the dog was out of striking distance she gave the blade a last push, dropped the handle and made a dash for the back door.

She didn't get far. A slightly smaller rattlesnake was crossing her path. Two more were curled up on her back porch! Incredulous, she climbed onto an old rickety picnic table, hoping it wouldn't collapse under her weight.

"Phoenix, come!" The order was more than forceful. It was filled with alarm.

Sophie braced herself as the dog vaulted to the bench, then joined her atop the table. Encountering one venomous snake wasn't that unusual in the desert but this… This was incredible. Why in the world had they suddenly invaded? There was no wildfire to drive them into her yard. And if there had been a den located nearby she should have noticed problems right away, not several years after moving in. Such reptile gatherings tended to be seasonal and this was her third summer here.

Wide-eyed, she scanned the ground around the table and noted three more reptiles. They instinctively knew that direct August sun would kill them and had taken refuge in shady spots. Unfortunately, some were resting between the picnic table and her kitchen door. Once night fell they'd move. But by then she'd have trouble seeing well enough to avoid being bitten, not to mention keeping Phoenix safe.

Sophie was trapped. Frustrated. Mad at herself. She hadn't even brought the hoe to the table with her. How long could she stay crouched without her legs and feet going to sleep? And how long could she keep the new dog from attacking the reptilian menace and getting himself killed?

Easing into a sitting position and preparing to fold her legs, she glanced down. One of the smaller snakes was climbing onto the bench. Once he got that far he'd be able to reach the top of the table! Sophie lowered one foot over the edge, hooked a toe under the side of the bench, and kicked.

It wobbled. Teetered. When it fell all the way onto its side it was farther away, hopefully far enough to keep all but the largest rattlers from getting to her.

And speaking of those… A triangular head poked over the edge of the table. Its forked tongue vibrated. There was no way she was going to try to kick this one away.

Drawing her gun she started to take the standard two-handed aim, then thought better of it and used one hand to grab the dog's collar so he wouldn't bolt when she fired so close to him.

The first shot hit the reptile under the chin and threw it backward. Trembling, Sophie leaned over the table's edge to make sure she'd killed it—and came face-to-face with its bigger brothers. More shots finished those. By this time, she sincerely hoped her neighbors had heard enough to call the police because she didn't want to take her eyes off the snakes for a second.

Up until then, Phoenix had held his position pretty well, considering. Now, however, he rose slowly, hackles bristling, and stared past the side yard to the street beyond. Sophie recognized the dog's attitude immediately. He was no longer concerned with chasing dangerous snakes. There was something else in his sights. Something he'd sensed was evil without even seeing it.

She swiveled, kneeling, looked in the same direction and brought the muzzle of her gun up, ready for self-defense.

A sudden thought stripped away her bravado. How many shots had she fired at the snakes? How many bullets were left? Did she have *any*? In the heat of the moment she'd failed to count and if she dropped the clip out now to look, she might not be able to replace it fast enough.

Only one thing was certain. There was at least *one* shell left in the chamber or the slide would have stayed back.

Was one shot going to be enough?

THREE

"You'd better get over here, Chief," rookie officer Shane Weston said, once Ryder answered the phone. "And don't bring Titus. I think we've killed all the snakes but we could have missed one or two."

"That was what all the ruckus was about? There was enough radio traffic to have handled a small war. I could hardly make out a thing the way you were interrupting each other's transmissions."

"Sorry, sir. It was pretty hectic for a while. I'm surprised she managed to keep that dog safe."

Ryder scowled. "Dog? What are you talking about? Was the call at the training center?"

"No," Weston said. "I thought you knew. Sophie Williams had a backyard full of rattlers."

"What? The dispatch was for the corner of Desert Valley and Second, so I didn't realize they meant her house down the block." His pulse jumped when he imagined the scene. "I might expect a bunch of snakes gathering like that in the spring but not now. How many were there?"

"Hard to say. We're still counting. That's why I called you."

"Go on." Ryder was losing patience. With Lily at

home and no one to watch her, any action on his part was going to be delayed until he could drop his daughter back with his babysitter, Opal Mullins.

"There's more. Sophie insists somebody else was here, sneaking up on her. I'm not convinced. The snakes had her cornered in the yard and she was pretty paranoid about it."

Ryder clutched his phone so tightly his hand throbbed. "Is there a chance they may have been dumped there?"

"I suppose it's possible," Shane said. "Some lowlife sure has it in for our head trainer. Since the bullets missed her this morning, I did wonder if they tried to kill her with a batch of rattlers."

"Kind of hard to plan ahead for an attack like that," Ryder said. "Although I suppose they might have gathered them to release at the training center and changed their minds."

"Terrific." He snorted wryly. "Look, the worst of the danger is over and nobody was bitten. I just thought it would be good to get your input on this. You know how Harmon and Marlton can be when they're trying to avoid paperwork."

"Yeah. The sooner they retire the better," Ryder replied. "I can't believe Louise didn't call me right away. Isn't she covering the desk?"

"Not this late. So, should we hang around? Are you coming out?"

"Yes," Ryder said. "I'll have to drop Lily at the babysitter's. Give me fifteen minutes, tops."

"Copy," the rookie officer said as he prepared to end the call. "Wear your boots."

Ryder looked over at his drowsy, little blonde five-year-old and had to smile. He'd been reading her a bedtime story and she'd laid her head on the cushiony arm of the sofa when he'd stopped to answer the phone.

The sight of such a loving, beautiful child made his heart beat faster, yet constricted his gut as if he'd just taken a body blow. He'd failed to protect her mother. He was not going to fail Lily. The mere concept was abhorrent. This child was his life, his legacy, his and Melanie's, and nobody was going to harm her. He'd *die* before he'd let that happen.

He gently rubbed Lily's bare feet. "Wake up, honey. I have to go out. I'm taking you back to Miss Opal's."

"Uh-uh. It's story time. You can't go away again."

Ryder felt guilty and compensated as best he could. "How about we go out for ice cream after I get back?"

That seemed to brighten the child's mood although she was still making a face. "With sprinkles?"

"If that's what you want," Ryder promised. "Now put your shoes on while I get my boots. I need to hurry."

Lily's innocent blue eyes focused on him. "What happened, Daddy?"

"A lady found rattlesnakes in her yard."

"Are you gonna shoot them?"

Ryder couldn't tell whether the child was asking because she needed reassurance or because she felt sorry for the snakes. "I'm not sure about all of them. I imagine my officers had to shoot some."

Sadly, she said, "Oh."

"They had to protect the lady and her dog."

"Dog? She had a dog?"

"Yes."

"Like Titus?"

"Uh-huh. Kind of."

Lily began to smile. "That's different." Sitting up, she rested her bare feet on the big yellow Labrador retriever lying against the front edge of the couch and wiggled her toes into his fur. His tail thumped but he didn't rise. "I love Titus."

"Me, too," her father replied with a sigh. There was only one thing worse than having to retire a faithful canine partner and that was losing one in the line of duty. He knew it was time to give the old dog a rest, but he also knew that Titus would brood about being left behind. That was a given.

He reached down and patted the dog's broad head. "No other dog will ever work as well as you do," he said soothingly. "I don't care who says otherwise."

"Can Titus go with us?"

"Not this time, honey. You know Miss Opal's cats don't like to play with him."

The scowl returned. Nevertheless, the child had her sandals on when Ryder returned wearing his boots.

He held out his hand. "Ready?"

"No." Lily tossed her blond curls, dropped to her knees and hugged Titus's furry neck, placed a kiss on the top of his nose, then jumped to her feet. "Okay. Now I am."

The poignancy of the scene almost choked him up. So did the trusting way she grasped his fingers. Losing Melanie had nearly broken him—would have—if he hadn't had Lily. Every day that passed he loved her more. And every time he went out on a call he prayed even harder for her continued well-being.

Yes, he could have sent her away when Carrie Dunleavy's crime spree was uncovered. But that would have meant trusting his little girl to someone else's care 24/7 and he simply could not do that. No one's vigilance could be as sufficient as his because nobody could possible love Lily as much as he did. Nobody.

He'd die before he'd let anything happen to her.

* * *

Sophie wondered who in the crowd of officers combing her backyard was going give the all clear. Rookie Ellen Foxcroft was probably at the hospital visiting her comatose mother, Marian, but Shane Weston, Whitney Godwin, James Harrison and Tristan McKeller had responded. They'd done most of the actual work while Eddie Harmon and Dennis Marlton, the old-timers, had stood back and relaxed, occasionally barking an order or chuckling when one of the novices found and dealt with another snake.

"Typical," she muttered, preparing to call out to either Eddie or Dennis and insist that one of them release her to go back to the house. Before she could, they both straightened and began to feign being busy. That could mean only one thing. The chief was here.

To Sophie's amazement, the sight of Ryder's six-foot-two, athletic self brought instant relief and more than a touch of joy. He looked just as good out of uniform, in jeans and a T-shirt, as he always did with his badge on. She waved. "Over here!"

Though he paused to speak with Shane and then James, he didn't tarry long. Sweeping the beam of a flashlight ahead of him to double-check his path, he came directly to her.

"You okay?"

"I am now," she replied, having to restrain herself from leaping into his arms like a scared kid. "Thankfully my neighbors heard me shooting and reported trouble. It's been a very long evening."

"So they tell me. Why aren't you and that mutt in the house?"

"Because nobody has given us the all clear." Scowling, she eyed the part of the yard she could see from her perch. “How bad was it? I heard enough shooting and shouting to last me for the rest of my life.”

A smile quirked at the corners of Ryder’s mouth. “Fortunately, that will be a long time thanks to my officers.” He held out his hand. “Come on. I’ll get you to the house.”

“I’d rather you carried Phoenix, just in case,” Sophie told him. “What if they missed one?”

“Carried him?”

“Yes.” She tried not to smile. “Please?”

Ryder handed her his flashlight and arched a brow. “If he bites me, we send him back where he came from tomorrow. Deal?”

That wasn’t fair. She hadn’t had enough time to fully assess the dog’s quirks. Still, he was eventually going to have to work with the chief and had performed amiably in his initial placement so she nodded. “Okay. Go for it.”

One of the important aspects of Phoenix’s training regimen was going to be reinforcing his ability to adapt to many situations. This would be a good test. She snapped her fingers to get his attention, looked directly into his eyes and held up her hand, palm out. “Phoenix. Stay.”

Although he flinched and tensed when Ryder slipped his arms under him and lifted, he didn’t struggle. Sophie wanted to cheer.

Instead, she dropped to stand beside man and dog, pointed the light toward the house and led the way back to her porch. It was impossible to miss seeing a portion of the carnage as they passed, and its portent made her shiver.

So did the nagging feeling that someone had been watching her while she’d been trapped on the tabletop.

Ryder was spitting dog hair when he bent to lower

the Aussie to the kitchen floor. To make matters worse, Phoenix turned in the blink of an eye and gave his cheek a slurp.

Sophie laughed. "Guess he won't be going back tomorrow."

"Guess not." Brushing off his civilian clothes, Ryder made a sour face. "Shedding all over me has never been a problem with Titus."

"How often do you carry him?" she asked, still chuckling. "He weighs a ton."

"I could still lift him if I needed to." Judging by the way the head trainer was eyeing his flexed biceps she wasn't going to argue. Flattered but slightly embarrassed, he changed the subject. "Let's talk about this call."

"Coffee first?" Sophie was already on her way to the counter so he nodded. "Sure."

"How about the others?"

"I told Weston to inform them they were free to return to the station. I'll send a team out at first light to clean up and make sure any possible stragglers are gone."

"Thank you."

Watching her fill two mugs with hot coffee he hoped she could carry them without spilling, since her hands were shaking so badly. "Want some help?"

"No. I've got it. Have a seat. There's sugar and creamer if you want."

"Black is fine." It didn't escape Ryder's notice that the new dog had made itself at home beneath the kitchen table and was sniffing his boots. For an animal that was supposed to be painfully shy, it seemed pretty mellow.

"Looks like you've made a friend," Sophie remarked

as she joined him and slid one of the mugs across the table.

"Apparently. All I had to do was rescue him."

"And me. Thank you again."

"You're safe in here."

He saw her suppress a tremor as she replied, "For now."

He eyed the slick floor, checking shadows beneath the edge of the lower cabinets and next to the stove and refrigerator to be certain they were clear. "Do you want me to inspect the house for you?"

Sophie shook her head. "That won't be necessary. The rookies already checked. Phoenix will sense any new danger. He's the one who alerted me about the yard."

"Then why in the world did you go out?"

As he watched, she lowered her gaze and began to pick at a nonexistent spot on the tabletop. That was enough to open Ryder's eyes for the second time that day.

He cleared his throat. "I'm sorry for raising my voice, Sophie. I was just worried."

"I know." She breathed a noisy sigh. "It's been a rough evening and I put your dog in danger by not being vigilant enough. You're entitled to be upset."

Reaching for one of her trembling hands he grasped it gently. "Who said anything about the dog?"

The small kitchen seemed to shrink until all Sophie was conscious of was the strong man seated across from her. He was just being kind, she knew, yet it was awfully nice of him to hold her hand. She could certainly use the moral support.

"I've never been so scared in all my life," she admitted, blinking back unshed tears. "I took care of the big one Phoenix saw first and others near the picnic table but there were so many…"

"I know."

"And there was something else. Did your men tell you I thought there was somebody hiding and watching me while I was stranded?"

"Yes. Any idea who it might have been?"

"None. The only reason I suspected it at all was because of the way the dog bristled. I wasn't sure but he was. That's good enough for me."

"Maybe someone heard you shooting and came to see why."

Sophie scowled. "Or maybe they were already there and hoping I'd use up all my ammo and be defenseless." She trembled. "I almost did."

Feeling him squeezing her fingers a little more, she pulled her hand away. It was time to stop thinking and reacting on a personal level. She was a trained professional. She'd better start behaving like one.

Sophie sat up taller in her chair and took a sip from her mug. "All right. We can either assume it was Carrie sneaking around, unhappy that I've been talking too much to you lately, or we can look for somebody else. You and the team believe that Carrie likely didn't have an accomplice because of the journal and so-called *shrine* you found at her place, right?"

"Right."

His jaw muscles knotted visibly as he spoke, and when he clasped his hands in front of him on the table, Sophie noticed his muscles flexing. She was entitled to be upset because of her recent ordeal but Ryder had a much deeper reason. After all, Carrie's collection of memorabilia about her victims had included more than just pictures and clippings of the two blond rookies she'd killed because they'd reminded her of him. A central feature was Melanie Hayes, Ryder's late wife. Photographs and newspaper clippings on Melanie lined a wall of Carrie's bedroom. But no one figured more prominently than Ryder Hayes himself.

Empathy filled her and she placed her hand lightly atop his clenched fists. Although he flinched, he didn't withdraw until she said, "I apologize, Ryder."

"For what?"

"For being insensitive to your loss."

"Never mind that. Right now, we need to be thinking about who's trying to hurt you. Start talking."

"About what?"

"Anything. Everything. You might explain why a raised voice bothers you so much."

"I never said it did."

"You didn't have to."

"Hey, I passed my psych eval."

He didn't reply immediately and she wondered what painful questions he'd ask next. Until now she'd managed to quell her adverse reactions to triggers that mentally transported her back to her abusive childhood and she'd just as soon not awaken those feelings further.

"All right," he finally said. "Let's talk about the night your partner was shot and why you quit the force after that."

"I'd rather not."

He propped his elbows on the table and leaned forward. "I don't think you have a choice, Sophie. We have to start somewhere and that's as good a place as any. Did you receive any death threats after that incident?"

"Police officers are always being threatened," she insisted. "Almost nobody follows through."

"Maybe this guy is the exception. Criminals can be very vindictive."

The truth stuck in her throat. Was it possible Wes's brother had made good on his wild threats and come after her at this late date? Why now and not sooner? Part of her mind wanted to brush away suspicion while another part felt as if the upcoming anniversary of Wes's death might hold the answer. To voice that, however, was repugnant. The poor man and his family had suffered enough without blaming them needlessly and causing more pain.

Ryder had been studying her. "I want you to make a list of possible suspects. Don't leave anybody out no matter how innocent you think they may be. Understand?"

She nodded as she noted his darkening mood and resigned herself to complying. "I'll do it, but I don't think you realize how difficult it will be for me."

As soon as the words left her mouth she knew she'd inadvertently been insensitive again.

Ryder's demeanor changed in a heartbeat. His eyes flashed, his jaw clamped and he stood so rapidly he almost knocked his chair over backward. Even before he said a word Sophie knew he was angry.

"Difficult?" he began. "You want to know what's difficult? Looking at my wife's picture posted with Carrie's other victims and remembering how blind I was to the evil that was right under my nose every day. *That's* difficult."

She wanted to tell him how sorry she was, how sympathetic, but she knew better than to offer platitudes when he was upset so she clasped her hands around her coffee mug and remained silent. In seconds he'd turned and stormed out the door.

Ryder was absolutely right. His loss was worse than hers in many ways. Not only had he lost his beloved Melanie and been left to raise their baby alone, he blamed himself for not considering his wife's killer could be a colleague. Carrie had presented such a mild-mannered facade they'd all been fooled.

As Sophie started to clear the table she recalled Ryder's outburst and froze in place. He'd raised his voice again. And sounded furious. So why wasn't she shaking like a leaf?

A glance toward the closed door allowed her to envision him slamming it behind him. No panic ensued. As a matter of fact, there were surprisingly warm and tender feelings flowing over and through her.

She closed her eyes and leaned on the table with both hands. Something momentous had happened tonight and it had nothing to do with snakes, at least not directly.

The emotional healing she had prayed for since she was a child had apparently begun. The scary question was, *Why?*

An even more disquieting answer came in the form of the admirable chief of police whose raised voice no longer set her nerves on edge. Why not? What had made the difference?

Phoenix came out from under the table and bumped her leg, wagging his tail and panting as he looked up expectantly. That gave Sophie her answer. She wasn't afraid of Ryder for the same reason Phoenix had accepted her.

Trust. Plain, old, heartfelt trust.

And to nurture those feelings between herself and the chief she'd eventually have to break down and name her deceased partner's disruptive brother Stan as one of her suspects.

She couldn't expect Ryder to reflect her growing sense of trust if she weren't totally honest with him.

Starting immediately.

A shiver sang up her spine and prickled at the nape of her neck. When Wes had died she'd blamed herself even more than Stan had blamed her, so his tirade at the grave site had seemed fitting.

In retrospect, it had been a lot worse than she'd realized. It wasn't merely his voice, because the threat had been whispered. It was his eyes.

There had been hate sizzling in his gaze. Hate and murderous fury. The kind that lasted. Simmered. And sometimes boiled over.

FOUR

As soon as Ryder left Sophie he headed straight for Mrs. Mullins's home to pick up Lily. When he arrived at the small, Spanish-style house, he lingered outside in his cruiser long enough to regain the strong self-control on which he prided himself. A man in command could not afford to show anger or weakness or any other emotion that would be detrimental to his position. More importantly, he didn't want to upset his little Lily.

He found her in the living room, playing with Opal's cats and telling them all about her wonderful dog. Maybe it was time to retire Titus. Yes, he got very excited when Ryder strapped on his official K-9 harness or vest but Sophie was right. He also tired easily.

Opal joined him in the archway to the living room when he paused to listen to the involved tale Lily was telling.

"She's been like this ever since you dropped her off," the middle-aged woman said. "What in the world did you tell her? She keeps warning my cats to look out for bad snakes."

"We had a call tonight, over at the head trainer's place. She was shooting snakes."

"The slithery kind or the two-legged kind?"

"Slithery. She just about emptied her gun until she remembered about the human kind of snake and saved a shot or two. Maybe now she'll carry an extra clip."

Opal smiled, brown eyes twinkling, and patted the waist of her jeans. "I keep mine on an empty chamber, for safety. Staying alert is important for old ladies who live alone, particularly when there's so much trouble in town. Besides, I have your girl to think of."

"Why do you think I trust you with Lily?" Ryder asked, returning her smile. "Anybody who was an MP is bound to be a good, safe guard."

"That was a long time ago."

"You never forget," he countered. "It's like riding a bicycle. The programming sticks in your mind."

"And muscle memory." Opal's grin spread. "Wanna see me fieldstrip a .45 auto blindfolded?"

"Maybe later." Ryder eyed his child. "I promised the princess some ice cream."

"You spoil her."

"And love every minute of it," he said.

That made Opal chuckle. "Wait until she's a teenager, and then tell me you feel the same way."

He sobered. "I'm not in any hurry."

Her touch on his arm was gentle, motherly. "You should think about a mama for her, you know. Every girl needs a mother, particularly as she gets older."

Ryder chose to turn the serious moment into a joke and arched an eyebrow. "Are you applying for the job?"

"Hah! I sure would if I was about thirty years younger. Of course, if you like your ladies real mature..." Opal patted her short cropped hair with one hand and rested the other on her hip.

"I'll keep you in mind," Ryder promised. "I know you can cook."

"Yup. And I shoot straight, too."

"Yeah." His eyes were on Lily. "I just wish this was a peaceful little town again. Even after losing Melanie it seemed relatively safe here. Everybody thought her murder was an isolated incident for a long time."

Opal sighed. "I know what you mean. How were we to know those other two fellas were victims, too? How'd that Carrie person choose 'em in the first place?"

"Because they reminded her of me," he said quietly. "I told you she killed Melanie out of jealousy. After that, she apparently fixated on a rookie officer who had light-colored hair like mine. When Mike Riverton didn't ask her for a date to the Police Dance two years ago she made his death look like an accident by pushing him down stairs. The following year, Brian Miller ignored her too and ended up dying in a fire when his house went up in flames."

"You never told me all that before."

Ryder nodded. "We held back details about the case and Carrie's motive to keep from causing a panic. Besides, Veronica Earnshaw didn't fit the victim profile."

Staring at him earnestly, the older woman said, "No, but Carrie might have thought you were interested in her."

"We can't rule it out," Ryder told her. "That's a big reason why I don't dare show favoritism to *any* woman. Not until Carrie's caught and jailed."

"Meaning, no dating." Opal turned to gaze fondly at Lily. "That's too bad."

"It's more than just dating. It's what goes on at work, too. If Carrie even imagines I'm spending too much time with another woman, that woman will be in danger." *Like Sophie has been.*

He shivered, then pulled himself together and banished destructive thoughts as he called out to his daughter. "Time to go, Lily. If we don't get there before the Cactus Café closes, we'll have to buy our ice cream at the mini mart."

She proceeded to tell each cat goodbye before getting to her feet. "They want to go, too, Daddy."

"Miss Opal doesn't want them outside," he countered.

"'Cause of the snakes, huh?"

"Right. And traffic and coyotes and all kinds of dangers. They were raised inside. This is what they know."

"But you could protect them, Daddy. You can do anything," Lily said, gazing up at him in adoration.

"I wish I could." Ryder was thinking back to the night he'd been too caught up in his job to pick up his wife from town. That was the night Melanie had been ambushed.

In Ryder's mind, no matter who had actually shot and killed her, part of the blame belonged to him. He'd be atoning for the rest of his life.

Grasping Lily's hand and holding tight he led her to the door, then paused to peer out into the yard. Nobody, Carrie Dunleavy included, was ever going to take someone he loved from him again. Not while he still had breath in his body.

And after that? He set his jaw. He knew he should trust God in all things, even the life of his darling Lily, but he kept remembering Melanie. They had believed together that the Lord had blessed their marriage, so why had He allowed her to be taken?

An overwhelming sense of doom enveloped him. He scooped his daughter into his arms, held her tight and jogged to the patrol car. This must be the way Sophie had felt when she'd imagined a menace besides the snakes, he concluded. Instinct for self-preservation had kicked in and she'd reacted to it on a basic level.

One thing was clear. Some gut feelings were God-given and had better be heeded. To ignore them was not only foolish, it was akin to laughing in the face of his heavenly Father.

"Forgive me, Lord," Ryder whispered as he fastened Lily in the backseat. A scripture verse popped into his head. "Lord, I believe. Help Thou my unbelief."

No lightning bolts shot down from heaven. No angels sang. But Ryder was calmer, stronger, more self-assured as he circled to the driver's side of the car. The Desert Valley police were going to catch whoever had been threatening Sophie, whether it turned out to be Carrie or not. As chief, he would see to it.

Only one thing took priority. The innocent little girl in the backseat. She always would.

Nervous despite her dog and reloaded pistol, Sophie had trouble sleeping. It didn't help that Phoenix hogged the bed. She shoved him over and threw back the covers as soon as the sun began to peek over the top of the red rock horizon. Morning was usually one of her favorite times in the desert, with fresh, cooler air and pristine silence.

Today, however, she had enthusiastic company. Phoenix spun in circles at her feet and raced from the room as soon as her bare feet touched the floor. "Okay, okay. I'm coming."

Not knowing how well he was trained, she figured it would be smart to slip some clothes on and let him out quickly. Boots didn't exactly go with cargo shorts but she wasn't letting her dog set foot in the backyard until she was sure there were no live snakes left.

She snapped a leash on his collar, tucked her gun into one of the pockets on the shorts and opened the back door. Except for remnants of last night's carnage, the place looked deserted. Sophie hesitated. There was no guarantee that her front yard was clear, either, but at least it wasn't messy, so she opted to reverse direction and lead Phoenix out that way instead of turning him loose inside the fenced area.

While he sniffed and wandered, unconcerned and therefore safe, Sophie checked the ground around the sides of her house. During her nocturnal unrest she'd reasoned that she'd been imagining hidden menaces so it was a shock to come upon wadded-up gum wrappers in the very place where she'd thought she'd sensed danger lurking.

"Oh, my..."

Her reaction was strong enough to cause the dog to take up a defensive position with his side pressed to her leg and hackles raised.

She laid a comforting hand on his head. "Good boy. I think we're all right now but I'm going to call this in."

Backing off, she led Phoenix away in order to keep from contaminating possible clues. As soon as she started to dial 911 she thought better of it. The last thing she needed was to cause a full-blown police response when the clues might mean nothing, and she sure didn't want to phone James Harrison and ask for his bloodhound when he was romantically involved with *Canyon County Gazette* reporter Madison Coles who would be likely to want to put her in the news. Sophie then thought about summoning Whitney but she was a single mother with a baby to take care of and it was barely dawn.

"Face it," Sophie muttered, disgusted with herself. "You aren't fooling anybody. You want to call Ryder."

He also had a child, but Lily was old enough to bring along if he chose. Besides, it would be advantageous to introduce Phoenix to Lily on neutral ground.

"Right. I need to be sure the dog likes kids," Sophie told herself, immediately recognizing the excuse for what it was. Lame. However, that was not enough to keep her from calling him at home.

Instead of making small talk, Sophie began with, "I found some clues—chewing gum papers and foil—next to my house. I'm pretty sure they weren't there before."

"I take it this is Sophie."

"Of course it is. I told you I was being watched. Suppose there's DNA on the gum wrappers? I didn't stop to see if there was any old gum lying around. I didn't touch a thing and I kept the dog back, too."

"Good for you."

"Look, do you want me to call somebody else? I don't particularly want a bunch of red lights and sirens charging over here again, not after the uproar last night. Which reminds me. Didn't you say you'd come check the yard this morning? How is that any different than coming by now?"

"Well, for one thing Lily wouldn't be with me later."

Sophie suddenly saw his concerns. "You're afraid to bring her here?"

He huffed. "I'm afraid to let her out of my sight, period."

"I understand. Now that I think about it, I know I've noticed that brand of gum at either the police station or training center. I just can't place exactly where. I could pick up the evidence and keep it clean but it wouldn't be admissible in court since I'm no longer an officer of the law."

Ryder yawned. "What are you asking me to do?"

"Come and get it."

"I have minions for that."

Sophie could tell he was chuckling and was not amused. "I was trying to keep from making a big fuss about it and getting everybody all riled up. You want to keep the good citizens of Desert Valley calm, don't you?"

"Yes." Another yawn. "Okay. Leave your evidence alone and keep the dog from getting into it. I'll get dressed and be there as soon as I can."

"Why don't you come for coffee? If you change your mind and bring Lily I can fix pancakes for us all."

"Not a good idea," Ryder countered. "I don't think it's wise for me to be seen spending any private time with you."

Sophie wanted to ask him if he was afraid of Carrie or of himself. She didn't. Instead, she said, "Consider it a part of Phoenix's training. I'd like to make sure he's good with children."

"Then meet us at the office some afternoon."

"You're right. Sorry. I'll stay here and wait. Will you come by as soon as you drop her off?"

When Ryder said, "Yes," Sophie felt such relief she almost sighed aloud.

She wasn't afraid of facing enemies she could see. It was the hidden ones that set her nerves on edge. The ones like the gunman who had killed her partner while she was tracking another criminal.

Or the ones who patiently lurked in the shadows and chewed gum while they watched her try to keep from being poisoned by snake venom. No matter what anybody said, she still suspected that those snakes had been dumped over her back fence to do what vipers did best. To kill.

Ryder had donned his full uniform so he could go on to work once he was finished gathering evidence at Sophie's. Her front door swung open before he reached the porch.

"Thanks for coming."

He touched the brim of his cap. "Where's the evidence?"

"Over there." She gestured. "I'll come with you."

Waiting at the corner of the house until she joined him, he scowled. "Where?"

"Right..." Her jaw dropped. "It was right *there*."

It went against his high opinion of her to doubt but he certainly had questions. "Could you be mistaken?"

"No, I saw foil and paper gum wrappers. Most of them were crumpled up so they wouldn't be likely to blow away. Besides, there's no breeze stirring this morning."

Ryder arched an eyebrow. "That was my conclusion. So, what do you think happened to them?"

"How should I know?" Her voice was raised, her eyes wide. "They have to be here somewhere."

"All right. We'll circle the house first, then bring in a dog."

Clearly, Sophie believed she'd seen clues, which was a point in her favor. Being unable to lead him to the scene was not.

"It was near this back corner," she insisted. "The same area that had me spooked last night. Remember what I told you about saving ammo just in case? Well, this was where Phoenix was looking when I started to feel as if we were being watched."

"So you assumed you'd see clues this morning?"

"No. I wasn't even thinking of that when I stumbled on the gum wrappers."

"Maybe. Maybe not."

Whirling, she fisted her hands on her hips. If Ryder hadn't been so disgusted to have been talked into participating in a wild-goose chase, he might have smiled at her uncompromising demeanor.

"I did not imagine a thing, Chief," she said with conviction. "There were clues on the ground. Look. See the footprints?"

"Most every cop in Desert Valley was walking out here last night," Ryder reminded her. "Any of them could have been chewing gum."

"Okay, okay. Suppose you radio the station and ask if they were before you assume I'm lying."

"I never said you were lying. I do wonder if your imagination isn't working overtime, though. You were pretty freaked out last night."

"Do you blame me?"

"Nope. It did surprise me that you assumed the snakes were part of a planned attack. The Arizona desert is their natural habitat. You must know they den up for winter."

"It's August and hotter than ever," Sophie countered. "I know how snakes behave. If there was a den in my backyard I think I'd have discovered it by now. I've lived here for two summers."

"Something around you may have changed. They could have lost their regular underground access to tunnels and been forced to seek another way in."

"I'd think you'd be the first to suspect an attack, especially after I was shot at in the depot."

As she spoke, Ryder was slowly making his way around her house. Roadrunners and flocks of smaller birds were busy cleaning up the mess near the back fence, making his job easier in one way.

He straightened when they returned to their starting point. "I suppose jays or some other species might have been attracted to the shiny wrappers and carried them off."

"Birds? You're blaming birds?"

Ryder let her barely controlled anger roll off him. Even if Phoenix didn't strike a trail, Titus would let them know if there had been a prowler. "Go get the new dog and let's see what he does."

"Not on your life."

"I beg your pardon?"

"You should," Sophie told him. "If you gave my opinion a shred of credit you wouldn't tell me to get a dog we know so little about. You'd bring in Titus and do the search properly."

When she was right, she was right. Ryder nodded. "My apologies. I'll go get Titus out of the car."

"I should hope so."

He could tell that Sophie was still miffed. Unfortunately, she'd been right when she'd guessed that he wasn't treating her so-called report of clues seriously. Either she'd imagined seeing signs of a lurker or she'd invented one. There was no way things like that just disappeared on a totally windless morning. At least not so completely. When he'd mentioned the birds in the area he'd been giving her a chance to alibi away her error in judgment. Now she was going to be stuck with it.

Opening the rear door of his SUV he fitted the working dog with a special K-9 vest, snapped a long lead on his collar and signaled him to get out.

Titus's tail wagged as eagerly as ever but his steps were slightly halting until he got warmed up. Knowing that the head trainer was observing them made Ryder extra cautious. Since they had nothing with which to offer a scent to the dog, he began to lead him in a circuitous path before rejoining Sophie.

She didn't greet the happy dog as she would have under casual circumstances. Instead, she motioned to the ground where she'd noticed the bits of trash and said, "Seek."

Ryder didn't expect any reaction, let alone a strong one. The old dog snuffled the ground, disturbing dried grass and leaves, then kept his nose to the ground, wheeled and headed directly for the street.

Playing out the light lead, Ryder followed. Titus had not only struck a trail, he was acting as if the scent was fresh!

If he hadn't been so biased in the first place, Ryder would have easily concluded that someone had returned recently and picked up the gum wrappers that Sophie had spotted. Now he was forced to reconsider.

Titus led him to the curb, then up the street several houses before he lost the trail.

Disgusted with himself and slightly contrite, Ryder turned to Sophie. "I owe you an apology. Somebody was in your yard, probably this morning, and they got into a car right here. We'll need to check with the nearest residents to see if they noticed."

"We can hope," she said.

Frowning, he took her by the elbow and ushered her back to her house as quickly as possible.

"What's the hurry? The gum chewer is gone."

"Now, maybe," Ryder said gruffly. "But stop and think. The only way anyone would have known you'd stumbled on those wrappers was by watching you do it."

To his relief, Sophie took him seriously. "And coming to clean them up before you arrived."

"That would be my conclusion, yes."

She paled and rested a hand on his forearm before she said, "I'm so glad you didn't bring Lily."

Heart racing, he scanned the surrounding properties for any sign of danger. Not seeing anything out of the ordinary didn't mean there wasn't a lingering threat.

One he might have walked his little girl right into if he hadn't been so worried about letting Carrie see him visiting another woman.

Now he was left wondering if she actually had.

FIVE

After their fruitless time outside, Sophie had hoped Ryder would stay for coffee. He begged off.

She vented by talking to the dog. "It's just you and me, boy. We can have scrambled eggs if you want. What do you say? A little people food won't hurt you."

Phoenix responded to her lilting tone with enthusiasm that left no doubt he'd be thrilled no matter what she fed him. Gazing up at her adoringly, he wagged his stub of a tail so rapidly his whole rear half did a frenetic hula.

"You're going to make it, aren't you, boy? Yes, you are. And as soon as we've eaten you can have the first lesson in your refresher course."

Taking Phoenix to the training center was a given. Keeping him with her at home was optional. It was hard for Sophie to admit she wished she could keep him indefinitely. He was not only company, he was a kindred spirit.

"Just like Ryder," she murmured. "Only I understand dogs a lot better than I do people. Guess I always have."

And that's where my God-given gifts lie, she added silently. It was a lot easier to picture herself in the midst of a litter of wiggly puppies than working at a preschool surrounded by sticky-fingered toddlers. The silly impression made her chuckle.

Being around Phoenix had lifted her spirits more than she'd expected. His joie de vivre was infectious. It was going to be a real pleasure to rescue him from his doldrums and give him a new purpose in life.

That goal was still on her mind an hour later when she pulled into the training center lot and parked. There were fenced areas for off-lead work, obstacle courses, search areas where officers could hide drugs for the dogs to find, and even a yard for pups that she was evaluating and training.

Then there was the Desert Valley Canine Assistance Dog Center. When Ellen Foxcroft had suggested starting that program she'd met with a lot of resistance, including Sophie's, but everybody was now convinced the project was worthwhile. It took a special mentality for a dog to provide stable, reliable assistance to the disabled without getting excited and endangering them. Police dogs were very different from companion animals.

Sophie smiled down at Phoenix as she led him toward her K-9 facility. He had all the intelligence and instinct needed to partner with a police officer. He'd succeeded once. He'd do it again—if she had anything to say about it.

Entering the building she led the Australian shepherd on a meet and greet, beginning with Louise Donaldson's desk. The dark-haired, sixtyish widow smiled slightly. "So, this is the infamous Phoenix. Do you expect him to rise from the ashes like his mythical namesake?"

"I certainly hope so," Sophie replied.

"He seems to be pretty calm this morning."

"We're making progress."

As she turned to proceed, Gina Perry, her junior

trainer, was entering with Shane Weston and his German shepherd, Bella. He kept his suspect apprehension dog on a short leash. Her fawn-and-black coat bristled and her body language predicted aggression.

Sophie acknowledged his sensible actions. "Thanks, Shane. I don't want Phoenix in a dogfight. Bella could have him for breakfast and never even breathe hard."

"He is kinda cute," Shane said. "What's his specialty?"

Gina answered for her boss. "Search and rescue. He used to be really good at it. We're hoping we can rehab him."

"If anybody can, you two can," Shane said. Considering the fact he had eyes only for Gina, Sophie was surprised he'd included them both in his praise.

Whitney Godwin breezed in, her light blond hair pulled into a tight knot, blue eyes wide. "Sorry I'm late. Shelby was fussy this morning. I think she's teething."

"I won't tell," Sophie said, picturing Whitney's adorable baby daughter. "Meet Phoenix."

"Oooh, can I pet him?"

"In this case, yes. I'm trying to accustom him to crowds and help him relax. He really is a sweetheart."

From behind her, Sophie heard a familiar voice ask, "Who's a sweetheart?" Her first thought was of Ryder but the speaker was rookie James Harrison.

"This Aussie," Sophie countered. "And your bloodhound. Hawk is more laid-back, though. Phoenix was pretty hyper this morning."

"Maybe he knows he has a new lease on life. Which reminds me," James drawled, "Madison would like to interview you about the depot shooting."

"It's all in the official reports. Nothing more to tell." Turning away, Sophie hoped neither he nor his reporter girlfriend would tie the snake incident and the shooting together. At least not yet.

"So, where's Tristan this morning?" Sophie asked.

"Investigating a possible arson in a seasonal cabin," Louise explained. "Probably vandalism. City kids think it's fun to come out here and do things they'd never try at home, as if we're too rural to figure things out."

Sophie nodded and looked over the room with its scattered desks, some of which had to be shared due to space and funding. "We do have an advantage right now," she said. "Once Carrie's in custody, I wonder if Marian Foxcroft's money will stop coming in to fund us." Just as she finished speaking she noticed Ellen Foxcroft in the background and apologized. "Oops. Sorry, Ellen. I didn't mean to sound disrespectful. How is your mom? Any better?"

Ellen smiled wistfully. "The specialists keep saying she'll come out of the coma soon. She's been showing hopeful signs."

"Good. I'm so glad. How's your special guy, Lee Earnshaw?"

"Going back to school to become a veterinarian," Ellen said, beginning to beam with pride.

"That's wonderful. He was so good with dogs when we met in the Prison Pups program."

"Good can come out of anything, right? Even Lee being framed for something he didn't do. I think Veronica would finally be proud of her brother."

The mention of her murdered predecessor, Veronica Earnshaw, dampened Sophie's mood. Phoenix sensed the change immediately and became more subdued.

"Well, I guess we'd all better get back to work before the chief catches us gabbing," Sophie said, trying to appear lighthearted. She looked around for one more rookie. "Where's Tristan going after he finishes investigating the fire?"

"Probably to make sure his teenage sister stays out of trouble," someone joked.

Sophie felt a smile coming on and encouraged it. "I never got into trouble when I was a kid."

She hadn't noticed Ryder entering the office so when he said, "What did you do, save it all for now?" she whirled. Her cheeks warmed. She barely managed, "Morning, Chief."

He nodded and proceeded to his office. Sophie figured this was a good time to make her exit, so she headed for the training center, a quarter of a mile up the street from the police station.

The aroma of freshly brewed coffee told her that Gina had stopped there before joining Shane at the DVPD. The gentle, auburn-haired, junior trainer was a perfect foil for Sophie's personality. They were a much better fit than either of them had been with Veronica. Nevertheless, the deceased woman had been great with dogs. It was her approach to humans that had been hard to take.

Sophie took her time, checked phone messages, followed up on some donations of young dogs she was considering and sipped a cup of hot coffee. All the while, Phoenix lay at her feet, tucked into the knee space beneath her desk.

The officers and rookies had unanimously decided to turn the upstairs apartment into a break area and storage after Veronica's murder. Sophie certainly didn't want to live there when she was well settled in the house on Second Street. Besides, they needed the extra room for equipment. One thing on her to-do list this morning was fitting Phoenix with a work vest and harness to see if they made any difference in his behavior.

As soon as she completed her paperwork she rinsed her cup, put it away with the others and led the dog upstairs. Even with the AC running, the rooms were stuffy. She'd have opened a window for ventilation if she'd arrived earlier. By now, it was too hot. Outside temps climbed fast in summer and fall, even though desert nights tended to be cool.

Boxes of collars, harnesses and vests were stashed in the main closet. It didn't take Sophie's trained eye long to choose the correct size working vest and fit it to the Australian shepherd. He didn't act pleased.

"Hey, buddy, you have to wear your badge and patches or you'll look just like every other cute pet out there," Sophie lectured, keeping her tone mellow. She ruffled his ears and patted his head. "Come on. Time to practice."

Phoenix threw himself to the floor and rolled onto his back.

Not good. She straightened and exerted control by voice, stature and actions. "Phoenix, heel."

Although he did stand, his head was hanging. If he'd had a tail he'd have tucked it between his legs.

Sophie began to walk away as if she fully expected him to behave. He did. Up to a point. By the time they reached the ground floor Phoenix had almost caught up to her.

Pausing in front of the door to the training yard, she waited for him to sit at her side. When he eased his rear down as if being asked to sit on cactus needles, she almost laughed. Poor guy. He wanted to be good but instinctive fear kept him from it, and until he was over that, there was no use setting up a search and rescue scenario.

The dog lover in her wanted to hug away his fears but she knew that wouldn't help. If she demonstrated concern she'd only reinforce his reluctance to perform.

"Heel," she said firmly, stepping out into the training yard.

Head drooping, he nevertheless obeyed. That was a good sign. It meant he was willing to follow her into unfamiliar territory. Score one point for the trainer.

Sophie marched around the obstacles in the large yard, keeping Phoenix at her side. Few commands were necessary. Even better, he was no longer acting as if he was being led to his own execution. He wasn't exactly jubilant but at least he looked reasonably self-assured.

She took out a canvas training toy and waved it at him. His eyes brightened. Paws danced. Stubby tail wagged.

"Aha. You do remember, don't you, boy."

She unclipped the leash, told him to sit, then gave him the toy as a reward. The change was complete. Phoenix was happy again. Deliriously so. He did want to work. And he did want his reward for doing so.

Sophie was so engrossed in watching the new dog play, she failed to pay attention to her surroundings.

Phoenix suddenly dropped his toy at her feet and growled. It took Sophie several seconds to figure out he was looking through the chain-link fence at a dark-colored car slowly passing in the street. There was no reason for him to be concerned so she reprimanded him. "No."

The dog was not deterred. His snug vest kept his hackles from rising visibly but there was no doubt he was being protective.

She shaded her eyes with one hand. The car came to a full stop. The driver's window rolled down. Something was sticking out the opening. It almost looked like…

"Gun!" Sophie shouted, reverting to her police training. She dived for cover behind a wooden training structure that looked like a tiny house.

The sharp crack of a bullet being fired split the morning air.

Gina appeared in the office doorway. "What's going on?"

"Get back!" Sophie shouted, waving her arms. "Call 911. Somebody's shooting at me!"

Gina screamed and disappeared.

Sophie stayed behind the small structure. *Phoenix! Where was Phoenix?* Could the attacker have been aiming at him? Surely not. The dog hadn't done anything wrong.

No, but police dogs were occasionally killed by criminals, Sophie reminded herself. Reading about such senseless loss always made her sad—and angry. Very angry.

She drew her pistol and rose up high enough to see the street. The car was still there. The dog was flat on the ground about ten feet from her.

"Phoenix! Come."

He raised his head and began to crawl toward her while she kept her aim directed at the black vehicle. If anybody tried to fire again she intended to stop them.

The dog was at her side in seconds, panting and trembling. Sophie pulled him close and checked for injuries as armed officers raced to surround the strange car and block its path.

There was a little blood on the dog's front paw. Sophie was about to try to carry him to the vet's office next door when she realized the blood she saw was dripping from her own forehead!

Only then did she notice a slight stinging sensation. She poked the spot with her index finger. It came away red.

Ryder and his men boxed in the black vehicle with their own cars, approached with guns drawn, and ordered the occupants to raise their hands and get out slowly. The side windows had been darkened so much it was impossible to see the interior.

Several of the K-9s were more interested in the ground around the car than the car itself. Once Shane had worked his way to the front and peered through the windshield, he signaled for Marlton and Whitney Godwin to breach the doors. The car was empty. The shooter or shooters had gotten away.

If Ryder hadn't left Titus behind in the office he would have put him on the trail immediately. Instead, he pointed to Ellen Foxcroft and her golden retriever, Carly. "Start your dog tracking. Weston, you back her up with Bella. If the scent splits, you two do the same. I want this guy."

Shane touched two fingers to his brow. "Yes, sir. We're looking for a man?"

"I wish I knew. It might be Carrie Dunleavy, and it might not. I have Sophie making me a list of possible assailants. I'll start Louise working on it as soon as I get the names."

As some of his officers dispersed, he assigned Harrison to work up the evidence, not that he expected this perp to have left behind any clues. He'd already noted no shell casings on the floor of the vehicle or outside on the road. That much caution probably meant there would be no fingerprints, either.

There were times, like now, when he almost wished he could blame Carrie for everything. At least that way they'd be able to focus entirely on capturing her. One of his worst fears was that she might have joined forces with some other criminal, maybe one she'd met while working for the DVPD. The concept made him shiver despite the blinding sun.

Ryder was headed back to his patrol car when his cell phone rang. It was Tanya Fowler's number. "Hayes here."

"Hey, chief," the veterinarian said. "I've got a little problem. I may need your help."

"I was told there were no injuries. Was one of the dogs hurt?"

"Nope," the vet said.

His pulse had just begun to slow when she added, "This patient is much harder to handle. I can't put her in a cage and a muzzle won't fit."

Ryder was in no mood for jokes. "What are you talking about?"

She lowered her voice until she was rasping into the phone. "There's a stubborn trainer sitting on my exam table right now and insisting I bandage a scalp wound. I don't want to get in trouble with Doc Evans or the clinic. Do you think you could convince her to go to the ER?"

"Sophie?" It had to be. His heart returned to double time. "What happened to her?"

"She's not hurt badly. I just think she should have Evans check her over, for her sake as much as mine."

"I'll be right there." Ryder threw himself behind the wheel of his car. *Sophie again.* She drew trouble the way flowers drew honeybees. So what did that make him?

"Crazy," he murmured to himself. If he wasn't already, he would be soon, thanks to the trainer facing one disaster after another.

He made a face, said, "I can hardly wait for the next incident," before he realized that the next attack might do her much more serious harm. Or worse.

SIX

"I'm fine, I tell you. Just clean it up and slap a butterfly bandage on it," Sophie insisted.

Tanya shook her head and backed away, hands raised as if she were being robbed. "No way. I could get in legal trouble."

"I won't tell."

"It's still wrong. If this is a gunshot. I'm not touching it."

Sophie had been pressing a paper towel to her forehead, just below the hairline. She flashed a contrite look. "It's not. I'm sure I just whacked my head on the corner of one of the training structures when I dived for cover. There's no sense making a big deal out of it and going to the ER."

She swiveled at the sound of running boots in the hallway. The sight of Ryder was welcome despite the thunder in his expression when he burst through the door.

It was Sophie's turn to hold up her hands to reassure him but she didn't want to move the paper towel so she used only one hand, raising it like a traffic cop on a busy corner. "I'm okay. Relax. It really isn't serious."

She thought for a moment he might sag against the doorjamb but he recovered quickly.

"What happened? I was told nobody was hit."

She winced. "I was just telling Tanya. I think I bumped my head when I took cover. I wasn't shot."

"How do you know? Have you been shot before?"

"No, but..."

He grabbed latex gloves from an open box on the counter and pulled them on before approaching Sophie. She wanted to fend him off, to tell him she'd take care of herself, but given his concern and commanding nature she decided to hold back.

His touch was gentle as he moved her hand away and disposed of the paper towel. "The bleeding has almost stopped. How long since you had a tetanus shot?"

"I hate shots."

"So do the dogs, but you make sure they're immunized."

She shrugged. He had a point. "Okay. I can call the clinic and have them check my records."

Ryder was stripping off the gloves. "Where's Phoenix?"

"Gina has him. Why?"

"Because you and I are going to see David Evans in person. He can check your medical records then."

"And assure you I wasn't shot. He was an army medic in Afghanistan. He'll know on sight."

Ryder took Sophie's arm and helped her off the steel table. "Evans is a good man," Sophie continued. "Whitney's blessed to have him in her life. He'll be a good father for her baby. It's nice for kids to have two..."

She stopped herself but not in time. Ryder's closed expression proved he knew she'd been going to refer to two parents, something his Lily didn't have. Sophie could have slapped herself for being so thoughtless.

In an effort the soften the blow she added, "I had both parents and I'd have been better off with neither. They fought all the time. I felt as if I was raised in a war zone."

They were nearly out the front door. "Is that why you chose law enforcement?" Ryder asked.

Surely he already knew that, she reasoned, meaning he was probably making conversation in hopes of distracting her from where they were going. Nevertheless, she played along. "Yes. And dog training. My best friends were animals. They still are."

His grip on her arm tightened almost imperceptibly, but it did change. She'd have loved hearing why, particularly if he was feeling sorry for her. That sentiment was not permitted. She'd wasted too much time brooding as a teen to allow anybody to drag her back down into despair. Her life was fine. She was fine. And no good-looking, bossy cop, chief or not, was going to get away with pitying her. No sir.

Straightening, she reclaimed her arm and quickly climbed into his cruiser. When he slid behind the wheel she was ready for him.

"If you won't do this my way, at least take me by my house so I can get a change of clothes."

"You keep spare clothes in your locker."

"I used them and forgot to bring more."

Although he arched an eyebrow he capitulated. "All right. But the clinic first."

"You're really stubborn, you know that?"

Ryder stared. "I'm stubborn? Compared to you I'm a pushover. Which reminds me. Do you have that suspect list ready for me? I want Louise to get on it ASAP."

"Well..."

"Have you even started it?"

"In my head," Sophie said.

He pulled a clipboard from beside his seat and handed it to her. "Write."

"Now?"

"Yes, now. Before your thoughts get any more scrambled than they already are."

Sophie huffed. "My thoughts are not scrambled. I just have a lot to think about and my brain is always busy."

"If you expect me to accept that as the reason why you didn't notice you were under fire, forget it." He rolled his eyes. "Considering all that's happened to you in the past few days you should be on high alert at all times."

"I am. I was." She gestured at her clothing. "As hot as it is, I still wore my bulletproof vest this morning."

"And now?"

"It's back at Tanya's office because I didn't want to drip on it. I'll get it later."

Sophie noticed his white-knuckle grip on the steering wheel right before he said, "I hope nobody takes another shot at you before you do."

Evans had confirmed Sophie was not shot, given her a tetanus booster and done exactly what she'd asked of the vet. That didn't particularly please Ryder. The woman was already so self-confident she was almost unbearable. Adding support from other professionals was likely to make her worse. If that was possible.

"I still want to go to my house," she insisted after they were back in the car.

Ryder wasn't surprised. "I figured you would."

"Smart man."

"No," he said flatly. "If I were smart I'd have put you on paid leave as soon as you were shot at the first time."

"I wouldn't have left town."

"Yeah, I figured that, too." He made a sour face at her. "This way, at least I know where you are and there are plenty of cops nearby. If you aren't worried for yourself, you should at least be concerned about the dogs you train."

"I am. But whoever is upset with me doesn't seem to be targeting animals," she argued. "That's a plus."

"A plus would be finding a viable suspect on the list you finally made. I've decided to have you work with Louise to track those people down. The sooner we have addresses for each of them, the sooner we can start crossing off names."

"More paperwork?" Sophie sighed. "I have Phoenix to work with and a couple of younger dogs to assess for Ellen's assistant dog program. I don't have time to waste shuffling papers."

"Do you have time to waste in the hospital?" Ryder considered adding the morgue and thought better of it. Sophie was intelligent. She'd make the correlation without him spelling it out.

"I can't run forever."

"No, but you can keep your head down." He let himself smile at her look of consternation. "Pun intended, by the way."

"Ha-ha." She lightly touched the bandage. "I did this ducking. If I'd stood still I wouldn't have a scratch."

"Providing the shooter didn't fire again." He scowled at her. "Do you argue with everybody or is it just me?"

"I'm not arguing."

"You could have fooled me." Ryder wheeled into her

driveway and shut off the motor. Instead of allowing Sophie to enter the house alone, he followed. Closely.

"I don't need help."

"I'm not here to help you. I'm here for protection."

Although she rolled her eyes, she didn't refuse his company. That was a plus. So was her cooperation when he insisted on searching the house before parking himself in the living room to wait for her to freshen up.

From there he could hear her banging doors and mumbling to herself. It was when she grew quiet that he tensed. "Are you all right?"

"Yes."

The answer was satisfactory but her tone was not. As he started down the hall he heard water running. "Are you dressed?"

"Yes. I'll be out in a minute."

The door to the bathroom stood ajar. Sophie was leaning sideways over the sink and trying to rinse her blond hair without wetting the injury. There were tears in her eyes.

He sighed. "Here. Let me do that. You're making a mess."

"I can wash my own hair."

"I'm sure you can. But you can't see what you're doing without looking in the mirror and if you do that, the soapy water is going to run right into that cut."

She winced. "I know. I already tried."

This is a mistake, Ryder's conscience insisted. Yet he reached for her. Touched her silky hair. Cupped his hand beneath the faucet and slowly rinsed her hair.

She'd closed her eyes and was breathing deeply, as if his ministrations had calmed her. Time stopped. Ryder didn't want it to ever start again. He watched the water stream through her hair and over the fingers of his other hand. He had not been this close to a woman since Melanie and it didn't matter how innocent his actions had been in the beginning, they were now eliciting feelings that were far too tender, too extraordinary.

Ryder snapped himself out of the emotional trap and reached for a towel. He started to press it to her scalp, then changed his mind and stepped back.

"There. You're presentable. Just dry it a little and I'll take you to work."

When Sophie opened her eyes and looked at him she seemed every bit as off-kilter as he felt. Her cheeks were rosy, her hazel eyes glowing, glittering.

Ryder touched her shoulder when she wavered. "You okay?"

"A little dizzy," she said, then smiled. "From hanging over the sink, not from banging my head."

"If you say so." Backing away as he spoke, he kept one hand reaching toward her in case she faltered again. "I'll go check the yard and street. Come out when you're ready."

"Wait." She straightened. Her smile lessened into an expression that was very different from what he was used to from her. "I want to thank you. For everything."

For making a fool of myself just now? Ryder asked himself before rejecting the idea. Only he knew how special it had felt to help her, to touch her hair, to be that close without letting his emotions show.

"Doing my job," he alibied, turning away. "I'll be outside."

By the time he reached her front door he was back in cop mode. He'd better be, he cautioned himself. Somebody was out to get his head trainer and until they were able to whittle down the list she'd given them, there was no telling who or what awaited Sophie Williams.

Easing the door open, Ryder kept one hand on his holster. The sleepy little desert town he'd been charged with protecting had turned into a jungle, filled with predators ready to attack.

As long as he never let down his guard everything should be all right. But he couldn't be everywhere. Neither could his officers, even with the rookies working as temps and his veterans putting off planned retirements.

All any of them could do was try. And pray. And hope that the shooter, whoever he or she was, continued to miss. The way Ryder saw it, it was only a matter of time before more fatalities occurred.

Visualizing the whiteboard in his office he pictured Sophie among the victims.

What shocked and surprised him the most was that his vivid imagination had inserted her photo in place of Melanie's.

Sophie studied herself in the bathroom mirror. She didn't see the difference she was feeling. She didn't have to. When Ryder had helped her rinse her hair there had been a connection between them that was inexplainable. And amazing. And other perceptions she wasn't willing to name or explore. Moreover, he had clearly noticed, too.

Staring at herself she swiped on lip gloss. Too bad she couldn't dim the glimmer in her eyes or dull her flaming cheeks. She had always liked Ryder and looked up to him as a consummate professional, but this—this was unexpected.

Was the surprising emotional connection between them something she should nurture or bury? That was a good question. As long as the chief continued to treat her as if she were not special to him, the wisest thing she could do was act detached, as well. This was certainly not the proper time to try to talk to him about it. He already had a full plate and the more she was involved in ongoing incidents, the less likely he was to open up.

Reason told her he cared. Logic insisted he should be worried about anyone who worked too closely with the police force. Underlying doubts insisted that his solicitousness arose from a sense of duty rather than personal concern.

She could live with that assumption more easily than the notion she might be falling for Ryder Hayes. Phoenix saw small kindnesses as a call to abject devotion. Humans were a lot smarter. They—she—was able to think things through and come to sensible conclusions. So, the man had acted tender toward her. So what? He'd have treated anybody who needed help the same. Wouldn't he?

Sophie had no idea but she was sure she had dawdled in front of the mirror too long already. Tucking her damp hair behind her ears she straightened and gave herself a strict assessment. Her professional face was on. Her clothes were clean. And the bandage on her forehead was still in place.

"Good to go."

Yet she failed to move. Ryder was out there, waiting for her. Could she maintain her firm facade once she rejoined him?

Placing both palms on the vanity she looked into her own eyes. "I can do this. I *will* do this. I'm just feeling needy because I was scared, that's all."

Assuming anything else was not only foolish, it demonstrated weakness. The part of her life in which she was a victim had ended long ago. She was a grown woman. A strong woman. She could stand on her own two feet and face anything.

"God willing."

Now that she was an adult it was easy to accept that she was stronger and more self-assured. The idea that was hard to swallow was that she was not indestructible. Nobody was. Not even cops in bulletproof vests.

That thought took her straight back to the night her partner, Wes, had died so needlessly. Where had God been then?

Immediately contrite and asking forgiveness from her heavenly Father, Sophie turned and headed for the front door. There were many events in life that seemed wrong, unfair, even cruel, yet if she failed to trust God she'd have nothing.

Faith could be a tenuous thing, particularly when a person was mired in difficulties that seemed inescapable. But a world without faith, without God, was too terrible, too frightening to even contemplate. To her, it would be akin to diving into a pitch-black sea of despair with no chance of return, nothing to grab onto for survival.

If she did not believe in heaven she could not have faced death daily as a patrol officer or trained the dogs those officers counted on for their own well-being.

And speaking of officers… Sophie joined Ryder on the porch, locked her door behind her and let him escort her to his car without argument. They had both reverted to their professional personas and the wall around her heart was firmly in place.

Good. She scanned the street as he did the same. They were a team and they were good at what they did. Sooner or later they'd uncover a clue to her attacker. Or they'd locate Carrie and blame it all on her, a result

Sophie preferred over the likelihood that Wes's brother was behind the attacks. The time was coming when she was going to have to break down and tell Ryder about the funeral and she dreaded having to remember, let alone talk about Stan's vitriolic rant.

Sophie stifled a shiver and cast a sidelong glance at Ryder to see if he'd noticed. He apparently had not. That was good, because the last thing she wanted was for him to realize that the more she searched for her shooter, the more she imagined danger behind every tree, every fence, every car.

The basic drawback was not that she was paranoid. The problem was that she had strong cause to be. Somewhere out there was an unfired bullet with her name on it. She had escaped so far. How much longer could she hope to do so?

SEVEN

The weary expression on Louise Donaldson's face told Ryder she and Sophie had not managed to link anyone on the list of suspects to the recent crimes.

He paused by the desk. "Well?"

Both women shook their heads. "I've put the names through our state databases and just accessed FBI," Louise said. "It's not looking promising."

"What about you?" Ryder asked Sophie. "Have you thought of any more names?"

When she shook her head, she averted her gaze the way a guilty suspect might. He didn't like that. "Look at me."

She raised her hazel gaze to meet his blue one. That was all it took for him to be certain she was keeping secrets. He clenched his teeth, jaw muscles working, and tried to stare her down. She didn't yield. Nor did she look away again. If anything, her resolve seemed to strengthen.

"Are you sure?"

Although she failed to voice her reply she did nod.

"All right. Keep searching. I'm going to check with state troopers and ask if they've had any sightings of

Carrie. In spite of the rifle, I still think she's our most likely suspect."

"I agree," Sophie said, getting to her feet. "I need a break. How would you like to do a little training with Phoenix this morning? He's really coming around. His attitude is better even after the shooting incident in the yard."

"How about you?"

She smiled and his rigid persona nearly faltered. "Me? I'm always ready to play with dogs."

"I was referring to your head wound."

"Oh, that. I told you I just banged my head. I have a headache, that's all."

"Yeah, I have a headache, too," Ryder muttered, glancing at her and frowning. "Her name is Sophie."

She chuckled low. "Funny. I named my headache Ralph."

"Who's Ralph?"

This time she laughed more loudly. "It's a joke, Chief. Lighten up, will you?"

"Not until Carrie Dunleavy is behind bars."

"I want her caught, too," Sophie said, "but that doesn't mean life can't go on. I have dogs to train and refresher courses to give until we can resume our regular classes. You're here, I'm here, Phoenix is in a run out back. Can you think of a more opportune time to get in a short session with him?"

"I suppose not." Ryder glanced at his office. Titus's bushy Lab tail was sticking out from behind the desk where he was napping. "I'd like to get the dogs acquainted, too, once we decide for sure if the Aussie is staying. Titus can be pretty protective, particularly of Lily."

"That's pack instinct," Sophie told him. "Lily's the littlest member of your family so he guards her."

"Which may be another good reason for him to stay home with her instead of coming to work, but my babysitter is a cat lady."

"We can overcome that problem," Sophie assured him. "I'll need to work with Lily, too, since you won't be at the babysitter's with her. I can give her a few simple commands and Titus will behave for her."

"Tell that to Opal Mullins the first time he bites a cat," Ryder said cynically.

Sophie chuckled again. "Unless she's had them declawed they should be able to fend him off. Anyway, don't borrow trouble. There's enough around already."

"You can say that again."

"Don't borrow trouble, there's…"

Ryder glared at her. "I wasn't being literal, Ms. Williams. You go get the dog ready. I'll meet you over there in a few."

As she started to walk away he called after her, "And wear a vest. That's an order."

He could tell by the arch of her eyebrows that she was considering an argument even before she said, "If I die of heatstroke it will be your fault."

"I'll take my chances."

And then she was gone. Ryder felt as if all the light had left the squad room. If anything happened to Sophie he knew he'd feel the loss deeply. Would it be the same as losing Melanie. No. Not yet at any rate. But the potential was there. He could sense it.

His late wife had been grounded, sensible, cautious and still had been murdered. How much worse was it for a woman like Sophie; someone who laughed at danger and made fun of his precautions?

The idea of telling her to leave town had occurred to him more than once. She wouldn't, of course. He didn't have to present the plan to know she'd reject it. Was she truly brave or was her stubbornness a by-product of the turbulent childhood she'd mentioned briefly? Perhaps even she didn't know.

Grabbing a bulletproof vest from his office he slipped it on over his uniform shirt and headed for the training complex. One goal was firm in his mind. He was going to get Sophie to tell him what she was hiding; who she had left off the list she'd compiled.

There wasn't a shred of doubt in Ryder's mind. Somewhere in her past lay another suspect. His biggest worry was why she had failed to disclose pertinent information. What was she hiding? And why?

Bright sun made Sophie squint as she stepped outside with Phoenix. Heat radiated off the pavement so she headed straight for what little grass they had managed to keep alive all summer and plopped down in the shade of one of the training obstacles.

She had complied with Ryder's order to wear a vest but had not fastened it tightly around her torso. Having it on was bad enough without cutting off air circulation, too. Besides, it was ugly. Not that she was worried about fashion, she countered. But ever since she'd been forced into more and more proximity with Ryder she'd started to notice when she needed lipstick or when her hair was tousled.

Reminded of his kindness when she'd been trying to wash her hair, she lightly touched the bandage at her temple. The cut barely hurt although there was a raised, bruised area around it.

"Better that than a bullet hole," she muttered, feeling a shiver shoot up her spine despite the August heat. Lying beside her, Phoenix raised his head.

"I'm okay, boy," Sophie told him. She stroked his head and scratched behind his ears, enjoying the velvety feel of the fine, gray-and-white hair. If she hadn't been waiting for the chief to join them she might have laid her head on the dog's back and closed her eyes. Animals, especially canines, affected her that way. Being around them was calming, relaxing to the point of almost dozing off when she let herself stop working long enough.

"Here I am," she whispered pensively, "in a place I thought was perfect until we discovered Carrie Dunleavy had been killing off her competition and any guy who had the misfortune to resemble the chief."

Slowly shaking her head she found she was still coming to grips with the truth. How could she—how could all of them—have missed the signs of the police department secretary's mental unbalance and hidden agenda? How, indeed?

"Because she never made waves," Sophie concluded. "She baked us cookies, she was always willing to take on extra work and help out, she was everything and yet nothing."

That was probably the crux of the problem, Sophie concluded. Nobody really took Carrie seriously. If they noticed her at all it was to ask her to do more work. Socially, she was disconnected despite her efforts at ingratiation via food or little gifts to selected people.

In a way, Sophie felt sorry for the woman. She understood feelings of alienation. They had nearly destroyed her during adolescence. If it had not been for turning her fractured life over to God, to Jesus, she didn't know how she'd have survived.

And speaking of survival… She spotted Ryder crossing the distance between them. The brim of his cap shaded his eyes but she could already tell he was a man on a mission. Hopefully, his goal was to train a dog, because if he intended to keep probing into her past she was not going to be a happy camper.

Instead of smiling or greeting her verbally, he stopped at her feet and dropped something small and light into her lap.

She started to thank him until she realized what it was—a package of chewing gum with a blue wrapper!

Sophie did exactly what Ryder had expected. She picked up the gum and stared at it.

"Is this anything like what you say you saw in your yard?" he asked.

"It's exactly like the trash in the yard, only this is new and the other was unwrapped." Wide-eyed, she looked up at him. "Where did you find it?"

"In a box in the station," he said. "Carrie's personal items were checked for evidence tying her to the murders, then stored. I thought I remembered seeing something blue like that package of gum. When you said you vaguely remembered the same thing, I decided to look."

Color left Sophie's cheeks. "*She* was the one outside my house?"

"Possibly. Can you think of any other reason someone might have been watching you?" He crouched in front of her, willing her to open up to him. Because she began to slowly shake her head he raised a hand. "Stop. Don't insult me by denying it. You and I both know you're holding back information. I just can't decide if it's because you don't trust me or because you think you can handle the situation by yourself."

"It's neither." Sophie sighed deeply. "I guess it's an

old loyalty. One person made serious threats but that was years ago. I can't imagine Stan still blaming me for his brother's death."

"He wasn't on your list, was he?"

"No." She began to pluck blades of dry grass and crush them between her fingertips. "Stan Allen is the brother of my late partner, Wes. He accosted me at the cemetery after the funeral. At the time, I thought Stan was going to hit me. He might have if my fellow officers hadn't pulled him away."

"Have you heard from him since?"

"No. We both left Mesa. I went one direction, and he went another. I never would have thought of him if you hadn't kept pressing me."

"All right." Holding out a hand to her, Ryder pulled her to her feet. "Here's what we'll do. First, I want you to tell Louise everything you know about this guy. Then use your own sources to try to track him down while she checks databases. Call old friends in Mesa. Whatever you have to do. Just find him."

Sophie held up the pack of gum. "What do you want me to do with this?"

"Put it on your desk where you'll see it every day."

"Why? If Stan is my stalker, what difference does it make what kind of gum Carrie liked?"

"It doesn't. I'm hoping it will become a symbol and remind you to be more cautious."

"No matter who is after me, you mean?"

Ryder's jaw clenched. "Exactly."

Sophie managed to accomplish everything the chief had told her to do, plus introduce Titus to Phoenix without incident. The older dog seemed unconcerned about the energetic Aussie, particularly because Phoenix practically tiptoed once he realized the senior Lab was boss. Not only was there no challenge for dominance, Phoenix flopped down in front of Titus and rolled onto his back, the recognized canine signal for surrender.

Sophie was seated on the cool floor, legs folded, when Ryder came back into his office.

"You were supposed to be looking for info on Stan Allen."

"I was. I found him. Or, rather, Louise did."

"And?"

"And, his last known address was an apartment near Flagstaff. Louise called the building manager. Stan still rents there but she says she hasn't seen him for weeks."

"Uh-oh. Any idea where he went or why?"

"No. I've been giving it some thought, though, and I can see a reason why he might have decided to come after me at this late date."

Ryder perched on the edge of his desk and looked down at her. "Go on."

"The news. When you uncovered Carrie's crimes, this department made all the papers and TV news. They published lots of pictures and all our names, at one time or another. If Stan recognized me, maybe that's what set him off."

"Logical," Ryder told her. He circled his desk and picked up the phone. "I'll check with Mesa's chief and fill him in on our suspicions. We can get the state troopers involved as soon as we know a little more."

"You mean as soon as you catch Stan trying to kill me again?" She couldn't help sounding sarcastic. "Sorry. I know there's no proof. It just seems possible."

Ryder scowled at her. "Yes, it does. Think of how much closer to answers we might be if you'd given us his name sooner."

She knew he was right, yet felt compelled to defend her decision. "I am responsible for his brother's death. I didn't see any reason to cause him further trouble if he was innocent, so I held back."

It surprised her when Ryder quickly circled his desk and grabbed her shoulders. "Let me explain something to you, Ms. Williams. Criminals who shoot cops are the guilty ones. They make the decision to fire, not you."

"I should have seen it coming. Warned him."

"And if you had, he might still have died. Nobody knows why these things happen. It's so unfair it makes me want to scream at God but that doesn't do any good."

He paused and Sophie could tell he was struggling to continue. When he said, "I know. I did that when Melanie was murdered," Sophie wanted to weep for him. So much pain. So much suffering that continued to haunt him.

Her voice was soft, barely audible, when she said, "I can still see Wes in that dark alley, falling and just lying there."

"And I see my wife on the path where she died, but I make an effort to remember the other times, the good times. There were plenty of those if I choose to call up the sweet memories. You need to do that. And stop blaming yourself for what happened. It will only hurt you."

Did she dare voice her innermost thoughts? Was this the right time? Given Ryder's efforts to temper her own lingering guilt she decided to speak her mind.

"That's good advice," Sophie said gently, meeting his blue gaze bravely. "Have you taken it, yourself?"

He abruptly released her shoulders and stepped back. "I don't know what you mean."

"Yes, you do. You have always blamed yourself for

letting Melanie walk home that night. Everybody knows it. And now that we know Carrie killed her you're probably thinking you should have seen the symptoms of her mental instability, but none of us did. You are no more responsible for the senseless attack on your wife than I am for Wes's. If you want me to stop feeling guilty, I think you'd better do the same."

He turned his back to her. Sophie could tell how close he was to breaking down so she silently left the office, closing the door behind her. Healing of a broken heart was a lot like doing surgery on a real one; sometimes you had to cause more pain in order to effect a return to life and health.

What about herself? Suppose the repeated attacks on her had been Stan's doing? If so, he believed he had good reason and for that she still could not blame him. She wasn't going to be foolish and expose herself to his anger, if that were the case, but she couldn't help wishing he was innocent.

On her way through the main office she was stopped by Louise Donaldson. "We got some info on a print in that black car your perp left behind in the street."

Sophie brightened. "Carrie?"

"Nope." Louise shook her head. "It came back as unidentified in local databases so I sent it to IAFIS."

"It wasn't Carrie's?" Touching the small bandage on her temple at the memory, she winced.

"No. Sorry. I'll keep trying."

"Okay. Thanks." What else could she say? If Stan had been a police officer like his brother they'd have his prints. The same went for the military. Since Wes had never mentioned much about his younger brother she was at a loss. All she did recall was how worried her late partner had been about his only sibling committing petty crimes and perhaps starting down the wrong path in life.

Had Stan graduated to felonies? If so, his fingerprints should be on file, assuming he'd been arrested and charged.

And if he hadn't? What if he had been hardened by a life of minor crimes and was just now progressing to one that could prove deadly? To her?

That notion was enough to set her nerves on edge and keep them there, as if danger lay around the next corner or hid behind every closed door.

In truth, it did.

EIGHT

Passing days seemed to drag. With no more threats to anyone and no sightings of a woman resembling Carrie, even Ryder began to relax a little.

He'd spent some time with Sophie while training Phoenix and was starting to see what the dog was capable of. He was an excellent tracker, even with distractions that might throw off most dogs. And he got along with Titus, another plus in his favor. That was why, when Sophie suggested he take both dogs home with him, he wasn't too surprised.

"You think he's ready for that?" Ryder asked.

"If I come along and make sure he and Lily are okay together. She's used to a dog that lazes around a lot. It's going to be different to have one that wants to play all the time."

"Will it spoil him?"

"Not if you never let her take charge when he's in his working vest and on leash." She smiled, making Ryder wonder if the air-conditioning in his office had failed. "It was the same with Titus," she reminded him.

"I know. But he was already used to me by the time Lily started to walk. He let her hang on him when she was just learning to stand. I should have taken pictures. It was really cute to see the two of them together."

"Well, now you'll have three. What time do you want me to have him ready?"

Ryder eyed the two dogs lying beneath his desk. Titus had claimed the prime spot in the back of the kneehole while Phoenix shared as best he could. "What do you have to do to get him ready? Pack his bags?"

That made Sophie's smile widen to a grin. Ryder ran a finger under his collar.

"Don't let on, but I'm giving him a bath and a pedicure. While I'm at it I'll do Titus, too, since they're such buddies."

"Well, don't forget his toothbrush," Ryder quipped. "I know for a fact that Titus hates to share."

She nodded. "I know you're kidding but I really will include separate toys for each dog. I don't want Titus to think he has to fight for the ones at home. Actually, it might be wise for you to gather them up at first."

"Okay. Anything else?"

"Not that I can think of, other than making sure Titus doesn't try to protect Lily. That's one of the reasons I want to be there."

Ryder noted the fondness in her expression when she looked at Phoenix. "You could keep him a while longer," he suggested. "It won't hurt, will it?"

"Only if he gets too attached to me."

"Or you get too attached to him? I can tell he's a favorite."

"Which is another reason I need to pass him on to you," Sophie admitted. "I can't tell you how proud I am of his progress, and of him. He's a really great K-9."

"Thanks to you," Ryder said. "I'll phone Opal and

tell her we're picking up Lily early today. Do you want to ride with me or drive separately?"

Again, Sophie's grin lit up his office. "Separately. Definitely. Now that I have my SUV back I want to use it."

Seeking to ease his own concerns about her, he joked, "Just see that you don't park it in the middle of another gunfight, will you?"

She mimicked a salute. "Yes, sir."

Ryder waved her off, managing to keep smiling until she'd gone. Recent peace in Desert Valley had given them all a respite, but he knew their problems weren't over.

This period was akin to the lull before a storm that brought flash floods to the arroyos and swept away anybody who was thoughtless enough to be caught in the wrong place at the wrong time.

He gazed out at a clear blue sky, imagining the seeds of black, roiling clouds just over the horizon. Even when the sun was shining and the air still, the only thing a desert dweller could be certain of was that when the rains did come, they would arrive as a deluge.

So would the danger that was temporarily on hold, Ryder told himself. Until they had Carrie Dunleavy and perhaps Stan Allen in custody, nobody was safe.

Particularly not Sophie.

Sophie was taken aback when the chief approached her to suggest a change of plans. She was also barefoot and knee-deep in a dog-washing project. When she straightened to speak with him, Phoenix shook, sending blobs of suds flying.

She blew her hair out of her eyes and flung shampoo off her hands. "Phew! That was fun. Take off your shoes and jump right in."

"No, thanks. Is it safe to get soap in the cut on your head?"

"That's all healed. I'm fine."

"Good. I was just thinking."

"Clever plan. Wandering aimlessly isn't productive." She chuckled at her own lame joke.

"I'm serious. I think you should keep Phoenix with you until we have your shooter in custody."

"You must be kidding. I don't do all this for fun—although it is—I do it because I want to help law enforcement. That does not include making pets of working dogs."

"I know, but..."

Leaving the dog tied to keep him from running off, Sophie released the water spray nozzle and faced the chief. "But, nothing. This is my job. Let me do it."

"I wasn't trying to stop you. I just thought you'd appreciate having a watchdog in your house at night."

"If I feel I need a watchdog I can always take one of the younger dogs home with me. I've had my eye on those shepherds we got from Marian Foxcroft six months ago."

"You're serious?"

"Of course I am." Truthfully, Sophie had had to force herself to arrange to relinquish Phoenix. That was the main reason she was sticking to her decision. Every day she spent with him was one more day to love him more. If a person and a dog could be said to be soul mates, she and the Aussie were. He seemed in tune with her, and she with him. That kind of bond had occurred in the past, of course, but not often.

"All right. Have it your way." Ryder started to turn

away, then looked over his shoulder long enough to point to the sudsy, dripping dog. "You missed a spot."

Sophie knew she shouldn't listen to the urging of her mischievous side. Before she had a chance to talk herself out of it, however, she grabbed the handle of the spray nozzle and squeezed. A spurt of warm water hit Ryder between the shoulder blades. *Splat!*

He shouted. The look of astonishment on his face when he whirled, hands up in self-defense and eyes wide, was priceless. Sophie wasn't sure which of them was most shocked; him for being hit or her for spraying him.

Everybody froze. Gina peeked around the corner from the kennel area. Her mouth gaped. Sophie laughed until tears dripped down her already-damp cheeks.

Not Ryder. He slowly stepped away, removed his watch, took off his belt with the holster and laid it aside, too. Then he bent to untie the dress shoes he wore instead of boots when he expected to spend the day in his office. Those went on the seat of a stool to keep them off the floor surrounding the open shower and dog-bathing area.

Sophie watched, incredulous, as he started toward her, arms extended as if he were entering a wrestling match.

"Uh-oh. Sorry, Chief. I don't know what came over me. My brain must have skipped a beat." She backed up, nozzle at the ready. "Stop! Don't make me use this."

She heard a growl. It was Phoenix. The last thing she wanted was for the dog to bite Ryder to protect her so she commanded him to stay and stepped away, making sure his leash was tied tightly.

Grasping the nozzle with both hands and taking a

shooter's stance she shouted, "Don't come any closer. I'm warning you."

Someone in the doorway let out a whoop. In the few moments it took Sophie to check who was there, Ryder charged for the closest other hose nozzle.

Instinct tightened Sophie's grip. The blast of water hit him in profile. He didn't falter. Instead, he grabbed the separate hose, took aim and returned fire.

Sophie was ducking, screeching and laughing hysterically. Any stream that didn't meet its equal between them hit her hard. Shutting her eyes she tried to regain enough balance to fight back but it was futile. He was dousing her while the rookies in the impromptu audience cheered and applauded. Even Louise got in the spirit of the water fight when she yelled, "Soak her good, Chief."

"Ack. Eeek. Phooey." Phoenix had shaken enough suds in her direction that she could taste soap.

All the fight left her at about the same time Ryder stopped spraying. She staggered back against the wall of the shower. Water streamed from her hair, swirling down the floor drain with the soap from the dog.

Sophie gasped for breath. Saw his larger, strong hands resting on the tile beside her. She might look like a drowned pup but he was far from dry himself.

A sidelong glance proved to her that he was no longer feeling playful. He straightened and addressed the watching crowd.

"If anybody mentions this incident outside the office or I hear even a hint of rumor on the street, you will *all* be in deep trouble. Got it?"

Multiple versions of "Yes, sir. Yes, Chief," echoed and faded away as the parties dispersed, leaving Sophie and Ryder alone with Phoenix.

She faced him with enough smile to hopefully prove she wasn't mad but not so much he'd think she was mocking him. Leaning to one side she twisted her long hair to wring it out. "Well, that was different."

"You shouldn't start something you can't finish," he grumbled.

Hesitating to assess his expression, she decided he wasn't truly angry. "I thought I did fairly well. You'll have to go home to change."

"I have a clean uniform in my locker."

"Oh."

"Did you ever replace the clothing in yours?"

"Not with good clothes. I brought stuff to change into when I was doing something messy, like washing a dog."

Ryder eyed her soggy self. "You already changed?"

"Nope. That would make too much sense. Besides, I was in a hurry to get Phoenix all spiffed up for you."

"Well, you may as well finish before you dry off." One eyebrow arched. "I'm going to turn my back and walk away now. Don't get any funny ideas."

"Who, me?"

"Yes, you."

There was no impishness left in her after their playful tussle. In its place were surprise and joy and an all-over sense of relief from the tension that had been plaguing them all.

Sophie smiled to herself as she returned to her dog-washing chore. "That's what we should do during the street fair instead of a dunking booth," she told Phoenix. "We should organize a good old-fashioned water fight and invite the whole town to take part."

The soggy dog didn't act impressed. He hung his

head as she carefully rinsed and toweled him before taking him out into the sunshine. Dry desert air did the rest.

Sophie's hair was almost dry, too, by the time she returned to the training center to give Titus his bath.

The old dog plodded into the shower room obediently and stood still while she shampooed him. "What a good boy. You're better behaved than I am," she cooed.

From somewhere in the hallway came a familiar voice. "You can say that again."

Sophie had to smile. "Which part?" she called back, "the 'good boy' or the 'better behaved'?"

It didn't surprise her that Ryder chose to not answer. Losing control and becoming playful the way he had when she'd sprayed him had to be terribly embarrassing. If anyone else had tried the same thing they'd probably have been reprimanded for insubordination.

But not her. Not this time. How long had it been since that man had felt comfortable enough to play with anyone besides his little girl? Probably years.

Sophie felt immensely blessed. Even if nothing more came of their relaxed friendship after Carrie was apprehended, at least they had shared a little enjoyment today.

And, she suddenly realized, Ryder wasn't the only one lacking fun in his life. She was just as bad. The cares of the days, the threats of violence, had usurped the place of simple pleasures. Yes, they needed to be vigilant. But they also needed to remember to live. That amounted to more than merely stopping to smell the roses. It had to be based in thankfulness for what they had been given and backed up by faith in the One who had blessed them.

Funny how that was a lot easier to think about than to put into practice, particularly when being shot at.

* * *

Lily was ecstatic when her daddy told her they were finally going to bring Phoenix home. Climbing out of the car as soon as Ryder parked, she bounced on her toes waiting for Sophie to bring her new playmate.

Ryder let Titus out, as planned, and watched Sophie leash Phoenix before telling him to jump down. So far, so good. Titus had wandered off to sniff the yard and paid no attention, even when Lily launched herself at the Australian shepherd and gave his ruff a hug.

"He smells good," the child said. "Like lemons."

"That's because I gave him a bath," Sophie said with a sideways glance at Ryder. "Your daddy helped."

He knew he was blushing when he scowled back at her. Why he had acted like a kid was beyond him. What had felt okay at the time now seemed outlandish and totally unacceptable. Of course it was. He had a position of authority to maintain. Chief officers did not go around having water fights with staff. It didn't really matter that as head K-9 trainer, Sophie didn't work for him. They functioned as part of the same team and had always treated each other as equals. At least he had. By spraying him, she had proved otherwise.

Ryder knew he should be furious but for some reason he wasn't. After all, he could have walked away despite the obvious challenge. There was just something about Sophie that had insisted he retaliate.

"I wanna play hide-'n-seek," Lily said.

"In the house. Not out here," Sophie replied.

Ryder led the way, opened the front door of his ranch house and ushered them all inside. He had a woman who came to clean once a week and Lily was good about picking up her toys, so he wasn't embarrassed about any clutter except the dog toys scattered in the living room. "Hold on a second. I'll pick up after Titus."

"It may be all right," Sophie said, eyeing the old dog. "He's not acting possessive at all. The time together in your office has helped a lot."

"All they did was sleep," Ryder countered. "Speaking of which, look."

Titus had already curled up in his favorite spot on the sofa and laid his chin on his front paws, relaxed but watching Lily.

"Don't forget what I told you on the way home." Ryder made sure he had his daughter's attention. "You can't just play with Phoenix or Titus will be sad. You have to give them both lots of love."

"I know." She darted to the couch, planted a smooch on the yellow Lab's broad nose, then dashed back to Phoenix and Sophie. "You hold him while I hide, okay?"

"Okay. I'll help him count to ten."

The sweet, agreeable way Sophie handled Lily warmed Ryder's heart. Adults often tended to belittle or ignore children but not Sophie. She was as in tune with Lily as she was with the dogs she trained. Maybe that was what he found so attractive. She had a natural way of behaving and accepting things that made her easy to like.

And lowered his defenses, he added, chagrined. The vivid memories of holding her under the spray with water going everywhere and her screaming like a kid kept popping into his mind. If word that he'd tried to drown the head trainer ever got out he'd never live it down.

"Ten!" Sophie called out. The instant she released Phoenix he was on Lily's trail. So was Titus. They rounded the corner into the hallway, nails scrambling on the hardwood floor.

Lily was giggling by the time Ryder and Sophie reached the spot where the dogs were. Phoenix had his head and shoulders under the bed. Titus was down on his front paws, rear in the air, tail wagging in circles.

"Looks like they found her," Ryder said.

Sophie was laughing. "I guess so. Where's his reward toy?"

"Around here somewhere." Ryder shrugged. "Sorry. I know I'm supposed to stick to training protocol but sometimes when they're playing I forget."

"It's okay. Lily can be their reward. Neither of them is wearing his vest so technically they're not working."

Sobering, Ryder eyed her. "Neither are you."

"Give me a break. It's hot outside and we haven't had any trouble for a week or so. I don't need to run around in body armor all the time."

"You should. We both know it."

The roll of her eyes was not the least bit comforting. He knew she wasn't a fool, yet she continued to defy logic.

All he could hope for, pray for, was that if and when the unknown menace struck again, his or her aim would be as bad as it had been in the past.

Unfortunately, that wasn't a given. Fire enough shots and sooner or later, one of them was likely to hit its mark.

NINE

Leaving Phoenix behind with Ryder wasn't nearly as hard on Sophie as going home alone turned out to be. Her house was dark, the front yard illuminated only by a distant streetlight. She parked the SUV so its headlights would shine on the back porch, then hurried inside before the automatic system shut them off.

So quiet. So lonely. So empty. She ate a solitary supper of leftover tuna fish on wheat bread, then tidied up the kitchen before heading for bed with a good book. It was times like these when she almost wished she had a permanent pet like a cat. Almost. If she could find one with the temperament of a dog she might consider it. In the meantime, she'd have to be content to foster her trainees, even if that did mean eventually letting them go.

The pages on the paperback soon blurred and she began to nod. Just before falling asleep she switched off the bedside light. Her dreams were filled with myriad dogs. And one man. He stood afar, his face in shadow, yet she knew it was Ryder Hayes as surely as she knew… That noise in the background was out of place.

Staying very still, Sophie opened her eyes. Nothing was moving. There was no unusual sound coming from anywhere, inside or outside. A dog would have been able to tell instantly if she should be afraid, of course, and she'd always believed anything a canine tried to tell her. Too bad she was on her own tonight.

A glance at the bedside clock showed three in the morning. Darkness would have been complete if not for a waxing moon. Sophie knew she should forget the rude awakening and go back to sleep but her heart was still beating too fast and her eyes refused to shut.

They were adjusting to seeing in the dimness when she heard glass shatter. A window? A drinking glass hitting the floor in her kitchen? It didn't matter. All she knew was that her home was being violated. She was not going to simply lie there and act the victim.

There was no time for a robe over her long gown, at least not until she was armed and ready. Scooping up her cell phone she slipped the revolver out of its holster and headed for the walk-in closet, easing the door closed behind her. Walls and doors weren't bulletproof, despite what TV and movies showed. They were, however, good hiding places. If no one could see her they wouldn't know to shoot.

Her hands were shaking. And the cell phone beeped when she pushed the call button. Sophie was hesitant to speak after that. Listening for footsteps she cradled the phone, only then remembering to send up a frantic prayer.

"Nine-one-one. What's your emergency?"

Rats, it was Missy Cooper instead of Louise. "This is Sophie Williams on Second Street. I have a prowler. In my house!"

"Can you get out and go to a neighbor's?"

"No."

"I'm sorry, ma'am. You'll have to speak up. I can barely hear you."

"Tell you what, Missy," Sophie almost hissed. "You can send help or leave the guy to me. I'm armed and will shoot if I have to."

"Units are on the way," the dispatcher said.

That's more like it. Sophie broke the connection. She knew the phone would continue to beep while she navigated to silent mode so she buried it under a pile of blankets in the hopes it wouldn't make any more noise.

Then she eased open the closet door and peeked out the thin slit. At first there was nothing. Then she heard a slow, steady series of footsteps. Someone was trying to sneak in by tiptoeing.

She was about to ease the door closed again when she heard the metallic swish and click of the slide on an automatic pistol. The shooter chambered a bullet.

Never before had it been this hard to hold perfectly still. Shaking to the core, she leaned on the doorknob for stability. The hinges squeaked.

Sophie stifled a gasp, returned both hands to her own gun and raised it, ready to fire.

A shadow fell over her bed. Watching it, she realized she'd thrown aside her light comforter rather than turn the air-conditioning down too low and had left behind a raised ridge of bedclothes that resembled a body.

The prowler took aim. All she could see were his hands and the barrel of the gun but she knew it was a man. She gritted her teeth, anticipating earsplitting noise. When he fired, the blast shook the windows.

The muzzle flash was temporarily blinding. The temptation to shoot back was great, but unless she could actually tell who and what she was shooting at she wasn't going to fire. Besides, he still didn't know he hadn't shot her in the bed and it would be foolish to give away her position.

Distant sirens made beautiful night music. Sophie heard her attacker running down the hall. A door slammed. That was *not* enough to draw her out of hiding. She wasn't going to move until she saw a police badge, preferably worn by one of the rookies she had trained, or, even better, by a certain chief she happened to be unduly fond of.

The sirens wound down, then stopped. Boots clomped down the hallway. She heard officers hollering, "Clear," as they checked the front of the house.

Releasing the cocked hammer on her own gun, Sophie was finally able to breathe.

She shouted, "In here," then slid to the floor to sit and wait because her bones felt as if they'd been left on the dash of a hot car in the Arizona summer sun and had melted into useless puddles like a box of wax crayons.

Scared? Sure. But it was more than that. She'd been less afraid of losing her own life than she was of being forced to take someone else's.

That was not a good sign.

Ryder had ordered Officer Tristan McKeller to stay with Lily when the rookie had brought the message about the attack on Sophie. They'd been unable to reach him because Lily had been tinkering with Ryder's pager and had shut off his cell phone, as well. Tristan had been chosen to check on the chief since his K-9, Jesse, was trained to pinpoint arson, not track humans.

What Ryder wanted to do first was set eyes on Sophie and see for himself that she was okay. He took the stairs to her front porch at a run, then halted a few feet short of sweeping her into his arms when they came face-to-face. Neither of them moved for several seconds. Finally he asked, "You all right?"

She nodded. "Yes, but I need a new bedcover. Mine has a bullet hole in it." Glancing past him she asked, "Did you bring the dogs?"

"Yes. Both of them. I wasn't sure if Titus could last long enough, and we don't want to lose this trail."

"Shane was first on scene," Sophie told him. "I think he's got the area around the house covered."

Ryder's feet were still planted and so were hers. "I should go."

Sophie nodded. He reluctantly left her and joined the operation in progress.

"We have dogs deployed in three directions," Shane reported. "Do you want to take command, Chief?"

"You're doing fine. I'd rather be tracking."

"Okay. The only area that hasn't been checked yet is the open field on the other side of the fence behind her house."

"We can take that," Ryder told him. "I brought both dogs. I'll leave Titus for backup and start with Phoenix. It's pretty rough walking out there. I don't want to tax Titus if I don't have to."

"Agreed," Shane spoke into his radio, then nodded at Ryder. "All set. They know you're coming. I'd hate to have one of the other rookies make a mistake and take a potshot at you."

"So would I. Do we have a description?"

"Big guy. Probably dressed in dark clothing. That's about it."

"No chance it's Carrie?"

"Not this time," the officer said.

In a way, Ryder was glad. If Carrie wasn't after

Sophie, that meant the extra time he'd spent with the trainer had not been at fault.

He smiled faintly as he prepared Phoenix and donned his own bulletproof vest. It also meant it would be safer to spend time with Sophie once this was over.

Nothing sounded better—except capturing whoever had tried to kill her tonight. He set his jaw and drove around the block, more than ready to track down the assailant.

Left behind, Sophie was far more nervous than she would have been if she'd been taking part in the search. Granted, it was no longer her job to go into the field with the dogs she trained but she really wanted to break the rules now and then.

There was plenty of activity in her yard to keep her interested, yet all she could think about was Ryder—and Phoenix. She approached Shane Weston. "All clear around here?"

He smiled and gave her a casual salute. "Yes, ma'am. Your place has been cleared and we have dogs searching the neighbors' yards."

Satisfied by the report she stepped out onto her back porch and paused to scan the darkness. Headlights swept the distant street where no houses blocked her view. A vehicle came to a stop, red lights spinning. A floodlight played over the desert terrain before someone—Ryder—brought Phoenix out of the back of the patrol car.

Sophie didn't have to see clearly to know who was out there and what he was doing. Instead of using a flashlight and making himself an easy target, Ryder let the dog bring him to the bare ground and sniff around.

One of her main concerns was snakes, like before.

This time of year they were only active at night and this was the perfect time to stumble across one. If the chief hadn't been working a dog she would have had a lot more concern. That was the great thing about K-9s. Their keen senses more than made up for a human's lack.

Peering into the hazard-filled night, Sophie was reminded to pray. She certainly had while hiding in her closet, she recalled, although not one word had stuck in her memory. That was the trouble with frantic prayer. It came in a rush of fear rather than organized thought. And, she concluded, it was the kind that sped straight to heaven because it wasn't all cluttered up with a person's ego or foolishness.

"Thank You, Jesus," she whispered, truly grateful for her escape and for the men and women who had come to search for the would-be assassin. Especially one man.

A shout echoed. Her hands tightened on the railing at the edge of the small porch.

Suddenly, the rear yard was filled with running figures and barking dogs. Another dog barked in the distance. If that was Phoenix, he'd certainly recovered his courage. His bark sounded a lot more menacing than ever before.

People were yelling. Sophie tried to ask rookie James Harrison for details as he passed, but the baying of his bloodhound, Hawk, drowned her out.

The melee stopped at the back fence. Some of the officers were playing lights over the scrub brush and rocks dotting the field.

"There! There he is. Eleven o'clock from my position."

Judging by his bark, Phoenix had to be coming at a

run and Ryder with him. Five flashlights zeroed in on the unknown man.

Shots cut through the darkness. Sophie instinctively ducked and stayed in a crouch. She was not going to hide inside. Not when so much was going on out there. Not when her friends and colleagues were taking fire.

"Jesus, help Ryder," she prayed. "Keep him safe." As far as she was concerned, his survival far outweighed the capture of her deadly stalker.

The officers at the fence began to cheer. That was more than Sophie could take. She had to join them.

Two shadows were grappling in the field. Phoenix had the pant leg of one of them in his teeth and was shaking it. The other had to be Ryder.

Sophie could hardly breathe. Hardly think. When a gun fired again she stifled a scream.

The pursuit was almost over. Ryder had launched himself at the quarry as soon as he'd gotten close enough.

The man had whirled and fired but the shot had gone wild when Phoenix had hit him below the knees and taken a bite of his leg.

Ryder left his own gun holstered rather than chance sending a bullet into the officers still at Sophie's. He'd seen them gathering when they'd helped him locate the fleeing criminal and knew the fence would slow them down enough that he'd have to finish this job himself.

He ducked a punch, then landed one of his own before wrapping the shooter in a bear hug and shoving him to the ground.

Phoenix immediately went for the arm holding the gun.

The wiry attacker tried to bring the muzzle to bear on the dog. Ryder was on him too fast. "Drop the gun!"

The captured man shouted curses and thrashed.

"Drop it," Ryder ordered again.

"She killed my brother. She deserves to die," he yelled.

And Ryder knew without a doubt who he had caught. The one person Sophie had left off her list of suspects was the menace after all.

Wrenching the gun from Stan Allen's hand he called off his dog, then rolled the man over and cuffed him.

As Ryder stood and pulled his captive to his feet, a group cheer arose.

"Good job, Chief," someone called. Others agreed.

He listened for Sophie's voice, hoping she had seen how well her dog had worked in a crisis situation. Although he couldn't hear her cheering above the cacophony he was certain she'd be celebrating, too. After all, this meant she could finally relax and start to live her life more normally.

Perhaps, God willing, he could, too, he mused as he led his prisoner back to his car, loaded him and let Phoenix jump into the front for a change.

Closing his eyes, Ryder pictured his darling Melanie. Would she mind if he took Opal's sage advice and began to think of finding a mother for Lily?

Expecting peace and assurance, Ryder was disappointed. It was easy to understand why. With Carrie Dunleavy still at large nobody could really go back to living freely, to enjoying life as it had once been.

"But that day will come," Ryder told himself with a sigh. He—they—would put an end to Desert Valley's fear and strife, one way or another.

If the state troopers didn't locate Carrie she might even come back to town and give him another crack at catching her.

That thought sent a shiver up his spine. Some witnesses had been positive the shooter at the depot had been a woman. Was it possible they had been so agitated they were mistaken? Maybe. Hopefully. This guy was about the same height as Carrie and had plenty of matching brown hair.

Ryder was looking forward to questioning him and getting him to admit to all the attacks. He'd better. Or they'd have to rethink everything.

TEN

To say Sophie was tired was the understatement of the year. She'd dozed off twice in the meeting Ryder had called at the DVPD the following morning to brief his staff and the dog trainers.

She heard her name and jerked. "Sorry. What?"

"I said we need to work out assignments for the homecoming celebration and street fair. I was planning to pair rookies and dogs with local officials and send them out on regular patrols. Since the fair is only open Friday and Saturday I think we can split the duty without everybody having to work all the time."

"I'd like to take some of the older pups out," Sophie said. "And I know Ellen wants to use the crowd for service dog training, too."

"Will Lee Earnshaw be around? If he is, he can handle some of the dogs for her, maybe in shifts. I'll need her on the street with Carly at least part of the time."

Sophie nodded. "He's going back to vet school, but he expects to be here for the homecoming." She had to smile. "He's not too crazy about Desert Valley after spending two years in Canyon County Prison for a crime he didn't commit, but he can't bear to stay away from Ellen."

"I guess that's understandable," Ryder replied, "even though he was exonerated."

"True. And they might never have met if he hadn't been involved in the Prison Pups program."

"Enough personal discussion, Williams. Let's get back to working out a schedule."

She almost snickered at his efforts to act so formal in front of the group. Those who hadn't seen their water fight had surely heard about it. After that, there was little chance she and the chief would be viewed as anything but friends. Which suited her just fine.

"All right," Sophie said, stifling a yawn and stretching her arms overhead. "I'd like to be included, as I said. You can either put me down as a regular or let me float to wherever we need extra coverage." That innocent suggestion brought a grin. "No pun intended. I didn't mean to bring up anything connected to water when I said *float*."

Muted snickers popped up. Ryder's cheeks colored. "That's enough. There will be no more jokes about *water* while I'm chief, is that clear?"

"Yes, sir." Sophie was giggling. "We'll consider the incident with the dog shampoo as *water under the bridge*."

Watching the expressions flashing across his handsome, if somewhat rosy face, she wondered if she'd gone too far. There was a point past which she should not go, if only to preserve the chief's decorum.

She waved both hands. "Sorry. That just slipped out. I'm so happy to be alive and kicking after last night, I guess I'm feeling a little childish."

Ryder seemed to forgive her teasing. "Understandable."

"Is Stan still refusing to talk?"

"Yes. After we brought him in I had Doc Evans look him over and prescribe something to calm him down. We'll have another go at him when he's acting more rational."

Sighing, she let her glance pass over the others in the meeting. "I suppose you all know the story by now. It's not something I'm proud of. Wes Allen, Stan's brother, was a good cop and a good man. He should not have died."

"Lots of people shouldn't have died," Ryder countered. He wasn't exactly frowning but he certainly didn't look happy. Not that Sophie blamed him. If she was having this much trouble getting over losing Wes, how much more difficult must it be for the chief to go on with his life after Melanie's murder?

And this was not the right time for platitudes or scripture quotes. Well-meaning friends and colleagues had bombarded her with what they had considered consolation and had only made her sorrow deeper, her loss more painful. Words had been inadequate then and they still were. The people who had brought the most comfort were the ones who had simply patted her shoulder or offered a hug without comment. Or wept with her later, she added. It had taken her weeks to cry and yet, even now, when she least expected it, some little thing might trigger more tears.

Wishing she had a dog lying at her feet, Sophie clenched her hands together in her lap and fought to appear relaxed. All but one of the people in the room seemed to accept her ruse.

The instant she let her gaze lock with Ryder's she knew she hadn't fooled him. In a strange way, that was comforting. Once again they were silently, unobtrusively, sharing empathy. She could not have accepted his pity any more than he'd have welcomed hers. But this was different. It was a connection she had not sought, yet it existed. Or did it?

Averting her eyes, she began to wonder if this kind of feeling was normal or if she was as deluded as Carrie Dunleavy had been. *Correction, as Carrie still is.*

That conclusion caused Sophie to ask, "What about Carrie? Are we going to have to worry about her crashing the homecoming or have there been reports of sightings elsewhere?"

"State troopers have posted a lot of possibilities," Ryder replied. "Most were in the southern part of the state, around Phoenix." At that, the dozing K-9 at his feet perked up and cocked his head. "No, not you," he said, finally smiling slightly.

That was the way Sophie felt whenever she was accompanied by a dog so she, too, smiled. "Maybe you'd better say Mesa or Tempe."

"Looks like it." Ryder concentrated on Louise. "Try to accommodate everybody when you make up the special duty roster, then bring it to me for approval. McKeller will want to be free enough to leave if Ariel Martin hasn't had her baby by then." Ryder knew that Tristan, one of his rookies, had gotten very close to Ariel, his daughter's teacher, during a case last month. Ariel was nine months pregnant and due any day. "Other than that, suit yourself."

He closed a tablet on the table in front of him and stood. "If that's all..."

"What about the civilians?" Louise asked.

"Use your discretion," Ryder said flatly. "Except for Williams. She's with me."

Blushing and positive it showed, Sophie quickly added, "To continue to train Phoenix. Right?"

The chief arched a brow and nodded. "Of course. Why else?"

Okay, I am certifiably loopy, Sophie concluded. She made a wry face and turned away. *I may not be coveting the chief and planning to eliminate anybody who got in my way as Carrie has, but my imagination is just as wild.*

Here she'd been, happily entertaining visions of their emotional and perhaps even spiritual connection, when he'd been all business, as usual. His reasons for wanting her around weren't personal, they were merely practical.

She shrugged. Well, one thing about it was good. If Carrie did show up and start killing again, at least Sophie wouldn't end up in the crosshairs.

The subconscious reference to a rifle scope made her frown. Think. Try to clarify an unsettling feeling. *That* was what had been hovering in the back of her mind! Stan had used a pistol when he'd shot her bed. So, where was his rifle?

Lily drove Ryder so crazy about the homecoming celebration and street fair, he let her come to work with him that Friday. The booths didn't open until 10:00 a.m. but he figured she could entertain herself playing with puppies at the training center, if necessary.

That was exactly what she was doing when he went looking for her. Someone, probably Sophie or Gina, had slipped an old shirt on over Lily's good clothes and she was sitting on the floor, laughing, while half-grown pups vied for spots next to her or in her lap.

She beamed up at her daddy. "They love me."

"I can see that. It's almost time for the fair. Tell the dogs goodbye and come with me."

"Okay." It took her several tries to get up amid all the licking and giggling.

"Sorry," Sophie said, hurrying to help. "I lost track of time."

Before Ryder could intercede she scooped up his daughter and carried her inside as he asked, "Are you ready?"

"In a sec. Lily needs her face and hands washed. Did you bring a hairbrush?"

"No. Why?"

"Never mind. It's a girl thing. I'll fix her hair."

The way her mother would, if she had one, Ryder thought, chagrined. Opal Mullins usually took care of readying Lily for school after he dropped her off, so except for church on Sundays, he rarely had to help the little girl primp. Truth to tell, it seldom occurred to him to smooth her tousled, blond hair. He liked the elfin way it made her look.

"Thanks for putting the shirt on her," Ryder said, lingering in the doorway to Sophie's office. "I didn't bring a change of clothes."

"What did you do when she was a baby?"

"I had some help. Her babysitter used to stay with her at my house back then. She took care of laundry and stuff."

Watching while Sophie gently brushed tangles out of the silky blond hair, Ryder remembered to pass on news. "By the way, Tristan won't be on patrol until tomorrow. Ariel just had her baby."

"A girl, right? That's what Ariel said she was expecting."

"I didn't think to ask." He had to smile when Sophie rolled her eyes at him and said, "Men. You never ask the important questions."

"All I know is, the baby is healthy and everybody is doing fine. Tristan is as proud as if he were the natural father."

"I know Ariel wishes he were, but at least her ex can't try to hurt her or the baby anymore. Not ever. I'm glad she has Tristan to lean on. He'll make a great dad."

"And probably remember to bring a hairbrush?"

Sophie laughed. "I wouldn't count on it. He's a man." She presented the purse-size brush to Lily. "Here. You can keep this one. I have others. Let's go."

The child continued to pull the brush through the ends of her hair long after Sophie had finished, as if she were suddenly grown-up. Ryder wasn't sure he liked that.

Another thing he wasn't sure about was spending the entire day with the pretty, head trainer. On a professional level it made perfect sense. On a deeper level it bothered him. A lot. If there was the slightest chance that Carrie was in the vicinity of Desert Valley, his keeping company with any woman was a bad idea.

He supposed he could have asked Gina, the junior trainer, to accompany him but only if he wanted to do battle with rookie Shane Weston to whom she was engaged. Besides, they were a compatible team.

Nor was he willing to endanger another person. Sophie and he already had something of a history, thanks to the criminal actions of her stalker, so why rock the boat?

Ryder huffed and began to smile as he drove toward the town square. Rocking a boat reminded him of sailing which reminded him of *water* which reminded him of—Sophie.

He couldn't even remember the last time he'd had real fun. Felt good enough to actually be playful. Or trusted anyone enough to revert to a former version of himself—a younger, less jaded version. Here he was, nearly thirty, and he had already begun to act like a stuffy old man. Until Sophie had forced her way into his psyche.

Glancing in the rearview mirror, Ryder saw her following in her SUV. She'd asked to transport Phoenix so he'd agreed. It was evident that she'd become attached to the needy dog. He could relate. There was something about the Aussie that brought out similar feelings in him. Plus, Lily loved playing hide-and-seek. Titus wasn't good for more than one or two times but the younger dog usually outlasted his energetic child.

"I want you to stay right with me and the dogs today," Ryder reminded Lily. "Remember what we talked about. You have to behave so Phoenix and Titus will. It's very important."

She nodded sagely. "I'll be good. I promise. Can I take my brush?"

"Why don't you leave it in the car so you don't lose it? You don't want to disappoint Ms. Sophie."

"She's nice." Grinning, she looked up to her daddy. "You gonna marry her?"

"Whoa! What makes you ask that?"

"I just wondered." Ryder saw her gingerly handling the small brush. "I like her."

"I do, too, honey, but maybe she doesn't want to get married. Some people never do, you know. They prefer to live by themselves."

"Oh."

Satisfied that he'd ended the conversation, Ryder parked on a side street for easy access, then helped Lily out before putting a leash on Titus.

Sophie pulled up behind them with Phoenix. He was

dressed in his own bulletproof vest and Ryder hoped the extra level of protection wouldn't make him, or the human officers, too hot as the desert day warmed.

Lily was jumping up and down. "Phoenix is here!"

"That's right," her father said. "Now settle down so you don't get the dogs too excited."

"Okay."

He frowned at Sophie. "Where's your vest?"

"In the car. I'll get it if you insist."

"I insist."

"Okay, but I'm not keeping it fastened tightly."

Ryder was so intent on making Sophie as safe as possible, he failed to see what his daughter was doing until she tugged on the trainer's free hand.

"Ms. Sophie?"

"Yes, Lily?"

"Why don't you want to get married?"

"What makes you think that?"

"Daddy said."

Sophie shot him a cynical glance. "Oh, he did, did he. Well, honey, I'll tell you why. It's because I like living with dogs better than most people."

"Why?"

Ryder hoped her answer was not going to be too serious. When she said, "Because they can't make up stories about me that aren't true," he was relieved. He almost strangled trying to stifle a laugh and was succeeding until she added, "Do you like to play in the water? I know a really funny story about that."

"Too bad you don't take after the dogs more," he interjected. "It would be better if you couldn't talk, either."

Grinning widely, she started off toward the Main Street gathering with Phoenix at her side.

Ryder fell in behind her, one hand in Lily's and the other holding Titus's leash.

"I wanna hear the story, Daddy."

"Maybe later," he said, assuming the child would quickly forget. "We have to see the fair and have some fun first."

And work, Ryder added, holding tight to Lily's hand. He'd almost left her with Opal today but given the positive police reports and Stan Allen's capture, he was relieved enough to let her come along.

After losing his wife, he'd been paranoid about keeping baby Lily isolated. Opal had talked some sense into him in time to keep his fears from permanently scarring his only child. He couldn't keep her to himself forever. He had to let her experience life and just do his best to safeguard her, as any caring parent would.

Besides, Carrie had never seemed affected by the little girl. Her threats and actions had been directed against any adult who had gotten in the way of her romantic fantasies. Lily was probably safer in Desert Valley than anywhere else. Here, everyone not only knew she was the chief's child, they looked out for her as well as each other.

He followed Sophie to the edge of the crowd, paused to radio his position and listened while the other teams checked in. Theoretically, he should be as calm as Titus was acting, yet he was not.

There was something wrong. He could feel it. What he could not do was identify it.

"All set?" Sophie asked lightly.

Ryder nodded. "Yeah. Let's do this."

ELEVEN

Sophie walked a fine line between enjoying herself and working, particularly since Lily kept up a steady stream of chatter, half of which was inherently funny. The child wanted, and got, most of what she begged for.

Lily would tug on Ryder's hand and point, and he would divert to do as she asked. His expression was more than benevolent. It was filled to overflowing with love. Whether she knew it or not, Lily Hayes was a very blessed little girl.

They paused at a booth festooned with paper streamers and filled with gaudy costume jewelry while Lily oohed and aahed.

"Made it all myself," the saleslady said.

Sophie could see tags and markings that indicated otherwise, which was probably why the baubles were so cheap. A sweet child like Lily deserved better. Perhaps, come Christmas, it would be okay for Sophie to buy her something suitable for a little girl. A locket, maybe?

Once, long ago, Sophie recalled having had a golden locket she'd cherished, although where it had come from was buried too deeply to remember. The only clear memory she had of it was the day her mother had been in a foul mood and had ripped it from her neck, saying it was too good for such a naughty girl. The chain had broken. So had Sophie's heart.

It was futile to entertain past hurts, she knew, so she forced a smile. While she'd been daydreaming, Lily had made her selection from the array of plastic jewels and Ryder was paying for her purchase.

"I wanna wear it," Lily shouted above the surrounding din.

When Ryder dropped to one knee in front of his daughter to fasten the clasp of a bright blue-and-green necklace, Sophie was so moved she had to don her sunglasses to hide her eyes. His tenderness was remarkable. More than touching, it was awe inspiring. If more parents were like Ryder, maybe their children would turn out better and the police wouldn't have so much to do.

Contrite almost instantly, Sophie whispered, "Sorry, Father. I know they probably do the best they can." *Like my parents did*, she added. They had an unhappy marriage and sometimes took out frustrations on their only child. That kind of treatment could have left her beaten down, but it had had the opposite effect. It had made her stronger. More independent.

In a strange way, everything in Sophie's life seemed to have directed her choices, to have brought her here at this very time. She did believe that God had a purpose for everyone but had never narrowed it down this way before. That conclusion was enough to refocus her concentration on the milling crowd.

Ryder straightened and touched her arm. "Did you see something?"

"No. I just realized I was daydreaming and decided to pay better attention."

"Good point. I plan to drop Lily at Opal's after we've made a couple of turns around the square."

"Aw, Daddy…"

"I can understand doing that," Sophie agreed. "If she stayed here all day you'd have to take out a loan."

"I want a hot dog."

Sophie laughed. "Just don't let her ride in my car on the way home. I don't recommend the bounce house, either."

"Yeah! I wanna go in there."

"Before lunch, not after," Ryder said, taking her hand and starting toward the ticket seller for the inflatable apparatus.

"You are one soft touch, Chief."

"I know. But Lily and I don't get much chance to do things like this. I'm usually working or she's in school."

"Kindergarten?"

The little girl shook her golden curls. "Uh-uh. First grade. I'm almost six."

"That old?" Sophie couldn't help chuckling along with Ryder when he said, "Six going on sixteen."

"I believe it. I was an only child, too. We tend to mature faster, I think, because we spend so much time talking to adults."

Sophie scanned the crowded street while Ryder escorted his daughter into the play area, then returned.

Lily didn't waste any time getting into the spirit with the other children. She waved at them from behind the black mesh safety net. "Look, Daddy! I can go high!"

"Do you have siblings?" Sophie asked him.

"No. My folks always said they got it right the first time."

"You made that up."

"Actually, no. It was one of Mom's favorite quotes."

"They must not live around here or you'd have her watching Lily while you're at work."

"You're right that they don't live in Arizona. But I'd still use Opal, even if my parents were local."

Sophie's forehead narrowed as she frowned. "Why? Are they inadequate parents like mine were?"

"No." He was shaking his head. "The reason I favor Opal Mullins is because she used to be an army MP. She knows how to handle herself in a crisis and I figure she's the best person to safeguard Lily." He paused and smiled slightly. "The only drawback is her cats. I can't send Titus with Lily because they don't like dogs."

"I can help with that if Opal will let me. I'd like to see Titus stay with Lily during the day."

"So would I." The radio buzzed. Ryder replied. "Hayes here. What's up?"

All Sophie could catch was a few fragments of words because he was using the earpiece.

"All right. Hold your positions. I'll be right over." His eyes narrowed on the amusement device where Lily was still happily jumping around and bouncing off rubbery supports.

"If you need to go, I'll watch Lily and bring her to you when her time is up." A chill skittered up Sophie's spine. "They didn't sight Carrie, did they?"

"No. Nothing like that. An elderly vendor caught someone shoplifting a pot holder. The buyer is insisting she bought it across the square. She's asking for me because she knows me. If it's who I think it is, she's older than Methuselah. She can wait a few more minutes."

The radio called again. Ryder made a face. "They're actually trying to hit each other now? Okay. I'll hurry." He turned to Sophie. "I won't be long."

"No problem. Which dog do you want to take with you?"

"Probably Titus. He's calmer. Is that okay with you?"

"Sure. Go. I've got this."

She could tell Ryder was hesitant. After he turned and started away he looked back several times. Nevertheless, Sophie was gratified that he trusted her with his daughter.

Shouting from the opposite side of the courthouse was starting to draw an influx of fairgoers. It sounded as if the fight had escalated. Leave it to two elderly women to start a ruckus over a pot holder.

Peering into the bounce house, Sophie didn't see Lily. She started forward. The operator stopped her at the rope fence. "No dogs."

"I just can't see my—my little friend."

"If I put her in there, she's still in there," he insisted. "Now back up, lady."

"This is a police dog," Sophie countered. "Let me through."

"You're no cop."

"No, but the dog is. And I'm with him," she argued.

"I don't care if he's the chief of police. You aren't allowed..." His eyes widened. Leaving her, he sprinted around the apparatus and out of sight.

Trying to figure out why he was agitated, Sophie continued to look through the heavy mesh for Lily. *There she was! Praise God.* But she had to stoop to see her.

That was what was wrong. The whole contraption was collapsing! Not only was it full of children, it was bound to be suffocating once the air leaked out.

Sophie raced toward the place where she'd seen the entrance. Elastic mesh was hooked to grommets in the thick plastic shell. If she could manage to get one or two of those open she could begin to rescue children.

They were starting to panic and call for their parents by the time she gained access. Adults crowding in behind her took children from her as she lifted them out and passed them back.

Phoenix remained beside her even though she'd had to drop his leash to free both hands. Pressure from above was starting to close the opening as support pillars lost form.

"Lily!" Sophie screamed. "Where are you?"

"Over here." The call was nearly swallowed up by the roar of the frantic crowd and the sound of the air compressor that was supposed to keep the structure full.

"Can you stand up?"

"No," Lily squealed.

"Then crawl to me," Sophie ordered, fighting to keep the exit open with her own shoulders and praying the child could make it before they were both crushed.

"I can't. I'm scared."

"You have to, Lily. I can't hold the door up much longer."

All Sophie heard in reply was weeping. Where was Ryder? Surely he must know he was needed here.

Crowding in beside her, Phoenix put his front paws on the curved edge of the base tube and barked.

"Yes!" Sophie edged aside and used all her strength to push a wider opening. "Go get her. Get Lily."

The dog slipped through the slit between the top and bottom of the structure without hesitation and plunged into the tighter space the way an agility dog would attack a flimsy fabric tunnel.

"Phoenix is coming to get you," Sophie shouted. "Grab his collar and let him bring you out. Lily? Lily, can you hear me?"

Passersby were shouting. Ryder overheard enough to make the hair stand up on the back of his neck. He outran his old dog getting back to Lily.

What he saw when he got closer was a disaster. The heavy rubber frame of the house was barely inflated. Gravity had forced most of the remaining air into the lower portions as the roof and ceiling collapsed. Locals and the operator of the attraction were trying to hold up one edge of the mesh opening while some fool…

His breath caught. That was Sophie. Her legs were kicking.

The reason why the trainer would have put herself in harm's way was immediately evident. Lily must be inside. And, as he listened, he realized a dog was, too.

Ryder flashed his badge and a path cleared in front of him. "What happened?"

"Pump musta failed," the operator said. "We got all the kids out but that crazy woman let her dog in."

"She would only have done that in an emergency," Ryder shouted. "Is there another way in?"

"No. All the other mesh is anchored solid. This is the only part that has a door."

"So far," Ryder said, leaving the others and racing around the four-sided structure. He could see through the rear portion. Lily and Phoenix were hunkered down in a corner that had yet to fully collapse. He couldn't see Sophie from there.

Several slashes with his knife made a hole in the elastic mesh without damaging the inflatable. "Here, Lily. I'm here."

She didn't move even though Ryder enlarged the hole and stuck his arm through. "You have to come to bring me the dog," he said. Nobody would get out of this alive if he had to crawl in and trap himself, too.

The perceived need to help her dog was enough to get Lily moving. She and Phoenix reached the opening together and the dog sailed through in one easy leap.

Ryder grabbed his little girl, pulled her out and held her close. There was no time to rejoice. Not when Sophie was still trapped.

The men who had been supporting the weight to relieve her were perspiring. Their hands kept slipping. He tapped one on the shoulder, said, "You. Help me," then commanded Titus, "Watch," so Lily would be guarded.

Each man grasped one of Sophie's ankles and began to pull. To Ryder's relief, she slid easily and came up dripping with sweat and fighting mad. "No! Let me go. I have to get Lily."

"She's out. She's safe. So is Phoenix," Ryder shouted, fending off her blows. The astonished relief on Sophie's face was more than welcome. It reconfirmed that she was also unhurt, although she was laboring to catch her breath.

As he helped her to her feet and steadied her, she threw her arms around his neck and began to sob. Ryder let her. He could feel tears of joy in his own eyes. Not only was his darling Lily safe and sound, this brave woman had risked her own life for her.

Overcome by the reality of what had just happened, he held Sophie close and stroked her back without hesitation. He didn't care if the whole town saw him and the rumors started to fly. No amount of thanks or hugs would repay this debt. He owed her everything.

At his side he felt the tug of a small hand. "Daddy?"

His arms opened. He bent down and scooped up the child he could have lost only moments before.

Sophie backed off barely enough to allow room for Lily, then wrapped an arm around her, too, and showered her with kisses.

Ryder did the same. He even made a few errors and

kissed Sophie's damp hair. When he thought about what could easily have happened, it chilled him to the bone.

"Hey!" the attraction's operator yelled. "You owe me for a ruined net."

Ryder ignored him until he added. "It wasn't my fault the thing collapsed. Somebody messed with my air pump!"

"Can you stand?" Ryder asked Sophie.

Sniffling and wiping her cheeks, she nodded.

"Then take care of Lily again. I'm leaving both dogs with you."

He used his radio to summon the rookies on duty and circled the apparatus. Parts of the large compressor looked dented but it seemed to be running okay.

Ryder put Shane in charge of setting up a perimeter and told James Harrison to use Hawk's bloodhound's nose to scout for evidence. Ellen Foxcroft and Carly, her golden retriever, tried to strike a trail but there had been too many people milling around for the dog to work well.

"Probably vandals," the operator remarked. "Kids love to hang around back here. I saw more of 'em today. It's not the first time they've fooled with my equipment. But it is the first time it's gone down so fast. I usually have plenty of time to evacuate. You should see my insurance premiums."

"Here," James called. "Look at this damage, Chief."

The operator stuck his head in to look, too. "You cops must've done that when you cut the mesh."

Ryder didn't bother arguing. He knew better. He might not have a clue who had stabbed the base of the inflated house but he knew it hadn't been him. If he ever got his hands on the kids who had thought it would be fun to bring down the attraction, he was going to lock them up long enough to make an impression they'd never forget.

He scanned the crowd, looking for guilty expressions. The only ones who seemed upset were the parents of the other children Sophie had saved. If the town didn't give her a medal for what she did, he might see about getting her one himself.

Returning to her and Lily, he saw that someone had given them bottled water. He smiled and patted Phoenix. "Good boy."

"I never taught him that," Sophie said proudly. "I suppose he could have picked it up by watching me training other dogs but it may have been instinctive. Either way, I was surprised when he followed my commands to get Lily."

"We play that game at home," Ryder told her. "I'm glad you sent him to live with us before today."

"Me, too."

"I want to thank you. For everything," Ryder said quietly. His vision blurred. "I could have lost Lily." *Or both of you.*

Sophie coughed and chuckled at the same time. "In case this ever comes up again, please keep in mind that I *hate* closed spaces."

"Noted. I hope it wasn't that far down when you crawled in."

"No. I saw it going and started to pull kids out." Her eyes widened. "I got them all, didn't I?"

"Yes. Lily was the last."

"You're sure?" Shivering, she glanced toward the police line. "If there's anybody still..."

"I'm sure. They took a head count as they went in and we've talked to the parents. The kids are all accounted for."

"Thank the Lord."

"I already did. And I thanked Him for you, too, Sophie. What you did was above and beyond. It took quick thinking and decisiveness. Most people stood there and screamed but nobody else acted."

She coughed again and grinned at him. "Just remember that the next time you accidentally get wet in the training center bath area."

It was impossible for Ryder to keep from smiling back at her. "After today, I might actually let you get away with it again."

"Often?" she quipped.

"Once," he said, faking a scowl. "You weren't amazing enough for twice." But she was, he reasoned. His heart swelled with the thought of her selflessness and he yearned to pull her and Lily back into his arms again.

Closing his eyes he thought, *Lord help me. And continue to protect those I love.*

The simple prayer shook him to the core. He couldn't argue, though. What he could do was continue to keep his distance and pray somebody took Carrie Dunleavy into custody soon.

He looked out over the crowd. Most of the fairgoers had resumed their meandering and stopped paying much attention to the deflated bounce house now that the excitement was over.

They didn't even seem to care that their chief of police had stood in the street embracing his daughter's pretty rescuer. Teasing from his own officers would come later, of course. That was a given. It wasn't them he was worried about.

Surely, if Carrie had returned to a town where she'd lived for years, somebody would have noticed her. There had been plenty about her crimes reported in the newspapers, both locally and statewide.

Except that she was the kind of person who was so plain, so unremarkable, she was practically invisible. For all he knew, dozens had stared right at her and paid no attention, especially if she'd made any effort at disguise.

Like it or not, in the mob they had in Desert Valley for this homecoming and fair, almost anybody who tried to move around undetected would succeed.

TWELVE

Sophie wasn't a bit surprised when Ryder took Lily to her babysitter's early. Between the radiating heat and the excitement, both good and bad, they were all wrung out.

She ducked under the colorful canvas canopy of a booth where a friend from church was selling cookbooks. "Whew! Shade."

"Here, have a seat. I need to stretch my legs."

Sophie gladly collapsed into the folding chair. "Thanks, Hazel. It's sure a scorcher."

The elderly woman laughed and patted her own brow with a tissue. "Honey, it's always hot here. I'd move up to Flagstaff in a flash if it wasn't for my aching bones."

"I guess there are advantages," Sophie agreed. "And it does cool off at night pretty well."

"Want more water, dear? I've got a cooler full."

"In a minute. First, Phoenix needs a drink." She bent over, gave the proper command and slowly poured water from her own bottle into her palm so he could lap it up.

"Smart pup you got there. I see he's one of them police dogs. It always surprises me that they don't all look like Rin Tin Tin. You know, German shepherds."

"A lot of war dogs are," Sophie explained. "We like

to use a variety of breeds for their specialized skills. I never turn down a dog that shows promise."

"What about them other dogs, the ones that help folks? You know, Ms. Ellen's."

"Companion dogs? For the most part they have a different temperament. They're more owner oriented and less outwardly concerned. It's hard to get a dog to open a door for you if he's more interested in barking at what may be on the other side."

"True." While Sophie relaxed and momentarily closed her eyes, Hazel turned away to wait on a customer for a cookbook. When she finished she asked, "What's wrong with him?"

Sophie straightened. Tensed. "Who?"

"Your dog. See?"

Phoenix pressed against her calf and stood as rigidly as a show dog in the judging ring. His ears perked, his body quivered.

Following his line of sight, Sophie saw nothing unusual. But clearly the dog did. Was he picking up vibes of danger or sensing something familiar? If she had worked with him longer she'd have had a better idea. Since his specialty was search and rescue, she wondered if Ryder was back. That was a possibility. So was the idea that another rookie officer and dog had come closer. Most of the animals got along pretty well with the exception of the ones trained for attack and apprehension. By necessity they had to have an edgy temperament.

Phoenix growled.

Sophie rose slowly, deliberately and stepped away from her friend, just in case.

"What's got his hackles up?" Hazel asked.

"Beats me. I'm going to walk around a bit. Thanks for sharing your shade."

"Anytime."

It would have pleased Sophie greatly to have spotted Ryder in the crowd. Not only was his presence comforting, he had their radio. Without him, she was cut off unless she chose to use her cell phone.

"What a great idea." She whipped it out and paged down to his name and number.

"Hayes."

"Where are you?" Sophie asked.

"Just coming up on the square. Is there a problem?"

Frowning, she continued to search for familiar faces. "I'm not sure. Phoenix alerted and I can't figure out why. I thought he might have seen you."

"Hang on," Ryder said. She heard him contacting the other officers by radio before he came back to her. "Might be he scented Ellen and Carly," he said. "They're over by the Friends of the Library used book sales booth. Why don't you join them? I'll be there in a few minutes."

"Okay. Thanks."

"Sophie?"

Waiting for him to continue speaking, she noticed that she had begun to feel as jittery as the dog was acting. "Yes?"

"Be careful."

"I am. It's just hard to see trouble coming when there are so many happy people all around me." *But better than having to go down a dark alley like the night Wes was shot*, she added to herself.

"You keep telling me that dog is as good as Titus. If you really think so, you need to trust him."

"I do. I'm on my way to the library booth. See you there." She ended the call and stepped out.

Phoenix kept pace, his side brushing her calf. He looked every inch a police dog on duty. Even if he had not been wearing his ID halter and vest he would have been formidable. With them, he was magnificent.

And extremely tense, she added, keeping a lookout. The formerly frightened animal had transformed into the working police dog she had envisioned when she'd first seen him. Even better, he was intuitive beyond measure.

So, what was he sensing? What familiar odor was he picking up that had put him on high alert? She had never introduced him to anything taken from Carrie's desk or her home, so it couldn't be that. Unless…

Sophie almost broke and ran for cover when she made a leap of reasoning. Phoenix had been with Lily in the bounce house and had exited near where the vandal had stood when he or she had slashed into it. Was he clever enough to have remembered that scent and recognized it again? It was normal for him to recall people he knew. Strangers were another matter.

She spotted Ellen and waved as she quickened her pace. Carly wasn't acting strange, yet Phoenix was. What did that mean?

They met beneath a bunch of balloons tacked to an upright board above the awning. "Boy, am I glad to see you're okay," Ellen told her.

"Yeah. You, too. Has your dog been nervous?"

"Not that I've noticed." The rookie officer eyed Sophie. "Maybe Phoenix is mirroring your mood. You're still keyed up."

That brought a sigh. "I suppose I am. I was afraid I

was going to run out of air in that stinky prison of rubber and plastic."

"But you saved a bunch of scared kids."

"By the grace of God." She kept searching the gathering. "Have you heard any more from the chief?"

"Not since a couple of minutes ago when he told us to keep an eye out for you," Ellen said.

"Radio and tell him I'm okay, will you, while I try to figure out what's wrong with this dog."

"Whatever it is, it seems to be catching," the rookie said. "Look at Carly."

Both dogs were now erect, alert and facing the same direction.

"I thought Phoenix might be reacting to the scent of whoever sabotaged the bounce house but Carly wouldn't be, would she?"

"She might. We took part in that search."

Sophie rested her palm on the butt of her gun, leaving it secure in the holster on her hip.

Ryder appeared in the distance with Titus at his side, bringing joy to her heart and calm to her nerves. She began to smile. Her partner was back. Their working relationship might be temporary but at least it would last for the weekend.

A bang sounded. The professionals ducked while most fairgoers merely looked around, confused.

One of the balloons arrayed above the booth had burst. Sophie was about to laugh at herself for being afraid when a second one exploded.

She shouted, "Shots fired. Everybody down!"

From Ryder's viewpoint the scene was chaos. All he could do was clear that portion of the street. It took several tries to convince revelers to take cover but he was finally satisfied.

A radio call assembled his staff. "Williams and Foxcroft say the shots hit that board up there with the balloons. Harrison, take it down and check for bullets. If you find anything, bag it and save it for the state crime lab."

"Yes, sir. Did you get your daughter out of here okay?"

Ryder nodded. "She's at Opal's." His gaze drifted to Sophie again. After the arrest of Stan Allen he'd thought she'd be safe. Now he was not so sure.

These shots had been even farther afield than the ones at the depot had. Still, if that was due to poor targeting, why had balloons burst every time? This shooter seemed to be aiming all right, just not at people. *Or at Sophie*, he concluded with relief. That had to be a good sign.

He approached her as soon as he'd put the others to work. "I think you should call it a day."

"Why?"

"Because you're not a cop anymore."

"As you keep reminding me," she countered, making a face. "It was my dog who alerted first."

Frowning, he studied the Aussie. "Really? Why would he?"

"I haven't figured that out yet. I thought it might be because he smelled the perp who slashed the bounce house but that seems a little far-fetched."

"Yes, it does. We never put him on that trail."

"Right. But Ellen had Carly tracking and she did perk up after we joined them. I suggest you and I stick together and let the dog go where he wants. He might strike a trail again."

"You're determined to stay here no matter what, aren't you?" When a smile lit Sophie's face and made her hazel eyes sparkle, he was positive.

"Well..."

"All right. But if one more thing happens, if you even sneeze, you're done. Understood?"

"Yes, *sir.*"

"And don't you dare salute me," he warned. "We've already provided enough material to keep the gossip mill running for months."

"Hey, it wasn't my fault I got stuck in the collapse and had to be yanked out."

Against his better judgment he slipped an arm around her waist and briefly pulled her closer. "No, but it was my fault I hugged you. I was so grateful I couldn't help myself. I still am."

"No problem," she quipped. "The next time I feel a good cry coming on I'll know whose shoulder to choose."

"Anytime," Ryder said.

"You mean that, don't you?"

"Absolutely." His gaze switched from her to the distance, where his men were taking down the board with the balloons. Once again, he could have lost her.

The notion of spending the rest of his life without Sophie in it was unacceptable. Even if they never progressed past being good friends, he wanted her around.

Now, all he had to do was see to it that nobody robbed him of the *second* woman he had ever loved.

As far as Sophie was concerned, it didn't matter where the dog led them as long as Ryder stayed beside her. She was less frightened than angry. This wasn't the last straw but it was getting close. There was only so much harassment one person could take. Of course,

Stan's attacks had been serious threats. But those were over now that he was in jail. The notion that he may have had accomplices had been refuted. He'd grieved his brother alone and his attempts at retribution had been committed solo. They were sure of that because he had proudly admitted to stalking Sophie and invading her home.

One unsettling thought made her touch Ryder's arm. "Stan didn't get out on bail, did he?"

"Not a chance. Besides, he hasn't been arraigned yet."

"Oh. I just thought maybe..."

"Pinning today's problems on him would be nice. Trouble is, he can't have done it." Ryder was shaking his head thoughtfully.

"Is it possible that the incident today involving Lily is connected in some way?" Sophie asked.

"We can't rule it out. It's normal to imagine conspiracies everywhere when we've experienced them before. Try not to let it get you down."

"Okay. I just wish we'd heard something about Carrie lately. The business with Stan was unfortunate because it distracted us."

Looking somber, Ryder nodded. "Anything that threatens you is distracting. That doesn't mean I can't do my job."

"I didn't mean that." She made a face. "Well, maybe I did, just a little. There's only so much your police department can do, even with the extra officers Marian is funding."

Again, he gave her a grim look. "Yes. And Ellen says her mother is starting to show real improvement. Doctors expect her to come out of the coma very soon."

"That's wonderful! I hated to keep asking poor Ellen

about it and make her keep telling me how bad Marian is doing."

"I know what you mean."

"So, what do you think will happen when Marian recovers? It's been months since she agreed to pay for all the rookies to stay to solve the murders. If she'd been conscious when Carrie's crimes were discovered, do you think she'd have withdrawn her support?"

"I don't know. It doesn't matter right now." Ryder paused at a street corner, deciding which way to proceed. Neither dog seemed inclined to patrol further. He shaded his eyes with one hand beside the brim of his cap. "Which way?"

Sophie shrugged. "Beats me. The four-legged officers seem to be ready for a drink of water and a nap in the shade."

"That makes three of us."

"Four," Sophie said. "I think my adrenaline is wearing off. I'm practically asleep on my feet."

"Which is why you should go home. Take a couple hours' break, then come back if you want to."

"I could freshen up, too," she added, glancing at her damp clothing and feeling the effects of perspiration.

Ryder gave her a lopsided smile. "Now *there's* a good idea."

"What? You don't appreciate the perfume of old plastic and sweaty kids? Imagine that."

"You could just go bathe the dogs again. I've heard that can be refreshing."

"Oh, have you?" The urge to apologize again for dousing him was strong. She squelched it. After all, he was the one who had brought it up this time and was acting as if he'd forgiven her. So why destroy the mood of camaraderie by being contrite, particularly since she didn't feel all that repentant any more.

"It would be simpler to use the facilities at the training center instead of going all the way home," Sophie said. "Is there a guard posted today?"

"Just Benny. He's stayed more alert since he was attacked a while back but he's not a young man."

"It still helps to have somebody there." She checked the street that led to where she'd parked her official SUV. "Walk me to my car?"

Ryder fell in beside her with Titus. "This poor old guy is really tired. Why don't you take him back with you and kennel him? I'll continue to work Phoenix. Maybe he'll alert again and I can figure out what upset him."

"Fair enough." Smiling, Sophie swapped the ends of the dogs' leashes and the K-9s switched places as smoothly as if they had recently practiced.

"I need to run more refresher courses soon," Sophie said as they strolled toward her parked vehicle. "These rookies need it and I have a long list of queries asking for retraining."

"Dogs or handlers?"

"Both." Sighing, she stopped beside her SUV. "What's going to be tough is making sure any department where they go is still in the market for a team, both K-9 and handler. Keeping these rookies here in Desert Valley for six months may have messed up their former plans."

"I'd thought of that. I'd never let myself be separated from Titus no matter what."

Sophie smiled. "That won't happen once he's retired and becomes your pet. I know how hard it is to let go of a wonderful companion and great student like Phoenix. Even though you'll be keeping him in town I miss having him at home with me."

At the mention of his name, the dog's ears pricked.

"Yes, you," she responded quietly. Breaking one of her own cardinal rules she patted his head while he was supposed to be working, then loaded Titus and bid Ryder goodbye.

The sight of the chief, standing tall with Phoenix at his side, almost choked her up. It didn't matter how many times she told herself that she was merely the dog's trainer, she felt a swelling of pride every time she was able to pair a great dog with a deserving officer.

The same went for Ellen's service dog project. Although the commands differed, the animal's willingness to listen was just as vital to success. All in all, Sophie had to repeatedly thank God for putting her in this place at this time and letting her do the work for which she was best suited.

Feeling gratitude, she drove toward the training center. If it weren't for criminals she'd be out of a job. Nevertheless, it would be awfully nice to have a respite from being shot at. That thought made her smile. Chances were that once Carrie Dunleavy was captured they'd all begin complaining about life being too dull!

Right now, however, when she was bone weary and in desperate need of a shower and clean clothes, not to mention a chance to wash her hair, Sophie was ready for a little R & R.

Habit made her check her rearview mirror. There was nobody there who looked dangerous. No black car with dark windows like the one that had been abandoned in the street when she'd cracked her head. No long, evening shadows that might hide rattlesnakes.

She should have been able to take a deep breath,

relax and chill out. Should have. But couldn't. Evident threats were not the worst kind.

It was the enemy who remained unseen that always proved the deadliest.

THIRTEEN

Now that the two most important people and one dog in his life were away from the street fair, Ryder was better able to concentrate. He'd argued with himself constantly that his capabilities were not affected by the presence of others, but the facts spoke for themselves.

Well, at least he wasn't ignoring the special ones in favor of focusing only on his job the way he used to. Yes, it was necessary to prioritize. But it wasn't always possible to separate earthly responsibility from God-given duty. Take Shane and Gina, for instance. He'd paired them for a reason. They were good together and, if parted, might worry about each other too much.

His pastor had recently preached that worry was a sin because it showed a lack of faith and trust in divine providence. Perhaps. Probably. Unfortunately, it was also a human trait and he was very human.

Human enough to fall in love again? Ryder asked himself. Maybe. Although it was also possible that forced proximity was affecting him, making him believe that what he felt for Sophie was love when it was actually deep concern.

All that was sensible. And logical. So why did his pulse start to speed when he saw her and why did his spirits lift when she smiled? Moreover, why did he feel devastated when he thought he might lose her?

His cell phone buzzed. "Hayes."

"We've had a possible sighting of the boys who slashed the blow-up house," Tristan said. "I didn't want to use the radio and take a chance of being overheard."

"Where?"

"East end of the square, near where it's piled up," he reported. "I guess they're admiring their handiwork."

"Copy. On my way. Keep them in sight but don't apprehend until I get there."

"Affirmative."

Wending his way through the thinning crowd, Ryder kept an eye on Phoenix, looking for a reaction. He got a strong one as soon as he stepped off the curb next to the collapsed attraction. The Aussie bristled, his hair sticking up between the straps of his vest.

As soon as the dog stopped, one front foot in the air like a bird dog, Ryder saw the teens, too.

They stopped laughing and jostling each other when one of them spotted the dog and pointed. All four boys exchanged glances. Ryder wasn't close enough to hear what they were saying to each other but their body language was clear.

He keyed his mic. "Move in. It's them."

The teens scattered as if they were a flock of wild birds and he was a circling hawk. He was glad Phoenix wasn't trained for apprehension because he wanted to bring these hoodlums down himself.

One jumped over a stroller, narrowly missing the baby in it, and sped off down the sidewalk, right into Tristan McKeller's arms. His yellow Lab, Jesse, helped and Tristan had him in custody immediately.

The second and third suspects went left together.

Shane and German shepherd Bella made short work of them.

That left a blond one for Ryder and Phoenix. The dog was almost as determined as his human partner. Zigzagging through a gathering of old-timers, sitting in lawn chairs and reminiscing, Phoenix followed the fleeing vandal step for step. Ryder released him and cut around to where he thought the kid would end up.

He was right. And almost too late. Ryder tackled the teen around the legs. Phoenix leaped on top of them both, barking and growling.

By the time the chief was back on his feet and had his prisoner ready to be handcuffed, the kid was crying like a baby. "I didn't do nothin'. It was all Sammy and Brad's idea. Honest."

"You got drugs on you?" Ryder asked.

"No, I swear."

"Prove it."

Reacting without thinking it through, the boy reached into the pockets of his jeans and came up with a handful of change, dollar bills—and a pocketknife.

Ryder smiled. "You're under arrest." Cuffing him he started to lead him away. "Since you're a minor, I imagine you'll want to call your parents."

"Hey, we was just foolin' around. You know. Kids can't be held for real crimes. They said."

He spun the youth and grabbed him by the shoulders to bring them face-to-face. "*Who* said?"

"Nobody, man, nobody. I was just tellin' you. You know?"

"What I know is that you and your buddies almost killed a bunch of little kids. That's assault, at the very least. About fifteen separate counts of it. And if I find out that somebody paid you to vandalize the ride, it'll be even worse."

"Hey, it was an accident. We didn't know it would go down so fast, man. Why are you so mad?"

"Because one of those kids was my daughter," Ryder said, reminding himself to behave professionally when what he wanted to do was turn this would-be thug over his knee then and there. Granted, he hadn't been a perfect citizen while growing up but he'd never endangered any lives. And he'd certainly never have done someone else's dirty work for any amount of money. That was the difference.

When he recalled the sight of Sophie, stuck half in and half out of the weighty apparatus, it made his blood boil. And the image of Lily, trapped inside, would be with him for the rest of his life. He knew that as surely as he knew his own name.

Anger is unproductive, Ryder kept insisting. Nevertheless, he was still riled when he turned his prisoner over to Shane, Tristan and the others.

"The booths will be closing soon and there shouldn't be any foot traffic until tonight when they have the hometown concert and street dance. I'll transport these prisoners to the lockup while the rest of you finish here. We'll regroup at the station at seven."

Nodding to James he added, "Since your girlfriend, Madison, is still hanging around looking for news for the *Gazette*, you can be the last to leave."

James Harrison nodded. "What about the booths for overnight? Most of the vendors are leaving their stuff right here."

"They say they have their own after-hours patrol," Ryder answered. "Personally, that suits me fine. Has anybody seen Sophie since I sent her to the training center to put Titus up and take a break?"

Each, in turn, answered in the negative. Ryder wasn't too worried. After all, they had Stan in custody and now the idiotic vandals were also out of commission. That left only Carrie Dunleavy and no matter how many old-timers and other locals he had asked, nobody had seen hide nor hair of her.

"Tell you what. Tristan, you're probably more than ready to go visit Ariel and that new baby. You take our prisoners to the station and I'll go to the training center. When you've locked them up you can go. I'll take care of the paperwork when I get there later."

"Yes, sir. Thanks. My sister, Mia, has been staying with Ariel but I need to check for myself."

"Understood."

Ryder certainly did understand. Although he had not ordered Sophie to come back to the square by a certain time, he'd expected her by now. Or sooner. She was the kind of person who always wanted to be in the thick of things.

He headed for his car with Phoenix at his side, not running but not dawdling, either. With each step his anxiety built.

By the time he was on the road back to the station, all he could think of was making sure that Sophie was all right. It would have helped if scenarios of danger and harm had not kept popping into his fertile mind.

If the following day of the street fair was half as troubling as this first day had been, he was going to need a long rest afterward. Preferably one that did not include nightmares of the former police department secretary. Carrie had been so clever, so unassuming, so good an actress, that everyone, Chief Earl Jones included, had never suspected her evil, manipulative side.

Chances were, that was the characteristic which would eventually bring her downfall. She'd wanted him enough to kill to get him. When that plan had failed she'd transferred her fatal fantasies to two other blond officers, murdering them in turn when they'd cluelessly ignored her. There had not been anything Carrie wouldn't try in the past. Her makeshift shrine to unrequited love had demonstrated that.

Nothing had changed. She might not be here yet but she would be. It was a given. And when she reappeared, Ryder and his officers were going to catch her.

They had to.

Sophie had showered and changed into the clean clothes she'd left in her locker at the training center. The cargo shorts and faded T-shirt were fine for kennel work but not up to the standards she felt would properly represent the K-9 Unit, so she didn't go back to the fair. Instead, she busied herself by cleaning pens, exercising pups by letting them play in the fenced yard and getting the evening meal ready for all her furry charges.

"This stuff actually smells good," she told the two German shepherds and three golden retrievers vying for position at her feet. "I must be really hungry."

Their response to her light conversational tone was to wiggle and jump and pant as if she were about to present them with the tastiest meal they'd ever enjoyed.

Sophie glanced at the wall clock. "It's half an hour early but I guess you guys can eat." Holding stainless steel bowls high she led the way to their nighttime quarters and edged the gate open with her foot. "Okay. Everybody in."

The eager pups not only entered, they sat for her. Well, almost. Their hind legs were bent but their rears were barely planted. "Is that the best *sit* you can do?" she asked, emphasizing the command.

Coming close and holding the position for a few seconds was good enough for dogs this young and excitable. Sophie was quick with the food reward and command to eat so they wouldn't lose control.

She was grinning as she closed and latched the door to their kennels. Puppies were always fed first because they had such a hard time settling down if they thought they might miss a meal.

A metal door clanked somewhere in the building. At least she thought it did. With so much barking and yipping around her she wasn't sure.

"This roof could collapse and I probably wouldn't hear it," she mused, still smiling. Many of the runs for older working dogs were empty because those K-9s were still out with their handlers. She fed some half-grown dogs she was testing for suitability, then went back for more food.

"It's just you and me, Titus," she told the old Lab as she passed his run. "So, what shall we have for supper? I'd like a steak, myself."

His otter-like tail thumped on the floor. Now that she was finished with the more rambunctious dogs, she opened his gate and let him walk with her into the kitchen area. "What does the chief feed you at home? I imagine it's not all kibble. You are probably spoiled rotten."

Panting so that his mouth resembled a smile, he gazed up at her and wagged his tail. "Uh-huh. I thought so. I'll give you a few treats to tide you over until your handler gets here. I'm sure he has something wonderful at home to eat." She thumped his broad back with the flat of her hand. "You don't look as if you've missed many meals."

"Woof."

"Exactly," Sophie joked, behaving as if he were agreeing with her. "The chief is a good guy. You should be thankful you ended up with him."

And so am I, Sophie thought.

She was scratching the mild-mannered yellow Lab's ears when he suddenly stopped panting. The fur at his ruff stood up, making him appear lion-like.

Sophie wished she'd closed the door from the runs because the constant noise was drowning out less prominent sounds. She stood still and strained to listen.

"I don't hear anything, Titus," she whispered. "Are you sure?"

A growl rumbled. What she couldn't hear, she felt as a vibration beneath her touch on his back.

"Okay. I believe you." Reaching for her holstered gun she realized she had taken the belt off when she'd showered and changed. That meant it was still upstairs in the break room, the apartment that had once belonged to her predecessor, another of Carrie's victims.

Thoughts of Carrie were enough to get Sophie moving. "Titus, heel," she whispered, knowing the well-seasoned dog would obey without fail.

Keeping her back to the walls as much as possible, Sophie inched into the office space, then down a short hallway to the stairs leading to the unoccupied apartment. Even if that was where the bothersome noises had originated, she needed to reach her gun. Laying it aside was a rookie move, one Sophie was not proud of.

Each step brought her closer to her goal. She would

have donned the uncomfortable bulletproof vest if it had not also been discarded with her dirty clothes.

Titus paced her most of the way, then stepped ahead at the last moment. Sophie reached to stop him and missed his collar.

The sound of a slamming door came from below. The dog hesitated. Cocked his head to listen. Then he left her, turned and galloped back down the stairs.

Sophie didn't know what to do. If there was a menace in the break room she needed to see about it. If Ryder or one of the other K-9 officers had just come in, however, it would be foolish to investigate by herself.

That would mean she'd have to admit to leaving her sidearm unattended, she realized. But this was not the time for pride over prudence. Wheeling, she followed Titus.

Ryder dropped Phoenix's leash and let him drag it while he greeted his faithful old Lab. When he looked up and spotted Sophie he didn't know whether to hug her or chastise her.

"Where have you been?"

"Here. Why?"

"I've been trying to call your cell for the last hour."

"Ah, well, that's a long story. When I came back to change, I took off my holster and vest and left them with the phone. I was just about to go upstairs to get them."

"Well, go." He could tell by the way she was shifting from one foot to the other that something else was up. "What's wrong?"

"Titus acted as if he'd heard somebody up there. We were about to see when you came and he forgot about everything else."

"It's not like him to abandon a search."

"He wasn't wearing his working harness so he probably figured it wasn't important. That, or he really is losing his edge."

"Maybe a little of both," Ryder said. He drew his gun. "You stay down here with the dogs. I'll go check it out."

"I left my stuff on the little table by the bathroom door," Sophie said. "Sorry."

"You're not supposed to have to defend yourself in here. Where's Benny Sims?"

"It's still too early for him to be on guard duty."

There had been a time when they hadn't felt the need for any extra protection, Ryder remembered with chagrin. Those were the days.

As he started for the stairway, he was totally alert. Each step was calculated, controlled. Using a two-handed approach he whipped around the corner into the upper rooms.

They were deserted. There was a lingering scent of flowery shampoo, undoubtedly a result of Sophie's earlier presence, but no prowler. No menace. Nothing out of place except the equipment she had left behind.

Ryder holstered his gun and picked up hers, handling it carefully. He was turning to go back down when he heard Titus and Phoenix begin to bark.

Sophie screamed.

A door slammed. Echoed.

Ryder sailed downstairs, his boots barely touching the wooden steps.

"Sophie!"

FOURTEEN

She flew straight to Ryder as soon as he reappeared in the stairwell. Though he did slip one arm around her waist he kept his gun hand clear. “What happened?”

“I don’t know.” It was embarrassing to have screeched like a dog that had tried to eat a beehive, but her nerves had been so on edge lately she was glad that was *all* she’d done. “You went upstairs, then the dogs started to bark and something crashed into me.”

“Did you get a look at whatever it was?”

“No. As soon as I hit the floor my so-called bodyguards were all over me.”

“I should have left Phoenix in harness. Titus is the one who really surprises me. I thought he had more sense.”

“Dogs can get senile. We don’t usually notice it because they don’t talk, but they may forget things.”

“Like chasing the bad guys instead of licking the victims?”

Sophie huffed. “Yeah. Something like that. I suppose, if they were really worried about me, they’d have given chase.”

“Not if they knew the prowler.”

“Carrie?” She could hardly make herself say it.

"Or one of the volunteers or cadets who help out. It could also have been a stranger, somebody who knew we'd all be busy at the street fair and thought it was a good time for a raid."

"Here? What were they after, kibble?"

"Or vests or ammo or even the dogs. You never know with crooks."

"True. It seems to me that if Carrie were involved she wouldn't have run off. She'd have confronted me or tried to hurt me."

"Logically, yes. Stay here. I'm going to go check the entire building."

Left with the dogs and rearmed for self-defense, she kept both of them leashed and close. Nevertheless, she was filled with relief when Ryder returned.

"Nothing?"

"Nothing. I'd already done a walk-through upstairs when you yelled. There was nothing wrong up there, either."

"Okay. We'll chalk it up to my nerves. Now that I think about it, it may have been Phoenix who bumped into me from behind and sent me flying."

"What changed your mind?"

"The fact that they didn't try to chase anybody. All they were interested in was licking me. Maybe they felt guilty."

"Or maybe you tasted good. Did you have a corn dog at the fair?"

"Hours ago. Titus and I were talking about getting a steak for supper before he alerted to the upstairs rooms. He thought steak was a great idea." The smile she had expected bloomed on Ryder's face.

"He would."

"Of course," Sophie quipped, "he's very smart." She

lowered her voice as if the dog might actually understand what she was about to say. "At least he used to be. I'm so glad you've agreed to retire him."

"Not so fast," Ryder countered. "He can still take part in things like stakeouts and help with tracking. All we have to do is make it easy on him."

"Speaking of which," she added, "what do you propose to do about Eddie, Dennis and Louise. Eddie's a little younger than the others but they're all vested so they can safely retire at any time."

"And make room for a few of the rookies who might want to stay on once Carrie is caught and we can officially tie her to Veronica's murder and the attack on Marian Foxcroft? I'd thought of that." He glanced at her. "So, how about that steak dinner? Minus the dogs. The Canyon Steakhouse serves a good rib eye."

Sophie blushed and made a face. "I can't go to a nice restaurant when I'm dressed like a refugee from a hobo jungle."

"You're not *that* bad." Ryder was chuckling.

"Thanks a heap, Chief."

"You're welcome. As soon as some of the others drift back to the station, I'll have a couple of them dust doors and the upstairs for strange fingerprints. Until then, you have time to go home and change."

Her eyes narrowed and she peered at him. "This is starting to sound suspiciously like a date. And I don't think that's a very good idea."

Laughing, he shook his head. "You have quite an imagination, Ms. Williams. Tell you what. I'll order a couple of large pizzas delivered to the station and you can come join us over there if you want to. Is that impersonal enough to suit you?"

"It's better, even if I won't get my steak," she said,

hoping she was successfully concealing her disappointment. Everything she'd said was true. They should not give anybody ideas about them dating, yet she couldn't help wishing he'd have argued with her about dinner, at least a little. He didn't seem to have trouble disagreeing about pretty much everything else.

As for the notion of a prowler, Sophie was beginning to realize that Ryder had been placating her.

He obviously believed she had imagined a threat this time—and maybe he was right. The whole town had been on edge for months, not to mention the heightened awareness once Carrie's crimes were identified and made public.

After the harrowing day she'd had, Sophie figured her own nerves had to be as overstimulated as those of a puppy chasing a favorite toy. She was a thinking, reasonable human being who needed to settle down and stop letting her imagination carry her away. If she kept calling for help when there was no need, Ryder and the others would soon stop racing to her rescue.

Oh, they'd respond. It was their duty. But they might not hurry enough to keep a real threat from ending her life. And she wasn't finished living. Not by a long shot.

Ryder kept his promise. He and Shane had time to discuss the day's events while rookies James Harrison and Whitney Godwin went with Officer Harmon to fingerprint the training building.

"You told everybody to use the side doors?" Ryder asked.

Shane nodded. "And to stay downstairs. Do you think they'll find any usable prints?"

"This time? No." Ryder shook his head.

"Then what scared Sophie?"

He shrugged. "I have no idea. The stress on all of us has been bad. It's possible she has the kind of mind that invents trouble."

"You don't really believe that, do you?"

Sighing, Ryder said, "Beats me. She hasn't acted like herself since the depot shooting. Trouble has followed her like a lonely pup."

"She was a cop once. Maybe she misses the excitement and is seeing danger everywhere."

"Possibly. But that doesn't explain everything."

"You mean since we arrested her late partner's crazy brother? Before that, the attacks come back to him. Right?"

Ryder's brow knit and he slowly shook his head. "I wonder. Do they? He hasn't admitted to anything besides making threats and breaking into Sophie's house. That leaves all the rifle attacks unexplained."

"So, he had two guns. He probably stashed the rifle after missing so often."

"What about today? In the square? Somebody else shot at those balloons right over her head."

"Somebody whose aim is a whole lot better," Shane reminded him. "If the shooter had wanted to hit one of us, he could have."

"I suppose so. I'll be anxious to get the ballistics report back. If we find out that the bullets at the depot match the ones fired at the training center and the fair, we'll have to rethink the whole scenario."

"You still think it's Carrie?"

"No. The MO doesn't fit her. She likes to be face-to-face."

Ryder could tell that the rookie was struggling. "Go ahead. Spit it out. Say what you're thinking."

"Okay. You asked for it." Shane cleared his throat.

"Think all the way back. Her first victim was shot, perhaps from a distance. Then one was pushed down the stairs. That was a hands-on crime. But the next was arson. Then Veronica Earnshaw was shot while microchipping a pup without a clue to who was about to kill her. Next, Marian Foxcroft was attacked and hit on the head. Once we ID'd Carrie as the perp—at least on Melanie and the rookies' murders because of the crazy evidence in her home—a rifle came into play. Seems to me our Carrie, if it is her, is an equal opportunity assassin."

"You may have a valid point."

"Thanks. Some of us have discussed it and we agree. Nothing is beyond that woman. We can't expect her actions to make sense to us when her thinking is so distorted."

Ryder shivered. "It makes me queasy when I think of all the delicious baked goods and other food she brought to work. There could have been poison in any of it and we'd never have suspected until it was too late."

"Only if she could have made sure you didn't eat any," Shane reminded him. "As far as we know, she still thinks you belong to her and fate will bring you together."

"Yeah. Too bad for her that psychopaths are not my style."

Shane chuckled at the bad joke. "Right. You prefer women who are so independent and spunky they only ask for help as a last resort."

"I wouldn't go quite that far." Nevertheless, Ryder was smiling and looking in the direction of the training center, a quarter of a mile away. He sobered. "I was afraid I'd lost Sophie when that inflatable collapsed. It could have suffocated her if bystanders hadn't helped hold it up until we could pull her out."

"Did you hear what you just said? You said, '*I* could have lost her,' not *we*. Sounds pretty personal to me."

"Slip of the tongue," Ryder alibied.

Shane laughed as the door opened and the rookies who were coming off duty filed in. Gina was with them and went straight to her fiancé. It did Ryder's heart good to see the couple so happy. Once this special assignment was over and Shane transferred to a permanent position the way he'd planned, Gina would go with him and Sophie would be short an assistant. Would she leave, too?

That idea settled in Ryder's chest like a boulder. Without Sophie to tease and laugh with, he'd be nearly as bereft as he'd been after losing Melanie.

"Not a good sign," he muttered to himself.

The pizzas were delivered just as Shane asked, "What?" saving Ryder from having to answer, and by the time everyone had grabbed a slice and settled down to eat, he figured he was going to escape having to explain.

Then Sophie walked in. Not only did the conversation lag, all focus turned to her. She had not only spruced up, she had tied her hair back, leaving ringlets loose around her face. Her cheeks were a natural pink, her lipstick rosy and her hazel eyes sparkling.

Greeting the group, she ended with Ryder and gave him the most beautiful smile he had ever seen.

His face warmed, and he grinned back at her.

Judging by the whoops and catcalls from his officers and others, he wasn't the only one who had noticed the mutual reactions.

But *he* was the sole problem. Carrie had already proved she'd do anything to have him for herself, including murder. Any personal changes in his life would have to wait.

Ryder grabbed a half-empty pizza box and held it out to Sophie, keeping her from coming too close.

"Your steak, Ms. Williams?"

She accepted a slice, held it up and made a face. "Looks like a poor substitute to me. Titus would be very disappointed."

So am I, Ryder thought. Keeping his distance from the attractive trainer was getting harder and harder. He didn't mind if his staff noticed. All he needed to be sure of was that their growing attraction didn't spill over to their times in public and give a practiced murderer another target.

Okay, I did my best, Sophie told herself. Short of dressing in her church clothes, she'd spruced up well. At least she'd thought so. And Ryder's initial reaction had been favorable. So why had he shut down as though he was sorry he'd acted glad to see her?

She'd bided her time long enough for most of the others to leave before she cornered him to ask. "Can I have a word with you, Chief?"

He finished cleaning up napkins and stuffing them in the empty boxes before he said, "Sure. I'll run this out to the Dumpster so the office doesn't smell like an Italian restaurant. Be right back."

"You can do that later," she insisted.

Ryder's left eyebrow arched. "Are you giving me orders?"

"Since you seem to need them, yes," she said flatly. Her insides were quaking but as far as she could tell, it didn't show.

"My office."

She preceded him, sensing his presence as he followed closely. When he shut the door, she had reached the edge of his desk so she turned and perched there, intending to appear casual.

"What won't wait?" he demanded, hands fisted.

The words she'd been rehearsing for the past hour deserted her and she was left with a disturbing void, both in thought and action. She clasped her hands in front of her. "Maybe this was a bad idea."

"Maybe it was. But I'm here now and I expect you to explain. Spit it out. What's on your mind?"

"You," she said honestly. "All the time. Night and day. On or off duty. And I wonder if I should have my head examined."

Ryder's slow progress toward her gave her hope—until he abruptly circled his desk, making it a barrier between them.

He sat, laced his fingers together on the desktop and looked up at her. "Has it occurred to you that by showing interest in me you are risking your life?"

Sophie rolled her eyes. "Oh, no, I never thought of that." Her voice rose. "Of *course* it's occurred to me."

"Then you understand."

"No. I don't. I can see not flaunting it but I'd sure like to know if my feelings are as far off base as Carrie's were. Do you like me or don't you?"

"Of course I like you."

The calmness of delivery and the lack of evident emotion in his affirmation made her wonder if he was merely being polite to placate a slightly unhinged coworker. That was certainly how it came across.

"Oooo-kay," she drawled. "And?"

Ryder took a deep breath and blew it out, apparently

making a decision. "And, it is killing me to have to stay away from you."

"Really? Why didn't you *say* so?"

"Because..." He paused to study his folded hands, then went on, "Because I was afraid to."

"Afraid *for* me or *of* me?"

"Take your pick. If Carrie got wind of my interest in you she'd do all she could to eliminate her so-called competition. Maybe she's already started. Plus, if you didn't share my feelings or decided to move away from Desert Valley, I wasn't sure I'd survive. It was easier to keep my distance and let everything else work itself out first."

"Very logical. You must have green Vulcan blood, Chief."

He chuckled wryly. "Because I want you to live long and prosper?"

"Something like that." Feeling her courage swell as the seconds ticked by, Sophie approached him. "Stand up."

Cautiously, he got to his feet. She could see his breathing growing more rapid, his cheeks reddening. The handsome, powerful, commanding man did have gentle, loving traits. She'd seen them when he was working with the dogs. And it was even more evident when he spoke about Lily.

Her own heart fluttered. When Ryder had claimed he'd be hurt if she left, he had touched a nerve. It was one thing to be hugged after a near escape and quite another to share a quiet, mutual embrace.

Slipping her arms around his waist she took the last step and laid her cheek on his chest. The rapid pounding of his heart echoed that of her own speeding pulse.

He didn't push her away, nor did he complete the affectionate gesture.

"Sophie, I..."

There were unshed tears in her eyes when she lifted her gaze and said, "If you aren't going to kiss me, at least give me a hug."

Ryder's arms tightened. She felt his warm breath on her hair, sensed him kissing her there. Until she had begun to fall for him she had not realized how lonely she was. Now? Now she was head over heels for a man who had been as lonely as she was and had only recently let down his guard. She didn't want to push him. She only wanted the affection she now knew he'd been withholding.

His hand stroked her cheek, his thumb whisking away a tear. He crooked a finger beneath her chin and lifted it.

Sophie had dreamed what his kiss would be like but her fantasy had fallen far short of reality. The touch of his lips was light, tender and warm, yet infused with a sense of love beyond anything she had ever imagined.

All too soon Ryder released her and stepped back. Resting his hands on her shoulders he said, "There. Now you know how I feel. All I ask is that we bide our time before we try to explore our feelings for each other any more. Please, Sophie?"

The best she could do was nod. No wonder he'd worried about Carrie's jealousy. This was no simple fling. She and Ryder were falling in love.

Hiding that much serious emotion from a stalker and murderer was not going to be easy.

Could they? Sophie seriously doubted it.

FIFTEEN

The following week passed without incident. A cleanup crew made up of volunteers from Desert Valley service clubs and other helpful individuals had Main Street and the square swept and scrubbed, looking cleaner than it had before the homecoming.

Ryder was dreading having to send Lily back to school soon because that would mean she'd be vulnerable until he or Opal picked her up in the afternoon. Worse, the child had developed a case of hero worship regarding a certain female dog trainer. He didn't mind the crush; he simply wanted to keep his daughter away from any possible source of danger.

Right now, he felt as if he, himself, posed the biggest risk. He'd often been told that it was easy to see how much he cared for Sophie, whether he denied it or not. If his friends and staff could tell at a glance, it was likely that any observer could.

Still, there had been no local sightings of Carrie and the state police were clueless, too. That was a good sign providing she was gone—a bad sign if she wasn't.

Office hours were usually more of a suggestion than a rule, particularly concerning the law officers, and Ryder was often the last to leave.

This particular day he had told Opal he'd be late picking up Lily because he was going to work Phoenix in the evening. There were several reason for choosing that time. The first was to take advantage of less daytime distraction. The second was to keep from being noticed spending extra time with Sophie.

Unfortunately, Opal phoned just as he was leaving his office. "Hayes."

"I hate to bother you, Chief, but my sister in Mesa's been hauled to the hospital. She's a widow and I need to go be with her. Can you come get Lily now?"

Ryder sighed, disappointed. "Sure. I'll be there in a couple of minutes. Is there anything else I can do for you? Do you need a ride?"

"I drove a jeep in combat," Opal countered. "I think I can handle my own transportation. But thanks for asking."

"Well, if you need anything, just give a holler."

"I will. And while I'm gone, you might consider leaving Lily with Marilyn Martin. She already watches Shelby for Whitney Godwin. She's real good with kids and I hear her place is real nice."

"I'll think about it. I just have to cancel my appointment tonight and I'll be on my way."

"No real rush," the older woman told him. "I'm not packed yet."

"Okay. See you soon."

Assuming that Sophie had been looking forward to their training session as much as he had, Ryder decided to stop by the training center instead of phoning to cancel.

The moment he saw her begin to grin at him he wished he'd called. Seeing her enthusiasm for his presence and then having to turn around and leave was going to be disappointing.

"You're early," she said.

He nodded. "Something has come up. I can't make it tonight."

Sophie's arched eyebrows predicted argument. "Why not?"

"Opal has to leave town and can't watch Lily."

"Then bring her with you," Sophie countered. "You know she loves to work with the dogs. We can put her in the puppy pen and let them play while we train Phoenix."

"She would love that. I just…"

"Benny Sims will be on guard duty by the time the others leave. If you're nervous about it, keep one of your regulars around as backup. Eddie Harmon's always looking for overtime. Those six kids of his keep him broke."

"I suppose I could do that," Ryder said soberly. "If I can get a second officer to stand guard tonight then okay, I'll be back with Lily. If not, try to understand?"

"I do." Sophie approached slowly and laid a warm hand on his forearm, sending electricity shooting up Ryder's spine. There was unspoken pleading in her gaze.

It was all he could do to keep from pulling her into his arms and kissing her over and over. Judging by the misty look in her hazel eyes she was having equal trouble resisting the urge for closeness—for the affection and total acceptance that had been missing from both their lives for all too long.

"My dogs are in the car. I hate to drive all the way home to drop off Titus. How about I bring him back with Phoenix? If tonight works out, I mean."

Her smile returned. "Sounds fine. Titus can nap while he's here."

Stepping away, she removed her hand from Ryder's arm and he immediately felt the loss. He'd make tonight work. He had to. Everything in his heart and mind insisted.

They'd train mostly inside, he reasoned, staying out of sight of the public and setting up tracking scenarios for Phoenix. Lily might even be able to help. The eager dog could track her the way he did at home when they played hide-and-seek. Both the dog and the child would love it.

Instead of going through dispatch, Ryder called Eddie personally. When he begged off due to a birthday party for one of his kids, Ryder contacted Dennis Marlton. He was free and agreed to work overtime.

That settled it. Elated, Ryder called the training center to assure Sophie he and Lily would be there. "I'll need to feed her," he told the trainer. "Are you up for another pizza? Lily's been asking for one ever since she found out she'd missed the feast we had at the station after the fair."

"Sure. I'm easy to please," Sophie said. Ryder could tell she was grinning as she spoke.

"Okay. It's a date. You get me, a spoiled rotten kid and two dogs, all to yourself."

"Sounds like the perfect combo," Sophie gibed.

Ryder hoped she'd still think so after Carrie was captured and they could meet openly and socialize like normal people.

He was no stranger to the kind of stressed friendships trouble often brought about. Nobody thought clearly in the middle of a traumatic situation, and although no one had taken potshots at any of his staff or the trainers lately, that didn't make the emotional upheaval go away. Only time, and the capture of their nemesis, would do that.

So, where was Carrie Dunleavy?

Instinct made him glance in his rearview mirrors. Nothing was out of place. Nobody was following him.

Nevertheless, he continued to watch. Letting down his guard now would be more foolish than walking into the line of fire without his bulletproof vest.

Sophie heard Lily coming before she saw her. The little girl was singing at the top of her lungs and skipping down the hallway. Titus followed obediently while Phoenix ran interference in front of her.

Bringing up the rear was the chief, carrying a pizza that reminded her how hungry she was. "Wow, that smells good. Glad to see you all made it."

"Everything been quiet around here?"

"Totally. Dennis is out back. You probably passed Benny when you came in."

"We did. Lily promised him a slice of pizza. I hope we don't starve after she gives all our dinner away."

"I doubt that will happen," Sophie said, chuckling and leading the way to her office. "Unless we step away from the box and a certain Australian shepherd helps himself."

"He's stopped stealing food at home," Ryder reported. "I won't guarantee that my softhearted daughter won't slip him something, though."

Sophie took a moment to caution Lily. "Onions are bad for dogs and spices can sometimes hurt their tummies, so it's not a good idea to let them eat from the table." She made sure to keep smiling so the girl wouldn't feel too chastised. "I teach all the police dogs a special command about eating that helps keep them from getting poisoned. After we're done, I'll teach you how to feed him from your hand the right way. Okay?"

"Okay!"

"If I get you a paper plate do you think you can take Benny his piece by yourself?"

"Uh-huh."

Sophie prepared the plate, then cautioned Lily to use two hands while she and Ryder restrained the dogs. She caught him gazing fondly at his daughter as Lily walked away, taking great care to properly balance the flimsy plate.

"Kennel," she said, trusting Titus to obey but keeping a hand on Phoenix's collar just in case. To her delight, Ryder followed them. He'd stuffed his hands in his pockets and looked nonchalant but she figured he had to be at least as uneasy as she was.

Closing and latching the gate to the dog run she turned, not at all surprised to find him close behind. "Shall we get this over with so we can enjoy our meal," she asked.

"Get what over with?" His words may have been questioning but his facial expression was all-knowing.

"Another kiss," she said, noting added warmth that had nothing to do with the outside desert temperature.

"You liked the first one?" Ryder drawled.

"It was passable." That line would have been funnier if she'd been able to deliver it without giggling.

"Well, if you insist."

Sophie didn't need any more of an invitation. She slipped her arms around his neck and stood on tiptoe. There was no awkwardness, no hesitation. They kissed as if they had been practicing for years. Her only regret was that they had not.

It was Ryder who stopped them. “I suggest we cool it. Lily is already wondering when I’m going to get her another mother. Opal planted the idea.”

Speechless, Sophie averted her gaze. *Mother?* That meant marriage, and although she was pretty sure she was in love with Ryder she wasn’t convinced she’d be a good mother for anybody. She certainly hadn’t grown up with an adequate role model. Was it possible to learn to be a good parent or did a person have to absorb it via experience?

She broke away and headed back toward her office. Not only was the pizza still there, Lily was already picking bits of sausage off the top.

“Hey,” Ryder called. “No fair. You have to share with us, too.”

Instead of smiling the way Sophie had expected her to, Lily made a grumpy face, said, “Whatever” and plopped down into a chair with her arms crossed.

The moment Sophie’s eyes met Ryder’s she knew. They both did. The little girl had come back before they had expected her to and had seen them kissing. That had to be why she was pouting, since nothing else unusual had taken place.

“I’ll get you a plate and your own serving,” Ryder said. “Which one do you want?”

“I’m not hungry.”

“Fine. It can sit here until you are. Sophie and I are going to eat.”

Ryder seemed to make a point of keeping his distance after that. Sophie fully understood. It didn’t matter if the child had voiced a desire for a new mother, seeing her daddy paying special attention to any woman had to be a shock. After all, Lily had had Ryder all to herself her entire life.

I can love her through it, Sophie decided. *No parent is perfect. If I do my best and take advice from women with experience, like Opal, I'll be a good mother.*

Providing Ryder doesn't decide to drop me to make Lily happy, she added sadly. That was always a possibility. Her own parents had chosen to abandon her so why should anybody else behave differently?

This is a terrible way to think, Sophie told herself. She already had a good, productive life and a career she loved. If God didn't choose to bless her with more, so be it.

The pizza began to taste like cardboard and she was barely able to choke it down. One look at Lily told her the five-year-old wasn't in any better mood than she was.

Poor Ryder. His efforts at placating his daughter weren't working, and now his supposed girlfriend was moping, too. The guy had to be at his wit's end.

And, as Sophie had learned long ago, the best antidote for a bad mood was spending time with dogs. They loved without question and commiserated when necessary.

Catching Ryder's eye, Sophie nodded toward the kennel area. "Weren't you going to show Lily the new puppies?"

"That's right. I was." He reached for her hand and gave enough of a tug to draw her to her feet. "You get the training session ready while we go look at pups."

"Gladly." It was Sophie's fondest hope that the father would use his time alone with his daughter to try to smooth things over, although it might be better to wait and let Lily adjust slowly.

Or not at all. Sophie wanted to slap herself for having such negative thoughts. Normally, she was far more upbeat. More self-confident. That happened when she felt comfortable and in her element with the dogs. People were another thing altogether. Hard to understand. Unpredictable and untrustworthy. They had been for as long as she could remember.

Some, like Carrie Dunleavy, were more than that, she concluded. They weren't just unknowable. They were evil to the core.

She shivered. The building was deserted except for her and the Hayes family. And the dogs, she reminded herself. Always the dogs. The one—the only—reliable element in her life.

Ryder thought about having a serious talk with Lily and decided against it. At this point they only suspected what was wrong with the girl. If he brought up his tender feelings for Sophie and that wasn't the reason Lily was sulking, he'd be adding to her melancholy.

"Stay in here with the puppies as long as you like," Ryder told her. "I'll put Titus right next to you and I'll be in the training room teaching Phoenix how to track for search and rescue."

"He already knows," Lily grumbled. "I taught him."

"I know you've played that game. What we need to do now is make sure he knows what we want when we tell him and can pick out the right scents."

"He's not as smart as Titus."

"They're both good dogs," Ryder argued, giving the arthritic old dog a clean blanket to lie on. "You were too young to remember what Titus was like when I first got him but he had to learn, too. For the same reasons you have to start back to school soon."

"I don't wanna go to school. I wanna stay with Opal."

Was *that* what was bothering Lily? "Well, you can't do that right now so get over it. Opal's sister needs her."

"I don't want a sister. Ever," Lily declared, surprising Ryder again. This was a kid who had once begged him to get her a baby sister or brother. Clearly, nothing he said or did was going to please her tonight. Actually, she reminded him of Melanie; like on the night she was killed. He had had to work late and rather than wait a few minutes for him to give her a ride, she had stomped off toward home, carrying the fancy dress she'd picked up at the cleaners.

Remembering that detail wasn't enough to smash all his guilt but it did put a serious dent in it. If Melanie had waited for him she might have lived, at least then. Given Carrie's mental illness, she would probably have found a way to eliminate his wife eventually, no matter what he had done or not done.

Which reminded him of Sophie. After closing and latching the kennel gates he hurried back to her.

"How's she doing?" Sophie asked, clearly concerned.

"She's sulking because Opal had to go away, I think. I'm either going to bring Lily to work with me or put her in that day care Marilyn Martin runs."

"I understand Whitney uses her so she must be fine."

"That's what Opal said. I just have a terrible time letting go. It's as if I'm seeing Melanie in Lily and wondering how long it will be before I lose her, too."

"I see."

Ryder cupped her shoulders. "I don't think you do. I'm not looking for another Melanie. It's worrisome enough to see Lily acting so much like her mother."

"I thought you two were happy."

"We were. But we were young and headstrong. The time we had together was cut short before we'd really come to terms with a shared life. I'd hoped having a baby would mellow us both out."

"And then you had to raise her all alone."

He nodded. "Yes. Opal taught me a lot. She was a good influence on Lily. I just wonder if she hasn't spoiled her."

A knowing grin spread across Sophie's face. "And you haven't?"

When Ryder's pager buzzed, he considered it a rescue from having to admit a fault. He checked in by radio, then told Sophie, "There's a major traffic accident out on the westbound."

"Will you have to leave?"

"No. I'm not needed. We may eventually have to kick Marlton loose, but I'm not going anywhere."

The look of relief on Sophie's pretty face warmed his heart. She wasn't the kind of woman who would resent him for doing his duty, but it was evident she wanted him to stick around. That was the best of both worlds. Someone who yearned for his company, yet was willing to let him go without pitching a fit.

That had been another sore point between him and his late wife, Ryder recalled. Melanie loved him. But she didn't want to share.

Just like Carrie Dunleavy.

SIXTEEN

It pleased Sophie when Phoenix successfully followed a scented drag through the building to the box where she'd hidden it.

"He's good," Ryder commented, giving the dog's silky ears a scratch and patting him on the head.

"I think he's great. How about trying him outside?"

"It's too well lit."

"That's what switches are for," Sophie teased. "When they're flipped up, lights come on. When you flip them down, the lights go off. Trust me. I can make it dark in the yard."

Ryder gave her a look of disgust. "You have a serious problem with your sense of humor, lady. It's warped."

"You're just now noticing?" To her delight, he laughed softly.

"Tell you what," she said. "How about seeing if Lily wants to be our missing person and hide while I give Phoenix a drink of water and let him rest?"

"Not out there. In here. I'm not comfortable with risking her or the dog in the training yard."

"Not even with the lights off?"

Ryder shook his head. "Not even with the lights off."

"Okay. Have it your way. I'll make a pass through

to check with Benny and Officer Marlton, then hold Phoenix back there until you're ready."

"Where shall I hide her? In the keyhole under your desk?"

Sophie was chuckling as she clamped her hands over both of the Aussie's ears. "Shush. Don't tell him."

"Right. You think he understands English?"

"Some. He headed right for my refrigerator the first time I mentioned food."

"That's not really as ridiculous as it sounds. Titus knows Lily by name."

"Of course he does. When I was a kid, I had to spell to keep my dog from figuring out what I was doing. He was my best friend."

"Dog friend, you mean."

Sophie gave him a wistful smile and explained. "No. Any friend. He lived up to the name Buddy all the time. He even defended me from my own parents a few times." She waved her hands in front of her as if erasing her words. "Forget I said that."

The wary look in Ryder's eyes as he turned to go get his daughter convinced Sophie he would never forget her telling admission; one, because it had shocked him and two, because it was part of her background and would undoubtedly affect her for the rest of her life. She had learned to be wary. Untrusting. And cautious beyond normal boundaries due to her dysfunctional upbringing. If nothing else kept him from regarding her as a potential mate, that would.

Remembering how Shane had managed to overlook Gina's mentally unbalanced fraternal twin brother and form a lasting relationship made Sophie both happy and sad. She was happy that two nice people had found each other, yet sad that she, herself, felt so isolated and alone.

"It's high time for a puppy session," she told herself, hoping Lily had received the same kind of emotional relief by keeping company with the exuberant youngsters. If anything could lift spirits it was a lap full of warm, squirmy pups.

There had been times when her predecessor, Veronica, had caught Sophie sitting on the floor of one of the runs, laughing and letting puppies crawl all over her. Such behavior had not pleased the inflexible head trainer but Sophie had continued to do it during her breaks, anyway. It was a good way to socialize the dogs and the best antidote for loneliness.

Speaking of which… She checked her watch and wondered if she should make another round between the two guards just for something to do. Neither had reported any problems and Benny had even been awake when she'd contacted him.

Although she and Ryder had only been apart for a few minutes, Sophie missed him terribly. Judging by the tension in Phoenix's leash, he did, too. That was a good sign. They had obviously bonded as handler and K-9 should. Instinct had told her they'd be perfect for each other so that was a gold star for her, too. She knew she had a gift for making successful pairings the same as Veronica had, only in Sophie's case she did it more by gut feelings than by strict rules. Thankfully, her junior trainer, Gina Perry agreed. Good training was part science, part intuition.

Sophie shivered. If Carrie had been a mad dog instead of a human murderer, she might have discerned enough to have stopped her years ago.

And now? Now, it was no secret that Carrie was guilty. The senses Sophie needed now were ones that would telegraph danger in time to head it off.

The problem was, all the previous attacks had left her so jumpy she no longer trusted her own sensations of apprehension and fear.

Such as those which she was feeling right now.

Ryder found his daughter curled up on the clean blanket with Titus. She had apparently tired of the rambunctious puppies and had let herself out so she could join the more peaceful dog. His ribs rose gently with each breath and cradled Lily's head as they both snoozed.

The dog detected him, opened one eye and thumped his tail. Crouching, Ryder petted him. "Good boy."

God, please watch over Lily, Ryder prayed silently. He had always said special prayers for his only child but lately they had become a lot more frequent and tinged with a touch of desperation. If he was this worried about her well-being at five, what would it be like when she was fifteen?

Titus's panting awoke Lily. She rubbed her eyes. "Can we go home now?"

"Pretty soon," her father told her. "I want to stay in town a little longer. There's a bad wreck out on the highway and they may need me."

"Oh." Cuddling against the warm dog she closed her eyes again.

"Would you like to help us train?" Ryder asked.

"No."

"You can hide and let Phoenix find you."

"Uh-uh."

"There's pizza left, too," he added, slightly relieved when she sat up. "We could warm it for you."

"Can Titus come, too?"

Ryder wasn't about to argue. "Sure. You can give

him your crusts as long as you eat all the good stuff off first."

"*She* said *no*." Lily glared toward the offices.

"That was for Phoenix. Titus is going to be staying home with us more from now on so we can treat him like a pet."

"Okay." The child was on her feet, stretching and yawning, in seconds. To Ryder's amusement, the old dog mimicked her. Letting Titus trail them he took Lily's hand. "How did you manage to get the gates open? I thought you were too short."

"I'm big."

"You certainly are. But that catch is outside."

"It was open already."

"That's impossible."

She shook her blond curls. "Uh-uh. It was open. All I had to do was jump up and knock the handle over."

Doing his best to mute his disbelief, he continued to press her. "What about the one for Titus?"

"It wasn't fastened, either."

"Okay." Leading her back to the office, he remembered that Sophie was waiting out of sight with Phoenix. She'd been in the kennels after he had clipped those gate latches. Maybe she'd undone them without thinking. He'd ask her ASAP. In the meantime, he had a test to set up and a hungry child to finally feed.

"Do you want your pizza nuked?" Ryder asked Lily.

"No. That makes it too hot to eat. Titus doesn't like it that way."

Ryder had to smile. "All right. We need to find a good place for both of you to hide so Titus doesn't tell Phoenix where you are."

"I know." Lily brightened. "Upstairs!"

"I'm not sure that's a good idea."

"Awwww."

"Sophie is right. I'm a sucker for you," he muttered. "Okay. Bring your supper and follow me. I'm not letting you go up there without checking it, first."

"You'll stink up the trail," Lily said wisely.

She may have put it crudely but she was right. "Then you'd better pick a place down here, because I'm not going to let you hide until I check where you'll be."

Lily tiptoed across the room and peeked into one of the large crates they used for training.

It was going to be an easy tracking task but at least it was safe, Ryder reasoned. "That's perfect. You and Titus get inside and be very quiet. And don't let him steal your supper."

"Okay, Daddy."

A grin spread across Ryder's face as he left to fetch Sophie. He didn't have the keen senses of a tracking dog but even a human could smell that aromatic slice of pizza. If Phoenix failed this test he belonged on a farm herding sheep the way his ancestors had.

After a glance back to be sure all was well, he left the room. By the time he reached Sophie his pager had sounded again. The officers at the wreck were asking for more backup and additional ambulances.

Sobering, he greeted her smile with a frown.

"What's wrong? Is Lily okay?"

"She's fine. Eating, actually. But I may have to cut Marlton loose to respond to that earlier collision. Apparently the pileup was hit again by at least two speeders and it's pretty bad out there."

Sophie gently touched his arm. "Do you have to go, too?"

"I hope not." He managed a lopsided smile for her benefit. "Come on. Bring Wonder Mutt. If he can't find a kid eating pizza and hiding with another dog, he's not the search and rescue tracker we'd hoped."

"I'm not worried."

Neither was Ryder. At least not about the K-9's tracking abilities. He had plenty of other things on his mind that kept his gut tied in knots. Such as whether he was neglecting his sworn duty by not responding to the multivehicle accident. Recent reports had specified needing more traffic control, not another chief officer. If that changed, he'd have to leave Lily behind for her own good. No way was he taking his little girl to a grisly accident scene.

Sophie had concerns about the victims of the traffic collision and had silently prayed for them when the first reports had come in. She had faith in the first responders, too. Desert Valley law officers and firefighters had a sterling record. They were extraordinary, particularly for such a small town.

She led the way back to the office area and paused at her desk. "Do you want me to use the pizza aroma or do you have something of Lily's for Phoenix to smell?"

Ryder presented a small, pink sweater. "Here you go. She keeps insisting she's not cold but she was curled up with Titus on a blanket out back."

"Cute. You should have snapped a picture with your phone," Sophie said, smiling. "Stand back. Here we go."

Instructing the dog to sit and watch her, she carefully presented the sweater and let him sniff it thoroughly. Then she commanded, "Seek."

In her peripheral vision Sophie saw Ryder shift. She was the one who was supposed to be nervous, not him, and she was amused until he shouted, "Hey!"

"What's the matter?"

"He's going the wrong way. Lily's in that crate over there."

"Well, she has walked through here several times tonight. It's a forgivable mistake. Let's let him sort out the newest scents from the previous ones." Giving the dog his head, she let him take her where he would. "This is one reason I thought we should do the test outside. She hadn't been running around in the training yard today."

Phoenix cast back and forth in a sweeping motion, moving forward with care. Ryder's pacing and fidgeting was beginning to get to her. "Stand still, will you? I'd be confused, too, if I thought you were trying to direct me and the instructions went contrary to what my nose was telling me."

"He's way off."

"Fine. Then we'll end this before you come unglued. Go get your pizza lover and bring her out."

As Sophie restrained Phoenix, Ryder jogged across the room and bent over the crate. When he straightened a moment later, his face was ashen and his eyes wide. "She's gone."

"What do you mean, gone? Are you sure that's where you put her?"

"Of course I'm sure." He spun in a full circle.

Sophie had already approached the crate and redirected Phoenix by the time Ryder said, "Turn the dog loose."

More urging wasn't necessary. The Aussie was almost pulling her off her feet as she struggled to unclip the long leash. His straining reminded her of a sled dog in an Alaska race.

Phoenix would have knocked Ryder down if he hadn't jumped aside. Once the dog struck the new scent trail, he careened around furniture and bounded up the stairs to the second story.

"I told her *not* to go up there," Ryder shouted.

He was so close behind when he yelled, he startled Sophie into stumbling. The excited canine disappeared around the corner at the top of the stairs in a blur.

Sophie yearned to be able to assure Ryder his child was safe but she kept silent. All she managed to mutter was, "Please, Jesus," over and over.

They topped the staircase at the same time. If Ryder had not grabbed her arm she might have been knocked down in his rush to shoulder past her.

"Lily! Lily, where are you?" he called.

Sophie raised her free hand. "Shush. Listen."

"I don't hear a thing."

"That's because you're making so much noise," she countered. Now that she was back on solid flooring she shook loose from his grasp.

"Where's that fool dog," Ryder roared, racing from room to room of the small, converted apartment.

Sophie stifled a grin and paused to catch her breath. For a guy who was the epitome of a calm, cool, sensible police chief, he was a basket case as a father. She snagged his arm when he ran past for the second time. "Stop!"

"I have to…"

"You have to stop and think and listen," she said, keeping her voice soft so he'd have to be quiet or miss what she was saying. "I hear giggling."

"I don't."

"Hold your breath before you hyperventilate. I think both dogs may be hiding with Lily. That's why we can't see Phoenix."

Ryder released the air in his lungs with a whoosh. His shoulders sagged. "I hear it, too, now."

Bending over and resting his hands on his knees, he continued to gasp as if no amount of air was enough.

Sophie placed a hand of comfort on his back and called, "You win, Lily. You and the dogs fooled your daddy."

The child didn't pop out of hiding but her laughter increased, soon to be accompanied by a bass woof from the old Lab and a tenor whine from Phoenix.

As soon as Sophie opened the closet where she stored equipment, all three tumbled out.

Titus plopped down on the rug, panting. Phoenix bounded around the room. Lily emerged, laughing and clapping hands sporting traces of tomato sauce, then ran straight to her father.

Ryder dropped to his knees, arms open to her, eyes glistening.

Sophie didn't want to embarrass him but she couldn't look away. The sight of father and daughter together was too precious, too awe inspiring.

What would it be like to be loved that much?

To have a parent who truly cared?

Ryder wanted to scold his little girl but he simply could not bring himself to do it. He was too glad to see her. And too ashamed of his show of weakness in front of Sophie. She must think he was a raving lunatic, like Gina's brother Tim had been when they'd apprehended him. Of all the times in his life when he'd been caught off-kilter, this was the first incidence where he'd lost his perspective. All he'd been able to think about was finding Lily the way he'd found Melanie. For a few terrible moments he'd thought that tragedy was happening again.

His cell phone rang as they were all making their way back down the stairs. Because he was carrying Lily on one hip he let it go to voice mail.

"You should get that," Sophie said.

"I will. Just give me a second." *A year would be better*, he thought, chagrined. Raising this child was bound to have turned him gray by then, not that it would stand out in his blond hair.

He gave her another squeeze. She protested. "Da-a-a-d. I'm not a baby."

"You don't act very grown-up, young lady. I told you not to go upstairs."

"You said it needed to be checked. So I took Titus." She beamed at the old dog. "He did a good job, huh?"

"I hope so," Ryder said.

His attempt to hand Lily off to Sophie met with little arms wrapping more tightly around his neck so he pulled out his phone and sat with the child on his lap. The voice mail message required a prompt reply.

Eyeing Sophie, he paused. "Sounds like they do need another chief after all. Opal's long gone by now. Any chance you can look after Lily for me? I shouldn't be out there long."

The child wailed, "No, Daddy. I'll be good. I promise."

"This has nothing to do with not obeying me," Ryder insisted. "An active accident scene is no place for kids. The officers and paramedics on scene need me to coordinate evacuation of the latest victims. It's not only ugly out there, it's not safe for you."

Instead of listening to reason, Lily wailed. "Nooooo."

"The dogs are staying here with Sophie," he offered. "Don't you want to be with Titus?"

She did him the favor of a sniffle and a nod.

"Well, then, get down and let me return this call. The sooner I go and do my job, the sooner I'll be back."

"You always leave."

"And I come back. Remember that, honey." If she had been old enough to have remembered Melanie he thought she might have argued, but she didn't. A baby whose mother hadn't been around to raise her was bound to be confused despite Opal's heroic efforts as a surrogate.

How hard might it be for Lily to accept a younger substitute? he wondered. Perhaps someone like Sophie. They certainly seemed compatible. And he felt affection for her. She was not only loving and understanding, she was fun to be around. Her approach to life might be a tad odd but it was never dull.

Ryder bent and stared into his daughter's beautiful blue eyes. "All right, Lily. This is how it's going to be. I'm going to go out to the accident scene and you're going to stay here with Titus, Phoenix and Sophie. Period."

She hung her head. "Yes, Daddy." Eyes widening, she apparently thought of an excuse. "What if I get tired? Where will I sleep?"

"You seemed to do just fine bunking with Titus in the kennel. If Ms. Sophie says you can sleep inside, you have my permission to keep both dogs with you."

"And the puppies?"

He could tell Sophie was struggling to keep a straight face. "Don't push it," Ryder said with a smile. "Two will give you one dog to pet with each hand."

"What about my toes?"

Sophie's shoulders were shaking and she'd pressed a hand over her mouth.

"Toes don't count unless we're on the sofa at home and Titus is lying in front of it."

"Why not?"

"Because you have to wear shoes here and your toes are inside."

"Uh-uh." She held up a foot. "Sandals. See?"

Ryder realized she had outmaneuvered him and stopped trying to be logical. He crouched to look her straight in the eyes. "Lily. You will stay with Sophie while I'm gone and behave yourself because I say so. Understand?"

Curly blond hair fell in cascades and masked Lily's rosy cheeks as she bowed her head and said, "Yes, Daddy."

Ryder looked to Sophie. "If she gives you any trouble you can call me on my cell."

"I'm sure that won't be necessary."

"I hope not. Benny's still on the front door and Marlton's in the rear so you should be fine."

"I'll take good care of her," Sophie vowed.

He dropped his chief's persona long enough to say, "I know you will. I trust you."

The thing that surprised Ryder the most when he said that was the depth of truth in his words. He was entrusting his precious child to Sophie Williams and was less worried than he'd ever been when leaving Lily with Opal.

Promising himself he'd sort out that epiphany later, he headed for his patrol car. Suffering strangers needed his help. His family would be fine until he returned.

Family? Yes, he concluded. He had begun to view

Sophie as the third member and realized he was finally at peace with that.

Forty-five minutes later, while directing an evacuation helicopter's landing, Ryder remembered he'd forgotten to ask Sophie about the unlatched gates.

SEVENTEEN

"What would you like to do?" Sophie asked Lily.

The pouting child merely shrugged.

"Are you still hungry? There's a little more pizza. How about a bottle of water? Aren't you thirsty"

A shake of the head.

Sophie made a face and blew a noisy sigh. "If you were a puppy I'd take you to the vet to see why you were acting so sad. But since you're not, and you can talk if you want to, I'll pick what we do." She looked around. "Let's see, there are dog bowls to wash and rinse. Or we could get down on our hands and knees and scrub cement with brushes so it's nice and clean for the next new dogs."

"Yuck."

"You have a better idea?"

Lily yawned. "We could play hide-and-seek."

"We could if we weren't all so tired. Titus is asleep and Phoenix is resting." She knew better than to list the weary child and trigger more argument. "Why don't we go upstairs to the break room and watch videos?"

"Cartoons?"

"Something better," Sophie told her. "You like dogs. I have some great training DVDs up there. And a sofa where you can sit with your shoes off and pet Titus with your toes."

"I can take my shoes off? Daddy said..."

"I know he did. But if you don't get up and walk around, sitting on this couch should be no different than the one you have at home."

To Sophie's relief and guarded delight, Lily looked happier. "Okay."

So far, so good. Their evening wasn't going to be all smiles, she knew, but this was a fair start at making peace. After all, she wasn't the child's mother so she really had no authority other than what Ryder had imparted when he'd left them together.

Lily rousted Titus, and Phoenix followed without hesitation. They had no trouble staking out positions next to the upstairs sofa as soon as Lily sat down and kicked off her shoes. Titus claimed his spot at her feet, laid his chin on his front paws and made himself at home. Less self-assured, Phoenix edged in next to the old dog until Sophie started the video player and joined the child. Then he took up a position by her feet.

"I like German shepherds," Lily said. "Why is that one so mean?"

"Because he's trained to act that way when he's on duty," Sophie explained. "Watch for a minute and you'll see how nice he is when he's at home."

"Titus is never mean."

"Dogs are like people." Smiling, Sophie patted Lily's knee. "Some are better at one job than any other. For instance, your daddy is good at catching bad guys."

"Yeah. He's real brave."

"I know. You must be very proud of him."

"Uh-huh."

"What's your favorite thing to do?"

"Tickle Titus." She raised a bare foot and giggled. "See?"

"I do see. He likes it, too."

"Yeah. Sometimes he licks my toes. The puppies did that tonight."

"I'm sure they did." Sophie began to relax. If she and Lily found nothing else to talk about, they could always fall back on their love of dogs. She cupped a hand around her mouth and leaned closer. "Can I tell you a secret?"

"Uh-huh." The sky blue eyes widened in anticipation.

"When it's really hot out and I'm hosing down the kennels, I sometimes take my shoes off and let the dogs chase my toes, too."

Lily covered her giggle. "I'll tell Daddy."

"That's okay. I don't mind." Remembering their water fight made Sophie grin. "When you do, ask him if he ever likes to play in the hose, okay?"

"Okay." Yawns were soon followed by a nodding head. Sophie slipped an arm around the child and let her doze close to her side. It was getting easier and easier to picture herself as a mother in spite of her own childhood woes. This wasn't so bad. It actually felt good to protect and shelter as if she were a mother hen tucking a chick beneath her wing. There was a Bible passage in Psalms about believers being tucked under God's wings. How did it go? "He shall cover you with His feathers and under His wings shall thou trust…"

Peace descended. Sophie was determined to stay awake despite the armed guards at both doors but her eyelids were growing heavy.

The DVD ended and apparently shut itself off, because when Sophie awoke the room was dark except for moonlight shining through the windows. The TV was silent. It took her a few seconds to realize that the warm creature half on, half off her lap was Lily.

Blinking to adjust to the dimness, Sophie was puzzled. Hadn't she left more lights burning? What about the hallway? The stairs?

A low rumble from the floor at the end of the couch came from Phoenix. She dropped her left hand and arm over the side and touched his silky fur. "What is it, boy?"

He slowly rose. Sophie kept her hand on him. "Easy. Stay." Although his muscles knotted he didn't leave her.

Easing aside to stand, she laid the sleeping child flat on the sofa cushions. There was a spare leash in the closet but Sophie knew better than to let go of the Aussie. Thankfully, he wasn't barking yet or he'd have awakened every dog in the place—and Lily, who was far less trouble than usual at the moment.

Keeping a hand on Phoenix's collar Sophie walked him to the storage closet where Lily had hidden earlier and located a leash. Once he was under control she led him to the top of the stairs. His nails clicked on the hard floor.

Sophie stopped. If the building's depths had not been so dark she wouldn't have been concerned. Power sometimes failed during storms, of course, but the weather had been mild lately.

One hand on the banister, the other holding the leash, she descended. From the main floor it was possible to see that other buildings obviously had electricity. So did the police department a quarter of a mile down Desert Valley Road. Did they have their own generator for emergencies?

"It doesn't matter," Sophie murmured. "What I want to know is why *this* place went dark."

The front door was the closest so she approached it. "Benny? Are you there?"

Louder. "Benny! Answer me. Are you okay?"

A hand in front of Phoenix's nose and a stern, "Stay" freed both hands. She drew her sidearm and released the safety on it before trying the door and finding it locked.

Sophie held her breath, turned the dead bolt and slowly opened the metal exterior door. The sidewalk outside was deserted. The only sign that Benny had been there was a half-empty soda bottle and a folding chair. She had known him to nap on the job but would never have dreamed he'd desert his post.

Phoenix was growling. He had stayed put, swiveling his head to look into the depths of the silent building.

She did the same, considering her options. If she left the area at the foot of the stairs, that would leave Lily open to attack from below. However, if she went to check on Marlton and found him, with or without Benny, she'd have reinforcements.

Because she had already called out and revealed her presence, she felt no reluctance to use her cell phone to inform Ryder of the strange situation. The call went straight to his voice mail. *911? No.* Not when so many officers and others were busy saving lives on the highway. She could handle this herself. She knew the layout of each room well enough to navigate without having to see well and the skylight in the indoor training area let in available moonlight. Plus, she was armed and had a dog with her. That magnified her human senses immeasurably.

Actually, given the situation, Sophie's decision was fairly easy. She'd get a flashlight, tell Marlton to check the fuse box and make sure all was well there, then contact the power company if the problem was not due to a fault in the training center's wiring.

An unexpected meow perked up the dog's ears. There was a *cat* in here? How in the world had that happened?

Sophie had not planned to release Phoenix. He had other ideas. He lunged. She lost her grasp on the leash. In a heartbeat he had outrun the beam of the flashlight and disappeared.

"Well, at least he can't get out," she grumbled, wishing she'd brought steady, predictable Titus with her before she concluded he was exactly where he belonged, upstairs guarding Lily.

Poor little kitty. It sure had picked the wrong building to invade. As soon as she'd gotten the electricity restored, Sophie planned to locate and save it from being overrun by canines. Most of them probably wouldn't hurt it but there were a few who might try, particularly if it was as young as it sounded.

Listening carefully, Sophie was puzzled that Phoenix was using a silent pursuit. That wasn't at all like him. Matter of fact, his barking was sometimes excessive.

The hair on the back of her neck prickled. "Phoenix? Phoenix, come."

No response. No barking, or whining. No sharp tapping of nails on the hard floor or scrambling sounds when he rounded a corner too fast and slipped.

Bile rose in Sophie's throat. Fright touched every nerve and demanded she run. As a dog trainer, her first responsibility was to the canines in her care, and if Lily had not been asleep upstairs she would have bravely pressed forward in search of the dog.

The presence of the helpless little girl changed everything. Phoenix had his speed and his teeth and the self-preservation instincts of an intelligent animal. Lily had nothing but an old dog and her; the woman who had vowed to keep her safe.

Wheeling, Sophie headed back toward the stairway. She had barely taken two steps when a searing pain cut through her head.

She remained conscious only long enough to feel herself starting to fall.

Then, blackness.

"Was that the last chopper?" reporter Madison Coles asked Ryder.

"Yes." He was hoping she wasn't going to take advantage of her relationship with rookie James Harrison to try to pick his brain for the *Canyon County Gazette.* A catastrophe like the one tonight was not something Ryder wanted to remember, let alone discuss.

"When you have a minute, you need to come see something, Chief," Harrison said. "One of the paramedics spotted it when he was cutting a victim loose with the Jaws of Life."

"What is it?"

"Take a look."

Ryder frowned, then crouched and began to clear scraps of debris off the object. It was about six inches wide and so long it disappeared beneath other wreckage. "A spike strip?"

"Looks like it to me. I wonder if the highway boys were in pursuit and laid it to stop whoever they were chasing?"

"I don't know. But I'm sure going to find out." He headed for the makeshift command post that had been set up in one of the patrol units parked safely off the road. A variety of uniforms showed the full complement of services that had been called in.

"Did one of you guys lay a spike strip?"

Denials were swift and loud.

Ryder held up both hands, palms forward. "That's what I figured. One of my men showed me something that sure looks as though there was nothing accidental about this pileup tonight. Somebody planned it."

As he spoke, a shiver shot up his spine. Who did he know who had the warped, evil mind necessary for such a horrible act? Who would harm innocent people like this? And why?

The *who* was easy. Carrie Dunleavy. But why? The only thing he could think of was creating a ruse to draw him and his men out of town. Carrie had never done anything without a reason. Even though it had taken years to figure out her twisted motives, they did exist. And they'd made a sick kind of sense once he'd seen the pictures and read her journal.

"Listen," Ryder announced, pointing to James. "This is Officer Harrison. He'll show you the device. I need to go."

The others were too focused on seeing the spikes to offer thanks. Ryder didn't care. He didn't need or want gratitude. What he wanted was to return to his daughter—and to Sophie—and hug them both as long and hard as possible.

Just because there had been no sightings of Carrie lately didn't mean she wasn't around. Criminal profilers in Flagstaff had warned she wouldn't go far. If they had been right, maybe she was in Desert Valley now.

Would she sabotage a highway just to get to him? Sure she would. She'd killed and maimed before. Stepping up her game after her crimes had been revealed made sense. She was running out of time. Out of opportunity. And hopefully, out of freedom.

He slid into his cruiser and flipped on the lights and siren, then made a U-turn in the median and sped back toward town. If his ideas were wrong, there would be no harm done.

If he was right and Carrie was on the offensive, he'd need more than mere speed. He'd need divine guidance and protection for his loved ones. Lots of it.

Sophie heard moaning before realizing it was coming from her. Dizzy and disoriented she touched her aching scalp. Blood made her fingers sticky. She tried to sit up and failed to find good balance.

"Well, well, look who's finally coming around," a bitter-sounding woman said. "I should have saved Marian Foxcroft's silver poodle statue to use on you, too."

Sophie could hardly breathe. *That voice. It had to belong to whom she thought. Did she dare even speak the name?*

Wide-eyed, she fought to focus despite the bright beam of the discarded flashlight. Starting by noting low-heeled pumps, she observed tailored beige slacks and a plain brown blouse that almost matched the woman's mousy hair. Everything was familiar except the menacing glare in Carrie's eyes. And the pistol she was pointing.

Sophie's gaze narrowed to the hole in the end of the barrel. "That's my gun."

"It certainly is. Kind of you to provide it, dear. I usually have to improvise, particularly since it's hard to lug a rifle around with me. Too conspicuous." She chuckled. "My aim is getting considerably better, don't you think?"

"You don't want to shoot me," Sophie offered, trying to reason with the madwoman.

"Why not? Do you think I don't know what you've been up to with my fiancé."

"I'm not up to anything, Carrie. Honest I'm not. All I care about is my dogs." A swell of panic almost closed her throat. "You, you didn't hurt any of them, did you?"

"Not yet. If you behave yourself I may not have to, either. Of course if you misbehave there are no guarantees. You saw what happened to Veronica, thanks to me. You should have celebrated. I got you a promotion."

There it was. The admission. Carrie Dunleavy had killed Veronica Earnshaw, Sophie's predecessor. The question was why. Veronica hadn't been interested in Ryder romantically. And he didn't particularly like her as a person, which would have made Carrie happy. So why had she killed her?

"You want my thanks for killing someone in cold blood?" The woman was insane.

Carrie nodded. "It might have been nice to get a little recognition for all the things I did at the police station. But no. Everybody ate my lovely baked goods and acted as if they expected me to keep treating them. Who ever treated me? Huh? Who? Even those mutts of yours didn't like me. Thank goodness I had my sweet kitties."

Two and two suddenly added up to four. "Did you bring a cat in here tonight to confuse the dogs?"

"Who, me?" Carrie meowed melodiously. "I didn't need to. My imitation was good enough to fool that stupid gray dog without endangering an innocent kitty. He ran through the back door and I locked him out." She cackled hoarsely. "He can keep those dumb guards company."

"Are they all right?"

Carrie shrugged. "Who knows!"

Sophie stared at her. "Why did you kill Veronica?"

"Boring question. But I have one. What I want to know is what happened to the girl."

"What girl?"

Carrie howled and raised the gun as if she were going to use it to backhand Sophie. "You know very well what girl. My daughter-to-be. Lily Hayes."

EIGHTEEN

Sophie felt helpless. Her head throbbed from behind her eyes to the base of her skull. The pain was not only nauseating, it kept her from thinking clearly.

How could this have happened? She'd been cautious to a fault. So had Ryder, even posting double the usual guards. If not for the traffic accident tonight he would have been there, too. What else could they possibly have done?

She supposed he could have shipped Lily out of town but his theory that the child was safer there with them was valid. He couldn't very well lock up his little girl while a crazed murderer ran loose. That was opposite to the way things should be.

Then again, who said life was fair? Even Christians fell victim to temptation. She should know. Her parents had been prime examples of people who'd talked about how to live a life of faith, yet had failed to do so. Sometimes she wondered if they'd realized how close she'd come to rejecting Jesus because of them. It was only afterward, with the insight of a believer, that she had come to terms with the pain of her past.

And now it seemed she was out of time.

Rising to hands and knees, Sophie labored to regain

normal equilibrium. Every breath brought another wave of nausea but each time it seemed to lessen a tiny bit.

"Get up," Carrie ordered. "Stop pretending."

"I'm not pretending. I'm dizzy."

"Good. You'll be less trouble that way." She picked up the flashlight and gestured. "I know you were upstairs when I let myself in with Marlton's key card, so march. We're going back up there."

Sophie would gladly have lunged at her and gone for the gun if she'd been herself. But she wasn't. The images of her surroundings were not only still dim, they vibrated like the shimmer of a mirage on a desert highway.

Nevertheless, she did manage to stand by extending both arms for better balance. Carrie sidled behind her. Prodded her with the gun barrel. "Move it or be shot right here. It's your choice."

Time was what Sophie needed; time to clear her head, time for one of the guards to come to the rescue, or even time for Ryder to finish on the highway and return. She was positive Carrie wouldn't shoot him, even if he confronted her. The rest of them were fair game.

One step at a time, Sophie staggered forward. Each step brought pain. And the pain caused a rush of adrenaline and made her heart race faster and faster until she wondered if it would pound out of her chest.

"Please, let me rest," she begged the older woman.

"Keep going before I change my mind and give you eternity to rest."

"Why?"

Sophie didn't really want to know what her adversary was thinking, she simply wanted to keep her talking and stall for time. It occurred to her to call to Lily and tell her to hide again, but what good would that do?

The converted upstairs apartment was familiar to Carrie as well as having no alternative exits. There was no way Lily could escape. None.

An overwhelming sense of doom pushed Sophie's mind from personal preservation into prayer for Lily. Silently, she pleaded for the child's life.

For Ryder's sake, too, she added. He simply could not lose his only child. *Please, Father. Please help me. Tell me what to do and give me the strength to do it.*

Purposely lagging, Sophie viewed each step as a separate hurdle. This was one race she didn't want to win because the goal at the top of the stairs was Lily. *Dear Jesus!*

Her foot slipped. She went down on one knee, still grasping the banister. Carrie poked her so hard in the ribs she gasped.

"One more trick like that and you're finished," the murderer warned.

Sophie stayed leaning forward and gained the final landing on her hands and knees. If she could trip Carrie from there, maybe she'd fall backward down the stairs and they'd have a chance to escape.

Unfortunately, Carrie's mind was as alert as Sophie's was hazy, and the plan failed.

"Up," Carrie ordered, circling wide.

Sophie obeyed. Titus knew the other woman from her years as police department secretary and didn't bark. Lily was rubbing her eyes as she sat up and peered through the dimness. "Where's my daddy?"

"We'll see him soon," Carrie said.

What amazed Sophie was how tender Carrie had sounded when speaking to the child. The change in demeanor was startling. And it was frightening because it showed how well she could fake an outward manifestation of kindness.

"I don't suppose you have handcuffs handy," Carrie crooned. "Well, no matter. Lily, go in the closet and bring me a leash."

The child didn't move.

"You heard Mama. Go get a leash."

Seeing how frightened Lily was, Sophie offered to do it. "I can get you one."

"No. The girl needs to learn obedience. She'll get it. Won't you, Lily, dear."

Sophie caught her eye and nodded. "Do as Ms. Carrie says, honey. Please. It's okay."

A slap caught Sophie on the cheek and echoed. She staggered and fell backward into a chair. The moment Carrie said, "Don't interfere," she realized her error. Still, she couldn't let the madwoman abuse the innocent child.

Teary-eyed, Lily returned with a braided leash.

"Good girl. Now go sit on the sofa and wait."

All Sophie did this time was give a barely perceptible nod. It was enough to encourage Lily. She perched on the edge of the cushions and petted Titus. He wasn't acting too defensive yet but he was clearly aware that something was wrong.

It took Carrie only seconds to lash Sophie's wrists behind her and tie them to the chair back. Then she went to the sink in the break-room kitchen and filled a glass with tap water. For a moment Sophie thought Carrie might intend kindness. When the woman laid aside the gun to reach into a pocket and produce several pink tablets, she knew better.

Water and pills were offered to Lily. "Here you go, dear. Take these like a good girl."

Lily vigorously shook her head, bringing wrath down on Sophie. "I told you not to spoil her. Now see what you've done."

There was no way Sophie was going to encourage Lily to swallow anything, particularly if it came from Carrie. "You don't have to do that," Sophie said, ducking and cringing when Carrie stomped across the floor and stood before her.

Suddenly, the madwoman wheeled. "Tell you what, Lily," she drawled, sounding half comforting, half menacing, "If you take these pills for Mama I won't shoot your dog."

Lily squealed and threw her arms around Titus's neck. "No! Don't hurt him."

Hand open, Carrie approached. "The pills, or else."

Every time she wasn't being watched, Sophie had struggled to free herself. One more loop and she thought she'd be able to wiggle her left hand out. There! Almost free!

Across the room, a sobbing child was sipping water and weeping as she tried to swallow.

With a final twist and pull, Sophie was loose. She came off the chair with a banshee yell and launched herself at Carrie.

The other woman was taller but less fit. They went down in a jumble of arms and legs. Titus placed himself in front of Lily and began to bark.

Carrie thrashed and kicked away. Sophie tried to hang on to her in spite of the pounding in her injured head and recurring dizziness.

The instant Carrie whirled, Sophie knew why. The gun was back in Carrie's hand. And it was aimed directly at her. All Sophie could do was try to wrest it from her. She gave another guttural shout and charged.

The report of the bullet being fired shook the windows and temporarily made her ears ring.

Shoved backward by the impact she grabbed at her shoulder. There was no pain yet, just a feeling of being punched. Hard.

Incredulous, Sophie stared at the blood flowing between her fingers. Shock softened the blow enough that she could reason, *She shot me. Now how am I going to save Lily?*

Her last thoughts were of Ryder as she closed her eyes and slid to the floor.

Red lights and siren running, the chief slid to a stop in front of the training center. He'd notified dispatch of his actions as he drove. Because of the manpower assigned to the accident he was the first to arrive.

The building was not only pitch-dark, he didn't see Benny Sims guarding the front door.

He drew his sidearm, found the door locked, and tried his key card. The mechanism clicked but the door remained closed tight. Wedged? Maybe. Frustrated, Ryder ran for the rear entrance.

Marlton was lying on the ground there, moaning. Sims was trying to revive him while Phoenix licked both their faces.

Ryder almost lost control and shouted instead of merely asking, "What happened?"

"Don't know," Sims said. "When I woke up I was back here and Dennis was actin' like he is now."

"What about Lily and Sophie?"

The older man looked chagrined. "Sorry, Chief. I can't say."

Ryder burst through the rear door with Phoenix at his heels. The flashlight on his belt was all he needed to follow the dog when he picked up a scent. This time, there was no hesitation. Phoenix bounded up the stairs so fast it looked as if his paws never touched the ground.

Breathless, Ryder caught up and played the light over the room. Phoenix had gone straight to a figure on the floor and was nudging it with his nose.

"Sophie!"

Ryder's heart nearly stopped. Pushing the concerned canine aside, he knelt at her side and touched her neck, looking for a carotid pulse. Tears of relief blurred his vision when he found one. It was strong.

He grabbed his radio and called for an ambulance, then gently rolled her over. There was a lot of blood on her shoulder but it wasn't pulsing. "Praise God." Whoever had shot Sophie had missed the subclavian artery. She had a chance.

It took only seconds to locate a small kitchen towel and press it over the entry wound. He put a second towel behind her shoulder where the bullet had exited leaving more damage.

His hands were shaking. "Sophie? Sophie, can you hear me?" There was no reply but he did think he sensed slight movement. "Hold still, honey. You've been shot. An ambulance is on the way."

Her lips moved. Ryder leaned closer.

"Lily..."

Ashen faced and barely able to think straight, he listened closely. When Sophie started to go limp again, he begged, "What about Lily?"

The hazel eyes he loved so dearly opened. Lashes fluttered. Tears gathered. "Carrie."

"Carrie was here? She's the one who shot you?"

Sophie licked her dry lips and tried to nod, groaning in pain instead.

"Lie still. It won't be long now," Ryder said as his heart shattered into a million fragments. Carrie had his little girl. Unless he got her back, life for him was over.

Gazing down at Sophie he added, *I need her, too*, and bent to place a tender kiss on her forehead.

Her pale skin felt icy, clammy with shock and loss of blood. If he hadn't known better he'd have pulled her into his arms and cradled her. The smartest thing he could do, however, was continue to slow the bleeding and pray that he'd have the chance to show her how much he cared after she healed.

She had to be all right, Ryder insisted. She simply had to be.

He spent a moment praying for her recovery, then leaned over again and kissed her lips, following with a whispered, "I love you."

Sophie drifted in and out of consciousness, happier when her dreams brought peace than when reality carried suffering. Somewhere, in the midst of all that, she sensed Ryder's presence, felt him touching her cheek. That was wonderful until she recalled bits and pieces of what had happened to Lily.

Strong hands held her down as she struggled to rise. "I—I have to go..."

"To the hospital," a paramedic said. "You've lost a lot of blood."

Behind that man she saw the blurry face of her dreams. "Ryder!"

He grasped her free hand. "I'm here. You're going to be all right once a doctor patches you up."

"No, I have to go after Lily."

"What happened? Can you tell me more?"

"Carrie was here. She took Lily."

"Did you see them leave?"

"No." Sophie sighed. "But she made Lily take pills. I tried to…to stop it."

Another medic urged Ryder to back off. "We've given her a shot for the pain. She won't be talking much longer. Let us load her so we can come back for the other guys."

"Is that when Carrie shot you?" Ryder asked. Sophie saw him brace himself to keep from being pushed away as she was lifted onto a wheeled gurney.

"Yes." Tears welled. "I'm so sorry."

"We'll find them," he promised.

She wanted to offer to go with him, to rise from the thin mattress and strike back. Instead, she sensed movement and heard men talking as they strapped her down before carrying her downstairs and pushing her out onto the sidewalk.

Bright, flashing lights hurt her eyes so she shut them and felt teardrops trickling down her temples. Where was Ryder? Was he going to come with her? To look after her?

A niggling fear lingered in the back of her mind as she succumbed to the effects of the narcotics. Something else was wrong, wasn't it? Something terrible.

Sophie fought to remember. It was important. Her thoughts cried out for Ryder. He would know. He would fix it.

Colors blinked at the edges of her closed eyes. A vortex of sound enveloped her with mechanical beeps and internal heartbeats and the wail of a siren.

Then, everything vanished, including her pain.

NINETEEN

Ryder gave the K-9 rookies their orders via radio. Some had to come from the accident scene and pick up their dogs. Others, like Whitney Godwin and Ellen Foxcroft, had not responded to the wreck and were a little closer.

Protocol insisted Ryder must wait for backup. His heart disagreed. Breaking the rules he'd been hired to enforce would set a bad example but he didn't care. This was Lily he was tracking.

Checking Titus, he realized that the old dog was already moving as if he was hurt, so he had no choice but to use Phoenix. Once the younger dog was in his working harness he stopped jumping around.

The sweater they had used for Phoenix's tracking test was gone, but Lily's sandals had been left behind. Ryder picked them up, stuck one in his pocket, and led his new K-9 partner out into the street.

"Sit." When he held out the small sandal for the dog to smell, the sight of it tied his gut in knots. "Seek."

One more quick sniff and Phoenix was off. He started down the sidewalk toward the police station, then stopped, circled and took off across the street.

Ryder gave him his head, slowing him only enough

to keep pace. He didn't dare release the dog and chance losing sight of him.

Phoenix strained against the restraint, pulling as if his life depended upon it. Ryder could totally identify. He, too, was pushing to the edge of his endurance.

Up and down curbs, around trees and away from town they went. The best part about the long run was that Carrie hadn't gotten into a car and driven away, leaving no discernible trail. If she had, there was no way any K-9, no matter how special, could have successfully tracked her.

Bristling and panting, Phoenix slowed. His nose checked the ground, then the air. They had come to one of the abandoned houses that had yet to be torn down or repaired as part of a Desert Valley beautification project.

Ryder ducked behind an overflowing trash Dumpster next to the ramshackle building and listened. Phoenix was making no effort to go on, nor did he seem confused.

As far as the dog was concerned, he'd done his job. He'd found Lily. All that was left was for Ryder to radio his position, which he immediately did, then figure out how to gain access to the house without being seen.

He circled to the rear with his K-9 partner at his side, pulling him back just in time to keep him from scratching on the door. "Sit." It was more a hiss than a command. He could tell that Phoenix was agitated. That was nothing compared to how Ryder felt. He was ready to smash his way in and tear Carrie Dunleavy limb from limb.

It took a series of deep breaths for him to regain emotional control. When he was sure he was ready, he slowly twisted the knob on the back door.

It turned easily.

A beam of light illuminated the face of a child stretched out on the kitchen table. Lily's face. And Carrie was standing next to her, stroking her blond hair as the child yawned. It was hard for Ryder to reconcile the mousy woman in front of him with the cold-blooded murderer he knew her to be—until he looked into her eyes and saw wickedness gleaming. She was every bit as evil to the core as he'd imagined.

"What took you so long," Carrie asked with a smirk. "One of my cats could have found us sooner than that miserable excuse for a search and rescue dog." She gave a maniacal laugh. "Too bad your old dog was out of commission right when you needed him."

"How did you know that?" He'd entered and closed the door behind him, isolating Phoenix to keep him from attacking Carrie and getting in the way. When Ryder made his move to disarm her, he didn't want to have to worry about the dog.

"Titus gave me trouble, just like I knew he would, so I kicked him in the ribs. Not too hard, mind you. Just enough to slow him down."

"What about Lily? What did you give her?"

"I don't know what you mean."

"Yes, you do. You made her swallow pills."

"Just cold pills." She frowned. "How did you know about that?

"Sophie saw you do it."

Carrie cursed, high and screeching. "She's still alive? I thought for sure I'd finished her." She eyed Lily. "Oh, well, at least that woman is out of the way and we can bring our perfect family together as it was meant to be."

Ryder didn't know what to say. Carrie obviously thought of the three of them as a family. He couldn't imagine anything more loathsome. Nevertheless, he began to build on her fantasy. "You wanted me and now you have me. We don't need Lily."

"Should I kill her, then?"

"No!"

"Humph. That's what I thought. We need our little girl to make a real family."

"Right, right." Ryder holstered his gun and raised his hands partway. "See? I'm unarmed. You don't need that gun, either. We're all friends here."

As the woman studied him, he hoped and prayed his expression masked his true feelings. Truth to tell, if he got his hands on her, the person who had taken one love from him and was threatening to take more, he wondered if he'd be able to do his duty instead of following the urge for retribution.

Instincts for revenge were strong, but his faith was stronger, although it fluctuated from moment to moment. If he had returned to the training center and found Sophie dead instead of merely wounded, he wasn't sure he'd have been able to control himself—then or now.

Carrie smiled. "We are friends, aren't we? It was such a thrill to see you enjoy my cooking when I brought treats to the station."

It took all the self-control Ryder could muster to keep from gagging at the thought. For five years he had treated his wife's killer as an equal, a friend and coworker. What a fool he'd been! They all had. And how convincing a true sociopath like Carrie could be.

"You—you can cook for me a lot from now on," he said. Sidelong peeks at Lily showed him her breathing was steady and deep.

"As a good wife should. That was another reason

Melanie was all wrong for you. She hated to cook. You were practically wasting away while she was pregnant."

Fists clenched behind his back, Ryder gritted his teeth. He had to take this, to go along with her fantasies long enough to gain the upper hand. If Carrie even suspected how much he hated her, there was no telling what she'd do.

Something inside of him countered the feelings of revulsion with a reminder that even Carrie was redeemable in the sight of God. He disagreed mightily. No one that evil was worth saving.

You're wrong, Ryder's conscience insisted. *Hate will consume you like a fire, leaving nothing but ashes.*

There was no way he was going to be able to instantly change his mind and find a way to forgive Carrie for all she'd done. Not without a lot of prayer and soul-searching, first. But maybe he could at least talk to her, stall for time until the rest of the rookies arrived.

"I put my gun away. How about you putting yours down, too?" Ryder suggested again.

"You'll be nice?"

"Of course. Haven't I always been nice to you, Carrie?"

She tucked the revolver in her pocket. "You never took me to the dance. I wanted to go every year and you never asked me. Nobody did."

"Is that what disappointed you about Brian and Mike?" The blond rookies who were like stand-ins for him in Carrie's mind.

"Well, duh. Of course. It was partly my fault. They had the same hair color and blue eyes as you do but they were poor substitutes. I should have been more patient."

"And waited for the right man," Ryder offered.

Carrie smiled sweetly. "Yes. For you. I didn't think

you'd ever get over the loss of your Melanie until I saw how you were treating Sophie. I gave up too soon, that's all. God was going to bring us together. I just needed to get some of the obstacles out of the way."

"If you really believe in God," Ryder said, "why would you act as if you're smarter than He is and separate a man from his wife?"

The sweet smile vanished. "You aren't listening. I told you. She was all wrong for you. You need to be with me." She gazed at the sleeping child. "And our little girl."

"But what bothered you about Veronica Earnshaw?" Ryder asked. "She and I had a professional relationship. That was all."

Carrie's brown eyes hardened even more behind her large glasses. "Veronica caught me staring at James Harrison, the next blond rookie that reminded me of you. She made fun of me. She even winked at me. And then she told James she'd come over to his room at the rookies' condo to give him and his dog a private training refresher. Private! I knew what that meant. James was mine. Mine! He was always so nice to me. He even said he would have asked me to the police dance if he didn't have to go on a stakeout to try to catch Veronica's killer." She laughed.

Ryder felt sick.

"Isn't that funny?" Carrie asked. "I'm glad James didn't disappoint me like the others."

Harrison had no idea how close he'd come to being killed, Ryder realized.

"And Marian Foxcroft?" Ryder asked. "How did she disappoint you?"

"That rich snob got a little too close to finding me out," Carrie said, shaking her head. "Nosy old woman."

"All right," Ryder managed to choke out. "Now I understand everything that's happened. Give me a hug and let's make up."

"Can I trust you?" She was eyeing him with suspicion and edging away as he tried to work his way close enough to grab and disarm her.

Smiling, he reached out to her. The instant she made her decision he saw it in her face. The wrinkles and frown lines relaxed. She circled the table.

"I want a kiss," Carrie said, giving him a dreamy look. "I've waited a long, long time."

Ryder grasped her wrists to keep her from going for the gun in her pocket, spun her around and snapped handcuffs on her before he relieved her of the weapon.

Screaming and cursing, Carrie reverted to the insanity that controlled her while Ryder reported by radio.

"We're ready to breach," Tristan McKeller reported.

"You won't have to. Come take custody of my prisoner," Ryder said. "And call another ambulance. My daughter needs to go to the hospital."

"I'm fine," Sophie kept arguing.

The two nurses who had been assigned to keep her quiet until they could transfer her to a regular room were taking their jobs seriously. "You've lost too much blood. You'll need a couple of days' rest before you'll be ready for discharge, let alone go back to work."

"You don't understand. They need me out there. I train search and rescue dogs."

"If they're already trained, they should work without you, right?"

"It's complicated."

"And you're stubborn," the darker-haired nurse said.

"I've had some cantankerous patients in my thirty years of nursing but you take the cake."

"What did you do with my clothes?" Sophie asked, looking around the cubicle. "I don't see them."

Younger and with spiked red hair, the other RN patted Sophie's free hand. "We had to bag them for the cops because this was a crime. Trust me, you're going to want to burn them. They'll never come clean."

"Can I at least have something to put on besides this thin gown. I'm freezing."

"I'll get you a warm blanket," the first nurse said. She eyed her coworker. "You can give her some scrubs if you like. She's not going anywhere barefoot."

Smiling, Sophie thought, *Oh, yeah? Watch me.*

Riding in the ambulance with Lily, Ryder kept trying to wake her and succeeded in getting a few mumbled responses. Two medics were monitoring her respiration and blood pressure.

"She'll be fine in no time," one assured him. "They'll want to do a blood test in the ER to make sure she wasn't given anything stronger than cold pills. It's just a precaution. Her vitals are good. I wouldn't worry."

Ryder was dubious. Carrie had sworn she hadn't given the child anything dangerous, but he wasn't about to take her home without a thorough checkup. Besides, he needed to see Sophie. To tell her Lily had been found and Carrie arrested.

"Were you the crew that picked up a gunshot victim at the Canyon County Training Center tonight?" he asked.

"Yeah. We dropped her at the hospital."

"Do you think she'll still be there?"

The paramedic draped his stethoscope around his neck and smiled. "I doubt they had to send her on if that's what you mean."

"Thanks."

"She one of yours, Chief?"

Ryder knew the man meant professionally. His answer was far from it. He smiled as he continued to hold Lily's hand. "Yes. She's definitely one of mine."

Getting the hospital garb on over her bandaged shoulder was painful. Sophie managed with the help of the red-haired nurse. By the time she was dressed she was breathing hard and perspiring. "Whew! That was not fun. I need a minute to catch my breath."

"Take all the time you need. I'll be back to check on you soon. Your warm blanket is right here if you want it."

"I'm good for now. Thanks."

"We're short on rooms due to the big accident."

"I'm so sorry. I should have asked. Were there a lot of serious injuries?"

"The worst victims were flown to Flagstaff so I can't really say. Ours are stable."

"Thank God. Literally," Sophie said.

"You've got that right. Do you want me to help you put your feet up so you can lie down here?"

"No. Thanks. I just want to sit for a few minutes and let the pain subside." That much was true. What Sophie did not say was that she hoped to be able to slip easily to the floor and walk, despite her condition.

She had no plans beyond that. First, she had to prove to herself that she was ambulatory. Then she'd find a way to rejoin Ryder and Lily, wherever they were.

That was the only goal that mattered. She had to know they were both all right. That Carrie had not killed them.

Her stomach knotted and she doubled over, almost losing her balance. The image of Lily, swallowing pills to protect Titus from harm, was one she would never forget.

All Sophie knew at this point was that Carrie had wanted to make Lily her own daughter. To do that, she either had to marry Ryder or get him out of the way and kidnap the child. Either could have happened while Sophie lay unconscious and bleeding.

Something vague kept drifting through her mind. It concerned Ryder and triggered tender feelings—the kind she'd been having for him since he'd first embraced her in innocence.

"Lord, help me do this," she whispered. Using her good arm, she pushed off the edge of the bed. The landing was soft, yet jarred her shoulder enough to send a wave of pain and nausea through her.

Deep breathing helped. She let go of the bed. Stood straight and determined. Took one step, then another.

She was halfway to the exit when she saw Ryder. He was accompanying a wheeled gurney and holding Lily's hand. The child was stirring!

Sophie gasped. Her pulse sped. Pain vanished. Ryder looked up and recognized her. The love in his expression was so overwhelming she couldn't move.

In seconds he was beside her, his arm around her waist.

She sagged against him, drawing on his strength. "Is Lily…?"

"She's fine. Just sleepy."

"I was afraid."

"I know. So was I. But it's over now."

"You got Carrie?"

"Handcuffed and hauled off to jail," Ryder assured her. "Are you okay?"

"I am now that you're here."

Relief swept through Sophie. She began to collapse, and he caught her up, taking care not to bump her injured shoulder.

"Do you remember much?" he asked.

"Not a lot after Carrie shot me. Lily was very brave."

"I get the idea you were, too."

She snuggled closer and laid her head on his chest. "I had to try to save her."

"I know." They were keeping pace with the gurney where the little girl dozed. "Do you remember anything about the time when I found you?"

"Not really. I've tried, but all I get is warm feelings."

"You're on the right track," Ryder said tenderly. "I was so worried when I saw you lying there, bleeding, I couldn't help myself. I told you I loved you."

Sophie lifted her head to smile up at him. "You did?"

"Uh-huh."

"I don't remember." The smile grew to a grin despite the throbbing pain of her wound. "Maybe you'd better say it again."

"Gladly." He paused to tenderly kiss her forehead. "I love you, Sophie."

She was fighting back tears of joy when she replied, "I love you, too.

Lily skipped into Sophie's hospital room and presented a bouquet of wildflowers that were more seeds and insects and broken stems than blossoms. Sophie had never received such a beautiful gift.

"Thank you," she said, taking the flowers with a wide grin and misty eyes.

"I picked them myself," Lily announced.

Ryder backed her up. "That, she did. I offered to buy some for her to give you but she had to do it herself. Reminds me of you."

"I just did what was necessary," Sophie said quietly, watching the little girl begin to play with an arrangement of get well cards on a side table. "They say I can get out of here this afternoon. Will you be available to give me a lift home?"

He perched on the edge of her bed and clasped her hand. "I will give you anything and everything you want, if you'll let me."

Sophie smiled. "I have all I need as long as the two of you are around." She arched a brow. "Well, except for a dog or two. Life isn't complete without furry friends."

"That's what Lily says. She wants a puppy, too, now that Titus doesn't want to play."

"He's healing okay?" Sophie asked, sobering. "I can't believe Carrie kicked him."

"Tanya says he'll be fine. Which reminds me," Ryder said. "Ellen's mother is awake and talking. Marian even remembers when Carrie knocked her out, which is another surprise. And another charge to add to the indictment, not that we need it to send Carrie away for keeps."

Sophie's heart swelled with thankfulness. "That's wonderful. Poor Marian. I was afraid the coma would last the rest of her life."

"I think we all wondered, despite plenty of prayers on her behalf."

"What happens now? I guess all the rookies will be reassigned now that the murders are solved. There's no way your budget can pay all those wages, is there?"

"Normally, no, but we're working on that." Ryder was stroking the back of her hand with his thumb. "Louise has already submitted her retirement paperwork and is helping Harmon and Marlton with theirs. I'll have at least three openings. Four, if you count Ken Buck's conviction for lying under oath and evidence tampering. I'm hoping I can convince four of the rookies to stay on permanently."

"Then only one rookie can't stay if they want to?" Sophie was so excited about the prospect she was almost giddy.

"If that's what they decide, probably," Ryder said. "James Harrison wanted to return to Wyoming, but unless Madison Coles can get a reporter's job up there he won't go. Tristan's happy because his sister, Mia, is staying out of trouble here. Besides, he's marrying Ariel and she has a teaching job to go back to as soon as her maternity leave is over."

"What about Whitney and the doctor? Evans took over management of the clinic and it's thriving. Surely he'll want to stay after he passes his licensing exams, so she will, too."

Ryder was smiling and nodding. "That's what I'd hope."

Sophie was counting silently. "That only leaves Shane and Gina, right? I wonder if I can convince her to stay on with me. She's a great asset to the training program."

"Don't forget Ellen Foxcroft," Ryder reminded her.

"It never dawned on me that she'd leave Desert Valley. Not now that her mother is recovering and she has the assistance dog center up and flourishing. With Lee Earnshaw going back to vet school, I suppose she might want to be closer to him, though."

"A little distance won't bother their romance," Ryder assured her. "Lee plans to commute on weekends as much as possible. With Ellen's money they won't have any hardship traveling back and forth."

Sighing, Sophie relaxed back against the elevated pillows. "Then they're all happy. My whole rookie class is taken care of."

He smiled in response. "I just realized something—all five rookies can stay if they choose to. Now that I'm the chief, my old spot is open too. That makes five. Now all we have to consider is us."

"Us? As in you and me?" Sophie eyed Lily. "Let's not rush things, okay? I want our marriage to be a joy for everybody, not just you and me." She detected a mischievous twinkle in Ryder's loving gaze. "What?"

"I don't recall asking you to marry me, that's all."

"You will," Sophie told him with a wry smile.

"Oh? What if I don't?"

Sitting up with a slight wince when her shoulder hurt, she reached to slip her other hand around his neck and pull him closer. "If you wait too long, then I will be forced to ask you, instead. I don't care who pops the question as long as the mutual answer is *yes*."

"Yes." Ryder whispered it against her lips just before he kissed her. "How about a Christmas wedding?"

"I prefer Valentine's Day," Sophie said. "But we certainly should plan to spend Christmas together. That will give me a chance to win Lily over. I can help her participate in the church Christmas pageant, for one thing."

Ryder laughed. "She told me last year that she wasn't going to be in that play again unless she got to be Mary and carry the baby doll, so you may have your hands full."

Sophie joined him with a soft chuckle as they both watched the little girl playing with the greeting cards. "I don't doubt that a bit," Sophie said. "I can hardly wait."

EPILOGUE

Spring spread an abundance of wildflowers across the desert, as if preparing the entire countryside for the nuptials of Sophie Williams and Ryder Hayes.

The yard of the Desert Valley Community Church was bedecked with the same kind of floral decorations, in keeping with the wishes of a certain little blonde girl who had scattered petals down the aisle between rows of folding chairs for her mother-to-be and matron of honor, Gina Weston. Gina's husband, Shane, was Ryder's best man.

Nervous—in a good way—Sophie paused to appreciate the wide blue sky, breathe pure desert air and thank the Lord for this day. Every member of last year's rookie class had married and all were in attendance, including their working dogs. Titus had accompanied Lily, carrying her basket of flower petals down the aisle for her and garnering broad grins.

With Phoenix at her side, Sophie smoothed her simple white sheath and grasped her bouquet. Lily had so admired the floral crown that held Sophie's veil she had fastened flowers to the dog's harness, making him strongly resemble a half-finished parade float.

The wind ruffled her veil. Sophie heard the music that was her cue and started toward the altar.

There was Ryder! She had asked him to wear his uniform instead of a tuxedo and he was so handsome he took her breath away.

Each step brought her closer to him, closer to the happiness she had long believed to be out of her reach, closer to a real home. A home she had almost lost before she'd had a chance to discover the possibility.

She passed her bouquet and the end of Phoenix's leash to Gina as she took Ryder's hand.

"Dearly Beloved," the pastor began.

Too soon it was over. Sophie knew she'd participated in the entire ceremony but her brain had yet to process the details. Everything was too wonderful. Too amazing. Too extraordinary to be real.

Lily tugged on her arm. "Can I hold your flowers?"

"All right. But you have to give them back later so take really good care of them, okay?"

"Okay." Her wide blue eyes looked up at her father. "Now?" she asked.

Ryder nodded. "Yes, now."

The child pulled to urge Sophie to bend down, wrapped her arms around her neck and said, "I love you…Mommy," then skipped off carrying the bridal bouquet.

Sophie was blinking back happy tears. When she looked at her new husband, his eyes were suspiciously sparkling, too. "You rehearsed that?"

"Not exactly. She kept pestering me about calling you Mommy and I told her to wait until it was official."

"She wanted to do it before? When?"

Ryder shrugged. "I don't remember. Probably around the time when the two of you Magi were leading dogs dressed as camels to Bethlehem in the Christmas pageant."

"And all this time I thought she was having trouble accepting me as her mother." Sophie made a silly face. "If I still had my flowers I'd be tempted to smack you with them for making us wait."

Laughing, he pulled his bride into his arms and kissed her again. And again.

Whoops and catcalls echoed in the balmy afternoon air. Someone hollered, "Hey, you gonna serve this or should we let the dogs loose?"

"I told you that second cake would be a problem," Ryder said. "Some of our rowdiest guests are animals. Real ones."

Sophie agreed. "Normal wedding cake is bad for them. I was just trying to make everybody feel welcome."

She kept hold of Ryder's hand as they approached the refreshment table. A three tiered wedding cake with white frosting and piped floral decorations stood at one end of the display, as expected.

At the other end was Sophie's answer to their canine guests. It was by far the most popular offering, particularly to the four-legged attendees. Liver paste was the glue that held row after row of crunchy, colored, dog treats to the sides of a pyramid almost as high as the real wedding cake.

Ryder laughed and looked at his team—all of whom had decided to stay on in Desert Valley. With six months under their belt on a twisty murder investigation, they were well on their way to moving from rookies to seasoned police officers.

And through it all, each one of them had found love.

Shane and Gina. Whitney and David. Ellen and Lee. James and Madison. Tristan and Ariel.

Himself and Sophie. Six months ago, he and Sophie had barely been on speaking terms. Now they were husband and wife.

He thought—for just a moment—of the insane woman who'd started them all down these unexpected paths. Former Desert Valley Police Department secretary Carrie Dunleavy had been quickly convicted of the murders of his late wife, Melanie Hayes, rookies Brian Miller and Mike Riverton, and lead dog trainer Veronica Earnshaw—and attempted murder of Marian Foxcroft. All thanks to her confession and guilty plea. She would be in prison for the rest of her life.

Ryder took his mind off the past and focused on the present—and his future. He took his new bride's hand and they stepped behind the dog-treat cake. Cameras and cell phones flashed.

"Together?" she asked.

"Absolutely. But if you make me taste that stuff I won't be happy."

"I'd never waste good liver on a man," Sophie teased. She plucked several treats from the top of the "cake" and Ryder did the same.

Before throwing them to the waiting dogs she called out, "Sit."

Every dog and half the guests obeyed as if the move had been rehearsed. One look at Ryder's smug expression told her it had.

"Are you going to keep surprising me for the rest of my life?" she joked, trying to make herself understood while laughing so hard that tears were streaming down her face.

"That's the plan," he said through his own laughter. "Are you ready?"

"Oh, yes."

Sophie proved it by wrapping her arms around his neck and kissing him soundly—before leaning back to dab a tiny spot of pâté on the tip of his nose.

Cameras flashed again. That was going to make a great picture to show their grandchildren someday.

* * * * *

SPECIAL EXCERPT FROM

Love Inspired® SUSPENSE

A K-9 cop must keep his childhood friend alive when she finds herself in the crosshairs of a drug-smuggling operation.

Read on for a sneak preview of Act of Valor *by Dana Mentink, the next exciting installment in the True Blue K-9 Unit miniseries, available in May 2019 from Love Inspired Suspense.*

Officer Zach Jameson surveyed the throng of people congregated around the ticket counter at LaGuardia Airport. Most ignored Zach and K-9 partner, Eddie, and that suited him just fine. Two months earlier he would have greeted people with a smile, or at least a polite nod while he and Eddie did their work of scanning for potential drug smugglers. These days he struggled to keep his mind on his duty while the ever-present darkness nibbled at the edges of his soul.

Eddie plopped himself on Zach's boot. He stroked the dog's ears, trying to clear away the fog that had descended the moment he heard of his brother's death.

Zach hadn't had so much as a whiff of suspicion that his brother was in danger. His brain knew he should talk to somebody, somebody like Violet Griffin, his friend from childhood who'd reached out so many times, but his heart would not let him pass through the dark curtain.

LISEXP0419

"Just get to work," he muttered to himself as his phone rang. He checked the number.

Violet.

He considered ignoring it, but Violet didn't ever call unless she needed help, and she rarely needed anyone. Strong enough to run a ticket counter at LaGuardia and have enough energy left over to help out at Griffin's, her family's diner. She could handle belligerent customers in both arenas and bake the best apple pie he'd ever had the privilege to chow down.

It almost made him smile as he accepted the call.

"Someone's after me, Zach."

Panic rippled through their connection. Panic, from a woman who was tough as they came. "Who? Where are you?"

Her breath was shallow as if she was running.

"I'm trying to get to the break room. I can lock myself in, but I don't… I can't…" There was a clatter.

"Violet?" he shouted.

But there was no answer.

Don't miss
Act of Valor *by Dana Mentink,*
available May 2019 wherever
Love Inspired® Suspense books and ebooks are sold.

www.LoveInspired.com

SPECIAL EXCERPT FROM

Love Inspired® SUSPENSE

When a guide-dog trainer becomes a target of a dangerous crime ring, a K-9 cop and his loyal partner will work together to keep her safe.

Read on for a sneak preview of Blind Trust *by Laura Scott, the next exciting installment in the True Blue K-9 Unit miniseries, available June 2019 from Love Inspired Suspense.*

Eva Kendall slowed her pace as she approached the training facility where she worked training guide dogs.

Using her key, she entered the training center, thinking about the male chocolate Lab named Cocoa that she would work with this morning. Cocoa was a ten-week-old puppy born to Stella, a gift from the Czech Republic to the NYC K-9 Command Unit located in Queens. Most of Stella's pups were being trained as police dogs, but not Cocoa. In less than a month after basic puppy training, Cocoa would be able to go home with Eva to be fostered during his initial first-year training to become a full-fledged guide dog. Once that year passed, guide dogs like Cocoa would return to the center to train with their new owners.

A few steps into the building, Eva frowned at the loud thumps interspersed between a cacophony of barking. The raucous noise from the various canines contained a level of panic and fear rather than excitement.

LISEXP0519

Concerned, she moved quickly through the dimly li training center to the back hallway, where the kennels were located. Normally she was the first one in every morning but maybe one of the other trainers had gotten an early start.

Rounding the corner, she paused in the doorway when she saw a tall, heavyset stranger scooping Cocoa out of his kennel. Panic squeezed her chest. "Hey! What are you doing?"

The ferocious barking increased in volume, echoing off the walls and ceiling. The stranger must have heard her. He turned to look at her, then roughly tucked Cocoa under his arm like a football.

"No! Stop!" Panicked, Eva charged toward the man, desperately wishing she had a weapon of some sort.

"Get out of my way," he said in a guttural voice.

"No. Put that puppy down right now!" Eva stopped and stood her ground.

"Last chance," he taunted, coming closer.

LISEXP0519